THE
RESISTANCE MAN

MARTIN WALKER

Quercus

First published in Great Britain 2013 by Quercus Editions Ltd
The paperback edition published in 2014 by

Quercus Editions Ltd
55 Baker Street
7th Floor, South Block
London W1U 8EW

A CIP catalogue record for this book is available
from the British Library

ISBN 978 1 78087 074 8
EBOOK ISBN 978 1 78087 073 1

10 9 8 7 6 5 4 3 2 1

Printed and bound in Great Britain by Clays Ltd, St Ives plc

Typeset by Ellipsis Digital Limited, Glasgow

In memory of Christopher Hitchens and Peter Scott,
two Balliol College friendships that lasted
for over forty years.

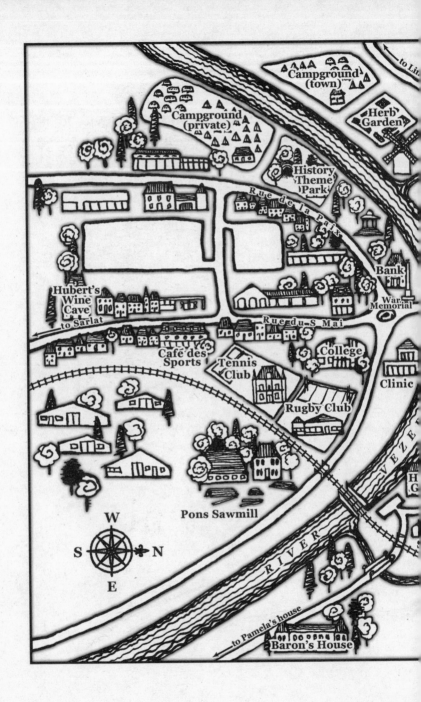

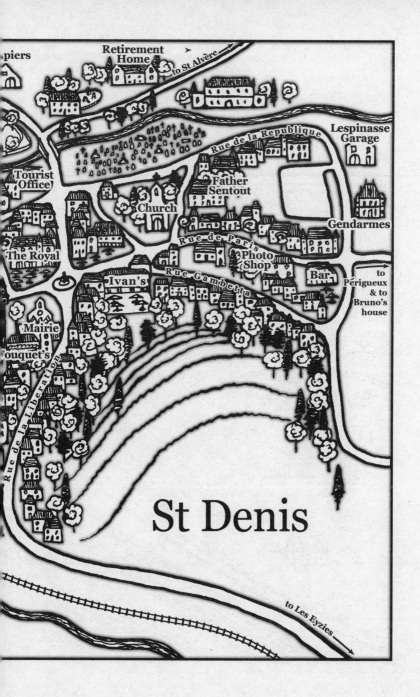

St Denis

Prologue

It was shortly after dawn on a day in late spring that carried all the promise of summer to come. The fresh green leaves were so bright they startled the eye, dew was already steaming from the grass under the first rays of the sun and the woods around the cottage were clamorous with birdsong. Benoît Courrèges, *Chef de Police* in the small French town of St Denis and known to everyone as Bruno, could identify the different notes of warblers and hoopoes, woodlarks and woodpeckers. But he knew these were just a fraction of the birdlife of the sweet valley of the river Vézère where he made his home.

Bruno wore his old army tracksuit in which he had just taken his morning run through the woods. His eyes were fixed on Napoléon and Joséphine, his two geese. These monarchs of his chicken run paced forward with slow dignity to study the quivering puppy held firmly in Bruno's grip. Behind the geese, twitching his head from side to side, came Blanco the cockerel, named after a French rugby hero. Blanco was followed by his hens and the two pheasants Bruno had added to his flock because he liked their smaller eggs and the careful way the hen pheasant would hide them in the undergrowth.

Raising a basset hound to be a hunting dog was slow work, but Bruno was becoming convinced that Balzac was the most intelligent dog he had ever known. Already house-trained, Balzac would even abandon an alluring new scent to obey his master's summons. Now he was learning that the birds in Bruno's chicken run were to be treated with courtesy as members of the extended family, and to be protected against all comers. Balzac was eager to bounce forward to play and send the chickens squawking and jumping into the air. So Bruno held him down with one hand and stroked him with the other, speaking in a low and reassuring voice as the two geese advanced to see what new creature Bruno had brought onto their territory this time.

Bruno had already familiarized Balzac with the deep and sensual scent of truffles and shown him the white oaks in the woods where they were usually to be found. He took the dog on his morning jogs and his dawn and dusk checks of the security of the chicken coop, and thought the time was approaching when Balzac would be able to run alongside when he exercised the horses. Bruno suspected he'd miss the now-familiar feel of the large binoculars case strapped to his chest, where the puppy was currently stowed when his master went riding.

Napoléon and Joséphine, who had grown familiar with Bruno's previous basset hound, Gigi, came closer. Blanco flapped his wings and squawked out his morning *cocorico*, as if to assert that however large the two geese, he was really in charge here. The puppy, accustomed to sleeping in the stables beside Bruno's horse Hector, was not in the least awed by the size of the geese. He cocked his head to one side to gaze up at them and made an amiable squeak of greeting. The geese cruised on past Bruno and his dog, leaving Blanco to stand on tiptoe and fluff out his feathers to enlarge his size and grandeur. Balzac looked suitably impressed.

Watching his birds and stroking his hound, Bruno knew he could not imagine a life without animals and birdsong and his garden. He delighted in eating apples plucked straight from his own trees, tomatoes still warm from the sun and salads that had still been growing moments before he dressed them with oil and vinegar. At the back of his mind lurked the question of whether there would one day be a wife and children to share this idyll and enjoy the stately progress of the seasons.

He turned his head to glance at his cottage, restored from ruin by his own hands and the help of his friends and neighbours in St Denis. Repaired now from the fire damage inflicted by a vengeful criminal, the house had grown. Bruno had used the insurance money and much of his savings to install windows in the roof, lay floorboards and create two new bedrooms in the disused loft. The plan had long been in his mind but the decision to carry it out felt like making a bet on his own future, that in time there would be a family to fill the space.

On the desk in his study lay the estimate for installing solar panels on the roof, along with the tax rebates he would receive and the terms of the bank loan he had been promised. Bruno had done his sums and knew it would take him almost ten years to earn back his investment, but he supposed it was a gesture to the environment that he ought to make. Now, gazing at the honey-coloured stone of his house topped with the traditional red tiles of the Périgord, he worried what the panels might do to the look of the place.

His reverie was interrupted by the vibration of the phone in his pocket. As he extracted it, Balzac squirmed free and began creeping towards the grazing chickens. Bruno reached out to haul him back, missed, dropped his phone and a furious squawking erupted as the puppy bounded forward and the hens half-flew and half-scurried back to the protection of their hut.

'Sorry, Father,' Bruno said as he recovered the phone, having seen that his caller was the local priest, Father Sentout. He picked up Balzac with one hand and headed back to the house.

'Sorry to disturb you so early, Bruno, but there's been a death. Old Murcoing passed away and there's something here that I think you ought to see. I'm at his place now, waiting for his daughter to get here.'

'I'll shower and come straight there,' Bruno said. 'How did you learn of his death?'

'I called in to see him yesterday evening and he was fading then, so I sat with him through the night. He died just as the dawn broke.'

Bruno thanked the priest, filled Balzac's food and water bowls and headed for the shower, wondering how many towns were fortunate enough to have a priest who took his parochial duties so seriously that he'd sit up all night with a dying man. Murcoing had been one of the group of four or five old cronies who would gather at the cheaper of the town's cafés. It had a TV for the horse races and off-track betting on the *Pari Mutuel* and the old men would nurse a *petit blanc* all morning and tell each other that France and St Denis were going to the dogs. Without knowing the details, Bruno recalled that Murcoing was one of the town's few remaining Resistance veterans, which could mean a special funeral. If so, he'd be busy. The decision about the solar panels would have to wait.

1

As if determined to make it his last sight on earth, the dead man clutched what at first appeared to be a small painting on canvas or parchment. Bruno moved closer and saw that it was no painting, but a large and beautiful banknote, nearly twice the size of the undistinguished but familiar euro notes in his wallet.

Impeccably engraved in pastel hues stood Mercury with his winged heels before a port teeming with sailing vessels and steamships. Facing him was a bare-chested Vulcan with his forge against a backdrop of a modern factory with tall chimneys belching smoke. It was a Banque de France note for one thousand francs of a kind that Bruno had never seen before. On the quilted counterpane that was tucked up tightly to the corpse's grizzled chin lay another banknote, of the same style and value. Picking it up, Bruno was startled by its texture, still thick and crinkly as if made more of linen than paper. It was the reverse side of the note the dead man held. Against a cornucopia of fruits and flowers, a proud cockerel and sheaves of wheat, two medallions contained the profiles of a Greek god and goddess. They stared impassively at one another against the engraved signatures of some long-dead bank officials, and above them was printed the date of issue: December 1940.

His eyebrows rose. For any Frenchman 1940 was a solemn year. It marked the third German invasion in seventy years, and the second French defeat. But it was the first time Paris had fallen to German arms. In 1870, the capital had withstood months of siege before French troops, under the watchful eye of the Kaiser's armies, stormed the capital to defeat and slaughter the revolutionaries of the Paris Commune. After the invasion of 1914, the Germans had been held and eventually defeated. But in 1940, France had surrendered and signed a humiliating armistice. German soldiers had marched through the Arc de Triomphe and down the Champs-Elysées and launched an occupation that would last for over four years. France under Marshal Pétain's Vichy regime had retained some shred of sovereignty over a truncated half of the country while the Germans took over Paris, the north and the whole Atlantic coastline. So this was a Vichy banknote, Bruno mused, wondering how long after the war's end it had remained legal tender.

There were more notes, all French and for varying amounts, inside a black wooden box that lay open at the dead man's side. Alongside them were some old photographs. The one on top showed a group of young men and boys, carrying weapons from shotguns and revolvers to elderly submachine guns. They were squatting on the running boards or leaning against a black Citroën *traction-avant*, one of the most handsome cars France ever made. A French *tricolore* flag was draped across the bonnet.

Bruno picked up the photo and turned it over to see the scrawled words *Groupe Valmy, le 3 juillet, 1944*. Mainly dressed like farmers, some wore berets and two had the old steel helmets from the 1914–1918 war. An older man sported a French officer's uniform with leather straps across his chest and ammunition pouches. He held up a grenade in each hand. Each of the men had an armband with the letters FFI. Bruno knew it stood for *Forces Françaises de l'Intérieur*, the name De Gaulle had chosen for the Resistance fighters. The next photo showed the same car and an ancient truck parked beside a train. The doors of a goods wagon were open and men in a human chain were passing sacks from the train to the truck. On the back were the words *Neuvic, 26 juillet, 1944*.

'I've never been allowed to see inside his box before,' said the woman. She eyed the photos but made no move to touch them or the banknotes. Her hands, work-worn and gnarled, remained clenched in her lap. She looked to be in her sixties. Father Sentout had introduced her as Joséphine, one of the dead man's three daughters. The priest was packing away the breviary and holy oils he had used to give the last rites. A spot of oil gleamed on the dead man's forehead where the priest had made the last sign of the cross and another on the eyelids.

'Eighty-six,' the priest said. 'A good age, a long life and he served France. Your father is with our father in heaven now.' He put his hand gently on the woman's arm. She shook it off.

'We could have done with that money when I was growing up,' she said, staring dry-eyed at the banknotes. 'They were hard times.'

'It was the banknotes that made me call you,' said Father Sentout, turning to Bruno. 'I don't know what the law says about them, being out of date.'

'They're part of his estate so they'll go to his heirs,' said Bruno. 'But those photos mean I'll probably have to plan for a special funeral.' He turned to Joséphine. 'Do you know if he had the Resistance medal?'

She gestured with her head to a small picture frame on the wall above the bed, below the crucifix. Bruno leaned across the bed to look closer. The curtains were open and the sun was shining but only a modest light came from the tiny courtyard. He saw the stone wall of a neighbour's house barely two metres away. A single light bulb hanging from the ceiling in a dingy parchment lampshade did little to help, but he could make out the small brass circle with its engraved Cross of Lorraine hanging from a black and crimson ribbon. Beneath it in the frame was a faded FFI armband and a photograph of a young Murcoing wearing it and holding a rifle.

'I'll have to check the official list but it looks like he qualifies for a Resistance funeral with a guard of honour and a flag for the coffin,' Bruno said. 'If that's what you want, I'll make the arrangements. The state pays for it all. You can either have him buried at the big Resistance cemetery at Chasseneuil or here in St Denis.'

'I was wondering if he'd left enough to pay for cremation,' she said, looking around the small bedroom with its faded floral wallpaper and a cheap wardrobe that had seen better days. 'He was waiting for a place in the retirement home so the *Mairie* stuck him in here.'

The old man had lived alone in the small apartment formed from the ground floor of a narrow three-storey house in one of the back streets of St Denis. Bruno remembered when the *Mairie* had bought the building and converted it for social housing. Four families were stuffed into the upstairs apartments and another from the waiting list would be moved into this place as soon as the old man was buried. The recession had been hard on St Denis.

'Paul should be here by now,' she said, looking at her watch. 'His grandson, my sister's boy. I called him as soon as I called the priest. He's the only one my dad ever had much time for, the only other man in the family.' She looked sourly at the corpse in the bed. 'Three daughters weren't enough for him.'

'I'll need your phone number to let you know about the funeral,' Bruno said, taking out his notebook. 'Do you know where he kept his papers, if there's a will?'

She shrugged and gave her number. 'Nothing much to leave.' She looked at her watch again. 'I have to go. I'll take whatever food he's left.' Through the open door they heard her rummaging in the small fridge and the food cupboard before she stomped down the narrow passage beside the garage that led to the street.

'Not much sign of grief there,' said Bruno, taking out his phone to call the medical centre. A doctor would have to certify death before Murcoing could be removed to the funeral parlour.

'He didn't have many visits from his family, except for Paul,' the priest said. 'All the sisters live down in Bergerac. Joséphine told me she works as a night nurse, so she probably sees more than enough of the old and sick.'

'How sick was he? I haven't seen him in the café for a while.'

'He knew he was dying and he didn't seem to mind,' Father Sentout replied. 'He had pneumonia but refused to go to hospital. That was the sickness we used to call the old man's friend. It's a peaceful passing, they just slip away.'

'I remember seeing him coming out of church. Was he a regular?'

'His wife dragged him along. After she died he didn't come so often at first, but this place is close to the church so he'd come along for Mass; for the company as much as anything.'

'Did he ever talk about the money?' Bruno gestured at the open box on the bed and the banknote still held tightly in Murcoing's dead hands.

The priest paused, as if weighing his words in a way that made Bruno wonder whether there was some secret of the confessional that was being kept back.

'Not directly, but he'd rail against the fat cats and the rich and complained of being cheated. It was just ramblings. I was never clear whether he reckoned his daughters had cheated him out of the money from the farm or it was something else.'

'Is there something you can't tell me?'

Father Sentout shrugged. 'Nothing directly linked to the money. I presume it's from the Neuvic train. Don't you know about it? The great train robbery by the Resistance?'

Bruno shook his head, reminding the priest that he'd only been in St Denis for a little over a decade. He'd heard of it but not the details. These days, the priest explained, the story was more legend than anything else. A vast sum of money, said to be hundreds of millions, had been stolen from a train taking reserves from the Banque de France to the German naval garrison in Bordeaux. Despite various official inquiries, large amounts had never been accounted for, and local tradition had it that several Resistance leaders had after the war bought grand homes, started businesses and financed political careers.

'If that was his share, he didn't get much,' the priest concluded, nodding at the banknotes on the bed. After the war there had been so many devaluations. Then in 1960 came De

Gaulle's currency reform; a new franc was launched, each worth a hundred of the old ones. 'In reality, that thousand-franc banknote is today probably worth less than a euro, if it's worth anything at all.'

Bruno bent down to prise the note from the cold fingers. As he put it inside the box with the photographs, he heard footsteps in the corridor and Fabiola the doctor bustled into the small room. She was wearing a white medical coat of freshly pressed cotton and her dark hair was piled loosely atop her head. An intriguing scent came with her, a curious blend of antiseptic and perfume, overwhelming the stale air of the room. She kissed Bruno and shook hands with the priest, pulling out her stethoscope to examine the body.

'He obviously didn't take his medicine. Sometimes I wonder why we bother,' she said, sorting through the small array of plastic jars from the pharmacy that stood by the bed. 'He's dead and there's nothing suspicious. I'll leave the certificate at the front desk of the clinic so you can pick it up. Meanwhile we'd better get him to the funeral home.'

She stopped at the door and faced Bruno. 'Is this going to stop you getting to the airport? I'll be free by five so I can do it.'

'It should be OK. If there's a problem, I'll call you,' he replied. Pamela, the Englishwoman Bruno had been seeing since the previous autumn, was to land at the local airport of Bergerac just before six that evening and he was to meet her and drive her back to St Denis. Pamela, who kept horses along with the *gîtes* she rented out to tourists, had been pleased to find in Fabiola a year-round tenant for one of the *gîtes* and the two women had become friends.

Bruno began making calls as soon as Fabiola and the priest left. He started with the veterans' department at the Ministry of Defence to confirm a Resistance ceremony and then called the funeral parlour. Next he rang Florence, the science teacher at the local *collège* who was now running the town choir, to ask if she could arrange for the *Chant des Partisans*, the anthem of the Resistance, to be sung at the funeral. He rang the Centre Jean Moulin in Bordeaux, the Resistance museum and archive, for their help in preparing a summary of Murcoing's war record. The last call was to the social security office, to stop the dead man's pension payments. As he waited to be put through to the right department, he began to look around.

In the sitting room an old TV squatted on a chest of drawers. In the top one, Bruno found a large envelope marked 'Banque' and others that contained various utility bills and a copy of the deed of sale for Murcoing's farm in the hills above Limeuil. It had been sold three years earlier, when prices were already tumbling, for 85,000 euros. The buyer had a name that sounded Dutch and the *notaire* was local. Bruno remembered the place, a ramshackle farmhouse with a roof that needed fixing and an old tobacco barn where goats were kept. The farm had been too small to be viable, even if the land had been good. Murcoing's last bank statement said he had six thousand euros in a *Livret*, a tax-free account set up by the state to encourage saving, and just over eight hundred in his current account. He'd been getting a pension of four hundred euros a month. There was no phone to be seen and no address book. A dusty shotgun hung on the wall and a well-used fishing rod stood in the corner. The house key hung on a hook beside the door. Left alone with the corpse until the hearse came, Bruno thought old Murcoing did not have much to show for a life of hard work and patriotism.

He wrote out a receipt for the gun, the box and its contents and left it in the drawer. Beside the TV set he saw a well-used wallet. Inside were a *carte d'identité* and the *carte vitale* that gave access to the health service, but no credit cards and no cash. Joséphine would have seen to that. There were three small photos, one a portrait of a handsome young man and two more with the same young man with an arm around the shoulders of the elderly Murcoing at what looked like a family gathering. That must be Paul, the favourite grandson, who was supposed to arrive. Bruno left a note for him on the table, along with his business card and mobile number, asking Paul to get in touch about the funeral and saying he'd taken the gun, the box and banknotes to his office in the *Mairie* for safe keeping.

As the hearse was arriving, Bruno's mobile phone rang and a sultry voice said: 'I have something for you.' The Mayor's secretary was incapable of saying even *Bonjour* without some hint of coquetry. 'It's a message from some foreigner's cleaning woman on the road out to Rouffignac. She thinks there's been a burglary.'

2

Bruno sighed as he set out for the site of the burglary. It was the third this month, targeting isolated houses owned by foreigners who usually came to France only in the summer. The first two families, one Dutch and one English, had been down for the Easter holidays and found their homes almost surgically robbed. Rugs, paintings, silver and antique furniture had all disappeared. The usual burglars' loot of TV sets and stereos had been ignored and the thieves had evidently been professionals. No fingerprints were found and little sign of a break-in. Casual inspection might never have known a burglary had happened. Each of the houses had an alarm system, but one that used the telephone to alert a central switchboard, since the houses were too deep in the country for an alarm to be heard. The telephone wires had been cut.

To Bruno's irritation, the Gendarmes had made a cursory inspection, shrugged their shoulders and left him to write a report for the insurance claim. He understood their thinking. Individual burglaries were almost never solved. The Gendarmes preferred to wait until they had a clear lead to one of the region's fences and offer him a deal: a light sentence in return for testifying against the burglars. Then they could report dozens or even hundreds of burglaries to have been solved.

This made their success rate look good on annual reports, which was what Paris wanted, and it led to bonuses and promotions. But it usually meant that few of the stolen items were returned to their owners. Bruno thought there should be a better way, and he'd suggested to the local insurance brokers that they ask their clients to provide photos of their more valuable items to improve the chances of tracking them down. Few bothered to do so.

But Bruno knew this house and was sure such photos would be on file. It was a small *gentilhommerie*, the estate agents' term for a building that was smaller than a manor house but bigger than the usual farmhouses of the region. Dating from the eighteenth century, it had an ornate entrance with stone pillars supporting a porch, two sets of French windows on each side of the entrance and five mansard windows on the upper storey. Stone urns for flowers, still empty at this time of year, flanked the French windows and each of the mansards had been topped with a stone pineapple, the sign of the handiwork of Carlos, one of the best of the local builders. The house had been impeccably restored, using old tiles on the new roof, and the old stucco had been chipped away from the façade to reveal the honey-coloured stone beneath. The drive was lined with fruit trees and rose bushes flanked the vegetable garden. At the rear, Bruno recalled, was a swimming pool and a stone terrace with a fine view across the ridges that sloped down to the river Vézère.

Bruno had been invited here twice for garden parties and another time for dinner. He had met the British owner, Jack Crimson, at the tennis club where the retired civil servant played gentle games of mixed doubles. He always signed up to take part in the annual tennis tournament, offered some gift for the prizes and made a generous donation each year for the children's tennis team. An affable man, always well dressed and with thick grey hair, Crimson spoke decent French. A little plump, but with the build of a man who'd been an athlete in his youth, he served excellent wines and threw an enjoyable party that had been Bruno's introduction to a deceptively potent English drink that they called Pimm's. He arrived each summer in a stately old Jaguar. When Bruno had seen that the house was filled with rare books, paintings and antiques, he had persuaded Crimson to take photos of them all for registration at the insurance office.

'*Ça va*, Bruno? I heard your van coming up the drive,' said Gaëlle, greeting him from the front door. 'They got in through the back and took the lot, all the good furniture, the rugs and paintings. They left the books. And they cut the phone line so I had to call the *Mairie* on my mobile.'

'Were all the shutters closed when you arrived?' he asked.

Gaëlle, a homely and competent widow in her fifties, nodded. 'I opened them myself to air the rooms. I always do. It's what Monsieur Crimson wants.'

She led him round the side of the house to the rear door, where the wooden shutter on a French window had been forced open. One of the small windowpanes had been broken by a professional; some glue had been smeared on the glass, a folded newspaper attached and then punched to make little noise and a clear break. The same technique had been used at the earlier burglaries. Inside, darker patches on the walls showed where paintings had hung.

'This was the dining room,' Gaëlle said. 'You can't tell, now the furniture's gone. He had some lovely old paintings of food, game birds and old-fashioned pots full of vegetables. They don't seem to have taken anything from upstairs.'

'I hope you haven't been using that,' he said, pointing at the feather duster she was holding. 'They might have left fingerprints.'

'I know, I watch those crime shows on TV. I just like to carry it.'

'Have you called Monsieur Crimson?'

'I phoned his number in England right after I called the *Mairie*, but I just heard some recorded English and then that beep, so I left a message. He'll call me back when he gets it.'

Bruno took a note of Crimson's number and established that Gaëlle, who came twice a week to clean, had last been at the house four days earlier. He went from room to room with his notebook, relying on Gaëlle's memory for the missing items. The desk and filing cabinets seemed untouched in the room Crimson used as a study and library, but Gaëlle said an antique rug had been taken. At the side of the stairs was another door, a broken hasp and padlock lying on the floor.

'That's his wine cellar,' she said, using the handle of her duster to turn on the light switch as she led him down the stairs. Bruno noted with approval the cellar's gravel floor, and the care that had gone into the labelling of the stacks. It made it easier to see what had been stolen: vintage Pomerols and Sauternes and a case of 2005 Grand Millésime of Château de Tiregand, the prince of the Pécharmant wines.

'They knew what they were stealing,' Bruno said, thinking that these were no common burglars. Cases of Cru Bourgeois reds and white Burgundies and even of champagne had been left in their racks.

As he returned to the staircase, Bruno noticed a small door beneath the stairs. He tried the handle and it was open, leading to a dark cellar room that smelt of fuel oil. In the ceiling to one side he saw a chink of daylight.

'This used to house the oil tank,' she said. 'It hasn't been used for years. He's got gas now for the central heating.'

Back upstairs, she led him to the side of the terrace, where she pointed to two metal plates held together by a sturdy padlock and said that was where the oil tank was refilled. Then she showed him some tyre marks on a patch of lawn.

'I think they brought their van round here to the back so they could load up easily,' she said. 'It rained all night the day before yesterday so maybe that was when they came.'

'You should be doing my job,' he said. 'It must be those TV shows you watch.' Bruno followed the line of the telephone wire to the place where it had been cut. He called the security number at France Télécom to see if they could establish a time when the line had gone down. It had been shortly before 1 p.m. two days earlier, a clever choice. If the house was occupied, they could come back later. If the wealthy foreigner was out, he was almost certainly at lunch and would not be back for an hour or more.

'It's a shame,' Gaëlle said, following in his footsteps. 'He's such a nice man, always polite and generous and he keeps the place very neat. You wouldn't know there wasn't a woman in the house.' She looked a little wistful, evidently fond of her employer. 'She died the year after they bought this place, his wife. He keeps a portrait of her in the bedroom, but that's still there.'

Bruno nodded but said nothing. The burglars must have

known that Crimson would be away, and that his house was very much worth robbing. They had come equipped with a van large enough to take a dining room table, chairs and cases of wine as well as the paintings and a valuable old clock that Gaëlle said stood on the mantelpiece in the living room. That suggested inside knowledge and that in turn meant, however unlikely it seemed, that Gaëlle had to be a suspect, or at least eliminated from suspicion.

'Where did you have lunch the day before yesterday, Gaëlle?' he asked, as casually as he could. Gaëlle eyed him steadily and replied: 'With my cousin Roberte from the *Mairie*, helping her bake stuff for her kid's birthday party. Don't worry, I know you have to ask.'

He tried Crimson's number in England, but like Gaëlle he heard only the automated voice and the beep that invited him to leave a message. He did so, briefly and slowly, giving his office and cellphone numbers and adding that he'd come back with a new padlock and hasp for the forced shutters and would try to secure the house. When Gaëlle pedalled away down the drive, Bruno debated with himself whether he should go the extra step. Remembering the fine dinner he'd enjoyed at Crimson's table, he decided that he should and he rang Isabelle's number at the Interior Ministry in Paris. Again, he was invited to leave a message and he gave Crimson's name and London number, asking if Isabelle could inform her Scotland Yard contacts to see if they could track him down.

How would the thieves get rid of such a mixture of stuff, Bruno wondered. Furniture, rugs and paintings could be sold at any one of the *brocantes*, the antiques fairs that were held in town after town throughout the French summer. There must be thousands of them, everything sold for cash and no records of the sellers. Unless Crimson's possessions ended up with a reputable dealer, the chances of tracking them down, even with the photos, were slim. The wine might be different, unless the thieves had very discerning palates and wanted it for themselves.

That triggered an idea, and as he re-entered St Denis Bruno checked the time and turned off into the driveway to the *collège*, parking in front of the row of modest apartments where the teachers lived. Subsidized and almost free housing was one of the ways the French state sought to lure well-qualified teachers to live and work in the country. For his friend Florence, a divorced mother of two toddlers with a science diploma who had found it tough to make ends meet, the teaching job had been a godsend.

Her arrival had been even better for St Denis. Now the mainstay of the town choir, Florence had also taken over the administration of the school sports teams, arranging fixtures and registrations. She had blossomed in her new role. The dispirited and somewhat dowdy young newcomer Bruno had first met had blossomed into a cheerful self-confident woman with a widening circle of friends. She had earned the respect of her pupils and turned science into the most popular subject. One of her first purchases with her new salary had been a new computer, and she had persuaded the local recycling centre to let her have all the discarded laptops and desktops so that she could repair them to launch a computer club at the school. The *Sud Ouest* newspaper had run a story about the way all the club computers, when not in use, were offering their free time to the SETI institute, helping process the reams of data from its radio-telescopes that were scanning outer space for signs of extraterrestrial intelligence.

Florence was giving her children lunch when Bruno arrived. They waved their spoons and chanted '*Bonjour, Bruno*' when she showed him into the small kitchen.

'Have you eaten?' she asked. 'I made Pamela's fish pie and there's more than enough.'

Bruno kissed the children and accepted gratefully.

'I know you like this bit,' said Florence, scraping off some of the crisp cheese *gratin* that covered the pie and transferring it to Bruno's plate. 'It's come to rival pizza as the kids' favourite meal.' She poured two glasses of Bergerac Sec from the 5-litre box in the refrigerator and handed one to Bruno. 'This is a pleasant excuse to have a glass of wine at lunchtime, but what brings you here?'

'Your computer club,' he replied. 'There's been a burglary and a lot of good wine was stolen and I was thinking that the thieves might try to sell it on priceminister.com or one of those other websites like eBay. Could your club come up with a program that would monitor such sites for these wines?' He handed over a copy of the list he had made of the gaps in Crimson's cellar.

Florence sipped her wine and scanned the list. 'It should be possible. You have the vineyard, the year, even some of the shippers. Your burglary victim must keep good records.'

'He's an Englishman, a retired civil servant. He has his cellar all catalogued like a filing system, along with what he paid for the wine. They took over ten thousand euros' worth. I can also get photos of the furniture, rugs and paintings that were stolen.'

Her eyes widened. 'Leave it with me. It's the kind of project that should get the kids thinking.'

'He's the kind of man who'd pay a reward, so you can offer them an incentive.'

'The thrill of the chase is all the incentive they need. You ought to see the way they've taken to hacking.'

Bruno stopped chewing. 'You're teaching them to hack? Is that a good idea?'

'They'd do it anyway, kids being what they are. I'm just teaching them about computer security, how to build fire-walls and search for malware. I don't let them practise on anything serious, but they've got behind a few of those pay firewalls some newspapers and magazines put up. The next project is to see if they can build their own version of an iPad, so they've been all over the web looking for technical tips. The English teacher says it's done wonders for their English, so now Pamela is helping us to set up a twinning system with a school in Scotland. We've already got a Skype link with their computer club.'

School had never been like this in his day, Bruno thought. This was an unusual generation that was about to be unleashed on St Denis, a rural commune where there were still farmers who drew their water from an ancestral well and in winter slept above their livestock for warmth.

'How are things between you and Pamela?' she asked, clearing away the children's plates and serving their dessert of stewed apple and yoghurt. 'I get the impression she's still depressed by her mother's death.'

'She's due to fly back from Scotland later today after some complicated business with lawyers about the will and inheritance taxes,' he replied, deliberately not answering her question. 'Her finances are none of my business, but it seems that she has arranged matters so that she can stay in St Denis.'

Bruno was not at all sure about the status of his relationship with Pamela, a woman with whom he'd had an on-and-off affair over the past few months. It was an affair where he sometimes felt he served at her pleasure, spending the night only at Pamela's invitation and not allowed to take anything for granted. A woman who guarded her privacy, she could nonetheless charm him with her warmth and generosity. And she could surprise him, bringing a flavour of the exotic and the unfamiliar. She was a woman unlike most of those he knew in St Denis, and it was no surprise that she had forged friendships with Fabiola the doctor and with Florence, similarly strong and independent women with their own careers.

He kissed Florence and the children when he left, the taste of the after-lunch coffee lingering pleasantly in his mouth, and was just climbing into his van when his mobile phone launched into the opening notes of the *Marseillaise*. He checked the screen and saw a Paris number that he recognized.

'I got your message,' said Isabelle. 'This burglary of yours is delicate stuff. Crimson is not just your usual British pensioner. His last job was running their Joint Security Committee in the Cabinet Office in Downing Street. That's the body to which both their spies and their security people report. He was their spymaster.'

'You mean like that "M" woman in the James Bond films?' He felt himself grinning at the absurdity of such a role being played by the genial old tennis player who had served him such excellent wine.

23

'Just like that. And he's an old friend or at least a long-standing colleague of the Brigadier, so I've been ordered down to St Denis to take over the inquiry. There may be more to this burglary than meets the eye.'

3

Bruno could tell from the way he took off his glasses and rubbed the bridge of his nose that his Mayor was not happy. His wife was in hospital for some tests that sounded ominous. The project for the new sewers was well behind schedule and the financial crisis meant that funds and grants from Paris were being cut. And now the commune was being hit by this wave of burglaries. The fact that one of the victims turned out to be an eminent Englishman with official connections in Paris was bad enough, but that neither the Mayor nor Bruno had known that a retired British spymaster had been living on their territory for years was even worse.

Burglaries were supposed to be the responsibility of the Gendarmes, but Bruno knew it would have been a mistake to make such a pitiful excuse. This was his turf and therefore his responsibility. However, Bruno knew how easily the Mayor could be distracted by anything to do with local history.

On the shelf by the ancient desk lay a thick file of handwritten pages, the Mayor's ambitious project of writing the definitive history of St Denis from Neanderthal man through the iron and bronze ages, the coming of the Celts to the arrival of the Romans and all through the centuries to the present day. At various times Bruno had heard him wax lyrical about the Merovingian kings and the ancient Duchy of Toulouse, the Hundred Years War against the English and the Albigensian heresy. There had been a whole year when the Mayor spoke of little but the passage of the conquering Arabs from Spain until they reeled back in defeat after Charles Martel stopped them at the battle of Tours in AD 732. The Mayor loved the coincidence that his three great French heroes shared the same name: Charles Martel, King Charles VII, who finally evicted the English in 1453, and, of course, Charles de Gaulle.

So Bruno solemnly laid one of his banknotes on the Mayor's desk, smoothed it out, and said: 'Old Loïc Murcoing died this morning and had this in a box on his bed. Father Sentout thinks it came from the Neuvic train.'

'The Neuvic train, really?' The Mayor replaced his spectacles and peered at the note. 'July 26, 1944. It was the very day the Americans were making their breakout from the Normandy beachhead.' His voice tailed off and he fell silent, his eyes fixed on some other place, some other time.

'I've only heard the legends. They say it was a lot of money.'

'Money? Over two billion francs. Two thousand three hundred million, if memory serves me right, which means something over three hundred million euros in today's money. Did you know it all began as a plot between two of our Prefects? One was a *Résistant* and the other was condemned as a *collabo*, although perhaps that's too crude a word.'

'I don't understand.' Bruno's head was still reeling at the idea of three hundred million euros in cash, and wondering how much it had weighed, how it had been taken from the train.

'I suppose it was a credit to the wisdom of our Prefects,' the

Mayor began. There had been the Vichy Prefect, a career civil servant named Callard, and Maxim Roue, the Gaullist one who would replace him after the Liberation. The two men knew each other, and remained in discreet contact. With the Allies already established ashore in Normandy and the Russian armies thundering through Poland towards Germany, Callard knew the Vichy regime was doomed. With an eye to his own future, he tipped off his successor that the Banque de France reserves were to be moved by train from Périgueux, where they had been stored to be safe from the bombing. The money was to be taken to Bordeaux for consignment to the *Kriegsmarine*. There was speculation that the German navy wanted to ship it out by submarine; perhaps to finance a new Reich in Argentina. Whatever the motives, the Resistance ambushed the train and took the money. A man calling himself Lieutenant Krikri even left with the train guards a signed receipt for the full amount, plus another fifteen hundred francs for the canvas sacks that held the money, each one sealed with lead and stamped with the seal of the Banque de France. Altogether, the haul had weighed six tons.

The Mayor explained that various official inquiries after the war had concluded that the money was spent on pay and supplies for the Resistance and money for their dependants. Even after the Germans lost Paris and retreated back into Germany some of their garrisons held out in La Rochelle and elsewhere. The Allies couldn't spare any troops for them, so the Resistance took over the task, transforming themselves into official units of the French army in the process. But they still had to be fed and paid and their families supported. That was the official explanation.

'And the unofficial explanation?' asked Bruno.

'All rumour. Some of the local Resistance chiefs enjoyed very wealthy lifestyles after the war, Malraux for one, although he was too close to De Gaulle to be touched. There was another, a man called Urbanovich who suddenly became extremely rich with a big place in Paris and another in Cannes and ran one of the most expensive art galleries in Europe. Not bad for a Communist who was probably a Soviet agent. But nothing was ever proved.'

'Three hundred million in today's money – there must have been a lot of cash left over.'

'Indeed, which is why the rumours persist. But you should remember that there were no public funds for political parties until the mid-1950s, and parties need premises, staff, printing facilities and newspapers, particularly a new party like the Gaullists. I think you'll find that most political scandals can be traced to money, that or sex.'

'You mean there's a difference?' Bruno said with a grin.

'So cynical, so young. Leave such unsavoury reflections to your elders.' The Mayor smiled back, more cheerful now. 'If you're interested in all this, there's a woman historian at the Sorbonne who has a house the other side of Les Eyzies. Her name is Jacqueline Morgan and she's half-American, half-French – her father was a diplomat in Paris after the war and he married a woman from the Périgord. I ran into her in the Bibliothèque Nationale when I was doing some research in Paris. She's gathered a lot of new material from the British and American archives on the Resistance and their post-war political roles. She's working on a book that I think should make quite a stir.'

'Sounds interesting.' Bruno would make a point of visiting this Jacqueline Morgan. 'Murcoing had just over five thousand of those old francs in his chest. Not a lot to show for such a haul.'

'The lads who took part were promised ten thousand each, but a romantic young lieutenant called Gandoin said that for his men of the Groupe Valmy, duty was its own reward. His men would take no fee. But at least one of the sacks of cash disappeared that night when they were moving the money.'

'Whatever happened to him?'

'No idea. Perhaps I should have asked Murcoing but it's too late now. I remember my father telling me of the brave and selfless Lieutenant Gandoin. A lot of those young heroes died that winter, once they were re-formed into the French army and sent up to liberate Alsace and then to invade Germany.' The Mayor looked up, forcing a briskness into his voice. 'I suppose these banknotes now belong to Murcoing's heirs.'

'Yes, I signed a receipt.' Bruno leaned over and took the banknote from the Mayor's hand.

'I'd like to have one framed and hung here in the *Mairie* with a suitable plaque of explanation.'

'You might ask Murcoing's daughter Joséphine if you could buy it from her. She struck me as the kind of woman who'd do a lot for twenty euros. You should have seen her perk up when I said the state pays for Resistance funerals. I've got her phone number here.'

The Mayor reached for his phone.

Bruno took the back road to Les Eyzies, a drive that always stirred him with memories of cases and incidents past, as well as for the stupendous limestone cliffs that rose to each side of the river. Off to his left up the hill was the *Grotte du Sorcier*, the cave with one of the very few prehistoric engravings of a human face, and a place dear in his memory as the spot where he had first kissed Isabelle. Further up the valley was the site of the archaeological dig where the body of a young man wearing a Swatch had been found alongside a grave dating from thirty thousand years ago.

He drove through the narrow main street of Les Eyzies, tucked between the cliff and the river, and mentally doffed his cap to the giant statue of Cro-Magnon man that loomed above the town. He took the sharply curving road that led along the Vézère valley to the Lascaux cave, and then at Tursac followed the Mayor's directions to the small house of Jacqueline Morgan. A white BMW convertible with Paris number plates, its roof down, was parked beside a well-tended vegetable garden. Bruno noted with approval her choice of cherry tomatoes, aubergines, courgettes, haricot beans and some sweetcorn.

Wearing jeans and a Columbia sweatshirt, clogs on her feet and a headband holding back a mass of iron-grey curls, Jacqueline Morgan took the cigarette from her mouth to extend a hand and greet him. She looked vaguely familiar – perhaps he'd seen her shopping in the market or standing in line at the Post Office. Behind her on each wall of the passage were loaded bookshelves. Bruno explained that his Mayor had suggested she might be able to help him learn more about the Neuvic train, and showed her Murcoing's banknote.

Her eyes widened. 'I've never actually seen one of the notes before,' she said. 'Come in, come in, you're very welcome. The Mayor has told me a lot about you.'

Off to the left he saw a small sitting room with old furniture that looked comfortable, although hemmed in by more bookshelves that lined all the walls. She led him to the room on the right, again filled with bookshelves but with a large round table in the middle that contained a laptop, boxes of index files and several books. They were held open at certain pages by pens, a pepper mill and a handsome silver coffee pot. From the kitchen came the unmistakable scent of lamb being slowly roasted with rosemary and garlic.

'I clear all this away for dinner,' she said, piling together some of the books on the table and clearing more from a chair to make some space for Bruno to sit. On the top of the pile sat a copy of Guy Penaud's *Histoire de la Résistance en Périgord*. 'You caught me working on footnotes, a scholar's drudgery. I was just about to make some coffee. How do you take yours?'

'Black, one sugar, please. Are you writing a new book?'

'Yes, on Franco-American relations during the Cold War, a fertile field. I've written on bits of it before, on nuclear cooperation and American policy toward France's wars in Vietnam and Algeria, but now I'm trying to put it all together.'

'The Mayor seems to think it will have quite an impact, that you have found lots of new material,' Bruno said.

'We'll see.' She went into the adjoining kitchen. Bruno heard a clatter of cups and the whir of a coffee grinder. She poked her head round the door and continued talking. 'He's a good man, your Mayor. It's such a shame about his wife. I'm giving him dinner tonight after he gets back from visiting her in hospital. Left to himself, he'd just have a sandwich, one of those men who are useless on their own.'

'We're hoping she'll be able to come home soon.'

'She's not coming home,' came the voice from the kitchen. 'You don't come back from galloping lymphatic cancer.'

Bruno was stunned. The Mayor had kept his wife's condition a secret from everyone, at least everyone but Jacqueline.

'You mean you didn't know?' she said, poking her head out again. '*Putain*, me and my big mouth. I'm really sorry, I thought his friends knew.'

Maybe some of them, thought Bruno. He'd thought he was pretty close to his Mayor, but evidently not. And he was sure nobody else at the *Mairie* knew. Obviously the Mayor's relationship with Jacqueline was closer than he'd thought.

'Let's forget it, OK?' she said, coming into the room. 'And don't tell him I told you. You were asking about the Neuvic train . . .'

She turned back into the kitchen and he heard a metal tray being placed on a counter. He'd never been close to the Mayor's wife, who had rarely appeared at the *Mairie*, but the news came as a shock. Cécile had never joined her husband in campaigning and seemed content to be a traditional wife, tending her home and her garden, politely greeting people in the market. She had stayed behind when the Mayor had gone to Paris to work in politics, and only joined him there once, for his investiture into the Senate.

Jacqueline re-entered the room with a tray, speaking as if the subject had never changed. 'Parts of my work led me into aspects of Resistance finance, which is why I got interested in the Neuvic train, the slush-fund to end all slush-funds.'

'Is this the manuscript?' he asked as he cleared some more space for the tray with its fine porcelain cups and saucers and a cafetière. He gestured to the typescript in front of him, post-it notes in different colours scattered through the pages.

'No, mine is still in the computer, with copies sent elsewhere round the net in case my hard drive dies. That happened to me once and it was hell. What you have there are my father's memoirs, typed up from his handwritten journals.'

'He was a diplomat, is that right?'

'Yes, he was in the American Embassy after the war and then on the Marshall Plan, the rebuilding of Europe's economies. That was where I first read about your train, where he called it the slush-fund.'

'The Mayor reckons it was worth about three hundred million in today's money,' he said.

She shrugged as she rested both hands on the plunger of the cafetière and began to press down. 'At the time it was worth a lot more in relative terms, at least until the devaluations. In 1945, the official exchange rate was just over a hundred francs to the dollar. But by 1949 it was over three hundred to the dollar. The money aboard the Neuvic train was certainly a vast amount, worth about five per cent of total government spending in 1946. Put it this way, the national education budget that year was 470 million francs, and the Neuvic train held about five times that.'

Five times the education budget? The proportion staggered him, but Jacqueline had just begun. There were at least three official inquiries into the fate of the Neuvic money, she explained, adding that they had all pretty much whitewashed the whole affair, claiming the money went to finance the Resistance and their families and some was used to bribe prison guards. That was true up to a point, she conceded, but only for a fraction of the money, maybe half or a little more. Millions had been stolen.

'How much do you know about French politics after the war?' she asked.

'De Gaulle came to power after the liberation of Paris in 1944 but resigned in 1946,' he replied. 'I'm not sure why.'

'That's simple. De Gaulle wanted a strong presidency rather than the unstable parliaments of the pre-war days. The parties, who'd been in a coalition of Communists, Socialists and Christian Democrats, naturally wanted a return to the party system and they accused De Gaulle of wanting to be a dictator. Then the other two wanted to get rid of the Communists as the Cold War got under way and the Gaullists started building their own party, the RPF. Politics are expensive, so that's where a lot of the money went, but maybe it was more virtual than real.'

'Virtual? I don't understand.'

She looked at him. 'Suppose you're an American diplomat in Paris in 1946 and 1947, and the Communists are the biggest political party. Remember the Cold War is just getting started. What would American policy be?'

'Stop the Communists, I suppose. And try to strengthen the other parties, the anti-Communists.'

'Right, and if you're an American diplomat, with all the money in the world, you'd use it to help the anti-Communists, right?'

'Yes.'

'No, wrong,' Jacqueline said firmly. 'At least wrong if you do it in public where there's immediately a scandal about Americans buying up the French political system. But if some loyal Frenchmen with fine Resistance records start handing out wads of money with a nod and wink and a discreet murmur about *le train de Neuvic*, nobody asks any questions, even if the money really came from the Americans.'

'But wouldn't they have to change it from dollars?'

'Yes, but remember how the Marshall Plan worked. The Americans gave dollars to the Europeans to buy food and goods and machine tools to restart their factories. They were repaid in local currency, which the Americans could do nothing with. There were no real exchange markets in those days. So the various American embassies suddenly found themselves sitting on this vast slush-fund of French francs, Italian lire, Dutch guilders and so on. The money went to stop Communism through funding election campaigns, subsidizing newspapers and student organizations, backing Socialist trade unions to undermine the Communist ones.'

'Two slush-funds, the Neuvic money and the Marshall Plan, and who knows which was which?'

'That's what I'm trying to find out,' said Jacqueline. 'That's why my father's memoirs are the key to all this. He was in it all the way through, from late 1945 to 1952 when the Marshall Plan became the Mutual Security Plan.'

'And how much was the Marshall Plan?'

'Altogether? About thirteen billion dollars. But another thirteen billion had already been sent in aid to Europe between the end of the war and the Marshall Plan starting in 1947. So the US pumped in a total of twenty-six billion, at a time when the American GDP was just over two hundred billion a year. Thirteen per cent of GDP is pretty generous if you ask me, but not too expensive to stop Western Europe going Communist. And it was certainly a whole lot cheaper than a war.'

'I had no idea,' said Bruno.

'Not many people do. If you want to know what really happened in history, it's like those two *Washington Post* reporters said in the Watergate scandal: Follow the money.'

'The Mayor is right about your book having a big impact,' Bruno said. 'I think you'll be rewriting the recent history of France.'

'Oh goody,' she said, an impish grin lighting up her face, making her look years younger and very much more attractive. 'And wait till you see what I've dug up on secret nuclear cooperation. French independent nuclear weapons aren't nearly as independent as you think.' She said it as casually as if she were talking of the vegetables in her garden, went to one of her bookshelves and handed him a slim paperback. He looked at the title: *Le partage des milliards de la Résistance*, the distribution of the Resistance billions.

'That will get you off to a good start; most of the background is in there. Let me have it back when you're done. More coffee, or can I offer you something stronger? You look like you could do with a drink.'

Even as he was thinking that a stiff scotch would be welcome, Bruno's mobile rang. It was Albert, head of the *pompiers*, the local fire brigade, which also acted as the emergency medical service.

'Got an emergency call from somewhere up in the hills by St Chamassy about somebody badly hurt with head injuries,' Albert said. His voice was faint, the signal weak. 'We've just got here and the Gendarmes should be on their way if they can find it.' He gave Bruno directions. 'And bring a doctor for a death certificate. The guy's dead. I think we might have a murder.'

4

There was still no sign of the Gendarmes when Bruno parked his van on the rough grass beside Albert's red emergency vehicle. A rather battered silver Renault Clio stood beside it. In front of the cottage on a small patch of gravel was a blue Ford Transit, its side and rear doors open to reveal an empty interior. It carried English registration plates and a small GB plaque on the rear bumper. Beside it lay a lumpish shape, two men standing over it. One was Albert and the other was a stranger, carrying a plastic bag.

The house behind them was like many others in the district, with a red tile roof in the shape of a witch's hat and walls of light-brown stone that turned in the sun to the colour of honey. Wooden shutters hung on the windows, painted the usual pale grey that had become ubiquitous after the French navy sold off its vast stocks of paint very cheaply. To one side was a small barn and to the other a pocket-sized swimming pool, flanked by two cheap metal chairs that needed a new coat of white paint. A couple of empty flower pots waited for the geranium season. The front door was open to show a floor of terracotta tiles. There were no personal touches, no patch of herbs or vegetables, no children's toys. It was a *gîte*, a farmhouse cheaply restored and transformed into a holiday rental.

'Salut, Bruno,' said Albert. 'This is Monsieur Valentoux from Paris, who called us. The silver Clio belongs to him. He was going to be staying here with the dead man.'

'Monsieur,' said Bruno, noting the pale, drawn face as he shook hands with Valentoux. He caught the smell of vomit, saw a patch of it by the rear wheel of the blue van. There were more spatters on the front of Valentoux's jeans and on his shoes, leather trainers that looked expensive. His hair was short with blond streaks and he wore a dark blue scarf around his neck, tucked into a cream shirt that Bruno guessed was silk.

'I put a cradle over the head,' said Albert, looking down at the body. It was covered by a fireman's red blanket and draped over something at one end. Bruno kneeled down and lifted a corner of the blanket and saw a spindly metal framework, rather like the ones he put over his winter seedlings.

'It's from my garden,' Albert explained. 'I was picking it up from my sister and it seemed like a good idea to cover him up. He's been dead for some hours. It's not a pleasant sight.'

'*Mon Dieu*,' said Valentoux. He raised his head to look at Bruno. 'I couldn't even tell you if it's him.'

'Perhaps the fire chief could help you to your car, Monsieur,' said Bruno, waiting until they left before uncovering the battered shape that had once been a human head. Blood had pooled beneath and behind the man's head. Bits of shattered bone and teeth stood out from the pool. The face was unrecognizable as human, the features savagely, perhaps deliberately, obliterated.

Bruno closed his eyes and tried to concentrate, forcing himself out from shock and back into professionalism by trying to think what weapon might have done this. Perhaps an iron bar, he told himself. He opened his eyes and looked at the rest of the body. One hand was blood-smeared and swollen, as if he might have tried to protect himself. The other hand looked to have been professionally manicured, the nails buffed and polished. An open and empty black leather wallet with brass reinforcements on the corners lay between the dead man's thighs.

Assuming the body was male, the dead man had been wearing khaki slacks and boat shoes without socks, a plain black T-shirt and a denim jacket. Only the jacket collar bore signs of blood, which suggested he had been knocked to the ground and then the head battered as he lay. His attacker must have stood over him, probably straddling the body, and then applied backhand and forehand blows to the head. That was the only way Bruno could interpret the way the blood had spattered. They had experts on that, these days, at the *Police Nationale*.

He replaced the blanket over its cradle, rose and took out his phone to call J-J, chief of detectives for the *Département*, and peered into the blue Ford as he waited for J-J to pick up. As usual, he got the recording, left a message and then sent J-J a brief text message.

On the floor by the passenger seat was an empty packet of crisps, some sandwich wrappings and a British newspaper, a *Daily Telegraph* with yesterday's date. Under the seat was a magazine called *Antiques Weekly* and he noticed some maps and other papers in the door pocket. He took a pair of evidence gloves from his pouch. One set of papers seemed to be a rental agreement for the van for three weeks from a branch of Avis in some town called Croydon. The renter was named as Francis

Fullerton. Tucked into the Avis folder was a ticket stub from the 7 a.m. Eurostar train the previous day. Bruno checked that the registration number on the ticket matched that of the blue Ford. The other sheaf of papers was from Delightful Dordogne, the local holiday rentals agency run by Dougal, a retired Scottish businessman. The *gîte* was rented to a Francis Fullerton for two weeks, starting as usual with such agreements on a Saturday. So why had Fullerton arrived early?

The rest of the van was empty and Bruno went back to the body. Some mixed euro and British coins were in a trouser pocket and he found a British passport in the denim jacket. He walked back to the Clio, where Albert and Valentoux were leaning against the side, smoking. Valentoux was still carrying his plastic bag.

'What's in there?' Bruno asked, gesturing at the bag. In the distance, he could hear a siren. The Gendarmes seemed at last to have found the place.

Valentoux lifted the bag and looked at it in confusion, as if he'd never seen it before. He handed it to Bruno. 'I was going to welcome him with lunch.'

Inside was a baguette, a *saucisson*, cheese, fruit and tomatoes and a bottle of champagne, no longer cold. Nestling at the bottom was a small wrapped package. Bruno asked him to open it.

'I'd rather not, it's a gift,' said Valentoux, and then caught himself. He took the package, tore open the silver bow and the gold wrapping paper. Inside was a gift box which he opened to reveal a Laguiole folding knife with a wooden handle and corkscrew and a leather pouch. 'Francis had always wanted one.'

'What time did you get here?'

'About one thirty, maybe a bit later. I left Paris before seven this morning to avoid the rush.' He tossed his cigarette to the ground, crushed it with a violent twist of his foot, then took a pack of Marlboro Gold from his jacket pocket to light another. Then he offered the packet. Bruno shook his head but Albert took one.

'Did you come by the autoroute? You should have a receipt.'

Valentoux went round to the side door of his Clio and took two pieces of paper from the well between the front seats. One was an autoroute *péage* receipt for that day and the other from a petrol station in Limoges, timed at 11.28 a.m. that morning. That was consistent with his arrival at about half-past one. Bruno nodded and put them in his notebook.

'His call to the emergency service came at 1.43 p.m. and he was transferred to us. He sounded panicked, said he thought his friend was dead,' said Albert. 'I got here about twenty minutes later and called you.'

'What brings you down here?' Bruno asked Valentoux.

'I'm going to be working here for the summer at the drama festival in Sarlat. We were going to start with a small holiday together, just the two of us.' His French was educated, the accent Parisian.

'How long had you been friends?' The approaching siren was louder now, distracting Valentoux.

'We were more than friends. I met Francis in London in January.'

'How did you meet?'

'I was guest director at a small theatre in Islington. He came to the opening night party with one of the actors.'

Bruno showed him the passport photo and Valentoux said that it was Francis Fullerton. He threw a quick glance at the blanket-shrouded body and shuddered.

'What do you know about him?'

'We spent a lot of time together in London and then he came to visit me in Paris last month. He's in France quite often.'

'Why's that?'

'He's an antiques dealer. He buys British antiques, mainly furniture, and brings them here to sell at French *brocante* fairs. Then he buys French furniture here to take back to England. He seemed to do well out of it, never short of money and always generous.' Valentoux's voice caught as he said this.

Bruno was about to ask why the blue van was empty and where Fullerton's clothes might be when his phone rang. It was J-J, returning his call. Bruno turned away to give J-J a briefing and directions and then a familiar Twingo came in sight at the end of the lane, followed by the flashing blue light of a Gendarme van.

'Wait here,' Bruno said, and advanced to greet Fabiola for the second time that day.

'They were lost so I showed them the way,' she said, gesturing at the van, its siren finally silent. She took her medical bag from the back of her Twingo and walked across to the body.

Two young women in uniform climbed from the front of the police van and a young male recruit unfolded his long limbs from a seat at the back. Ever since Capitaine Duroc had been suspended, the St Denis Gendarmerie had been run by a series of temporary commanders, all of them women.

The new one, Yveline Gerlache, had just arrived that week from Lorraine. So far, Bruno had met her only for a brief courtesy call and coffee at the *Mairie*. They were to have been guests at a dinner party thrown by the Mayor, but then his wife had been taken to hospital. Bruno reminded himself to organize a replacement dinner as she shook hands. In her late twenties and armed with a law degree, she had graduated the previous year from the officers' training academy in Melun. Solidly built but with delicate features and unusually long eyelashes, her grip was as firm as a man's. Beside her was Françoise, a Gendarme whom Bruno knew well. Ordinarily he'd have kissed her on both cheeks, but Françoise held back, offering him her hand.

The lanky young male recruit was weighing himself down with a forensic bag, camera, screens and other equipment that he took from the rear of the van. He tried to add a roll of crime-scene tape to his burden and one of the screens slipped from beneath his arm. He glanced nervously at Yveline, who looked at Bruno and rolled her eyes.

'You might not need all that,' said Bruno. 'The *Police Nationale* are sending a full forensics team. Their head of detectives is on his way. It seems that the dead man is a foreigner, an Englishman.'

'So it's too sensitive for us clodhoppers from the Gendarmes,' Yveline said with a grin, but her eyes were not smiling.

'And much too serious for a country bumpkin like me,' Bruno replied, and told her what he had learned. She heard him out and then asked: 'What's their relationship? Gays?'

Bruno shrugged. 'I haven't asked but I imagine so. The Englishman's an antiques dealer. His French friend Valentoux is a theatre director. They were planning a holiday here together.'

'A lovers' quarrel?'

'It's possible. But there's no blood on him and if he left Paris when he said he did the timing of his phone call suggests he wouldn't have had time to kill the guy and then clean up. Autoroute and petrol receipts fit his story.'

Yveline glanced across at Valentoux. He had at last put down his plastic bag and had a large white handkerchief pressed to his face.

'He's dead, sure enough,' said Fabiola, shaking her head as she returned from the body. 'As brutal a killing as I've ever seen. Jaw, teeth, cheekbones and skull all shattered by something cylindrical and almost certainly metal. An iron bar, maybe one of those things you need to change a car tyre. Time of death was probably between six and ten yesterday evening.'

Bruno still had his gloves on, so he opened the small hatch at the side of the Ford where the spare wheel and tools were kept. Nothing seemed to be missing. Yveline had donned her own gloves and was looking in the back of Valentoux's Clio. She looked at him and shook her head.

'Still, our theatrical friend could have killed him last night, washed and changed and driven away and then given himself an alibi on the autoroute this morning,' said Yveline.

Bruno nodded thoughtfully, and was about to follow her determined stride back to the body when Fabiola caught his arm.

'You're going to be stuck here with the body until they take it to the forensics lab in Bergerac. That means you won't be able to pick up Pamela at the airport. I'm meant to be off now so I can do it. Five o'clock, wasn't that when her plane lands? But we'll expect you for dinner.'

5

Bruno knew he would not quickly forget the expression on Yves Valentoux's face when J-J said he would be detained overnight at the Gendarmerie for questioning. He had cast a look of hopeless appeal at Bruno before Yveline pushed the Parisian into her van. Already devastated by the death of his lover, Valentoux was now being treated as the prime suspect on what Bruno thought was thin evidence. J-J had brushed aside Bruno's discreet suggestion that he was being too hasty. Bruno acknowledged to himself that Valentoux's alibi deserved further probing, and that his theatrical experience meant he could probably play the role of innocent with enough conviction to fool Bruno. But there had been something pathetic in the way he carried his plastic bag with the lunch ingredients, something genuine in his look of shock. And much as Bruno liked and respected J-J as a policeman, he was an old-fashioned type who made little secret of his dislike of homosexuals.

Bruno, by contrast, felt guilty about gays. This stemmed from an incident that he recalled uncomfortably as one of his own failures as a policeman. It was a memory that kept returning, a frustrating and ugly event that he remembered as the swimming-pool affair. Even this name made him feel guilty, since it concealed the reality of the brutal attack he had encountered and his impotence in dealing with it. It had been in his first year as a municipal policeman, when he was still limping slightly from the bullet he had taken in his hip in Bosnia. He'd been part of the French contingent in the UN peace-keeping force and the wound had invalided him out of the army.

He had been summoned by a phone call late on an August afternoon when the heat had begun to subside, the time when people begin to rise from their after-lunch naps and the bakeries reopen for the evening trade. A voice he did not recognize, slurred with drink, had informed him there was a mess to be cleared up at a remote farmhouse at the far end of the commune. The phone had then been slammed down with a burst of laughter.

Bruno had checked the map of the commune on the wall of his office to remind himself of the district that was just beginning to become familiar. There was no swimming pool there that he could recall. He phoned Géraldine, who ran the bar at the local tennis club and lived in that area. A disused farmhouse had been restored and turned into a *gîte* over the winter and a pool installed, she told him. It was mainly rented by British visitors, some of whom she'd persuaded to take out temporary membership at the club. Géraldine gave him directions which he traced on the map with his finger and then set off.

It took twenty minutes to get there, a pleasant drive along country lanes, fields of sunflowers giving way to grazing cows in the meadows and then to sheep as the road climbed and the grass thinned out. As he rounded the last bend on the dirt track that wound up the hill the scene appeared to be peaceful. The stone farmhouse had a new roof of red tiles and the gravel forecourt was so new and white it almost hurt the eyes.

The front door was closed and he strolled around to the rear, calling out 'Y'a quelqu'un?' Then his eye was caught by the trail of blood that ran over the terrace of flagstones and led to a swimming pool at the rear of the house. Shards of glass glittered in the sun from an overturned drinks trolley and at the pool steps he saw brownish swirls of blood hanging in the water. To the right of the pool was a white Range Rover with British plates, its windscreen starred and cracked and the headlamps smashed.

A voice challenged him in English. He turned to see a middle-aged man in very tight swimming trunks standing at the sliding glass doors that led into the house. He had blood on his chest, a swollen lip, two black eyes, and he was holding a pair of fire tongs. Bruno saluted, addressed him as Monsieur and said he'd had a phone call to say there had been trouble. Bruno remembered thinking he'd seen faces like that after a particularly tough rugby match. He'd asked if Monsieur needed driving to the medical clinic.

'An argument. Private. Much drink,' the man said in broken French. Bruno looked past him into the house where another middle-aged man was helping a naked youth to limp his way down the stairs from the upper floor. Despite the bloodied nose and battered features, Bruno thought he recognized the young man. At the sight of Bruno in uniform, the youth turned as if to climb back up the stairs again. Bruno gently took the fire tongs from the first man's hands and stepped inside the house. The two men on the stairs had also been beaten, with red marks on their bodies as if they had been hit with sticks. The older man, blood trickling from his mouth and nose, winced as he stood upright. The buttocks and thighs of the young man flared an angry red.

A pair of jeans and a T-shirt lay on a chair by the glass doors, a wallet peeking from one of the pockets. Bruno took it out, opened it and saw that the young man had a French ID card, age eighteen, with a name he knew, Edouard Marty. Just a few weeks earlier, Edouard had been at the tennis club with school-mates, celebrating their graduation from the *lycée* in Sarlat. Edouard was going on to university, planning to study archi-tecture at Bordeaux.

'What happened here, Edouard?' Bruno had asked, and the middle-aged man helping Edouard put a hand on the boy's shoulder as if to stop him turning to answer.

'We were enjoying a quiet day by the pool when we were attacked by a bunch of thugs with pickaxe handles,' the man said in good but accented French. His friend in swim trunks tried to interrupt but the one on the stairs was too angry to be silenced.

'They wore stocking masks over their heads. They beat us up, smashed the cars and drove off with two of our friends. Two more of us have gone to the clinic. One has a broken arm.'

Beside him, Edouard sank to his knees on the stairs and lowered his head, his shoulders heaving with sobs.

After a brief but angry exchange between the two Eng-lishmen in their own tongue, they refused even to give their names to Bruno. It didn't matter; Bruno found registration papers in the Range Rover along with a copy of the rental agreement for the *gîte*. But it was clear that one had told the other to say nothing. Nobody had answered when Bruno asked if they had all been at the pool when the attack had come or whether some of them had been indoors. They wouldn't even confirm how many attackers there had been, or if any of them had spoken. Edouard would not look at Bruno and remained silent throughout, shaking his head at Bruno's offer to take him to the clinic, or to call his parents to take him home.

And there it had ended. Uncertain of the legal rights of foreigners, Bruno had felt powerless and frustrated. He had been alone; the Gendarmes had been too busy with a traffic accident to be able to send any support. When Bruno reached the medical centre, one Englishman had been treated for a fractured arm and a young Frenchman for a broken nose. The French youth had not shown his *carte vitale*, which would have qualified him for free treatment. Another Englishman in an Audi with smashed headlamps had paid the medical fees and driven them away.

When Bruno went back to the *gîte* the place was empty, the crumpled drinks trolley and broken glass tidied away. An envelope containing two thousand francs had been left on the kitchen counter, the words 'for damages' scrawled on the outside. Edouard called his parents that evening to say he was joining friends for a vacation in England. His parents were too embarrassed to answer Bruno's questions in anything more than grudging monosyllables. Bruno had no statements, no formal complaints and no real basis for an inquiry, as the magistrate told him when declining to take up the case. What he should have done, Bruno now knew, was to seize the visitors' passports and their car keys, confiscate Edouard's ID card and say they could only have them back when they had made formal statements at his office.

Bruno knew that an injustice had been done. He had checked on the age of consent for homosexuals and established that Edouard and his English friends had committed no crime

49

under French law. Edouard being gay had neither shocked nor offended him; he had been too long in the army to confuse anyone's character with what they chose to do in bed. He could have let the matter drop, but Bruno had felt outraged that such deliberate violence could with impunity be inflicted on his territory.

He talked to several of Edouard's friends and tried to track down the other young Frenchman who had been treated at the clinic. It turned out he had given a false name and address in Bergerac. After a few days, all he had were the names of the four Englishmen who had rented the *gîte* and those of two of Edouard's schoolfriends who had decided to take a sudden camping holiday in Spain. One was the son of a local stone-mason and the other the son of a dairy farmer, both of them tough-looking men in their late forties whom Bruno knew from the rugby club. They claimed to have been fishing and drinking together on the afternoon when the attack had taken place.

'From what we hear, a bunch of foreigners were trying to turn some local kids into nancy boys,' the stonemason had said when Bruno tracked him down to the house he was restoring. He would not meet Bruno's eyes. 'Seems to me it's the for-eigners you ought to be locking up.' The other builders at the site had backed him up, muttering that there would have been more than a few bloody noses if they had known what was going on.

There was little more Bruno could do, but he called on Joe, his predecessor as the town's policeman, and was shocked at his advice.

'What's the problem?' Joe had asked. 'A couple of English queens get taught a lesson. They won't be messing around with any more of our young lads. It's not the first time something like this has happened and it won't be the last. I know there's a lot of talk about community policing these days. Well, this is community justice and you interfere with that at your peril.'

He was equally shocked when his Mayor congratulated him briefly as they filed out at the end of a staff meeting at the *Mairie*. 'Glad you managed to tidy up that mess without any fuss,' the Mayor had said, with a reassuring squeeze of Bruno's arm.

As he turned into the driveway that led to Pamela's house, Bruno's mood lifted when he saw her with Fabiola and his own riderless horse leaving the stables. He sounded his horn in a double peep, parked, and went up to take Pamela in his arms as she swung down from her mare. She kissed him squarely on the lips.

'If you must stand me up at the airport and then turn up late for the horses, I suppose a murder is just about acceptable as an excuse,' she said as she hugged him.

'Murder be damned, it's good to see you,' he told her.

She put her hand to his cheek, kissed him again and turned. 'We're heading for the ridge. Catch us up. Or there's no dinner for you.'

She slid from his arms and put her foot back into the stirrup to mount her horse. She tapped Bess's sides with her heels and trotted away while Hector ambled across to nuzzle at Bruno's chest, expecting his customary apple. Bruno stroked his horse's neck and gave him his treat. In the stables he greeted his puppy Balzac and installed him in the binoculars case that he strapped around his chest. He donned his riding boots and helmet, changed his uniform jacket for a windcheater, mounted Hector and set out after the two women.

The day had been too busy for reflection about the reunion with Pamela. Theirs was an affectionate friendship, based on a common love of food and horses and convivial evenings that often enough ended in bed. But she had made it clear that she had no wish to deepen their relationship, nor to make it permanent. Bruno wasn't at all sure what he wanted. He was comfortable in her company and content in their time together but there was the constant thought that he wanted something more. It was not as simple as saying that he wanted children and she did not, that he wanted to experience a full family life. Bruno knew that he also wanted passion in his life, and for all the delight he took in Pamela and the sensuality she could display and share in private, passion and emotional tumult were not what he knew with her.

That brought his thoughts back to Isabelle, mercurial and tantalizing, fierce in her ambition and her determination to carve a brilliant career. Sometimes moody, sometimes capable of a deep and embracing calm, she stirred him in ways that were so profound he felt himself exulting in the great gift of knowing her. But they each knew, however often fate and sexual need drew them back together, that there was no future for them; that she was as committed to the potential and power of Paris as he was locked in the deep peace of the Périgord.

Isabelle's phone call had come as he was driving to Pamela's to say that her train had just reached Bordeaux and she had rented a car to drive to her hotel in Périgueux. Might he join her for dinner? Or perhaps your Mad Englishwoman has returned, she had added, with a touch of something in her voice that was part frost and part mockery.

'She's not English and she's not mad,' he had replied, as he always did. The initial nickname the inhabitants of St Denis had given to Pamela had almost disappeared, except for Isabelle. It was one of the few things about her that he found tiresome; such a casual dismissal of another woman was beneath her.

'I'll see you at Crimson's house tomorrow, or we could meet for coffee in St Denis and I'll take you out there,' he had said.

'We've got the GPS address. See you there early tomorrow.' And she had rung off, leaving him to speculate what she had meant by 'We' as he allowed Hector to pick up the pace and canter after the two women. Hector quickly narrowed the gap, treating Bruno to the delightful sight of his two friends bouncing in their saddles. Pamela looked especially magnificent, with her trim waist and that red-bronze hair flaring out behind like a fox's tail.

Hearing the approach of his horse's hoofs, Fabiola glanced back, waved, and pushed her mare to a canter and then all three of them launched into a gallop along the lower slope of the ridge. Bruno heard Pamela whooping with joy as she rounded the edge of the woods and sent rabbits scurrying and a flock of crows exploding noisily from the trees. Balzac gave one of his eager little barks, just deep enough to hold the promise of the full-throated bay of a mature hound. For the first time that day, Bruno felt at ease with the world.

His mood continued through the soothing chore of rubbing down and feeding the horses and the ceremony of Pamela's return and the gifts she had brought. There was a bottle of Lagavulin for him, the magnificent scotch whisky that he had first tasted at Pamela's table, a cashmere sweater for Fabiola and food for them all. She had picked up a leg of Scottish lamb, a whole smoked salmon and some Lanark Blue cheese made of ewe's milk that could only be found in Scotland. The lamb had been roasting in the oven since Pamela's return and the rich, luscious smell pervaded the kitchen.

Fabiola set the table and then went into the garden to pick the early strawberries and the first of the *haricots verts*. Bruno opened the wine he had brought, two treasures selected from his cellar to go with the food he was sure Pamela would be bringing. For the smoked salmon, he'd brought a Bergerac white from Château de la Vieille Bergerie. For the lamb, he had sacrificed one of his last remaining bottles of the Grand Millésime 2005 from Château de Tiregand. The wines of Bergerac, he believed, were one of France's better-kept secrets. While half of him looked forward to the day when they took their place alongside the great vintages of Bordeaux, he also feared that he'd be less and less able to afford them.

The wines ready and the glasses polished, Bruno went out to the garden to dig up some potatoes. Back in the kitchen he washed and peeled them as Fabiola beside him topped and tailed the beans and Pamela began slicing the salmon at the big round kitchen table. Glancing up from the sink, Bruno could see Pamela's swimming pool and a corner of her grass tennis court, whose lumps and dips persistently frustrated his attempts to roll them smooth. The vivid green of late spring covered the slope that rose to the woods and the ridge that looked down on St Denis.

'Shall I collect some mint?' he asked. Pamela had introduced him and Fabiola to the British custom of eating mint sauce with lamb. 'Not today,' she replied. 'We're trying something different, something a little magical.'

She laid the slices of salmon onto the plates, black pepper and fresh lemons beside them, and began to slice the big round loaf of Meyrals bread she had bought on the way back from Bergerac airport. Then she took from her bag a small dark jar and chanted in theatrical tones: 'Rowan tree and red thread, keep all witches deep in dread.'

'My mother used to say that every time we had rowan jelly,' she said. 'The rowan tree is meant to be good magic, you find it often in churchyards. We used to bring a bough of rowan indoors on Good Friday to keep away witches and the dark forces. And my father liked to squeeze a little rowan juice into his gin and tonic. Made into jelly, it goes well with lamb, so I brought some for you to try.'

The potatoes and the haricots were bubbling in their saucepans as Pamela put a meat thermometer into the lamb and pronounced it done. She left it on the stove top to rest, took off her apron and ushered them to table.

'Welcome home,' said Bruno, pouring out the white wine.

'And welcome to you both,' she said, clinking the glasses and giving the good news that her mother's estate was now settled and her financial future looked reasonably secure. Her worst fears had not been realized; her mother had not left everything to the Battersea Dogs' Home or some charity that rescued old donkeys. She would be able to stay in St Denis with her friends and her horses and never have to see her ex-husband again.

'So this is a very good day,' Pamela declared, and turned to Bruno. 'And now I want to hear all about this murder.'

'You mean that under English law someone can bequeath their property to anyone they like? In France it has to go to the family heirs.'

'Yes, I know, it's part of your *Code Napoléon*. But come on, let's hear about the murder.'

The bare facts were easily told. But it was hard to describe the growing scepticism of Yveline the new Gendarme and J-J. Valentoux had gazed at them helplessly when they asked him to prove he had not killed Fullerton the previous day. The man was clearly in shock, still stunned by the sight of his friend so brutally killed and now aghast at the further stress of hostile questioning. He had insisted that he'd been at home in his Paris apartment overlooking the Buttes Chaumont on the previous evening, reading the manuscript of a new play. He had no visitors, had seen nobody and so could not prove that he had not driven down to St Denis, murdered the Englishman, driven back to Paris and then returned in the morning to establish an alibi. He was taken to the Gendarmerie for questioning and detained overnight under *garde à vue*.

'If it's not him, we have nothing, no clue, no motive, no idea of a suspect,' J-J said. Bruno replied that short of fingerprints or DNA evidence, they could not even be sure the dead man was Francis Fullerton. J-J had nonetheless asked Bruno to call the British consulate in Bordeaux while he sent a query to the British police through the usual informal channels.

'Two gays, they have a quarrel, crime of passion,' J-J sniffed. 'That's the working hypothesis, although I suppose whatever trendy young magistrate gets the case will say I'm prejudiced.'

'Not if Yveline says it first,' Bruno grinned. 'Anyway, you are prejudiced. We both know that.'

56

'That goes for most cops my age,' J-J grumbled.

The only new piece of evidence came from the dead man's trouser pocket; two paper receipts that Bruno had missed in his initial search. Fullerton had twice on the previous day filled his van with diesel, once in Calais and then from a station at the shopping centre outside Périgueux. J-J had sent a detective to check the tapes from the latter's security camera. Since the receipt gave the time of purchase, it was a simple matter to wind back the tapes, and the man filling his van was wearing the same clothes as Fullerton and looked sufficiently like him for a preliminary identification. After filling his van, he had gone to the air pump to check his tyres and had opened the rear doors, revealing that the van had been full of furniture.

'So that's the second mystery, apart from the murder,' Bruno said over the smoked salmon. 'What happened to the furniture? Did he deliver it somewhere before he picked up the keys to the *gîte* or was it stolen by his attacker? And why did he arrive a day early? Valentoux seemed certain that they had arranged to meet today, and Fullerton had said he'd get an early train through the tunnel and planned to arrive here early afternoon today.'

'And he has no alibi that could show he'd been in Paris yesterday evening?' Pamela asked.

Bruno shook his head. 'He was racking his brains trying to remember, but he'd been at home since the late afternoon. We asked if he'd had food delivered, gone out for a drink, had a phone call – anything.'

'What about his mobile phone?' Fabiola asked. 'Can't you find out from that where he was?'

'Yes, but if he was trying to fabricate an alibi he could have left the phone at his apartment in Paris and still come down here to commit the murder. At least he gave us Fullerton's cellphone number and we're trying to trace its movements, but there was no sign of it in his van or in the suitcase we found in the house.'

'Are you sure they were a gay couple?' Pamela asked.

'Valentoux confirmed that when he was being interrogated.'

Bruno did not mention the tension that had arisen with J-J and Yveline when Bruno had argued there was too little evidence to hold Valentoux for questioning. There had been another row when Bruno learned that Yveline had delayed sending a fax to the *Procureur*, the public prosecutor, until after his office had closed. Under French law, once a crime had been committed, the *Procureur* assigned a *juge d'instruction*, an investigating magistrate, to supervise the case. Delaying the formal alert to the *Proc* was a fairly common police tactic, giving them more time to question a suspect. Bruno's response had been to go to his car to call Annette Meraillon, a young magistrate he trusted. When he mentioned Valentoux's name, she perked up to say she'd seen a couple of his plays in Paris and had been impressed. She promised to follow it up.

It would infuriate J-J and Yveline, but that was their problem. Then as he'd driven to Pamela's house he'd heard a report of the murder on Radio Périgord. Albert must have tipped them off, but it meant that any inquiry from Annette could have been triggered by the media. Bruno put it from his mind and began to pour his treasured Pécharmant red.

'So what do you think?' Pamela pressed him when the lamb had been served, the rowan jelly tasted and praised along with Bruno's red wine.

'I don't think he did it. He seemed genuinely stunned by Fullerton's death. Maybe I'm overcompensating because of the way J-J and the Gendarmes seemed to leap to conclusions. But I'm also wondering whether there's a link to this spate of burglaries I mentioned.'

The coincidence had struck Bruno when Valentoux had described Fullerton's astute method of doing business, buying French antiques for sale in England and then doing the reverse in a neat back-and-forth across the Channel, taking advantage of the snob appeal of foreign antiques in each country. It was the kind of operation that would fit sweetly with burglaries, taking stolen goods abroad for sale where they would be less likely to be traced. Although the timing of Fullerton's travels did not work, whoever had burgled Crimson's house had known which items were worth taking. There was serious money to be made and perhaps a wider organization involved, and that could provide a motive for murder.

Over fresh salad from the garden and Pamela's Blue Lanark cheese, they finished the wine and Pamela looked thoughtfully at the painting of an extremely plump pig that hung on her kitchen wall.

'I wonder if I should think about getting some special insurance. That's quite a valuable painting and I've got some decent furniture.' Pamela had been stunned to hear that Crimson's house had been emptied; they were frequent tennis partners and she knew him well. 'I'd never worried about burglaries around here before.'

'You don't even lock your door, half the time,' said Fabiola. 'I keep telling you about it.'

'Nor does Bruno,' Pamela retorted. 'And he's a policeman.'

'I lock my shotgun and the shells away, but I've got nothing else worth stealing,' he protested. 'And Balzac's there most of the time.'

'Balzac is still too much of a puppy to deter any thief. And there's your wine – you'd be furious if that got stolen.'

After the fresh strawberries and the coffee, Fabiola helped them wash the dishes, then said a discreet goodnight.

'Would you like to stay the night?' Pamela asked, taking his hand. 'I'd hate for you to be stopped and breathalysed by this new Gendarme woman.'

'It wouldn't be her. There's a new rule that Gendarmes can't go on traffic patrol in their own commune, to stop them recognizing a friend and letting them off with a warning. And yes, I'd love to stay the night, but if you're tired I can use your guest room.'

'I could tell that's where you slept while I was away. Why didn't you use our bed?'

'Because it's your bed,' he said. He'd been exercising her horses as well as his own while she had been in Scotland, so he had usually had dinner with Fabiola and then stayed over at Pamela's rather than drive home after a glass or two too many. It was on the tip of his tongue to say: 'I don't think of your bed as ours.' But he'd caught himself, and said: 'Your bed isn't the same without you in it.'

'Silly Bruno,' she said, kissing him. 'In my bedroom the bath is en suite, much more convenient. Why don't we go up with a candle and take a nice hot bath together?'

6

'Murder in Périgord' said the headline in *Sud Ouest* the next morning. 'Englishman brutally slain in *gîte*. Parisian man held for questioning.'

'So you've got the guy already?' asked Fauquet with a hungry gleam in his eye as he served Bruno his coffee and croissant. Owner of the café tucked into the alley behind the *Mairie*, he had become one of the main sources of the town's gossip. Along with his excellent croissants and powerful coffee, it was part of his stock in trade. 'Albert was in earlier. Said it was a really vicious killing, the guy's head smashed to bits.'

All along the crowded counter of the café conversation stilled as customers waited to hear what new light Bruno might shed on the case. He knew them all well, local shop-keepers and office workers, people who worked at the *Mairie*. Whatever he said would flash around town within minutes and probably feature on the next news bulletin of Radio Péri-gord. And it would certainly be swiftly conveyed to Philippe Delaron, who spent much more time on his part-time role as *Sud Ouest* correspondent than he did running the family camera shop.

'Nobody's been arrested,' Bruno said, and took a bite of crois-sant. He could hear himself chewing, so attentive was the silence along the bar. 'We were just talking to the guy who found the body and called the emergency service.'

'That's the Parisian?' Fauquet persisted. '*Gai comme un phoque*, Albert reckoned. He was in here just now.'

How had the French dreamed up the phrase 'gay as a seal' to describe a homosexual, Bruno wondered. Whatever did seals have to do with it? He concentrated on his croissant.

'Takes one to know one,' said Fauquet with an unconvincing laugh. 'I always wondered about Albert.'

Bruno shook his head in mock despair. Happily married for thirty years to a woman who had borne him four children, there was nothing seal-like about Albert. Bruno finished his coffee, put a two-euro coin on the counter with some change, said '*Bonne journée*' to the crowded café and climbed into his van for the drive to Crimson's house. He was aware of a dryness in his mouth as he anticipated the reunion with Isabelle.

She was not alone. There was a large white unmarked van parked at the rear of the house and two men in blue overalls were taking in some electronic equipment. Isabelle was prowling the terrace. She still had a slight limp and was puffing at a cigarette as she argued with somebody over a mobile phone. As usual, she was wearing black slacks and a polo neck, flat shoes and a long black raincoat. A turquoise silk scarf worn as a belt provided a splash of colour. Her skin was bronzed from her holiday.

Part of him wanted to rush to her, take her in his arms and relive those moments when he'd felt closer to her than to any other human being. But another part of him felt – he groped for the right word – not dispassionate so much as detached, observing himself as he watched her, seeing her vulnerability as she changed her step to avoid an empty floral urn. Her profile came into view, the slim neck, the hair so short she looked boyish. Then she spun on her heel, chin out and head tilted high, imperious and hard. In that moment, he had a sense of how she would look in another twenty years, her ambition fulfilled and her heart cold, a woman at ease with power. He felt a moment of sadness that she might succeed in making a brilliant career and become one of the handful of people who ran the French state, returning each evening to a magnificent but empty apartment.

Her eyes widened in recognition as she spotted him. Did they soften? Bruno wasn't sure. She waved the cigarette at him in cursory greeting, turned and resumed her verbal duel. Bruno sighed, shrugged and began to examine the van, its rear doors open and revealing racks of electronic equipment. Behind it was a new-looking Peugeot with a rental sticker, doubtless Isabelle's.

'What's this?' he asked one of the men. He was carrying what looked like a very fat laptop.

'Ask her,' came the surly reply, with a glance toward Isabelle.

'They're with me,' she called to Bruno. 'He's got a secure phone line in there and we're checking to see if it's been compromised.' She returned to her call.

Bruno considered this. France Télécom had told him the line had gone down at 1 p.m. two days earlier. But would there not have been some kind of automatic alert on a special secure line? Why would Isabelle lie to him, unless she had been ordered to take this opportunity to make a different kind of search, or perhaps to install some microphones? Yet if they were going to plant bugs in the house of a retired British spy chief they could have done it at any time. And presumably Crimson was experienced enough to take his own precautions.

'Sorry, Bruno, some idiot in the liaison office at France Télécom in Paris trying to explain why they didn't notice the line had been cut.' Putting her phone away she kissed him on both cheeks and hugged him with fierce energy in that way she had. The embrace lasted a second too long for social nicety and her hand lifted to stroke his cheek. Over her shoulder, he saw the man with the big laptop watching with interest.

'It's good to see you again,' she said, reaching into her rain-coat pocket for her cigarettes. She had given up smoking when they'd been together in that magical summer before she had taken the job in the Minister's office in Paris.

'And grand to see you. How was Greece? And your leg?' Isabelle had taken a bullet during an operation against a shipload of illegal immigrants the previous year. She now had a titanium implant in her thigh. The latest stint in hospital had been for plastic surgery to repair the fist-sized hole in her flesh, and the cruise around the Greek islands was her convalescence.

'The docs say the op was a success,' she said. 'There's still a scar, but it's fading and the cruise ship was fine. I lay on my deckchair and read trashy novels. It's left me with a strange suntan and a couple of extra kilos.'

'You needed to put some weight on and they don't show.'

'How would you know?' she asked, and then gave him a flash of that private smile of hers, the one that came from her eyes. 'Enough chit-chat,' she said briskly. 'What do you make of all this?'

He explained about the previous burglaries, each using the same method to break in. He added that he'd confirmed the cleaning woman's alibi for the time the phone wire had been cut.

'Who's been handling the burglaries, the Gendarmes?'

'Yes.' He told her they had left him to file the insurance reports and he'd be emailing photographs of some of the stolen items to the national watch list.

'Big embarrassment in Paris,' she said. 'The Minister called his counterpart in London to apologize and the Brigadier did the same with his contacts. They virtually promised the Brits we'd clear it up, get all the stuff back and send the thieves to Devil's Island. That's where you come in. The Brigadier wants your local knowledge and has asked for you to be seconded to us to track down the burglars. I gave the Prefect his letter last night and I've got another one to give to your Mayor.'

As a municipal policeman, Bruno was officially employed by the Mayor and council of St Denis, part of the magnificent complexity of French judicial bureaucracy that had the Gendarmes employed by the Minister of Defence and the *Police Nationale* by the Ministry of the Interior. But the Ministry could always dragoon him into service when they thought his local knowledge might be useful. Bruno shrugged in reluctant acceptance of the inevitable. 'You know we've also got a murder on our hands?'

'I heard it on the car radio. Who's the guy being questioned?'

'A Parisian theatre director named Yves Valentoux. He found the body and J-J thinks he did it as a *crime passionnel*. I'm not so sure.'

'Leave that to J-J. The burglars are your priority. Apparently Crimson has been in Washington but the Brits got in touch with him and he's heading back.'

65

'I brought some tools to seal the broken shutters, lock the place up again and secure it.'

'We'll take care of that. I'll have someone here until Crimson returns.' Somehow she had taken his arm and steered him out of earshot across the terrace towards the pool, still covered from the winter. Dead leaves covered the plastic sheeting. Beyond it was a *potager* and young tomato plants had already been staked. He saw the filigree green of carrot tops, young courgettes and lettuce. Crimson must have a gardener to take care of the grounds. When had the gardener last been here? He would ask Gaëlle.

'I trust you had a pleasant evening,' Isabelle said. 'I was squeezed in at the last minute into the Prefect's dinner party. His wife took one look and put me way down the table, between the Mayor of Ribérac and the headmaster of the *lycée*. Once they learned I was a *flic*, they talked golf, which made me miss you a little.'

Her eyes sparkled with mischief, as they always did when she teased him. *Mon Dieu*, it was good to see her again.

'A career woman like you, perhaps you should take up golf.'

'It takes too long. And we have a perfectly good gym at the Ministry. My leg is almost healed and I have this plan to jog to Place Beauvau every morning, hit the gym and shower. I have my own locker so I can keep clothes there.'

That was Isabelle, always planning, always with some project. 'You always wear the same clothes anyway. Everything black.'

'When you first saw me I was wearing jeans and that brown leather jacket.' She grinned back at him.

'I liked you best when you used one of my shirts as a dressing gown,' he said, and she slapped his wrist in mock reproof.

'Those days are over.' She paused, giving Bruno time to absorb this. Then she made her face serious, one of her sudden switches of mood that often left him floundering. 'How's your Englishwoman?'

'She always wears the same things, too. Riding breeches mostly, and wellington boots.' A memory came to him of Pamela in a long green evening dress, her hair piled high.

'You smell a little horsy. I like it, very masculine.' Her tone changed as if she were changing gear. 'Do you have any leads on these burglars? The Brigadier really wants it cleared up.'

'Crimson's been retired for two or three years now. Is he still so important?'

'Guys like that never really retire. He's a consultant now with the Hakluyt Group, filled with ex-SIS types and charging big corporations fat fees for risk assessment. At least, that's what they say they do, but in that world who knows? Do you know him?'

'He's a good friend of the tennis club and he comes to the rugby games when he's here in winter. He's friendly to every-body and I've been invited to the house a couple of times.'

'Who were the other guests?'

'At the garden party it was a couple of local mayors, a bank manager, Hugo from the wine cave and lots of expats, mostly retired British diplomats and a couple of writers. At dinner it was the same mix but a smaller group. Oh, and the local deputy to the *Assemblée Nationale*.'

'Any Americans?' she asked, a little too casually. He looked at her.

'Not that I recall. There aren't many around here. Why do you ask?'

She shrugged. 'Just wondering how retired he really is. Apparently he was having some pretty high-level meetings while he was in Washington.'

They were in a garden now and he saw that the lawn had been mowed, but not recently. 'If I'm going to focus on the burglary I need to check on the gardener and see who might have known Crimson would be away.'

He explained why he thought it was one gang, and that they knew their antiques. Bruno could search criminal records but Isabelle would have access to much broader archives that would include suspected dealers who were too careful to have ever been caught. It would be useful to have that list, particularly if there were any local connections.

'How long are you here?' he asked.

'At least until Crimson gets home and settled in. Maybe we could find time for dinner. And I want to see our puppy.' Balzac had been her gift to him after his previous dog was shot by a Basque terrorist.

'Come to dinner. You can see the puppy and tell me what your plans are if the government changes with the next election.'

He said it lightly, but Bruno did not have to spell out his meaning. The Interior Ministry was always controversial, but there had been more and more scandals in recent months, over the wire-tapping of journalists, over some alleged cover-up of campaign finance from a rich industrialist's widow, and above all over a new department of the Ministry, the *Direction Centrale des Renseignements Intérieurs*. Combining the old police intelligence operation with counter-espionage and anti-terrorism, it had become a very powerful arm of the state. Critics, including the opposition parties, called it sinister and suggested its boss had become the President's private spy. If he lost the forthcoming election, the new government was expected to launch a wholesale purge and change of personnel.

'I'm not involved in any of that political stuff.' She turned to face him, looking vexed. 'I thought you knew me better.'

He held up his hands, smiled and said: 'I'm on your side, you know that.'

'It doesn't sound like it, Bruno.' Her eyes narrowed. 'Is this part of J-J's plan to get me back to Périgueux?'

'No, you'd hate it,' he replied. 'I can't see you spending a couple of years waiting to take over J-J's job when he retires,' he went on, wondering how to take the heat out of the conversation. He tried to make a joke of it. 'You'd be forced into a lot more tedious dinners with the Prefect and you'd probably have to take up golf.'

'So why did you bring this up? This is my career you're talking about.' She turned away. 'God, I hate being manipulated.'

'Why did I bring it up? Because I care for you and because I'm worried about your becoming a political football in a dirty match, that's why.'

Her back was toward him, shoulders rigid. Bruno knew Isabelle well enough to be sure that apologies would not work; she was not the sort of woman to be easily mollified. She insisted on straight talking and he was in a mood to provide it.

'I don't know what your connection is to this new organization, but we get the Paris newspapers down here, and the political magazines,' he went on. 'We don't even have to read

69

Canard Enchaîné to realize that there's something in your Ministry that's starting to stink. It doesn't matter whether you're part of it or not. The mud sticks.'

She turned again to face him, still challenging but less fierce. 'How come you're suddenly an expert on the election, let alone the internal politics at the Ministry?'

Bruno had never been clear which particular section of the sprawling Ministry employed the Brigadier's team. It seemed to occupy some vague middle ground between Defence and Interior and the DGSE, the foreign intelligence service.

'I don't have to be an expert. You're attached to the Minister's private office,' he said. 'If the government changes, you'll be assigned elsewhere. The new minister will want his own people.'

'That's just an administrative convenience. I'm a serving police officer with the rank of Capitaine. Nothing will change that.'

'They can always assign you to traffic management in some cold, grey *département* up on the Belgian border.'

She began a quick rejoinder but then stopped, as if debating with herself whether to say more. 'Funny you should say that. I might get reassigned soon, even a little further north than the Belgian border. I've applied for another job.'

Bruno raised an eyebrow and faced her. 'Anything you can tell me about?'

'Eurojust, the judicial coordination office of the European Commission based in The Hague. If it comes off, I'll be getting a promotion to Commandant.' She paused and looked back the length of the garden towards the house. 'It's a four-year assignment.' She let a silence build again as if expecting Bruno to comment. 'The Brigadier suggested I apply.'

'Good for him,' Bruno said, and meant it. He had wondered whether the Brigadier, a ruthless operative and consummate political survivor, was the kind of boss who would take care of his staff.

'I don't expect he'll go down with the ship.' Somehow they were walking amicably together again and she had taken his arm as if the brief row had never happened. 'Apart from your murder, what else is happening down here? And how's our puppy?'

'Balzac is fine, but I really need more time to train him. And there is something else – have you ever heard of the Neuvic train robbery?'

'A Resistance thing in the war? I heard somebody gossiping about it when I was stationed in Périgueux.'

'A couple of the old banknotes turned up on the deathbed of an old *Résistant*. I have to organize his funeral. If there's anything in your files at the Ministry, I'd be interested.'

7

Bruno wanted to check the list of burglary victims against the owners who used Dougal's rental agency to find tenants for the months when their houses would otherwise stand vacant. A retired businessman from Glasgow, Dougal had started Delightful Dordogne out of boredom after his first year of inactivity and had now become one of the leading employers in St Denis. The business employed his two daughters and their husbands, one French, and one Dutch. His first grandchild was already spending his summer holidays helping Dougal to keep track of the bookings.

'I've been expecting you since I heard about Fullerton's murder on the radio,' Dougal began. 'I suppose that's what you want to know.'

Bruno nodded. 'Did you ever meet him or was the rental arranged by phone and Internet?'

'I certainly met him. He rang me Monday and asked if he could take the place a couple of days early. It was empty that week and he seemed like a nice enough chap so I agreed.'

'Very trusting.'

Dougal shrugged. 'It's the way I do business. He'd already paid for the original booking with a bank transfer. I've made you a copy so you'll have his bank details.'

'Did you see him at all?'

'Yes, he came to the office here the day before yesterday just after five to pick up the keys and paid for the extra days in cash. You can see where I marked it.'

Dougal led Bruno to the giant wall chart. It dominated the large, airy room in the old public laundry that he had rescued from ruin and converted into offices. The houses he rented were listed from top to bottom on the chart and from left to right were columns for each of the weeks of the season. Crimson's name was not among them, although Bruno noted that the other burglary victims were listed along with the *gîte* where Fullerton's body had been found. Bruno ran his finger along the right line and saw Fullerton's name with a tick in the small box beside it to show the rent had been paid and another to show the cleaning had been done and sheets and towels installed and the swimming pool cleaned. There was a small hand-drawn arrow pointing to the current week, and a scribbled note that said: 'Three days paid.'

'I used to keep this on the computer as a spreadsheet,' said Dougal. 'But then I put it up on the wall so that the cleaners and other maintenance people could see when they were assigned to each property.'

'So anybody who worked here could see at a glance when a house would be available for rent, which meant the owners were away?'

'That's so. You must be thinking that was how the burglars chose their victims, but most of my people have been with me for some time. I know them pretty well and trust the ones working for me now. Still, I can print out a list of all the employees if you want.'

Bruno said he needed that and then a thought struck him. 'What if an owner doesn't want to rent out his house but still needs a cleaner or gardener or pool maintenance? Do you offer that as a separate service?'

'We do, mainly for the pool maintenance. There aren't many takers for the cleaners and gardeners. Most people have their own connections because it's cheaper. They pay cash whereas we have to pay the social charges for our employees. It damn near doubles the overall wage bill.'

'Is Monsieur Crimson one of your clients? His house is not on the list.'

Dougal led Bruno around his desk to another wall with another chart that listed the separate pool and garden and cleaning services and pointed to Crimson's name.

'He comes to us for pool and garden work. He used to have cleaning as well but then Gaëlle realized she could do better on her own than working for me. We always make our people work Saturday mornings because that's the changeover day for most rentals. She said she wanted the weekends off.'

One of his daughters brought in two cups of coffee from the espresso machine in the kitchen as Dougal called up the Crimson file on his computer. Bruno greeted her, asked after the children and then copied down the names and contact details of the gardener and the pool-maintenance man.

'Any of your staff that you have doubts about?' Bruno asked when Kirsten had gone.

'Not any more. One or two turned out to be unsatisfactory in the early days but we weeded them out. We do take on some part-timers at peak periods but usually people we've used in the past. I'll add their names to the list.'

'Could anybody else come in here off the street and look at the charts?'

'It's possible. We get a number of casual visitors, salesmen mainly, or people trying to rent out their houses, and we use this as a waiting room if I'm busy elsewhere. But if they don't know our system, I'm not sure whether someone off the street would be able to read the charts in the way you mean.'

Bruno gathered his printouts, thanked Dougal for his time, and walked round to the Post Office to look at the delivery rosters. Jean-Louis, the deputy manager, checked who had done the routes that would have covered Crimson's house and the *gîte* where Fullerton had been murdered.

'Pierre and Pascal,' he said, looking out of his office window to the yard where the yellow postal vans were parked. 'They're both on break now so you can see them on the porch. We aren't allowed to smoke in the building anymore so that's where they take their breaks.'

Pierre had made no deliveries to Crimson's house on the relevant days and recalled seeing nothing of interest. But Pascal had delivered a letter and a couple of circulars to Fullerton's *gîte* two days earlier.

'I was on late shift,' he said, his Gitane bobbing from his lips as he spoke. 'Must have been late afternoon, sometime around five o'clock. It's a long drive up the track and as I was driving back I had to stop and reverse because of the *chauffagiste*. He was in a big white van and he had trouble getting round me. That's how I saw the sign.'

'What did it say?'

'Chauffage-France or France-Chauffage. I'm thinking of putting in central heating so I remembered the address. It was in

Belvès, in a *Zone Industriel*, and I thought I might ask them for an estimate, see if they're any cheaper than the ones round here.'

'Did you get a look at who was in the van? One person or two?'

'Just the driver, a youngish guy I think, but I didn't really notice. I was trying to be sure I didn't take my own van so far over I'd end up in the ditch. The funny thing was, when I looked up the firm in the phone book I couldn't find any listing for a heating firm in Belvès.'

'Could have been a new one, not in the phone book yet.'

'That's what I thought,' said Pascal, glancing at his watch. 'So I looked it up on the master list we keep in the office that has all the new subscribers, and there was nothing on there either.'

Pascal looked across to the yard where his friend Pierre was already loading boxes of letters into the back of his van. 'Break over,' he said, rising. 'Got to go. It's not the place where they had that murder, is it? They said on the radio it was up by St Chamassy.'

'There might be a connection. We'll check it out and may have to come back and take a statement. Did you see anybody at the house or was there a car parked when you dropped off the mail?'

'Not that I remember. There might have been a vehicle but I can't be sure.' He shook his head.

'Do you remember anything about the driver of the van, what he was wearing?'

'The usual blue overalls.' Pascal shut his eyes as he tried to remember. 'His sleeve was rolled up and he had a tattoo on his arm, very striking with thick stripes. It was like an abstract design rather than one of the usual mermaids or an anchor. When we slowed down to squeeze the two vans past one another I got a good look at it. His arm was resting on the rim of the door and we were so close we were almost touching.'

'What about the van?'

'It was one of those extra-tall Renaults they use for moving furniture, big enough for people to stand up inside.'

'You said white. What colour was the sign?'

'It was in blue letters, quite big because I could read it easily. It had the Belvès postcode. There was a phone number, too, but I didn't write it down.'

Back in his office at the *Mairie*, Bruno called his counterpart in Belvès to ask what he knew of the industrial zone where the heating firm was supposed to be based. Bruno learned that it contained two construction companies, two warehouses, a commercial laundry and a firm that specialized in handmade staircases, but no heating company.

'What's in the warehouses?' he asked. One stored goods for a local chain of do-it-yourself stores and the other was run by a company that did household removals and parked big trucks in the zone's secure parking lot.

Bruno opened his phone directory and looked through the yellow pages for sign-makers. The fourth one he tried, in Bergerac, had the previous month made two truck signs for a company called Chauffage-France, with an address in Belvès. The customer, a young man, had paid cash, and said his name was Lebrun. The address he gave was the alleged workshop in the industrial zone.

77

'Had you seen him before?'

'No, but I wouldn't mind seeing him again,' said the woman on the other end of the phone. 'He was a good-looking guy.'

'So you'd know him if you saw him again?' Bruno asked.

'Sure. And if I need to jog my memory we've got him on tape. We've got security cameras now, for the insurance. You could come and see for yourself. What's he done, this guy?'

Bruno evaded the question but within the hour he was at the sign shop, part of a modern printing company that also did photocopies, business cards, posters and advertisements for billboards. The entire operation seemed to run on computers and the manager had prepared for him a plastic folder with several frames already printed from the security camera tapes. He also emailed copies to Bruno's office computer so Bruno could forward them to J-J and the Gendarmes.

They showed a young man in his twenties wearing dark blue overalls and a dark baseball cap that shadowed part of his face. The nose was clear enough, although the mouth and jaw were obscured by a moustache and small beard. There was one clear shot of his features, when a banknote slipped from his hand to the floor. The girl at the desk must have said something because he looked up smiling, almost flirtatious. Bruno felt a tug of memory, sure that he'd seen that face before but unable to place it.

'Who was the woman I talked to on the phone?' he asked the manager. He was steered to a girl with spiked hair and a nose ring who sat at a table at the front of the store that looked half reception, half cash-desk. He showed her the photo to check that it was the mysterious Monsieur Lebrun that she remembered.

'Do you remember what you said that made him smile?' he asked.

She laughed. 'I asked him if he always threw money at girls' feet and he gave this sexy smile and said it helped him see their legs better. I was sure he was going to say something else, maybe ask me out. But then he bit his lip, paid his bill and left quickly. It was a bit odd, that's why I remembered him.'

Armed with the printouts of the photos, Bruno pondered his next move as he returned to his van. He could go through the rogues' gallery, the books of photos of people who had been arrested, although he assumed J-J's team would be doing that. If the guy had used the ZI address and postcode, he was probably familiar with it. He started the van and headed for the old hilltop *bastide* of Belvès.

He always enjoyed visiting the *bastides*, those fortified towns built in the Middle Ages along the shifting frontier between the French parts of the region and the lands held by the English. Built on grid patterns around a central market square, with a church that could act as a fortress, they still dotted the region. Together with the caves along the valley with their prehistoric art, their Roman ruins and Renaissance châteaux, the *bastides* were a constant and satisfying reminder to Bruno that he and everyone else who lived around St Denis was part of an endless stream of history. He also relished the irony that while the *bastides* had been built to defend and reinforce the power structures of the Middle Ages, they had in fact helped to erode the feudal system. As incentives to get the peasants to move to these towns, where kings and barons hoped to make money from taxing the markets, they were offered freedom from serfdom. Along with the power of the English longbow and the crossbow to decimate the charges of the feudal knights in armour, the *bastides* had undermined the social and political order that the knights were dying to defend. That was often the way with political solutions, Bruno reflected; they produced dismayingly unexpected results.

Perched on its hilltop and still clustered around its central square, Belvès boasted a fine market and an antiques fair where Isabelle had bought Bruno the grand dining chair he still used. He smiled to himself at the memory as he circled the old town and headed for the *Zone Industriel* below. He paused only to make a courtesy call to the local municipal policeman, who replied that Bruno was most welcome on his turf and would he have time for a *p'tit apéro* after his visit? Bruno accepted the invitation with pleasure.

The Zone was part of the urban sprawl that in Bruno's view defaced more and more of the countryside he loved. There was always a giant supermarket, a do-it-yourself discount store, huge furniture and sports shops and low-cost petrol pumps. Behind this commercial centre stood the vast warehouses and small factories, each a single storey high and built with vinyl siding and cheap metal roofs. The industrial zone had a sliding metal gate, which opened automatically as the security guard saw the police van. There were cameras on the roof of the guard's kiosk, dotted around the buildings and on tall lighting poles that could illuminate the parking lot where the giant removal tracks were parked.

Starting with the security guard, he called at building after building to show the photo from the print shop and ask if anyone knew the young man. Mostly he got apologetic shrugs, but at the office attached to the removals warehouse a woman in her forties with heavily made-up eyes, and showing a generous amount of cleavage, looked at the photo twice. Dark roots were just beginning to show in her bright blonde hair.

'You're not our local *flic*,' she said. 'What's up with this guy?'

'Routine,' he said casually. 'He could have been a witness to something and he was driving a van with an address at this ZI.'

'Not any more, he isn't,' she said. Bruno suspected that her desire to show herself to be in the know had trumped her instinctive caution when talking to a policeman. 'We had to let him go. When was he driving this van? Was it one of ours?'

'No, it was another warehouse, but we're checking everywhere to see if we can identify the guy. Do you know his name?'

'Paul, handsome little Paul,' she said. 'We'll have something in the personnel files. He was with us just under six months, driving the small vans. He wasn't licensed for heavy goods.'

'I only saw big trucks in the yard.'

'Some customers don't have much furniture. And then we've got a sideline business, storing antiques and stuff for the *brocante* dealers who come down here every year for the summer trade. That's why we use the small vans.'

'A nice lad, was he?'

'A bit too nice, if you get my meaning. I rather fancied him at first, but I got the impression that women weren't his preference.'

Bruno deliberately let his eyes linger on the cleavage. 'More fool him,' he said.

Smirking, the woman rose from behind the counter, turned and swayed into a rear office, her hips swivelling in the tight skirt of royal blue that matched her eye make-up. She came back bearing a slim file and a teasing expression. She put a blue-painted nail to her lips and said: 'I'm not sure if I ought to let you see this . . .'

'Well, if you really want to disturb your boss . . .' he began. 'But then we wouldn't have our little secret, would we?'

'You guys in uniform, you're all the same.' She tapped him on the chest with the file and then let him take it. There was a job application form and copies of an ID card and driving licence. Paul Murcoing, he read, age 28, and three different addresses listed for him in the six months he'd worked there, one in Belvès and two in Bergerac. The elusive connection came to Bruno at once: he'd last seen Paul in a photograph in the house of his dead grandfather, the old *Résistant*.

She leaned forward on the counter, her hands together so her arms could squeeze the magnificent bosom into even greater prominence.

'I suppose now you'd like me to make you a photocopy.'

'What I'd like you to do could get us both arrested,' said Bruno, by now thoroughly enjoying himself. And it was certainly getting him the information he wanted. 'But a photocopy would be very kind.' He paused. 'My name's Benoît.'

'I'm Nicolle.' As she went into the rear office, she turned and waved her blue-tipped fingers and said: 'Be right back.'

Bruno called J-J's mobile and announced that he had a suspect. He gave Murcoing's name and last known address, read out his aunt's telephone number from his notebook and added: 'According to one woman he worked with, there could be a gay connection.'

'Hang on while I look him up in the records,' said J-J.

82

'Are you still questioning Valentoux?'

J-J grunted assent, and then Nicolle returned with the photocopies. 'Still warm,' she said, handing them to Bruno. 'Almost hot.'

'*Très bien, Monsieur le Commissaire*,' Bruno said into the phone. 'Right away.'

He clutched the photocopies, leaned forward to plant a kiss on Nicolle's cheek and said: 'Got to go, that was the boss. One last thing, did Paul have any friends here in the Zone?'

'He might have had one, but like I said, he wasn't interested in girls.'

As he opened the door to leave, she called: 'Hey, Benoît.' He stopped, turned. 'That was fun,' she said, and blew him a kiss.

8

At the first address Paul had listed on his personnel form, Bruno found an elderly North African woman in a headscarf with an imperfect command of French. A young man in a tracksuit with a shaven head and a large single earring turned from the blaring TV set and said: 'We've only been here three weeks.' He had never heard of Paul Murcoing and never seen the man in the photo.

At the final address in Bergerac, a curtain twitched when he rang the bell. After a minute, a young woman in a dressing gown opened the door on a chain, yawning, and asked him the time.

'Eleven twenty.'

'*Merde*, I only got off work at six. What is it?' She clutched at the neck of her gown where it was falling away to reveal a large rose tattooed on the curve of her breast.

Bruno explained and showed the photo and she gave a nod of recognition. 'That's Paul, alright. He doesn't live here but he sometimes used to come to visit his sister.' He tried not to look at the tattoo.

'Is she in?'

The woman shook her head. 'Yvonne moved out, a month or so ago, maybe more. She said she had a room offered near where she worked but she may have hooked up with some guy she met. She does that sometimes. I haven't seen Paul for ages.'

'How well do you know him?'

'I was at school with Yvonne so I've known him for years. What's *le p'tit pédé* done this time?'

Despite his surprise, Bruno kept his expression still. A *petit pédé* was a derogatory term for a young gay, and when she said 'this time' did she mean he'd previously had trouble with the law?

'He's been in trouble before?'

She looked at him levelly and began to close the door. 'None of my business.'

'This is pretty urgent. He could be a witness in an important case. Do you know where Yvonne works, where I could find her?'

She sighed. 'Promise I can go back to sleep if I tell you?' When he nodded, she said: 'She does part-time cleaning in foreigners' houses up around Les Eyzies, that valley with all the caves in.'

'You mean St Denis?'

'That's it, some company run by an old Scottish guy who wears a kilt. She took a photo of him on her phone. He gave all the staff a bottle of scotch one day, even the part-timers. Can I go back to sleep now?'

'Thanks,' said Bruno. 'Sweet dreams.' Back in his van he looked through the list of employees Dougal had given him. There she was, Yvonne Murcoing, on the second list of the part-time staff. If he'd gone through that first, the name would have jumped at him. The address Dougal had listed for her was the one he'd just visited. He called Dougal and asked if Yvonne Murcoing was still working for him.

'She's off sick, but I think she's been staying in one of the staff houses we use.' He gave Bruno a phone number and an address. He called the number but there was no reply. He tried calling J-J but got voicemail so tried one of his deputies, a young inspector in Bergerac who would have been assigned to any search for Murcoing. There was no news. The most recent address Murcoing had given the warehouse hadn't seen him for weeks. Bruno then called Joséphine, Murcoing's aunt, and left a message, asking her to call him and saying he had news about the funeral. That should guarantee she called him back.

He took the back route from Bergerac through Ste Alvère to avoid the traffic on the main road along the river. He parked opposite the Gendarmerie and noticed Valentoux's silver car in the lot, so he was still being held. He walked across to look at it; fingerprint dust was visible on the handles and mirrors. That meant the forensics should have finished with it. He put on a pair of gloves and opened the door, wondering if they had checked for discarded receipts that could buttress Yveline's theory that he could have driven down a day early to commit the murder. He found nothing.

He was about to close the car door when a thought struck him. He opened the glove box and pulled out the instruction book. There was a section at the back where careful drivers could note down their diesel purchases and the number of kilometres driven and work out their consumption. But Valentoux had never filled in a single page. Tucked inside it was the little plastic wallet where most people kept their *carte grise* and other documents that the police checked when a car was stopped. There was a receipt from a *Contrôle Technique* garage, an inspection station where older cars were required to be tested every two years. Bruno checked the date, nine days ago. The form listed the number of kilometres on the clock when the test was performed. He compared that with the clock. Valentoux had driven seven hundred and twenty kilometres in the past nine days. Paris to St Denis was nearly six hundred. If he had made a second journey to kill Fullerton, he could not have done it in his own car.

From behind the desk, Sergeant Jules shook his hand and said Yveline was in the interview room with the suspect. J-J was using the old Capitaine's office as a work room. Bruno handed over the *Contrôle Technique* and explained. 'I suppose he could have hired a car and done it that way,' he concluded.

'Only if he knew some place that let him have a car for cash,' said J-J wearily. 'We've been through his credit cards and bank account. There's no sign of any odd transactions.' He took off his glasses and eyed Bruno. 'Is it you I have to thank for that phone call we got last night from the *Procureur*'s office?'

'What phone call?' Bruno asked innocently.

'Your friend Annette Meraillon, asking if it was true we were questioning a murder suspect.'

'My friend?' said Bruno. 'She's a vegetarian feminist who thinks I'm a dreadful old meat-eating dinosaur like you. Anyway, she's too junior to be assigned a case like this.'

'One of these days you'll go too far,' J-J grumbled. He tried to glower at Bruno but his heart didn't seem to be in it.

'How's Valentoux bearing up under the interrogation?' Bruno asked.

'He seems fine, obviously has great faith in French justice. He keeps saying he didn't do it, has a little cry when he thinks of his dead friend, and then dries his eyes and answers everything we throw at him. He's been very cooperative, hasn't even asked for a lawyer. I was going to release him this morning when the *juge d'instruction* arrived, but Yveline was keen to have another crack at him and I don't want to start an argument with the Gendarmes. The *juge* is talking to him now.'

J-J turned to a young woman sitting at an adjoining desk and handed her the inspection station receipt Bruno had taken from Valentoux's car and asked her to explain its significance to the magistrate in the interview room. Then J-J looked at his watch. 'I wonder what your friend with the bistro is doing for his *plat du jour*?'

'Ivan usually makes *côtelettes de porc au céleri* today.'

'So what are we waiting for?' said J-J. He lumbered to his feet and headed for the door at a pace that belied his bulk. A bowl of *potage de légumes* later, mopped up with a fresh baguette and washed down with a glass of Ivan's house red, J-J sat back and looked at Bruno.

'So you can put this Murcoing guy at the murder scene at the relevant time, in a van with a forged sign, and you say he's gay, so that could be a connection with Fullerton. I ran his name through the records when you rang. He's got two convictions for car theft, another for hunting without a licence, and he was questioned last year on suspicion of selling stolen antiques but released for lack of evidence. He looks a likely suspect but it's all circumstantial.'

'And his sister is in a position to know which houses would be empty and open for burglary.'

'That's the problem. Why would he want to rip off a *gîte*? There's no furniture worth taking.'

'Maybe he knew Fullerton and knew he had a truckload of antiques with him.'

'It's a bit thin,' J-J said, surprising Ivan, who was about to serve the pork chops. 'Not you, and not this fine-looking dish,' J-J said hurriedly and then leaned forward to breathe in the aroma of the celery sauce. A wide smile appeared on his face as he waited for Ivan to return with the vegetables.

'I warn you, he's put his prices up,' said Bruno. 'Probably your fault for over-praising him. It's ten euros fifty now for the set lunch.'

J-J swallowed his first mouthful, nodded in approval and sipped at his wine. 'Soup, this fine pork chop with vegetables done to perfection, then a green salad followed by cheese and topped off with – what's the dessert today?'

'*Tarte Tatin.*'

J-J looked up to the heavens. 'Thank you, God.' He looked back at Bruno. 'Followed by *tarte Tatin* plus a quarter-litre of this very drinkable red for ten euros fifty? I don't know how he does it.'

'It will be an extra euro twenty for the coffee, and then you'll probably want a glass of Monbazillac with the *tarte* and then maybe a *digestif* and suddenly your bill is twenty euros,' Bruno said. 'That's how Ivan makes his money.'

'It's worth every penny and we'll economize. No *digestif* for you today. By the way, who's his latest girlfriend?'

Ivan's menu varied with his love life, which in turn was usually defined by those girls he met on holiday whom he could persuade to return with him to St Denis. There had been a Belgian girl who seduced him into producing endless *moules*. The Spanish lover had introduced St Denis to gazpacho and paella, which were greatly appreciated, although the sounds of crashing pans and murderous curses that came from the kitchen when she was angry with Ivan were also relished by the regulars. The new German girl had been a pleasant surprise; her Wiener Schnitzel, hammered so thin it overlapped the plate and served with a succulent potato salad, had become a local favourite that Bruno tried never to miss. Hugo from the wine shop had even started to stock an Austrian wine, Grüner Veltliner, in its honour.

'It's still the German,' Bruno said. 'But the signs aren't good. Ivan's been seen sitting alone at the bar and drinking after the place has closed.' As a result, he explained, there was now keen anticipation in the town of Ivan's next holiday plans. One faction was urging him to explore South-east Asia and bring back a Thai cook, while another was suggesting that the French Caribbean islands of Martinique and Guadeloupe might bring an exotic tropical spice to the *plat du jour*.

'And who's your latest recruit, the woman in the office?' Bruno asked.

'That's Josette, just completed her detective's course, transferred from Nontron. Married to a *motard*.' J-J used the slang for a motorcycle cop. 'Any day now, I'm expecting her to announce she's going on maternity leave. She's the one who looked up Murcoing's record. We're putting an all-points bulletin out on him.'

'So if you're no longer taking Valentoux seriously as a suspect, why are you still holding him?'

'I told you, Yveline wanted another go at him and then Bernard had to question him – that's the *juge d'instruction* they assigned, Bernard Ardouin. He's pretty good, a Socialist of course, but sensible. He used to play rugby for Sarlat. I told him I thought we'd wrung Valentoux dry and he seemed to agree. I don't think there's much point keeping him any longer. He'll be out this afternoon.'

'With a big sign round his neck saying Gay Murder Suspect. Can't you put out a statement saying he's been cleared?'

J-J shrugged and attacked his *tarte Tatin* as if he hadn't eaten for days. It disappeared in four large spoonfuls. 'Sure you won't join me in a little Armagnac with the coffee?' he asked. 'By the way, you didn't tell me Isabelle's back in town.'

'I saw her this morning.' Bruno explained Isabelle's interest in Crimson's background.

'I hate it when intelligence gets involved,' J-J said. 'Always screws things up. A little bird in the Préfecture told me the Brigadier has got you seconded to his team again.'

'Afraid so. I'm meant to find the burglars and get Crimson's goods back.'

J-J snorted. 'I'm surprised at Isabelle. She knows better than that how tough burglaries are to solve. She damn well should; I trained her.'

'There may be one possible way into this,' Bruno said. 'You say it's thin, but what if there really is a connection with the murder? Fullerton's an antique dealer, Murcoing has an arrest for stolen antiques, even if nothing was proved, and that's what the burglars have been taking.'

'And we have to find out whatever happened to that load of antiques Fullerton had in the back of his van.'

'So it's all the more important that we track down Murcoing,' Bruno went on. 'Perhaps you could put through a request to the British police to see if anything's known about Fullerton. We know he was an antiques dealer, but maybe he was a crooked one.'

J-J nodded, picked up his phone, called Josette and asked her to take care of it.

'Let me make sure I have your theory right,' said J-J. 'Murcoing could have had some dealings with Fullerton in the past, maybe doing the burglaries, and then Fullerton ships the goods back to England. He goes to meet Fullerton at the gîte to pick up Fullerton's latest shipment, which might even be stuff stolen in England. They transfer the stuff into Murcoing's van and then they have a falling out, maybe over money, and Murcoing kills him.'

'And then there's the gay angle. We know from Valentoux that Fullerton was gay and one of Murcoing's sister's friends called him a *petit pédé*. Maybe they fell out because Fullerton had found a new lover in Valentoux.'

'That corpse was a *crime passionnel* if ever I saw one,' J-J agreed. He sipped his coffee and called for the bill. 'So even though Isabelle and the Brigadier want you focused on the burglary, you want to be part of the murder inquiry because that's how you think you'll solve it all.'

He opened his wallet, put a twenty-euro note and a ten onto Ivan's saucer, waving away the change, and tucked the receipt back with the rest of his cash. 'Suits me,' he said. 'I'll make sure you're kept informed of everything we get: forensics, records, anything from the British police and the lads I've got making the rounds of the local antiques dealers.'

'And I want to be there when you question Murcoing.'

'We have to find him first. Inspector Jofflin from Bergerac is in charge of that. Now let's get outside. I'm bursting for a cigarette.'

'I'll come back to the Gendarmerie with you. I want a word with Valentoux once you let him out.'

'In that case, give me an hour to square things with Yveline and Bernard.'

Bruno headed back to his office to deal with his emails, phone messages and the usual pile of post. There was one from the British consulate in Bordeaux to say that Fullerton's brother would arrive by plane in Bordeaux the following day to take care of the funeral arrangements. He'd rent a car and contact Bruno on arrival in St Denis. The consulate had booked him into Les Glycines in Les Eyzies for three nights. There was an email from the adjutant of the 4th *Régiment de Transmissions* in Agen, confirming that a squad of troops would mount a guard of honour for Loïc Murcoing's funeral and asking him to verify the date and time. He had just got off the phone with Father Sentout to confirm the funeral arrangements and was about to call Florence when the Mayor put his head around the door, came in, closed it behind him and leaned against it.

'I had a phone call from Jacqueline Morgan. I gather you know about Cécile's condition,' he said. He looked exhausted.

'Yes, I was terribly sorry to learn it.' As he did whenever the Mayor entered his office, Bruno stood up. His instinct was to go over and embrace the old man who had been the nearest he'd ever known to a father. 'I will keep the information to myself.'

'It's her wish.' The Mayor put a hand to his brow, smoothed his fingertips over his temple as if trying to soothe a headache. 'She does not want her final days filled with a stream of weeping visitors. Nor does Cécile want people to see her as she is now.'

'I understand.' He felt helpless, wanting to do something helpful to show his sympathy and concern but with no idea what might be best. Bruno wondered how long this trial would last, not just for his Mayor but for the sweet and loyal woman who was dying in the same self-effacing way that she had lived. How little we can really do for one another at the time when it's most needed, he thought.

'It must be difficult for you, returning from hospital to an empty house. Would it help if you moved into my spare room?'

'Thank you, Bruno, but no. Jacqueline has taken on the task of seeing that I'm properly fed and I think it right to sleep in the room that Cécile and I shared for nearly four decades. It will be forty years next February, but she won't live to see it.'

9

Like Valentoux himself, the theatre director's silk shirt looked the worse for wear when Bruno collected him from the Gendarmerie and took him across the road to the Bar des Amateurs. When Bruno asked what he'd like to drink, Valentoux shook himself out of his daze and ordered a beer, then pulled out a pack of cigarettes, but it was empty. They sat at a table outside, the sunshine dappled by the leaves of the plane trees that lined the street.

'What will you do now?' Bruno asked.

'Buy cigarettes, take a shower and see if the drama festival still wants a director who's suspected of murder. Then I'd better head back to the *gîte* where Francis died. I won't be able to sleep a wink but it's the only place I have to stay.'

'You can't go there. It's been sealed off as a crime scene.'

'*Merde*. I'm in no shape to drive back to Paris. Can I take my car or have they sealed that too?'

'You're free. You can pick up your car whenever you want. I was going to suggest you follow me back to my place, take a shower there and change and you can have the spare room until you decide what to do.' Bruno turned and called to the barman to bring him a pack of Marlboros and some matches.

'I didn't know you smoked,' said Valentoux. 'That's a very kind offer – why are you doing this?'

'I don't smoke. They're for you,' Bruno said. 'You've been all night and half the day in a jail cell and interrogation rooms. You're out of cigarettes. I don't think you killed Fullerton and nor does the chief of detectives. If any evidence to the contrary turns up, we'll know where to find you. Will there really be a problem with your job at the drama festival?'

Valentoux shrugged, pulled out his mobile phone and said: 'Three messages from them asking me to call urgently. This job's supposed to last me all summer and I turned down other opportunities to do it.'

'Phone them. If there's a problem, I'll speak to them.'

Valentoux called, exchanged a few sentences, and then said: 'There's a policeman here wants to talk to you.' Bruno took the phone and Valentoux whispered: 'Festival director.'

'Chief of Police Courrèges on the line, *Monsieur le directeur*. I understand you have some concerns about Monsieur Valentoux.'

'The news reports have been troubling, but I understand Yves has now been released,' the director said.

'He was never arrested, simply helping us to understand what happened. He was the one who found the body of his friend. He is completely free and I know of no suspicions attached to him, whatever the media might be saying.'

'I've been asked to cancel his contract.'

'Excuse me, I thought you were the festival director,' said Bruno, putting some frost into his voice. 'Are you not in charge? Should I speak to somebody else?'

96

'I'm the director but there's the board chairman, the Mayor, the sponsors . . .'

'And there's a contract. If you cancel it, you'll have a lawsuit on your hands, and I'd have to testify that I had formally informed you that Monsieur Valentoux has been released with the thanks of the police for his assistance and without any shadow on his name. We don't want any unpleasant accusations of discrimination or homophobia.'

Bruno spoke over the protests that came down the line. 'I suggest you give me your email and I'll send you a message within the hour confirming what I have said and I'll put a hard copy in the post tonight. That should suffice for your sponsors and your board.

'No? Then I'll send those off to you and confirm to Monsieur Valentoux that his contract stands and he is free to come and see you tomorrow, if you wish. Thank you for your time and *bonne journée*.' He handed the phone back, took a long pull of the cold beer and watched Valentoux light a cigarette with shaking hands.

'Why are you doing this?'

'You've had a rough time. No need to make it worse,' Bruno said. 'Stay here, have another beer while I send off the email and letter and I'll pick you up back here in thirty minutes. OK?'

As he walked back up the main street toward his office in the *Mairie*, Bruno tried calling the house where Yvonne, Murcoing's sister, was staying and where she was supposed to be resting on sick leave. Again there was no reply. He called Annette to thank her for her intervention and explained that Valentoux had been released and that he'd be at the drama festival as planned.

'They've assigned Bernard Ardouin to the case, so you're in good hands,' Annette said. 'I told him that Valentoux had enough of a reputation in cultural circles to get the Paris newspapers interested. I also told him to make sure to talk to you about the case.'

'You'll destroy your reputation,' he said, smiling as he spoke. He liked Annette, a keenly competitive rally driver who had once scared the life out of him by putting him in the passenger seat for a hair-raising drive around a forest track.

'What reputation? Anyway, if Valentoux is out and in the clear, I'd love to meet him.'

'In that case, come and have dinner at my place tonight. He'll be there. Are you still vegetarian?'

'In principle, but as you know it's almost impossible to live in Sarlat and not to eat a little duck.'

'Duck it shall be,' he said. 'We'll see you about seven thirty. I have to exercise the horses first.'

He rang off and climbed the old stone steps of the *Mairie* to his office, where he sent off his email and letter to the drama festival director and called Dougal at Delightful Dordogne to ask who else lived in the staff house with Murcoing's sister. He was given three names and mobile-phone numbers. Two of the girls he knew from his tennis lessons when they'd been schoolgirls. He called the one he'd liked most, Monique.

'I'm trying to find Yvonne Murcoing,' he said, after the usual pleasantries. 'She's supposed to be at the house but there's no reply.'

'We haven't seen her for a couple of days,' Monique replied. 'She left a note on the kitchen table saying there'd been a death in the family and she'd been called away. I've got her mobile number if that helps.'

It was the same number that Bruno had been trying without success. 'Have you met her brother?' he asked.

'Paul? Yes, he drops by from time to time, usually just to pick her up. They seem to be pretty close. She has a photo of him by her bed. We had a couple of takeaway pizzas here together, watched a DVD he brought. I went to bed after a bit. The film was too arty for me, something Swedish in black and white, lots of moody silences.'

'Did you see him recently?'

'Not for a few days but I've been out a lot. Shall I ask the other girls?'

'Yes, please. Do you know if Yvonne has a car?'

'She drives one of those little Toyotas, I don't know what they're called. It's that grey-silver colour and it's not here now. I know she gets it serviced at Lespinasse's garage. He should have the registration number.'

On the way back to the bar to pick up Valentoux, Bruno stopped at the butcher's and bought a kilo of *aiguillettes* of duck. These were the long, thin strips of the finest meat that was left after the *magret*, the breast, had been removed. Too often ignored or left on the carcass to thicken a stock, Bruno loved them and planned to prepare them for dinner that evening. He had potatoes and the first of the strawberries under glass frames in his garden, lettuces, a lot of radishes and some early courgettes. Stéphane had dropped off some cheeses with the ham he'd been curing in salt since the ritual slaughter of the pig at the start of the year. That was all Bruno needed.

There was no sign of Valentoux at the table outside the bar, but Bruno looked inside and saw him standing at the counter, a large glass of what looked like whisky in his hand as he thumbed through the bar's copy of *Sud Ouest*.

'I see what the festival director meant,' he said, closing the paper with its front-page headline on the murder of Fullerton. 'It's only just hitting me, the knowledge that I'll never see him again.'

'Let's get you back,' said Bruno, and led the way to the Gendarmerie's parking lot so that Valentoux could follow him home. Once back at his cottage, Bruno showed his guest around, gave him a towel, showed him the shower and guest room and suggested he get some sleep after his night in the cells.

In the kitchen, Bruno filled a bowl with hot water and left it to warm. He poured a half glass of red wine into a flat-bottom dish, added salt and pepper and a crushed garlic clove and rolled the duck *auguillettes* in the wine. Then he took a large jar of old-fashioned mustard, thick with seeds, and put three heaped tablespoons into the emptied warm bowl. He added an equivalent amount of chestnut honey from a jar he'd been given by Hervé, one of the beekeepers who sold his wares in the St Denis market. He mixed the mustard and honey together, added the wine and the duck, and turned them until each of the *aiguillettes* was well coated. He covered the dish with plastic film and put it in the fridge.

Out in the garden with his basket, he dug up a couple of his potato plants, picked radishes, strawberries and courgettes along with some spring onions. He took the strawberries and the onions into his chicken coop and plucked them there, leaving the green stalks for the chickens to fuss over. Back in his kitchen, he washed the vegetables, leaving them in the sink as he checked that he had sufficient flour for the *beignets*. He peeled and sliced the courgettes, added salt and laid them in a colander to drain. He was just washing up when a clean-shaven Valentoux entered the kitchen wearing a silk dressing gown and carrying the bottle of champagne that had been in his plastic bag.

'That shower was just what I needed,' he said. 'I'd like to give you the champagne.'

'Put it in the fridge and we can drink it this evening. I have some friends coming for dinner, including a fan of yours who saw some of your plays in Paris. The other guests and I will arrive smelling of horses since we have to exercise them. They're due at seven thirty and we'll eat about eight or soon after. I'm heading out again but I'll be back after the horses.'

'I love riding. I had to learn for a film I was in, a costume drama about Catherine de Medici. I'd really like to take it up again, but not today. I'll get some sleep, if that's okay. You're being very kind.'

'I hope you like dogs. Better prepare yourself to meet a very affectionate and even more inquisitive young basset hound puppy. He's called Balzac and I'm supposed to be training him. I'll bring him back from the stables where he likes to spend his days.'

'Balzac's a grand name for a dog.'

Bruno dried his hands, picked up his cap and headed for his van. His first stop was Lespinasse's garage, where the owner scooted out from beneath a Citroën *traction-avant* he was restoring to look up the registration number of Yvonne's car.

'Is there a problem?' Lespinasse asked. A plump, jolly man who could still play a decent game of rugby, he wiped his hands clean with grease from a large open jar and then with a paper towel before turning to his files.

'No, it's her brother I'm looking for and I thought she might be able to help me track him down. You know their grandpa died?'

'Old Murcoing? Yes, I knew him from when he had me up at the farm trying to fix his old tractor. It was a Porsche so he said it should run for ever. I bet you didn't know Porsche used to make tractors. Here's her registration number, a Toyota Yaris.'

Bruno wrote it down, told Lespinasse that there would be a military funeral for the old man and stopped at the Gendarmerie just along the street to get Sergeant Jules to put Yvonne's car on the watch list.

'The magistrate was looking for you,' said Jules. 'I gave him your number but he had to get back to Sarlat. Nothing urgent and he said he'll be back tomorrow.'

'How's the new boss?' Bruno asked.

'Anybody would be an improvement on Capitaine Duroc, but she's only just got here. Too soon to tell but she's very polite, still got the officers' school polish on her.'

'You'll soon rub that off, Jules,' Bruno said. 'Anything else?'

'Philippe Delaron was asking about that Englishman that was burgled. He said he'd looked him up on Google and he thought there might be a story in it. Apparently the Englishman's a *milord* or something quite important. Delaron was a bit cagey about it. You know what he's like when he's after a story.'

Bruno made a mental note to make his own check on Google and headed for the house where Monique lived, to see if Yvonne Murcoing might by chance have returned, but the place was empty. It had been a long shot but not far off his route to Pamela's house and his spirits lifted and his mood mellowed as he drove up the familiar lane to the house where his puppy and his horse and Pamela all awaited. It would be, he told himself, an oasis of affection and calm after a long and frustrating day.

Instead, he found a controlled chaos, a plumber's van and a large truck in the courtyard from which came the unmistakable whiff of a problem with the septic tank. Pamela, in overalls and rubber boots, was sluicing out her kitchen.

'Don't come near me. I stink,' she called, blowing him a kiss. 'Antonio says he's almost done.'

Bruno nodded at Marcel, standing by the truck that was known locally as the honey wagon. Marcel had a steady business installing and emptying septic tanks all over the region, but somehow managed to shed the aroma of his trade in the evenings when he'd spend his time between Ivan's bistro and the Bar des Amateurs. All that could be discerned in the atmosphere around him in the evening was the pungent smell of the cheap cigars he smoked constantly. And who, Bruno thought, could blame him, as the throaty sound of the truck's pump signalled that the tank had nearly been emptied.

A new gust of fumes drove Bruno to the stables, to be greeted by Balzac trying to scramble up his legs while Hector gave a welcoming whinny. Bess and Victoria, Pamela's two mares, gazed at him incuriously and then went back to staring at the wooden planks of their stalls. He changed into his riding clothes, despite Balzac's best attentions, gave Hector his customary apple and saddled all the horses. He hadn't seen Fabiola's car but he assumed she'd join them. She knew it was his turn to cook this evening.

'It's safe to come out now,' said Pamela, dressed for riding and her still-damp hair pinned back. She could change faster than any woman he'd ever known. She reached for her riding hat and kissed him. 'We had a plumbing disaster this afternoon, but Antonio fixed the blocked loo and persuaded Marcel to come and pump everything out.'

'And somebody was just enthusing to me about the delights of life in the country. You'll meet him at dinner, that drama festival guy I was telling you about last night.'

'It's alright for him to wax lyrical. He lives in Paris where they have sewers, and on days like this I wish I did too. Fabiola rang to say she's on her way. She was held up by a broken bone she had to set at one of the camp grounds. We spent half the morning moving her stuff across.'

'Across to where?'

'Didn't I tell you? She's moving into the spare room in my house for the summer so I can rent out her *gîte*. Lucky you, you'll be sharing the bathroom with two women. With the rental I'll be able to install a second bathroom upstairs, at the end of the landing.'

'Do I get to scrub Fabiola's back, too?' he grinned and hugged her from behind.

'Absolutely not. Don't even think about it.'

10

Bruno returned home to find that Valentoux had explored his way around the kitchen and dining room. He had set the table and gathered wild flowers from the field behind the blackcurrant bushes. They filled the vase he had placed on the outdoor table, where Bruno's champagne flutes had been polished and made ready. Balzac had raced ahead and was already making friends with their guest. A few moments later he spotted Pamela and Fabiola coming up the drive bearing bottles of wine. Balzac tore himself from Valentoux to greet them and then darted back to Valentoux again.

'You look a lot better than you did yesterday,' Fabiola told Valentoux. 'At one point I thought of declaring you in shock, but you seemed to be pretty lucid in answering Bruno's questions. My sympathies on the loss of your friend.'

'I want to hear what you have planned for the theatre festival,' said Pamela. 'But maybe we'd better wait until Annette joins us.'

Bruno was pouring the champagne when Annette arrived in her small blue Peugeot with the wide tyres for rally-driving, sending Balzac into another frenzy of welcome.

Bruno excused himself to visit the kitchen to heat a pan of sunflower oil for beignets. Readying one bowl of spicy salsa, he took from the fridge a pot of Stéphane's *aillou*, fresh cheese flavoured with herbs and garlic, spooned it into a bowl and took both bowls out to the garden with some small plates and a pile of paper napkins. Back inside, he dipped the sliced courgettes into a light batter he made out of flour and water and then eased them into the hot fat. Once they were brown and crisp, he took the beignets out with a slotted spoon, sprinkled salt onto them, and slipped in a fresh batch to fry. He took the first plateful out to his guests and left Pamela to show Valentoux how to hold the hot beignet in a paper napkin and then decide whether to smear it with salsa or *aillou*.

The sound of laughter greeted him as he emerged with the second batch, Valentoux deploying a range of voices to play various roles in the story he was telling. He broke off to applaud Bruno's return.

'I never had courgettes like this, and adding this *aillou* makes a perfect couple,' he declared. 'It's like oysters and champagne or caviar and vodka; heavenly twins.'

'Wait till Bruno introduces you to his foie gras and Monbazillac,' said Pamela.

Nothing like food to get a conversation going, thought Bruno, smiling as he went for the final batch of beignets. But he wondered at Yves's surprisingly cheerful mood so soon after his lover's murder. Was it the thespian style, Bruno wondered, the tradition that the show must go on? He'd never come across someone quite like Valentoux before, a man quite so deliberately theatrical that Bruno suspected he'd never be able to tell whether Yves was being genuine or just acting.

When he returned to his guests, Valentoux had opened a bottle of Clos d'Yvigne, the dry white Bergerac that Fabiola loved. She must have brought it. Knowing his fondness for Pomerol, Annette had brought a bottle of Château Nenin from 2005, which he decanted at once since they were to enjoy it that evening. He opened it to let it stand awhile. Pamela had brought a Monbazillac from Clos l'Envège, which would go perfectly with the strawberries, and he went back to the kitchen to put it in the fridge to stay cool. He put the marinaded duck into the oven, sliced some ham from the haunch that hung from the main beam and put a plate of ham and his fresh radishes at each place on his dining-room table. He added a slice of unsalted butter to each plate and sliced a big *pain* from the Moulin bakery.

'*À table*,' he called from the kitchen window, 'and bring your wine glasses with you.'

He steered Annette to the head of the table, he and Valentoux to her left and right and then Fabiola and Pamela, and explained to the table how the ham on their plates came from a pig that had been treated since the previous summer to a regular diet of acorns and chestnuts.

'And I saw him pick the radishes from his garden today,' added Valentoux. 'This is an amazing way to live, I think I shall become exceedingly fat.'

'Bruno isn't fat,' said Fabiola.

'And nor are any of you,' Valentoux replied, looking at each of the women. 'How do you do it?'

'Riding,' said Pamela and Fabiola in unison.

'I've gained three kilos since I came here,' said Annette. 'I blame the cheese.'

Valentoux copied the way Bruno smeared a little butter onto each of the plump, red radishes, dipped each one in salt and then alternated a bite of bread, a radish, a piece of ham and then a sip of the white wine.

Pamela helped him clear away the plates. She prodded the potatoes and declared them ready as he removed the duck from the oven using bright red gloves emblazoned with a white Swiss cross that Fabiola had given him for Christmas.

'*Aiguillettes de canard au miel et moutarde à l'ancienne*,' he announced as they brought the dishes to table.

'I thought that was honey I could smell,' said Annette, as Bruno darted back into the kitchen to fetch the carafe of Pomerol. 'I never heard of that with duck.'

'It should go well with this wonderful wine you brought,' said Bruno, pouring it out.

'Tell us about the festival,' said Pamela. 'What can we expect?'

'For a start, you can expect some complimentary tickets,' Valentoux replied, and went on to describe the plays he planned, a mix of old classics and experimental new theatre, of French and foreign drama. The plates were cleared away, the cheese and salad brought, and then Bruno opened the Monbazillac.

'Do you know where you'll be staying while you're in Sarlat?' Annette asked.

'Not yet, I was going to look for an apartment to rent in the next few days. As long as it's fairly central, I'm not looking for anything grand.'

'I rent an old house with some friends on the Rue des Consuls, just around the corner from the festival office. We each have a floor to ourselves, two rooms and small bathroom, and we all share the kitchen, living room and garden. One of the tenants leaves this weekend for a summer school in Italy so his floor is free until the end of August.'

'It sounds perfect. Let me come and visit and then take you to dinner,' said Valentoux, and the two of them agreed to meet at her house in Sarlat the following evening. Bruno brought coffee, and as the dinner drew to a close, Valentoux proposed that he might cook and play host at a similar event. Pamela was the first to agree, placing her foot firmly on Bruno's beneath the table; as usual, she'd slipped off her shoes as she dined. When they all rose from the table, she made it clear that she intended to stay the night, so Fabiola and Annette left together. Valentoux marched into the kitchen declaring his intention to do the washing up.

'I meant to ask you, did Fullerton ever mention the name of Paul Murcoing, a young man from this area who seems to have been involved in antiques?'

Valentoux suddenly went still at the sink. 'I never heard that name. Is he somebody who might be a suspect?'

'Could be. Did you meet any of Fullerton's friends?'

'Only when we were in England, and none of them was French.' Valentoux was scrubbing at a pan that was already clean. 'This Paul Murcoing, is he gay?'

'So it seems. He's disappeared and we're keen to talk to him. I don't know if you're in a position to help.'

'Would you like me to make some discreet inquiries? I don't suppose you have many contacts in the gay community and I do know one or two people down here.'

'Frankly, I'd be grateful for any information about him. He's a bit of a mystery to me, and that's a problem, given the way I work. I'm a village *flic*, which means I know everybody. In a town like this, where these things are important, I know whose grandpa was in the Resistance and who was a collaborator. And as often as not I know who's having an affair, and if I don't know I'll probably get an anonymous letter of denunciation.'

'And you don't know any gays?' All the dishes washed, Valentoux had turned and was leaning against the sink, looking at Bruno with a slightly amused expression.

'Don't be silly. There's three thousand people in this commune. We get all sorts. But it tends to be very discreet and Paul Murcoing doesn't fit into any part of the closeted gay world that I know around here. He's an urban type, an outsider to the rural Périgord that I'm familiar with, and as a result I feel a bit lost in trying to track him.'

'I'll do what I can. Where was this Paul based?'

'Bergerac mainly, but he worked for a while in Belvès, which is very like St Denis. He seems to have worked mainly as a driver. Hang on a moment, I'll get a photo.'

'I'll be outside, having a much-needed cigarette.'

Standing on the terrace, moths beating valiantly against the outside light, Bruno handed Valentoux a copy of the photo from the security camera.

'Good-looking youth; with a smile like that he could be very popular in Paris. Can I keep this?'

'Yes, I have copies. Pamela and I leave quite early in the morning to go and ride the horses, but I'll probably be in the café by the *Mairie* by eight unless something comes up. And I can recommend the croissants. Goodnight. And sleep well.'

When he came in from the bathroom, Pamela was sitting on the bed draped in a large bath towel. She had applied some fresh perfume and his bedroom was lit only by a single candle.

'That was a lovely evening,' she said as he started to unwind the towel. 'I'm looking forward to your reminding me just why it is you prefer women.'

11

Bruno was enjoying his croissant at Fauquet's café when his phone rang just before eight.

'Have you seen the paper yet?' Isabelle asked, her voice sharp, almost shrill.

'I'm just looking at it.' He gestured to Fauquet to hand him the café's copy of *Sud Ouest*, where the second story on the front page was 'British spymaster burgled'.

'You're the only one who could have leaked that, Bruno. The Brigadier's furious and I don't want him taking it out on me.'

'Not guilty. Check with Sergeant Jules. He told me that the reporter had simply looked up Crimson on Google.' He scanned the report. It looked as if Delaron had transcribed the details of Crimson's career from some official biography. On an inside page was Delaron's photo of Crimson's house and a file photo of Crimson receiving his knighthood at Buckingham Palace.

'Well it's building up as a story on the news wires and on the radio. The BBC ran something, so now we're getting inquiries from the British press. The last thing we want is reporters running all over the place.'

Bruno's mental antennae alerted. Why would that be a problem if she were simply making an effort to find Crimson's burglar as a matter of professional courtesy?

'What are you up to, Isabelle?'

'Stop it, Bruno. You know perfectly well I need the Brigadier's backing to get this new job. He's on the warpath and coming down here with Crimson when he flies in tomorrow. Have you made any progress?'

'Maybe,' he said, leaving the café to speak in private. 'At least I've got a suspect. Name of Paul Murcoing, low-grade criminal record, last known address in Bergerac. J-J has a team looking for him now but he seems to have gone to ground. Where are you?'

'I'm at Crimson's house, babysitting the place till he gets back, and we've got forensics crawling all over it. If this Murcoing's been arrested we'll have his prints and DNA on file. Meanwhile I'll see if we can round up some Gendarmes to keep the press away from the house. The question is whether this is just a straightforward burglary or whether there's something more to it. Does this Murcoing have any British or American connections?'

'He's a suspect in the murder of the British antiques dealer,' he said.

'Jesus, this gets worse.' She rang off, leaving Bruno holding a dead phone. Why might it not be a straightforward burglary? And why had she asked about American connections? Apart from a retired New York lawyer, a widower, and two old dears who had taught French in Californian high schools, he didn't know any Americans in the area. There was Jacqueline, of course, but she was a French citizen. Suddenly he remembered why she had looked familiar when he'd called at her house. He had not simply seen her in the market or at the Post Office, it had been at Crimson's garden party the previous summer and she'd been wearing a black cocktail dress. They hadn't spoken, there must have been forty or fifty people present.

Jacqueline knew Crimson, and she was writing a book which could make a big splash in the media about American funding in French politics. But that was history, sixty years ago, the dawn of the Cold War. It wasn't the kind of issue that would have any serious political impact today. Most of the old parties had disappeared or merged into new ones; only the Socialist and Communist parties remained from the old days. He shook his head; that couldn't be it. However, there had been that cryptic remark Jacqueline had made about the French nuclear deterrent not being really independent. That was different; that could have an impact, he mused. If Crimson knew about it, and had just been holding high-level talks with the Americans, with French elections coming up the prospect of a scandal about the crown jewels of France's defence system was likely to worry the Brigadier and his Minister. This was all very fanciful, Bruno concluded, and way above his pay grade. He'd better talk to the Mayor.

His phone rang again. It was Monique, asking if he was still looking for Yvonne Murcoing. Indeed he was, he replied. Monique had just checked Yvonne's room, to see if she might have returned, and on the notepad by the bed she'd found a phone number with the words 'camper van'.

Bruno scribbled down the number in his notebook and thanked her. The woman who answered his call said Yvonne had rented their camper van the previous year and she'd recently asked to do so again. But she and her husband were about to take a week off themselves. When had Yvonne called, Bruno asked. In the evening, three days earlier, he was told.

That would have been the day of Fullerton's murder. Bruno rang J-J and left a message asking if his team could start checking van rental agencies. As he put his phone away, it gave the little ding that meant a call had come in while he'd been talking. The number showed it had come from Paris. He checked the voicemail and listened.

'*Salut*, Bruno. Gilles here from *Paris Match*. I'm interested in this burglary of your British spy chief. It's a quiet week otherwise so I thought I might come down to your delightful part of the world, maybe do an interview with Crimson with a sidebar on the Brits in Périgord. I'd be grateful if you'd call me back, *ciao*.'

Gilles was a reporter Bruno had known from his time in Sarajevo, during the siege, and they'd renewed their friendship recently when Gilles had been more than helpful in the case of the Red Countess. Gilles was a smart man. Once he realized that Isabelle, whom he also knew, had come down to St Denis he'd soon sniff that there was more to this burglary than met the eye. Bruno would have to handle this with care.

The Mayor looked rather more cheerful when Bruno knocked and entered his office. The delay with the new sewers had apparently been fixed and the Mayor asked Claire to make two fresh coffees. Bruno described his talk with Isabelle. Could her sudden interest in the Americans be somehow connected to the revelations in Jacqueline's book?

'I doubt it,' the Mayor said. 'Her book isn't finished and it won't be published until well after the elections.'

'Bits could leak,' said Bruno. 'Has anybody seen it but you?'

'I don't know. I imagine she has sent parts of it to her editor at the university press which is publishing it. And I know she's given a talk to a couple of historical societies. This is history, Bruno, old stuff; a lot of the old passions have died.'

'Not when it comes to nuclear weapons cooperation.'

'Hmm, I see what you mean,' the Mayor said. 'I don't know the details, of course, just what Jacqueline has told me in a general way. And it will come as no secret to the French and American officials involved. If they haven't publicized it in the past I see no reason why they'd want to do so now.'

'Presumably Crimson would know about this,' Bruno said. 'The Americans and the British usually work closely on intelligence, and on nuclear matters.' He put down his cup and sat forward. 'Maybe I'm adding two and two and coming up with five, but you know politics. This looks like a pretty close election we have coming up. Could something like this make a difference if it blew up?'

'Any little thing can make a difference in a tight race. Let me think about this. After all, I'm involved.' He leaned back in his chair, closed his eyes for a long moment and then opened them to look out of the window. 'I signed the paper that secured Jacqueline special access to our Senate archives. My name will be on the paper trail.'

Bruno waited but the Mayor had no more to add. He thought it best to change the subject.

'I meant to ask before about Cécile. I hope she's not in too much pain.'

'They give her morphine. I'll visit again this afternoon.'

'And dinner?'

'Jacqueline is doing something with last night's leftovers. She's a good woman.' Bruno took the cups and left him staring out of the window.

*

After an hour searching on *toutypasse.com* for ads renting camper vans in the region, Bruno had made over twenty calls but little progress. His labours were interrupted by a call from the curator he knew at the Centre Jean Moulin in Bordeaux, to report that nothing embarrassing had been found in Murcoing's war records. He had joined the Maquis in late 1943, after the Germans had occupied southern France and begun the STO, Service du Travail Obligatoire, the compulsory roundup of men and young women to work in labour camps in Germany. He'd joined the Groupe Valmy in early 1944, fought at Terrasson in June and took part in the battle to liberate Périgueux in August.

'Some of this we have confirmed by Marcelle Murat, a real Resistance heroine known as Le Caporal. She used her pharmacy as a postbox and informal hospital as well as acting as a courier between the various groups. I'll draft a complete paragraph that you can use in a press release or have read out at the funeral,' said the curator. 'I'll miss the old boy. He used to come and see us once a year, always to ask if there was anything new about the money he'd helped take from the Neuvic train. Are you familiar with that?'

'Yes, I even found a couple of banknotes he must have taken from the train. He had one clutched in his hands as he died.'

'We'd love to have one for the museum, if you could ask his heirs. That would be young Paul, I suppose.'

'You know him?' Bruno sat up with a jerk.

'Oh yes. He'd normally come along with his grandfather. I remember he sat in when we interviewed the old man for the oral archive. He was just as bad as his grandpa, railing against the thieves and crooks who stole the Neuvic money. It was all a capitalist plot, he said. Of course, his grandpa was in the FTP, the *Francs-Tireurs et Partisans*, the Communist wing. I don't know if Paul is in the party but he certainly sounds just like his grandpa. He's a regular on the bulletin board we set up on the Internet, always on the various history websites. The Neuvic train seems to be an obsession with him.'

'That's interesting because we're trying to track Paul for another inquiry. It's quite serious, so serious I doubt that he'll even turn up for the funeral. Can you give me details of these websites?'

'There are so many, I'll send you a list. And I'll look up some of Paul's postings, ravings more like. I've got your email address at the *Mairie* and anyway I'll see you at the funeral. There aren't many of the old veterans left and I'd like to attend.'

'What's Paul's email address?' Bruno quickly wrote it down, rang off and checked his watch. School had started, but maybe Florence had no early class this morning. He tried her mobile without success and sent her an email instead, asking if she could track any activity on Paul's account at orange.fr.

He felt he was making progress, step by step. An image of Paul was beginning to build in his head. There was the photograph, that cheeky smile with its flash of intelligence. There was his relationship with his grandfather and their shared obsession about the Neuvic train, his fondness for serious films and his relationship with his sister. How often did siblings in their twenties go on holidays together? But there was so much yet to learn, so much of the image that was fuzzy or blank. What of the connection to Fullerton? Was it business or pleasure or both? And what would Paul have done with the vanload of Fullerton's antiques? If he and his sister were looking for a camper van, they'd need somewhere to store Paul's white van and the furniture. The old family farm had been sold, so that was ruled out. Perhaps Paul knew of an abandoned barn up in the hills, but that would not stay long undiscovered.

There was a knock on his office door and a tall thin man with sloping shoulders and a mournful expression entered the room carrying a black briefcase. He shook hands as he introduced himself.

'Bernard Ardouin, *juge d'instruction*. We have a mutual friend in Annette, who says I have to be sure to listen to you.'

An interesting start, thought Bruno, and unusual. Under French law since Napoleon's day, a magistrate appointed to be *juge d'instruction* in a case had almost unlimited control of the investigation. He could interview witnesses and review evidence, define the lines of inquiry the police should pursue, authorize arrests and prosecutions. Finally he or she would present the case to a court. Unlike the adversarial system in Anglo-Saxon countries, where a prosecuting lawyer and a defence lawyer fought the case to win a verdict of guilty or not guilty, a French *juge d'instruction* was supposed to discover the full truth, and had broad powers to do so. That was why the French novelist Balzac had described such a figure as 'the most powerful man in the world'.

'You're very welcome,' said Bruno. 'Do you want to chat here in the office or go down to the café?'

'Let's start here. Cafés tend to have lots of ears listening for gossip. And it's not good for our reputation when people realize how little we know. All I have so far is the certificate of death and a preliminary pathologist's report which says death was inflicted by a succession of heavy blows causing multiple fractures to the skull and facial bones. It also says that the victim was HIV-positive and taking the usual drugs to keep it at bay.'

Ardouin removed a thin file from his briefcase and ran over the facts. The victim was a foreigner, Francis Fullerton, aged thirty-six, a British citizen and antiques dealer. The body was discovered by Yves Valentoux, aged thirty-five, of Paris, a French citizen, with whom the deceased was in a homosexual relationship. He looked up.

'I interviewed Valentoux yesterday and was satisfied that he could be released. I understand it was you who worked out his movements through the garage and *péage* receipts. The *Police Nationale* tell me they are looking for a possible suspect, Paul Murcoing. Perhaps you'd take me through this from the beginning.'

Bruno described the steps he had taken, the visit to Dougal, the postman's identification of the van, the sign-maker and the warehouse at Belvès.

'So the only evidence of his involvement is that this white van was seen by the postman approaching the *gîte* not long before Fullerton's death,' Ardouin said. 'Plus this Murcoing had been arrested on suspicion of dealing in stolen antiques and may also be homosexual.'

'He's disappeared and so has his sister. She tried to rent a camper van on the evening of Fullerton's murder.'

Ardouin looked up again from where he was scribbling notes on a pad and gave Bruno a look of amiable scepticism. 'And he's the only lead you've got.'

'True,' said Bruno. 'But if somebody goes to the effort of buying a fake sign for his van with a fake address and he pays in cash, then it's reasonable to assume he's up to no good.'

Ardouin nodded. 'But not necessarily murder. He could have met Fullerton by agreement, loaded his van with Fullerton's antiques and then left him alive and well. Then someone else comes along and kills him for entirely different reasons.'

'I agree,' said Bruno. 'Even so, he's someone we very much need to interview. He was close to his grandpa who died two days ago and is due to have a full Resistance funeral. If he misses that, he's on the run. Did the police send you the photographs of the furniture stolen from the other Englishman's house and the list of wine?'

'No, what other Englishman?'

Bruno pushed across the desk a copy of *Sud Ouest*. 'A very influential Englishman who has a team from the minister of the interior's office babysitting his property with their own forensics people looking for any trace that Murcoing had been there.'

'Could be coincidence.'

Ardouin's tone was matter-of-fact, rather than negative. Bruno got the impression of a solid, painstaking magistrate who would steadily let the evidence build, while remaining wary of hunches and theories. There were not many magistrates of this type. Many of them justified the usual police grumble that they were left-wing, feminist and Green. On balance Bruno had concluded that this was reasonable. The law leaned to the side of property and authority; and it was no bad thing for some magistrates to tend a little in the other direction. In any event, he'd much rather deal with a *juge d'instruction* like the lugubrious but dependable Ardouin than with someone more flamboyant.

'Of course it could be coincidence, but when we have so few other leads, coincidences are worth exploring,' Bruno replied. 'I've also launched some inquiries into the local gay community to see what's known of Murcoing, his usual associates, friends where he may be able to stay, that sort of thing. And we've circulated photos of the stolen furniture, in case something turns up.'

'What do you plan to do next?'

'I'm going to start looking into the *brocante* business, try to find people who might have known Fullerton and Murcoing. You probably heard from J-J that the *Police Nationale* have asked the British for any information they may have about the victim. His brother is arriving later today to make funeral arrangements and he may be able to tell me more about Fullerton that might help us. Apart from keeping up the search for Murcoing, I'm not sure what else I can do.'

'The *Police Nationale* tell me you've been seconded to the Ministry to focus on the burglary of this Englishman. Will that leave you any time to help me?'

'If I'm right in suspecting the cases are connected, I'll be working for you while working for them.'

'Right, I'll leave you to pursue your inquiries as you see fit, just keep me informed. An email each evening or a phone call will do.' Ardouin gave Bruno an unexpected smile, a warm and genuine expression that lit up his usually mournful face. 'And since it's a warm morning, let me buy you a beer in that café you mentioned. Annette tells me you're a keen tennis player, like me.'

12

Brian Fullerton had the look of a boxer going to seed and carried himself like a military man. He had big hands with a gold wedding ring and an amiable face with a broken nose, big ears and floppy grey hair that needed cutting. He wore a blazer with an unidentifiable club badge on the breast pocket, the bowl of a pipe poking from it, and well-polished brogue shoes. So far all Bruno knew of Francis Fullerton's looks was his passport photograph; from that formal snapshot he would never have guessed the two men might be brothers. Recalling that Fullerton had been thirty-six, Bruno estimated this man to be about ten years older.

'My condolences on your loss. You made very good time from Bordeaux,' Bruno began, glancing at his watch. He hadn't expected the man until much later in the afternoon.

'I cancelled the booking the Consulate had made for me and took the Ryanair flight to Bergerac instead,' said the brother, in excellent French. 'It seemed a lot closer. Here's my passport, just to confirm I am the brother you're expecting. I haven't checked into the hotel yet, it seemed a bit early. They'd booked me into Les Glycines in Les Eyzies but that's rather too pricey for me so I looked on the Internet and found a place in town, the Hôtel St Denis. It looked cheap but reasonably comfortable.'

It was the place Bruno would have picked.

'Where's my brother's body?'

'At the morgue in Bergerac. The autopsy should be finished by this evening. It will then be up to the magistrate whether the body can be released for burial. He was a bit worried about identification. Now that you're here, we can probably confirm that through your DNA. I'm afraid the head was too badly damaged to be recognizable.'

Fullerton frowned. 'That sounds bad.'

'It was an extremely brutal killing, and we're determined to bring the murderer to justice. Allow me to compliment you on your French.'

'That's mother. She's French, met my father when she came to work for some neighbours as an *au pair* back in the early Sixties.'

'Were you and your brother close?' Bruno pulled out his notebook and began writing.

'Not really, Francis was eleven years younger and we led very different lives. But we tried to do the usual family things like Christmas and the occasional holiday so he could get to know my children. I'm a civil servant, married with a family, rather conventional, and Francis was the complete opposite.'

'You mean that he was homosexual?'

'Ah, you know. Not only that, although it took our parents some time to adjust. We're an old-fashioned family.' He went on to explain that Francis had never really settled down, perhaps had never really grown up. He'd been intelligent and managed to get a degree even though he dropped out from university for a while, but he kept getting into trouble with drugs and debts.

'When Francis went to prison it broke my mother's heart. He was her favourite of course, the last baby, born long after my sister and me, and he always had this angelic look as a child.' Fullerton frowned again. 'I suppose I have to get used to referring to him in the past tense.'

'We didn't know he'd been in prison,' said Bruno, startled by the news but not altogether surprised. 'We've asked the British police if anything was known about him but these things take time to come through official channels. Why was he sent to prison?'

'Receiving stolen goods,' said the brother. After some wild years in London and then in America, Francis had settled down with a steady partner called Sam Berenson. He was an older man, in the antiques business in a part of Brighton called The Lanes, full of antiques shops. Francis claimed that he'd been the fall guy when the police found a haul of stolen silver at their shop. One of the burglars had turned Queen's evidence, and since Francis refused to testify against his partner he was sentenced to three years and was out in two.

'But he stayed in the business?'

'Berenson died of AIDS while Francis was in prison, and he left Francis the lot; a house in Brighton, the shop and all the stock.' Fullerton shook his head ruefully. 'Almost worth it for two years inside, that's what my wife says.'

'Did he specialize in silver?'

'No, that was the odd thing. The shop specialized in antique furniture, rugs and paintings. Francis sold it and the house he'd been left at the top of the market, just before the recession. He made quite a lot of money and then started his new business. He began going back and forth to France, selling

British stuff over here and then buying French furniture to sell back in Britain. He seemed to do very well out of it, drove a Porsche, bought a house in Chelsea when the prices dropped. He always had a good eye for a bargain.'

'So he kept up his links to his mother's homeland. How often did he make these trips to France?'

'At least once a month. He had a big warehouse outside Brighton where he kept his stock. And he went back to the States a few times, using his old contacts in Los Angeles. Then he started exporting English antiques over there.'

'Do you know if Francis made a will?'

'Yes, I checked with his lawyer before coming over here. Everything goes to me and my sister to be kept in trust for our children. I've got a letter from the lawyer saying I'm the executor. I made some copies so here's one for you.' He pulled a file from his briefcase and handed Bruno the letter.

'I suspect his dying in France may complicate the inheritance. You may want to consult a lawyer.'

'I've done so. I'm told his British property will be covered by the will, but the French property will be different.'

'What French property?'

'An old farm in the Corrèze, very picturesque but a bit remote for me and the children. We only visited a couple of times as a family. I came down again last year with him, just the two of us. He bought the place when he sold the shop. That's why I was surprised to hear that he died here at a *gîte* he was renting. It seemed a bit strange when he had a place of his own.'

'Does it have barns?' Bruno asked. 'Could he have used it as a warehouse?'

'Yes, that's why he got it. It was cheap, of course, but with the new autoroute he could get around to the various *brocantes* and estate sales from Bordeaux to Lyon.'

'I think we'd better go out and take a look at this place. Where is it exactly?'

'Just south of Ussel, about twenty minutes off the autoroute. I need to go there myself to see his *notaire*. Is there anything more you need me to do?'

'If you know what you want to do with your brother's remains, I can introduce you to the local undertakers. But first I must consult with the *juge d'instruction*. I think he'll want you to give a DNA sample, just to confirm the identification, and I'm sure he'll need to interview you. Let me see if he's still in St Denis.'

Bruno called Ardouin, who was still at the St Denis Gendarmerie, gave him a swift explanation of what he'd learned from Brian Fullerton and arranged to escort him there. On the way back to his office, he stopped at Father Sentout's house to check on the details for Murcoing's funeral and called in at Delightful Dordogne to see if Dougal had heard any news from Yvonne Murcoing. Not a word, he said, and he was about to clear out her room at the staff house to make way for a replacement. On his way out Bruno met Philippe Delaron coming in to pick up a list of new rental addresses to be photographed for Dougal's website.

'When's the English spy coming back to his house?' Philippe asked. He was wearing a new leather jacket that looked expensive. His sideline in news photos was evidently paying better than the family camera shop. 'I'll need to take a photo. Gaëlle says she thinks he gets back tomorrow.'

'In that case, she's probably heard more than I have.'

'Why have they got Gendarmes guarding the house?'

'Ask the Gendarmes.'

'Come on, Bruno, be a sport. Surely you can tell me something.'

'The *Procureur* has appointed a *juge d'instruction* into the murder inquiry and the victim's brother has arrived from England,' Bruno said, trotting down the steps. At the last step, he stopped. 'Have you had a request from the *Police Nationale* to publish a photo of anyone they want to find urgently?'

'You mean a suspect? Not that I've heard. Give me a minute.' Philippe thumbed an autodial number on his phone, fired off a quick question and then shook his head. 'Not so far.'

'I'll see what I can do,' said Bruno and called J-J as he walked back down the Rue Gambetta. J-J said that the press officer was supposed to issue Murcoing's mugshot from his earlier arrest later that day.

'What if I let *Sud Ouest* have the more recent photo from the surveillance camera? They'll give it more prominence if they think it's their story rather than a routine police request.'

'Go ahead. But don't get quoted saying this guy's a suspect. Let them take the responsibility for that and we'll give a no comment.'

Bruno described what he'd learned from Brian Fullerton and said he planned to drive out to the Corrèze farm as soon as he'd finished with the *juge d'instruction*. Back in his office, he texted Delaron to come and see him, prepared another copy of Murcoing's photo for the paper, and began printing out the pictures of Crimson's rugs, paintings and furniture that had been deposited with Crimson's insurance agent.

He was looking up the phone number of the *Police Municipale* in Ussel when Delaron appeared. Bruno handed him a copy of Murcoing's photo from the surveillance camera at the printing shop.

'This didn't come from me, understood? And I'm not saying he's a murder suspect, just that the police urgently want to interview him. I think the *Police Nationale* will be issuing his mugshot later today. He's Paul Murcoing, lives in Bergerac, makes a living as a driver – and his grandpa is getting a full-scale Resistance funeral here in St Denis next week. That's it.'

'Thanks, Bruno. Where was this taken? Looks like a print from a surveillance tape.'

'I'm not saying, Philippe. *Bon courage*. Oh, by the way, there's something you can do for me in return.' Bruno pulled out the photos of Loïc Murcoing as a young man in his Resistance unit and handed them to Delaron. 'I'd like these blown up as large as you can make them. It's for his funeral. I'd like to put them by the coffin in the church.'

Once Delaron had left, Bruno called Gilles at *Paris Match* to say he'd always be welcome in St Denis but he wasn't sure how much of a story there would be in a burglary.

'I see you've got a murder on your hands as well, the victim being another Brit. Any connection?'

'It's not clear yet. Look, Gilles, this is not an affair where I can give you much help. A *juge d'instruction* has been brought in and I'll be in real trouble if I start feeding you stuff. Crimson hasn't even got back here yet.'

'I was talking to one of the British reporters here in Paris. He said Crimson gets back tomorrow and he and some others are heading down to St Denis. I'll be joining them, but I'll arrive earlier. I'm booked into the Vieux Logis from tonight.

I'll be in that café of yours by eight tomorrow morning.'

'The Vieux Logis? I didn't know *Paris Match* was making that much money these days.'

'Let's just say I have a hunch about this story. See you tomorrow.'

When Bernard Ardouin called to say he was finished with Fullerton's brother, Bruno went to the Gendarmerie to pick him up and propose a drive to Francis's farm in the Corrèze.

'Nothing else for me to do,' Fullerton replied. 'They can't release the body until the identification is confirmed and then I'll have him cremated and take the ashes back to England. If you take the autoroute to Ussel, I think I remember the way. I need to see the *notaire* there, in any event.'

He pulled a mobile phone from his briefcase and began dialling. Bruno called J-J to tell him of his plans and then called Isabelle to keep her in the picture. Finally he made a courtesy call to the police in Ussel to say he was coming onto their patch. When he finished, Brian Fullerton was looking at him, a perplexed expression on his face.

'That's odd. I just called the number of the farm in Corrèze, wondering if my brother had left one of his usual messages about where to find the key. He's got these different hiding places each with its own letter. It was a sort of code he worked out with my kids when they spent a summer here, a family joke. But somebody answered, a woman, and when I gave my name and asked who she was she slammed the phone down.'

'*Merde*,' said Bruno. Could it have been Yvonne? Was that where she and her brother were hiding out?

He called the Ussel police again and explained the situation. They promised to send a car.

13

A single policeman waited by his van in front of the farmhouse. It was similar to those around St Denis except the stone was grey and the shutters were painted bright red. One long, low barn was attached to a wing of the house and a second, taller barn stood to one side. The garden was unkempt. Stalks of last year's dead geraniums lay forlornly in pots and there was jungle where the vegetable garden would have been. The trees planted to the north and west looked stunted, as though hunched against the wind. It would be cold here in winter, Bruno thought.

'By the time we got here, the birds had flown,' said the *flic*. He introduced himself as the town policeman from Neuvic, a name that startled Bruno. 'I know, you keep thinking it's the one in Dordogne. This is another Neuvic, best known for the lake. You can't see it from here but it's just over that ridge to the south.'

'Have you been inside?' Bruno introduced Fullerton as the new owner, brother of the murdered man.

'The main house was open so we took a quick look around. The beds had been slept in, dirty dishes in the sink and there's a cashier's ticket from Leclerc in the bin dated two days ago. I don't know if anything's been touched or stolen. The message from Ussel said it was that guy in the bulletin from the *Police Nationale*, the murder suspect.'

Bruno took two sets of gloves from his van, donned one and gave the other to Fullerton, who'd been peering through the windows. Nothing seemed different, he said. Bruno led the way into the house. It was an odd mixture. Some beautiful pieces of old furniture, an Empire clock atop an Empire table, two Louis XVI chairs, a large tapestry on the stone wall that Bruno thought might be an Aubusson, were scattered like islands of good taste among cheap modern stuff that looked like IKEA. The kitchen was filthy, layers of grime on the red tile floor and the stove was worse. Bruno noted empty bottles in a box and dirty glasses in the sink.

He kneeled down to look at the bottles. In two of them, the dregs were still moist. One was a Château Kirwan, 2005, and the other was Haut-Brion, 2001. He checked his notebook. They could have come from Crimson's cellar. In the dining room, some strips of wallpaper hung down forlornly and a large brown patch of damp covered part of the ceiling. His eye was drawn by an exquisite small oil painting of a young woman in eighteenth-century dress on a swing.

'School of Watteau, I believe,' said Brian. 'Were it a real Watteau it would be worth more than the whole place.'

Upstairs, the towels in the bathroom were damp and the floor of the shower was still wet. In one bedroom they found female underclothes and pair of discarded tights. In the other a pair of men's dirty socks were balled beneath the bed. Both beds had been left unmade.

'Looks like they left in a hurry,' said Brian. 'Maybe they were in a panic after I called.'

'Have you looked in the barns?' Bruno asked the *flic*. He said no, adding that they were locked. Bruno asked Brian if he remembered the codes for the keys.

'Gloria,' he said triumphantly, and laughed. 'G for the geranium pot, L for the ladder, O for the orangerie, which is what we called the little glass lean-to at the back, R for the rake in the tool-shed, I for the iron seat that came from an old tractor, and the last A is for that artichoke pot hanging on the wall.'

He lifted the terracotta artichoke from its hook to reveal a big iron key and a smaller one that looked like a Yale. Bruno and the *flic* followed him to the single-storey barn. He used the big key to open a large but partly broken wooden door. Behind it lay a much more solid metal door which he opened with the Yale. He flicked on an inside light, a fluorescent strip that flickered and buzzed before suddenly blazing into stark life.

Cases of wine were stacked against the far wall. In front of them were heaped rugs, rolled up and tied with lengths of orange plastic string. Alongside stood paintings wrapped loosely in canvas. Bruno went back to his van for the file of photos of Crimson's possessions. The first painting he uncovered was a thickly-painted scene from a window, dominated by a flapping curtain and overlooking a dismal garden with dirty brick houses in the background. It was marked in Crimson's file as a Bratby, valued at eight thousand euros, and Bruno saw the artist's signature in the bottom corner. To make sure, he unwrapped the next canvas and unveiled two rather gloomy watercolours of beach scenes, beautifully framed. Each was recorded in Crimson's photos, and listed as John Sell Cotman. They were valued at five thousand euros for the pair.

'No doubt about it, these are stolen goods,' he said, rising and showing the photos to the *flic*. 'They were stolen from a house in my commune at the beginning of this week.'

'You mean my brother was up to his old tricks?' Brian asked.

'Not as far as these paintings were concerned. He was still in England when these were stolen,' Bruno said. 'But for the rest, I don't know. Let's look in the other barn.'

It was locked, so in search for the keys Fullerton led them to the tool-shed and the orangerie in vain before going to the back of the house where an aluminium ladder lay propped lengthwise against a wall. He bent down at one end and slid a key from the hollow of one of the legs, held it up with a grin and the three of them trooped to the large barn. This had two wide wooden doors, each about two metres high. They were locked with a chain and a padlock. The key fitted and turned easily and they hauled the two doors open to reveal a tall white van. On its side were painted blue letters reading Chauffage-France with an address in the industrial zone of Belvès. Its rear doors were open and the interior was stacked high with furniture, mainly tall wooden dressers, each protected from its neighbour by blankets.

'Bingo,' Bruno breathed to himself. On the floor of the van by the open doors were four heavy iron tubes, each about a metre long, held together by elasticized bands with hooks at each end.

'Any idea what these might be?' he asked, pointing at the tubes. He wondered whether he might have found the murder weapon.

'Rollers,' said Brian, lighting the pipe he'd been filling. 'It's how they move heavy furniture, sliding them along on those rollers.'

More furniture was stored in the barn: large and small tables, more dressers, tall glass-fronted bookshelves with ornate carved headings and sets of handsome dining chairs.

Bruno called Isabelle, trying without success to keep the pride from his voice, to tell her that he'd found at least some of Crimson's belongings and that his suspicions had been confirmed of the link between the burglaries and the murder. He allowed himself a few moments to enjoy her praise, feeling like a schoolboy rushing home with a prize, and then rang J-J to get the arts squad and forensic team to the Corrèze farmhouse.

'We've found the white van and we may even have the murder weapon,' he went on. 'It ties Murcoing with Fullerton and we may be able to clear up a whole host of burglaries into the bargain.'

'On my way,' snapped J-J, and Bruno turned to see Brian delving into one of the dressers in the back of the white van. He was wearing gloves so he'd do no harm. It was probably all his property anyway.

'Is it OK with you if I head off home now?' asked the local *flic*, looking at his watch. 'I was due off at two.'

Sure, said Bruno, shaking hands and thanking him. He promised to send a copy of his report to the Ussel station, and to make sure they got some of the credit once Murcoing was caught. He watched the police van disappear down the bumpy track.

'Can you give me a hand to move this furniture a bit?' Brian asked from inside the van. 'Just lean that dresser over to the left so I can get this drawer open.'

Bruno complied, and was rewarded with a triumphant cry

from Brian as he eased from the drawer a white Apple laptop computer.

'That's where my brother always hid it when he was travelling,' said Brian. 'Do you think I might get it back when you're done with investigating what's on it? I always lusted after one of these.'

'I thought you said you and your brother weren't close,' Bruno said. 'You seem to know a lot about his habits.'

'We made the effort to keep up. I even came out here with him once, just the two of us.'

'What about his mobile phone?' Bruno said. 'We never found it at the *gîte*. Maybe that's here, too.' He sighed as he looked at the mass of furniture to be moved.

'No problem,' said Brian, took out his own phone, thumbed through the address book and dialled a number. 'If it's here, we'll hear the "Money, money, money" song from the musical *Cabaret*. That's his ringtone.'

No sound came. Brian shrugged and took the laptop into the house. Bruno followed him into a room that was used as a study, with a desk and crammed bookshelves and an old-fashioned phone. As Bruno glanced around, Brian ducked under the desk, and pulled up a power cord still attached to a converter plug.

'Francis always left a power cord here, in case he forgot one,' Brian explained, and plugged in the laptop. He began muttering to himself as the screen opened and demanded a password. Suddenly he looked up and struck himself on the forehead. 'Idiot!'

He turned to Bruno. 'I forgot to look at the shrine. It's that big cupboard. Is it open?'

He pointed to a giant built-in corner cupboard. It had two double doors that stretched from floor to ceiling, nearly three metres tall, in heavy, age-darkened oak. Bruno tugged at the handles but the doors were locked. Brian pulled the drawer completely out from the desk, and from the back of it took a key that had been attached with heavy-duty metallic tape.

'This may come as a bit of surprise,' said Brian, sounding apologetic as he inserted the key. 'I should have mentioned it before.'

'*Mon Dieu*,' breathed Bruno as the doors opened and a rack of guns met his eye. There were two rifles, two old submachine guns, a revolver, a small mortar and an antique radio set, all grouped around a large framed photograph of a young man in British army uniform of the Second World War. He wore three white stripes on his sleeve. A smaller photo of a pretty young woman of the same era hung beside it. Draped above the portrait was a flag from the FFI, the French Forces of the Interior. Below it was a row of medals, two Nazi daggers and an old Wehrmacht helmet. Between them, very expensively framed, was a Banque de France banknote that Bruno recognized – the same design and denomination as the one he had seen gripped in the hands of old Loïc Murcoing.

'Meet Grandpa,' said Brian. 'That's the shrine. And that photo of Grandpa is a much better likeness of Francis than that passport photo you've got. It was uncanny, how closely they resembled each other.'

But what caught Bruno's eye were the two empty slots in the display of guns, one shaped like a handgun and the other like a small machine pistol, with the velvet backdrop unfaded where they had been.

'I wonder where they've gone,' said Brian. 'That was where the Sten gun used to be. And the other one was a Browning nine-millimetre. I'll be sorry if we can't find those.'

'Are these in working order?' Bruno asked.

'They still work and he cleaned them regularly. We used to do a bit of hunting with the rifles. I used the Lee Enfield but Francis always used the French Lebel. We also tried some target shooting with the Browning that's missing.'

'If I were you, I'd not repeat that to anyone else, least of all to any policeman,' said Bruno. 'As far as they know, you never fired any of these and your brother told you they were harmless. Otherwise this could get very complicated for you. Now, what can you tell me about this shrine and your grandpa?'

Their mother had been French, Fullerton began, and so had their grandmother, a young woman from this part of the Corrèze whom their grandpa had met and made pregnant during the war. He'd returned after the war to marry her. Grandpa, known in the family as Sergeant Freddy, had been a wireless operator with the Special Operations Executive, SOE, the British agency established to build and train resistance movements across the Nazi-occupied Continent.

That was Sergeant Freddy in the large photo, and *Grandmère* Marie beside him. The medals included Grandpa's Distinguished Conduct Medal, the oak leaf for his mention in dispatches, and a series of the usual campaign awards. He had been dropped into France in March 1944, to operate the wireless communications that brought in the *parachutages*, the air drops of arms and equipment from Britain that went to the Resistance. The radio in the shrine was a genuine British mode B Mark II, a device as crude as it was weak, with a signal at best of only twenty watts and requiring at least twenty metres of aerial. Constantly on the move to evade the German radio direction finder vans, the wireless operators suffered a terrifying attrition rate. If they tried to transmit from towns, the Germans turned off the electricity in every substation until the radio died. Then they surrounded the street. If they tried to transmit from the countryside, they needed an accumulator, heavy, cumbersome and not easy to charge.

Sergeant Freddy was smart. He developed a system to charge an accumulator with parts from an old bicycle and never transmitted from the same place twice. He managed to evade the Germans until the final liberation of the region in August 1944. But in June of that year many Resistance groups rose prematurely, believing that the D-Day landings heralded imminent victory. They were slaughtered by German regular units. In Tulle, the nearest large town to the farmhouse, a hundred and twenty of them were hanged in a single day. A hundred and fifty more were sent to Dachau, where most of them died. Sergeant Freddy was also lucky, and the FFI flag was for the Maquis du Limousin unit that had helped him get away from Tulle.

The guns were all genuine from the period and some of the individual weapons had been used by the Resistance. Francis had bought them over the years, from collectors, from estate sales and auctions of family heirlooms. The Sten gun and the German Schmeisser had been obtained from what Brian described as 'very unsavoury sources', which Bruno assumed to mean criminals.

'That banknote's a new one on me. I never saw that before,' Brian added, leaning forward to study it more closely. 'Would it be from the Neuvic train robbery?'

'I think almost certainly, yes. Any idea how your brother might have got hold of it?'

'No, but I'm not surprised. Francis was fascinated by that incident and read everything he could get his hands on, went round interviewing people. It was all an accident, maybe more of a coincidence, the nearest town to here being also called Neuvic. That set him off. He spent a lot of time on it, going to the Public Records Office. I know he was trying to find out if Grandpa had been involved. He'd got hold of some account that confirmed Sergeant Freddy had arranged some of the parachute drops that went to Groupe Valmy.'

He stood up again, looked around the room and shook his head. 'All those bookshelves, full of stuff he gathered, but Francis never managed to find one of the original banknotes before. I wonder where he got it?'

'Did your brother ever mention anyone called Murcoing?' Bruno asked. 'Paul Murcoing, a young man. And an old *Résistant* called Loïc, his grandfather and one of the original Groupe Valmy members?'

'No, but I'll bet you'll find stuff about him in those files. Take a look in the bottom drawer of the filing cabinet, that's where he kept his photos. They'll all be in alphabetic order.'

Bruno looked under M and found a file labelled Murcoing (Valmy). Inside it were three decent portrait shots of the old man standing by a modern Neuvic road sign. There were also copies of the 1944-vintage photos of the Groupe Valmy that Bruno had seen in the dead man's box of treasures. But there was no file for Paul Murcoing.

Brian went back to the laptop, trying to guess passwords while Bruno searched the rest of the house. He examined the contents of the freezer section of the fridge, the cisterns for the WCs, looked under tables and on the tops of bathroom cupboards. Finally, taking a last look around the bedroom where he'd found the dirty socks, his eye fell on a framed photo on one of the bedside tables. There were Paul and Francis, arms around each other's shoulders, grinning for the camera while sitting at some café table in the sun. They were drinking what looked like Ricard and between them two cigarettes smouldered on an ashtray marked Dubonnet.

'I found the password,' came Brian's triumphant shout from below. 'It was taped to the back of another drawer. He used *Neuvic1944*. He was obsessed with that damn train robbery.'

Bruno turned to go downstairs to see what the laptop might reveal but his eye was caught by a second framed photo on the other bedside table. A moody portrait of Paul Murcoing half-smiling, something deliberately seductive in his eyes, was inscribed: *Pour mon très cher Francis, Je t'embrasse, Paul.*

14

The village of Paunat was one of Bruno's favourite places, a classic ensemble of old Périgord houses tumbling down a hillside to the stream and dominated by an austere Benedictine abbey. Seated at a table for two on the terrace of the restaurant, Isabelle and Bruno kept glancing up to admire its floodlit wall as the twilight deepened. Once J-J and Bernard Ardouin had arrived at Francis's farmhouse with the forensics team, Bruno had been able to leave and drive Brian back to his hotel. Isabelle had called to invite him to what she called a working dinner, saying she needed to get all the details before the Brigadier arrived with Crimson next day.

'You can pick somewhere discreet, if you're worried about word getting back to your Englishwoman that I'm back in town,' she had said, in a half-mocking, half-teasing tone.

Given the speed at which local gossip moved around St Denis, Pamela probably already knew. He'd called her earlier from the Corrèze to explain that he wouldn't be able to exercise the horses that evening but that he'd join her at seven the next day for the morning ride. The truth was that there was no restaurant within thirty kilometres where he could guarantee discretion.

For once, Isabelle had ditched her usual black and was

wearing a starched white shirt that showed off her cruise-ship tan, over a pleated skirt that flared enticingly as she turned to wave at him after climbing out of her rented car. When he'd admired the way it looked on her, she'd told him proudly that it was a Fortuny, bought at a vintage clothing shop in Paris.

'I'll take the menu with the *coquilles St Jacques* and then the *blanquette de veau*,' she said, looking appreciatively at the large blackboard with the day's menu that had been placed by their table. 'A bottle of Perrier and whatever wine you think most suitable. And then tell me all about what happened today and you can also explain why you didn't bring our puppy along.'

'Balzac still has some house-training to learn before I'd dare let him loose on a restaurant,' he replied, while trying to choose between the veal and the partridge. Finally he ordered the same dishes that Isabelle had chosen, along with a glass each of the restaurant's Bergerac Sec to go with the scallops and a half bottle of La Jaubertie's Cuvée Mirabelle to go with the veal. Then he told her how the day had unfolded from the moment Brian Fullerton had mentioned his brother's farmhouse.

'What worries me is the missing guns,' he concluded over the cheese course. 'From the brother, it's clear that Francis was in the habit of using them, so it's a reasonable guess that Paul had learned to fire them. He's on the run with his sister, fleeing in a hurry from the place they thought was a refuge, and he's armed and dangerous. I don't envy the traffic cops who flag him down or whoever has to go in once he's cornered.'

'They'll use the *Jaunes*,' Isabelle said, referring to the *Gendarmes Mobiles*, their elite unit. 'Nobody would shed many tears if Murcoing gets killed but there'll be trouble if his sister gets shot as well. But that's somebody else's problem. For today, it's a good result. It's obvious that Murcoing is the murderer and Crimson gets his stuff back, along with a lot of other victims. I imagine the local insurance agents will be giving you a very special dinner.'

Bruno was about to say that it could not be nearly as special as this evening when he remembered the sharp way she had said: 'Those days are over,' when he'd made some quip about her wearing his shirt as a dressing gown. And now she was off to some European job in Holland. There would be no more special missions for the Brigadier that sometimes brought her down to St Denis. Perhaps this was to be their last supper, her way of saying goodbye, taking the opportunity of a day when the blow would be softened by his professional success.

'But that's not the only reason I wanted to see you this evening,' she said. Bruno braced himself, preparing his face to display a look of wry affection tinged with sadness. It wouldn't even have to be faked. A part of him would always be in love with her vivacity and her fire.

'I thought I'd better warn you there's a buzz around the Ministry that there's to be some kind of pre-election surprise. People are nervous. And St Denis seems to be caught up in it,' she said, startling him. 'Maybe you are, too. I'm not sure exactly what this political intrigue might be, but the Brigadier told me to ask you about Americans, and when he did I noticed your army file was open on his desk. I think that was why he was so quick to seize on Crimson's burglary.'

'I don't understand. Crimson's an Englishman.' One part of his brain was thinking that this had to be about Jacqueline's book and therefore implicated his Mayor, while another was thinking that for once this was something he could not discuss with Isabelle. Her interest would be to protect the state; his would be to protect his Mayor.

'English, Americans, two sides of the same coin.' She waved his comment aside. 'You know these old Gaullists, it's always been an article of faith that there's no difference between *les Anglo-Saxons*. And in intelligence at least, they're probably right; the English tell the Americans everything. Just remember that as far as the Brigadier is concerned, you have no secrets. He'll even know we're together this evening.'

'Did you tell him we were having dinner?'

'No, but you remember in Bordeaux, after your phone was tapped and he gave you one of our secure ones? He can call up a screen that shows him where all of those phones are at any given time. And before you ask, yes, that means he knows when we've spent the night together.'

Bruno felt himself blushing. 'Is this rumour about an election surprise just in your Ministry?'

She gave a wry smile. 'You know Paris.' She said it as if she'd been born and bred in the capital, when they both knew she'd been based there less than a year and had spent much of that time in hospitals.

'Remember Gilles from *Paris Match*, the reporter I knew in Bosnia?' Bruno asked. 'He's coming down here along with some British journalists. He said it was because of Crimson, but I wonder.'

'Crimson is a good news story. Burglary solved, goods recovered, brilliant police work.'

'If that's all Gilles is planning on reporting. I know he loves the region but this is election time, political season. We both know he's a good reporter; relentless when he's after a story.'

She nodded thoughtfully and took a sip of wine. 'It's strange that we never talked politics, you and I, nor was there much of it when I was based in Périgueux. In Paris, after other people's love lives it's the main topic of conversation. I presume you lean to the right like most *flics*.'

Bruno raised his eyebrows. 'I don't think I lean in any direction, and I suspect the old traditions of lifelong loyalty to a single party are fading pretty fast. Take you, for example; I'd say you were progressive on social matters like abortion and gay rights, but conservative on law and order and maybe on defence.'

'That sounds like you as well,' she said, smiling.

'I don't pay that much attention to national politics. Locally, I vote for the man or woman I like.' Bruno recalled his last trip to the voting booth for the municipal election. He'd voted for the Mayor, who was centre-right, and for the kindly retired schoolteacher who'd chaired the local Socialist party for two decades. He'd also cast his ballot for Alphonse, an old hippy who was a passionate Green, and for Montsouris, the only Communist on the council. In the last national election, he'd voted one way for the presidency and in the elections for the *Assemblée Nationale* he'd voted for the other side.

'But you're anti-European,' she insisted. 'You're a French nationalist, a real *cocorico*. And I've heard you moan about those bureaucrats in Brussels often enough.'

'Absolutely not,' he declared. 'I love France but I'm a passionate pro-European. It's just this particular form of Brussels-based Europe that irritates the hell out of me.'

Bruno relished the way that other Europeans like Pamela

from Britain and his German friend Horst, the archaeologist, could live and work in France or anywhere in Europe they chose. He liked the principle of a single currency and travel without passports. But he was angry that Brussels spent a fortune on agriculture while farming around St Denis was being squeezed to death.

'So who are you going to vote for?' she asked. 'The devil we know or the devil we don't?'

'I don't know yet. None of them really impresses me but maybe it's time for a change. That's the best thing about democracy, the feeling that you can throw the rascals out.'

He signalled for the bill, but the waiter pointed to Isabelle and shrugged. She'd paid when he went to wash his hands.

'Don't worry, you're on expenses,' she said.

'Thank you,' he said, studying her and wondering whether to say what was in his mind. He decided to go ahead. 'For a while, I thought you'd invited me to dinner to say a formal Adieu.'

She looked at him in silence, almost sternly, took a deep breath as if about to say something important and then stopped herself. She picked up her bag from the floor beside her, rose and turned to take his arm. She flashed him a brilliant smile, gave the skin of his forearm a gentle nip and said: 'I thought I already did.'

'Several times,' he replied. 'That's the problem. I never know if you mean it.'

The kitchen and living-room lights were still on and Valentoux's car was parked in the drive when Bruno got home. He must have heard the Land Rover, because as Bruno emerged

147

he was standing in the doorway, a bottle in his hand, to welcome Bruno home.

'This is for you, to say thanks,' he said, handing Bruno a bottle of Lagavulin and leading the way back into the living room where two glasses were waiting alongside a jug of water. 'Annette tells me it's your favourite scotch and I'm celebrating. I'll be moving into her place in Sarlat tomorrow, if that suits you.'

Bruno thanked him, put the new bottle into his drinks cupboard and brought out the bottle of Lagavulin he'd already opened. He poured out two glasses and splashed a little water into each one. He noted with approval that there were no ice cubes.

'Annette told me how you drink it, no ice, just a touch of water.'

'Dougal, a Scottish friend, showed me how the Scots drink it,' Bruno replied. 'I'm glad you're settled and I've also got some reassuring news. It looks like you're in the clear and that it was Murcoing who killed your friend.'

'I'm not surprised. I've found out a bit more about him from one of the actors I've known for years, someone who's based in Bordeaux. He sounds like an unpleasant young man, rather mercenary, who makes a habit of living off older men. Apparently he speaks good English.'

Bruno was about to say that Fullerton would fit that pattern, but thought better of it and instead sipped his drink. Fullerton had been Yves's lover, after all. He liked Valentoux and did not want to offend him, so how did one embark on a discussion of Fullerton's other affair? And how far should he allow for some jealousy on Yves's part?

Valentoux noticed Bruno's hesitation and smiled. 'You're very polite for a policeman. I knew Francis was never faithful to me and I accepted that. I fell in love with him and I was very attracted to him. He was a wonderfully handsome man, full of energy and *joie de vivre*. There were times I thought I'd found the love of my life; times when we both thought that. But I think I always knew or perhaps feared that he was a bit of a rogue, not someone to rely on.'

A parallel with Isabelle came into Bruno's mind. He'd trust her with his life but he wasn't sure that he could rely on her, not if it came to a choice between her career and her heart. He dragged himself back to the conversation with Yves.

'When you say Murcoing was mercenary, you mean he went with older men for money?'

Valentoux shrugged. 'Perhaps, I don't know. But I'd imagine it was mainly for presents, expensive clothes and trips, always at the best hotels, perhaps the occasional painting. I can't see Francis being involved with someone quite so crude as to demand cash.'

Suddenly Valentoux took a notebook from an inside pocket and handed Bruno a small colour photograph. It showed a dark-haired little girl in a light blue dress sitting on the lap of a strikingly pretty woman. The picture had been taken in a garden, an ivy-covered wall behind them and another rather older woman stood beside them.

'You may be surprised but that's Odile, my daughter, and those are her parents, Francine and Hélène, an actress and a set designer whom I've known for years. They initially wanted to adopt, but when that proved difficult, they asked me to help and I was honoured to do so. Odile calls me *Tonton*, Uncle Yves.'

'Congratulations,' said Bruno, his eyes lingering on the little girl, looking for a resemblance. 'I think she has your eyes.'

'I have a whole photo album: her birth, her birthdays, going on holidays together at the beach in Normandy. Here's one of Francis with Odile, in my apartment in Paris. He thought she was marvellous and I think he fell in love a little with Francine and Hélène, just as I had.'

'She's lovely. How old is she?'

'She was four when that was taken, last summer, in my garden. Francine and Hélène are very kind, they make a lot of room for me to share in their joy. Perhaps they may have had some room for Francis as well. I know Francis hoped that might happen. That was something he wanted to talk about on this holiday we had planned. He was beguiled by his fantasy of giving Odile a little sibling.'

'She's a lovely child. You're a lucky man,' said Bruno, and meant it. He pushed the photo back across the table, poured two more drinks and asked: 'Did you know that Francis had another house not far away, in the Corrèze? That's where I was this afternoon.'

'I knew he had a place somewhere in the south, but he made it sound more like Languedoc or Provence. I had no idea it was so close.'

Bruno described his meeting with Francis's brother, the trip to the farmhouse and the loot he had found there. He didn't mention the guns or the shrine but he spoke of Francis's interest in his grandfather's wartime exploits and his obsession with the Neuvic train.

'On the evening we met he talked to me about his grandfather, Sergeant Freddy he called him, and his work with the

Resistance. I thought he might have been inventing it, a convenient chat-up line to attract a Frenchman. He sometimes talked about this mythical train with its billions of francs. I'd never heard of it and I'd thought it might be another of his fanciful stories. He had quite a few, about his wild times in Los Angeles and New York in those halcyon days before the plague came, before AIDS.'

'Did you know he was HIV-positive?'

'Yes, he was honest about that from the beginning, and absolutely assiduous about safe sex. That's why I was reluctant . . .' Yves checked himself. 'Francis was interested in gay marriage. I think it was as much the hope of having a child like Odile with Francine and Hélène as any great urge to settle down with me. But I was worried about the HIV being passed on.'

Yves passed his hand over his eyes. 'How silly that all seems now that I'll never see him again.'

Seeing his wistful expression, Bruno chided himself for being too intrusive. He finished his drink and rose to his feet.

'I'll be up early again tomorrow to exercise the horses, so I may not see you before your move to Sarlat. We've got each other's numbers and we'll doubtless meet through Annette. Just toss the sheets and towels in the washing machine before you leave.'

'One last thing before you go,' said Yves. 'I don't know if it could help but when I first mentioned to Francis that I'd be directing in Sarlat this summer he said he knew the area. Apparently he'd been renting a place somewhere around here, he said near Les Eyzies, ten years or more ago. He'd taken the place with some friends and met a young French boy. There had been some trouble with local people, I'm not sure whether it was a fight or just the usual gay-bashing and they'd all left in a hurry.'

Bruno felt a little shock of recognition and a renewed sense of his failure in an unresolved case whose memory could still occasionally trouble his nights. 'Did he tell you the name of the French boy?'

'No, never. But when we were at his place in London one evening he showed me some poems he had written. They were very intense, not to my taste. But there was one about listening to a lover speaking French.'

15

On his early-morning drive to Pamela's house, Bruno considered with some care how to refer to his evening with Isabelle. As they saddled the horses he said lightly that he'd been summoned to 'a working dinner with your favourite policewoman from Paris'. To his relief Pamela did not react. She was much more interested in his news that Crimson was expected to return to St Denis that day, that his belongings had been found and that the local burglaries would now cease.

'That poor man, coming home to a ransacked house,' she said. 'Tell him to join us for dinner, Bruno.'

Invigorated by the ride and glowing from his shower, Bruno led Balzac on a leash through the temptations of the Saturday morning market. The young basset hound stopped first to sniff and then gulp down the scraps of paté and crusts of brioche, the offcuts of great hams and rinds of cheese that kindly stallholders tossed in his path. Finally Bruno thought, Enough. He scooped up his puppy to carry him past these well-meant offerings and fastened his leash to the leg of the chair opposite the one where Gilles was sitting. His laptop was open before him and all the day's newspapers were piled alongside it. As Bruno turned to wave for his coffee at Mirabelle, the schoolgirl who earned pocket money as a waitress on Saturday mornings, Gilles began feeding Balzac chunks of his own croissant.

'You'll make him fat,' Bruno said as he shook hands. 'I'm going to have to stop bringing this dog to market. What's the news from Paris?'

'Not much, which is why I'm down here hoping for some more,' said Gilles. 'Is this guy Crimson arriving today?'

'So I'm told, and we've found his stuff. The *Police Nationale* will be putting out a press release later today saying that all of Crimson's belongings have been recovered. If you're still running news on your website you can have the scoop. You'll even beat *Sud Ouest*. We found them in a Corrèze barn belonging to the murdered English antiques dealer.'

'When you say "We" does that mean you were present?'

'Yes, but don't say that. Let J-J take the credit.' A coffee and croissant appeared in front of him and Bruno nodded his thanks to Mirabelle, one of Florence's favourite pupils.

'Let me tweet this first and then you can give me some more detail for the website.'

Twenty minutes and another coffee later, Bruno had made his rounds of the market. He climbed the steps to the upper square and gazed down on his town and his people. Farmers' wives with shopping bags were coming out of the bank and teenage girls in market-day finery were giggling together by the bridge and deliberately not looking at the boys. Everything was normal and all was calm, except that there was an armed killer on the loose.

His cheerful mood evaporated as he considered what he might do if Paul Murcoing suddenly appeared on the bridge carrying his stolen guns. He was paid to protect St Denis. Reluctantly, because he preferred to do his job unarmed, Bruno descended the steps, walked across to the *Mairie*, up to his office and opened the safe. He took out his MAB 9-millimetre, stripped, cleaned and lightly oiled it and then carefully wiped the bullets before loading the magazine. It could take fifteen rounds, but like most former soldiers he left out one to loosen the spring and reduce the chances of jamming. He reassembled his weapon, checked the safety catch and strapped his holster around his waist. Feeling self-conscious at its unaccustomed weight, Bruno went back to complete his patrol and watch over the market. To his surprise, none of his friends and neighbours seemed to notice he was armed.

An hour later it was, however, the first thing Isabelle spotted when he responded to her phone call and arrived in his van at Crimson's house. As he climbed out to greet her he could hear the distant sound of a helicopter and she called from the doorway: 'Perfect timing, they're on their way in and it's good to see you with a gun again. That usually means matters are about to get interesting.'

She opened the front of her leather jacket so he could see her shoulder holster but then went down on one knee as Bruno opened the rear of the van and little Balzac leaped out and sprinted towards her. Ears almost as long as Balzac himself flapped like giant wings as he leaped into her arms, his tongue raking her neck and cheek. She laughed and hugged him, and then seemed to lose her balance and toppled onto her back, Balzac standing four-square on her chest to nuzzle at her face. Bruno felt himself grinning even as he thought how much he would miss her.

'Don't just stand there, help me up,' she called from the ground, and laughing he stretched out a hand. The helicopter was much closer. She dusted herself down and watched Balzac follow his sniffing nose around the garden. Whether or not she missed him, Bruno thought, she'd certainly miss Balzac.

One of the men in overalls who had been with her on her first day at Crimson's house was standing on the edge of the covered swimming pool, holding a red flare, its smoke giving the pilot the wind direction. The military helicopter flew past the house, turned and came back into the wind as it dropped. Bruno clamped his képi firmly to his head, noticing that it was a Fennec, one of the unarmed models used to transport senior officers. Balzac, who had darted into the shelter of Bruno's legs when he saw the helicopter descend, now barked defiance as its rotors stilled. The door opened and the Brigadier, dressed in a suit and tie, groped with his foot for the little step bar attached to the skids and jumped down. He turned to help a rather older man in grey slacks, blazer and open-neck shirt.

Crimson was the only man Bruno knew who seemed to have his hair cut once a week. It was always of a perfect length and it never seemed to lose its parting, however strenuous the tennis or capricious the wind. At first, Bruno had thought it signified a touch of vanity, but now that he knew the man it seemed all of a piece with his self-possession and self-control.

'Bruno,' said the Brigadier, much more coldly than usual, reaching out for a curt handshake as Bruno's arm came down from the salute. 'I believe you know Monsieur Crimson.'

'Bruno and I have been on first-name terms for years,' said Crimson, in his grammatical but strongly-accented French. With careful courtesy he shook Isabelle's hand before surprising Bruno with a kiss on both cheeks. They had been amicable acquaintances but hardly good friends. Perhaps he was trying to send a signal to the Brigadier. 'I gather you've pulled off a remarkable bit of police work.'

'You'll need to check the hoard, but I brought this as a token of the eventual return of your goods,' said Bruno, and handed to Crimson the wrapped parcel he had brought with him from the back of his van. He was conscious of the Brigadier glowering impatiently at him. Whatever credit he'd gained from solving the burglary did not seem to have impressed the Brigadier.

'Let's do this inside the house,' Crimson said, and looked down to where Balzac was sniffing at his cavalry twill trousers. 'And who's this little fellow? You finally managed to replace dear Gigi?'

Inside his kitchen, he unwrapped the two Cotman watercolours, which Bruno had selected as the most portable and identifiable of the loot from the barn. He examined them both with deep satisfaction.

'These were the wedding presents my wife and I gave each other over forty years ago. I can't believe you pulled this off, Bruno. I'd been resigned to a long battle with the insurers and then when I landed at Paris, there was Vincent waiting for me with the good news and his helicopter. I can't believe that you got my wine back.'

Bruno had never known the Brigadier's first name, and from the way her eyes widened, nor had Isabelle.

'I'll want to see you at the Gendarmerie at five this afternoon, Bruno,' the Brigadier said briskly. 'I don't think we need detain you or your dog further. As soon as Monsieur Crimson has unpacked his things, we'll take the helicopter on to this place in the Corrèze so that he can check on the rest of his property and then we'll arrange to have them shipped back here.'

Bruno replied with a crisp salute. His attempt at a dignified departure was undermined by Balzac, who was alternating his attentions between Isabelle's black trainers and Crimson's English brogues. Bruno finally had to bend and scoop Balzac into his arms to take his leave, aware of Isabelle's averted eyes and the half-baffled, half-concerned look on Crimson's face.

'Ring me tomorrow because I owe you the best dinner in the Périgord,' the Englishman called after him.

16

His holster back around his waist, Bruno was in his office at the *Mairie*, dealing with accumulated paperwork, when his phone rang. He put down the leasing contract for the big screen on which the council would project the open-air cinema on summer evenings and answered.

'It's Jacqueline Morgan and I'm not sure whether I'm in your jurisdiction but I thought I'd better tell you first. I've been burgled.'

She was in another commune, so technically a break-in at her house was none of his business, but with the local government reforms linking different communes together the demarcation lines were blurring fast. He could have ducked this job, he told himself as he drove through Les Eyzies on the way to her house. But her tale was intriguing, she had been helpful in sharing her expertise, and any friend of his Mayor deserved his best efforts. He parked behind her white BMW, pulled from the glove compartment a pair of latex gloves and a couple of evidence bags and knocked at the door.

The first thing he noticed was that Jacqueline had been to the hairdresser. The iron-grey curls he remembered had been tamed into soft waves and given subtle streaks of gold. She was wearing a well-cut dress that flattered her trim figure. On her feet were the usual trainers but a pair of court shoes stood by the door, as if she'd kicked them off on entering. At their first meeting, she had looked American, or at least she looked like his expectation of an American female academic. Now, despite the shoes, she looked French and ten years younger. When she presented him her cheek to be kissed he detected an attractive scent.

Jacqueline explained that she had spent the morning at the market in Sarlat and had then met the Mayor for lunch before he went on to the hospital. Bruno didn't think she was the kind of woman who'd dress up to go shopping in the market, so she must have wanted to look her best for the lunch with the Mayor. He smiled to himself at the thought.

She'd then driven home to find no sign of forced entry. But the books and papers on her table were not quite where she had left them, and when she'd looked into the kitchen she found the back door open and one of the panes neatly removed. She had checked the rest of the house and a few small items of jewellery were missing from her bedroom, along with some silver, her TV set and laptop from downstairs.

She led him to the back and showed him the pane of broken glass on the kitchen floor, still mainly attached to a sheaf of greased newspaper. Automatically his hand went to the butt of his gun. That was the technique that had been used at Crimson's house. Could this be Murcoing's work again? Or perhaps somebody who wanted to make it look like Murcoing?

He told Jacqueline to stay inside and went out to check the garden and outbuildings. They were all clear but an army could have been hiding in the wooded slopes of the ridge that rose behind the house. Dirt roads led up through the woods, although he could see no other houses up there. About a kilometre back he had passed a duck and goose farm which seemed to be Jacqueline's nearest neighbour. A burglar would have had no fear of being seen. The ground was too dry for prints but there were tyre tracks in the grass behind the house, out of sight of the road. Jacqueline parked her BMW at the side of the house.

Inside, the house was strangely tidy for a burglary. Usually drawers were pulled out and upended, mattresses shoved aside and often ripped and cupboards dragged away from walls. In the bedroom a rather fine wooden box, obviously for her jewels, had been tipped onto the bed. A charming nude sketch of a woman sitting on a bed, her shapely back to the painter, hung between the two windows. Even the least artistic thief would have thought that was worth money.

'I haven't touched anything since I found the house like this, except for some of the books and notes downstairs to see if anything was missing,' she said. 'The most important thing is the manuscript of my father's memoirs. I have copies, of course, but not here in France, they're . . .'

Bruno put a finger to his lips to signal for silence. He was not one to leap to conclusions but there was a possibility that Jacqueline's burglars had been the kind of people who would also leave the house bugged. It was going to be a very interesting conversation with the Brigadier.

'Are you insured against theft, Madame?' he asked. She nodded, her eyes widening. 'And the value of your stolen silver and jewels would be what in your estimate?' He waved his hand upwards two or three times to encourage her to set the figure high.

'Well over ten thousand euros,' she said, catching his meaning. 'Probably more, some of them were antiques, irreplaceable family heirlooms. The silver coffee pot is eighteenth-century American, and since my father was descended from Mary Robbins there's a family legend that it was made by Paul Revere.'

Bruno looked at her blankly.

'He was a silversmith in Boston, a famous revolutionary who carried the news of the British raid that started the War of Independence. There are poems about him that children learn in school, at least we did in my day. Mary Robbins married his son.'

Bruno nodded, thinking that would be useful for the plan that was forming in his mind. 'Do you have a photo of this coffee pot?'

Jacqueline went to a two-drawer filing cabinet disguised as a wooden chest of drawers. He told her to wait and brought another set of gloves from his car. She put them on, muttering that the files seemed to have been searched, but finally gave him a postcard-sized print of a handsome coffee pot with a curved spout.

'I had to do it for the insurance once I'd listed it as a special item,' she said. 'I put the value at ten thousand.'

'And your laptop? How much would that be worth?'

'Over a thousand. Both it and the TV were quite new.'

'So altogether this could be up to twenty thousand euros in value that has been stolen? Perhaps we'd better see if anything has gone from the outbuildings before I call the Gendarmes.' He steered her outside and into the garden at the rear.

'You think I'm being bugged?' she asked in a whisper.

He shrugged. 'It's possible. What about the material on your laptop? Do you have it all backed up?'

'Yes, on the university mainframes, both in Paris and back in the States. It's tiresome but I won't have lost anything. But what are you thinking, is this some government operation, spying on me?'

'I don't know but we'll do this by the book.'

After a vain search of the barn and shed Bruno led the way back into the house and called the Gendarmerie at St Denis, where Sergeant Jules was on the desk. Jacqueline's house was roughly halfway between the gendarmeries in Montignac and St Denis, so he couldn't be accused of deliberately calling in the Gendarmes he knew. Bruno explained the burglary and the value of the items stolen and stressed the news value of Paul Revere's coffee pot. Most important, he added, was that the same method of entry had been used in the burglary of Monsieur Crimson, so that pointed to Paul Murcoing. That would get Yveline excited, Bruno thought.

He then went to his van and pulled out the cheap pay-as-you-go phone he'd bought in a previous case when Isabelle had wanted to contact him in a way that could not be traced. He used it to call Annette in Sarlat, and explained not only the burglary but also his suspicion that the real target of the thieves might have been Jacqueline's papers. Could she make sure that the report of the burglary got special attention when the *Procureur* came back to the office on Monday? Once the *Procureur* listed the case as a *délit*, a serious crime, there would be a paper trail that would make any attempt at a cover-up very difficult.

'This sounds intriguing, so let's talk about it over dinner tonight,' she said. 'I'm with Yves at the house and he's been shopping in the market to make that dinner he promised you. I already called Pamela and Fabiola.'

'Is there enough for a couple more guests? My friend Gilles from *Paris Match* is in town and I think you'd like to meet Jacqueline.'

'The more the merrier,' Annette replied. 'My place in Sarlat, about eight? And by the way, Bernard Ardouin has brought me in to help on the Fullerton murder, so I need to call to Sergeant Jules. I'll just ask him if anything has come up, and that way the *Procureur*'s office will be informed.'

Bruno rang off, called Gilles to tell him about dinner and smiled to himself at the difference between the way the French judicial bureaucracy was supposed to work with its separate jurisdictions and checks and balances, and the way that in practice friendships and personal connections could cut through the red tape. He took a mischievous pleasure in the way that he, a village policeman, could play the system. But this time he would have to be particularly careful. Usually he could count on discreet support from the Brigadier and Isabelle. This time the politics made that problematic, and he'd hate to have either one of them as an enemy. The Brigadier could squash him like a bug.

Suddenly he looked at the cheap phone in his hand and cursed himself for a fool. Isabelle had the number. If she decided to track the phone records, his careful manoeuvring could be uncovered. So much for his moment of self-satisfaction! He'd have to buy another disposable phone as soon as he got back to town.

Why was he taking this risk? He barely knew Jacqueline. But he knew he wasn't doing this for her but for his Mayor, to whom he owed just about everything that made his life rewarding: his home, his work and his place in St Denis. More than that, he had a visceral dislike of the way that agents of the French state often rode roughshod over the law. If the Brigadier, say, had staged Jacqueline's burglary to protect the government from embarrassment, it stuck in his throat. He remembered the cross words he'd exchanged with Isabelle over the growing number of scandals piling up at the door of her Ministry. At least she was making arrangements to move to another job.

'I thought you might like some coffee,' said Jacqueline, coming out of the house with a tray. 'I'm just sorry that I can't serve it in Paul Revere's jug.'

She took the tray to a small garden table with two spindly metal chairs, tucked into a sunny corner among the rose bushes.

'I think you ought to know what's going on, or at least what I think may be happening,' he said. 'Somebody in the French government is worried that the Americans want to unleash a scandal just ahead of the election. There is some suspicion that Jack Crimson is involved – I presume you know his background?'

Jacqueline nodded. 'And they think my research is somehow involved, is that what you mean? But it all happened so long ago. Anybody involved in that business with the slush funds and the Resistance money is almost certainly dead.'

'You mentioned that you were working on something else, about the French nuclear deterrent not being truly independent.'

Yes, she told him, and explained how it started with Nixon's summit with President Pompidou in 1970 and that by 1973 the French were being given assistance in developing their missiles, their multiple warheads, and even shown how to set up underground testing sites for nuclear weapons. They were also helped on missile guidance systems. She had a Pentagon document that recorded the French saying they didn't need their missiles to be accurate enough to hit Soviet missile silos, they just wanted to be able to take out cities.

'When you say you have a document, you had it here?'

She nodded. She had a whole file of documents, memos of talks between Nixon and Pompidou, between Kissinger and the French defence minister, Robert Galley. The cooperation had gone a lot further under Presidents Carter and Giscard d'Estaing. Most of the material was marked Top Secret, but she had managed to get some of it declassified. There was a whole lot more in the archives of the Nixon Library.

'So this material is now publicly available?'

'Only if you know where to look. Some of it's quite funny. There's a memo of a discussion between Kissinger and Defence Secretary Schlesinger when they say the French have, and I quote, "the worst nuclear program in the world", unquote. Because of US laws against the transfer of nuclear secrets they set up a system called negative guidance, under which the French nuclear technicians would say they were thinking of doing it this way and the Americans would shake their heads. They'd go on through the design until the Americans didn't shake their heads and that's how they built the triggers for the French nuclear explosions. I had fun writing the chapter with all that stuff.'

'Why would the Americans do this?'

'Kissinger makes it quite clear that the purpose was to ensure that the French were dependent on American technology and stressed that "the real quid pro quo is the basic orientation of French policy". Once De Gaulle was out of power, Kissinger could use the nuclear bait to turn the French into good little allies again, on the American leash just like the British.'

'Are these documents still in your files?'

'I photocopied them, turned them into pdf files and have them all stored on the cloud. Get me a computer and a printer and I'll print them out for you.'

'Have you told the Mayor all this?'

'Not in such detail, no. I told him the funny stuff. He was the one who said my book would make quite a stir. But I've given seminars on this material at the National Defense College and at the Woodrow Wilson Center in Washington. I have a couple of graduate students who'll get their doctorates out of this.'

'Is your book finished?'

'The text is finished and I'm just about done with the footnotes. I expect I'll be sending it to Yale University Press by the end of the month. My editor there has already seen most of it.'

'This is the English version you're talking about. What about the French edition, when will that be ready?'

'I'll translate it myself and I'm aiming to have it done by the end of the summer vacation, which would mean publishing it sometime next year.'

Bruno was thinking how this would play in French public opinion if extracts from the book or even a summary of its highlights turned up on the front page of *Le Monde*, a week or so before the election. Nuclear independence had been one of the cardinal principles of French governments for the last half-century and to learn that it was all a sham would come as a national shock. He could envisage a row in the *Assemblée Nationale*, public inquiries, denunciations and even fist-fights on TV talk shows.

'I can see why people might want this kept quiet,' he said.

'But it's our history, Bruno, yours and mine and that of every other French voter and taxpayer. Why shouldn't they know about it?'

Why not indeed, he thought. But the timing would be important, the timing and the way the information was released. Was it all that wicked for the Brigadier and his political masters to delay the information for a few weeks until the election was over? Would it not even be a huge distortion of the political process to have the final days of the election campaign dominated by an angry public debate over France's nuclear status?

Bruno shook his head, suddenly angry at himself. He was thinking like the Brigadier or like a politician. These were not decisions to be taken by agents of the state, thinking of the French electorate as so many children to be protected from monsters in the dark. This was a free country, a cradle of modern democracy and the home of the Rights of Man. This was for the French people to decide, not a handful of politicians who wanted to cling to power by suppressing the truth.

'You look like a man who's just made his mind up about something,' said Jacqueline. 'Are you going to tell me about it?'

'First, you're invited to dinner tonight with me and some friends in Sarlat, and if you agree I'd like to share this with them,' he replied. In the distance, he could hear the familiar sound of a police siren. The Gendarmes were on their way. 'One's a magistrate and another is a journalist with *Paris Match*. I trust them and I'm confident that you can, and this may be the only way that you can control how this story is released and presented.'

'Rather than suppressed by the kinds of people who burgled my house and bugged my home,' she said. 'That's fine with me. I wonder, can the Mayor come, too? I was going to make dinner for him but I think he'd enjoy this.'

17

His shoes polished and his uniform jacket and cap brushed, Bruno presented himself at the Gendarmerie at one minute before five, shook hands with Sergeant Jules and was shown into the Commandant's office. The Brigadier was standing beside the desk, studying a series of framed photographs on the wall of Yveline playing hockey. On top of the computer sat a small stuffed toy in red cloth. As Bruno came to attention before the desk he could see it was a monkey and was surprised that the Brigadier had not tossed it into a waste-paper bin. He braced himself for an encounter of the kind he had learned in the army was best handled by saying 'Yes, sir,' and as little else as possible.

'How are you, Bruno? Sit down, take your hat off and have a seat.' The Brigadier sat down at Yveline's desk, pulled a bottle of Balvenie scotch from his briefcase, poured generous slugs into two water glasses and added a couple of splashes of Evian. He pushed one across the desk to Bruno, who stared at it suspiciously.

'Well done on the burglary. Crimson is delighted and so am I.'

'Thank you, sir,' he replied, trying to keep the surprise from his face.

'You're no fool, so you'll have worked out why I was curt with you at Crimson's house.'

'Yes, sir.' It could only be because the Brigadier wanted to mislead Crimson. He had no idea why.

'I can't enjoy my drink until you do, so take a sip and stop playing the old soldier.'

Bruno obeyed, but hardly tasted the whisky as he watched the Brigadier pull a slim file from his briefcase.

'You won't be surprised to learn that Crimson is someone we keep a friendly eye on, but we're also interested in this Jacqueline Morgan and how they know one another. Just over a year ago she was invited to give a faculty seminar at the Wilson Center in Washington on her research into Europe–American relations in the Cold War. Crimson was her guest, invited along to give a commentary from the British point of view. Since it covered some very sensitive aspects of French nuclear policy, we were fortunate that a visiting French academic was in the seminar room and could tip us off.'

He fixed Bruno with a piercing look and asked: 'Why did you not tell Isabelle that you'd been to a party at Crimson's house last year with the pair of them?'

'I told Isabelle I'd been to parties at his house but I didn't know her. I didn't meet Jacqueline Morgan until the day before I met Isabelle at Crimson's house, and I called on her as a historian who knew a lot about Resistance finance. She was in work clothes; no make-up, her hair a mess. Having previously only seen her dressed up for a cocktail party I wouldn't have recognized her.'

'How well do you know Crimson? He seemed very fond of you this morning.' The Brigadier refilled their glasses.

Bruno recounted the tennis games, the drinks at the club bar, the garden party and the dinner. 'Until Isabelle told me his background I'd assumed he was just another retired civil servant.'

'You understand that it's him we're really concerned with rather than her. He's always been very close to the Americans and it was interesting that it was after meeting him that she got those documents declassified. I doubt whether the Americans give a shit who is the next president of France. But the British certainly do.'

'I'd have thought they'd be happier with the devil they know.'

'You could be right, I wouldn't know. But even if the Brits don't want to interfere in our elections, they may think it useful for us to know that they could upset our apple-cart if they chose to. There are things London wants from us – protecting their precious financiers in the City, concessions on European affairs. A little leverage is always good.'

'This is all way above my head,' Bruno said. That drink was looking very attractive but he restrained himself.

'In that case let's talk about Jacqueline.'

'She strikes me as an interesting woman,' said Bruno.

'You are known to have a soft spot for women, Bruno, a sentiment that in general I applaud. But it can lead to misapprehension.'

He pulled out another file from his briefcase and began reading phrases at random. 'Arrested in Paris, May 1968, at a barricade on the Rue St Jacques while a student at the Sorbonne ... arrested again August 1968 at the Democratic party convention in Chicago, received a broken jaw from a police baton ...

172

September of that year she takes up an exchange scholarship at University of California, Berkeley . . . December 1969, a delegate to the final convention of Students for a Democratic Society in Flint, Michigan, voted to wind up the SDS and reform into the Worker Student Alliance, a group closely associated with the violent extremists known as the Weathermen . . . Arrested again in May 1971 during a march on the Pentagon to protest the Vietnam war.'

The Brigadier paused in his reading, looked up and took a sip at his drink. 'Quite the little activist, this Jacqueline Morgan. A member of Redstockings, a radical women's collective, and a contributor to a collective book titled *Our Bodies, Ourselves*. And she never gave up. Arrested again in 1985, this time in Britain, when she was staying at the women's camp against American missiles at the Greenham Common airbase. She was arrested again that year during a demonstration over the miners' strike but was released without charge. She was supposedly a visiting professor at the University of London at the time. I suspect this is when she came up on Crimson's radar screen. Most recently she attended our own Green Party's summer university last year, where she spoke as a member of the advisory board of Greenpeace in the United States. I have to hand it to her, she never stops.'

He tossed the file onto his desk. 'And now the radical Professor Morgan is connected to a British spymaster. If this were the Cold War, I'd suspect a honey trap and start looking for a Moscow connection. These days, who the hell knows?'

'You know she was burgled today?' Bruno asked. 'Her laptop and documents were taken, along with some silver and jewellery to make it look genuine.'

'It wasn't us, but I hope you'll understand that I can't answer for all the less public arms of the French state, however much I may disapprove of what they do in the name of national security.'

Bruno sipped at his drink, wondering what the Brigadier's real agenda might be, but mainly thinking of the epic of Jacqueline's life: May '68, Vietnam, feminism, nuclear disarmament, Greenpeace. She'd plunged into the history of her time, and also made a distinguished career by writing some of that history. He did not feel surprised, rather a touch of admiration.

'Why not say what it is you want to do?' Bruno asked. 'Are you trying to suppress her work or do you just hope to delay it until after the election?'

'Why on earth would I want to do that? This is our history. The French public is entitled to know it.'

Bruno sat back in his chair, completely baffled. He reached for his scotch, took a long sip and then looked thoughtfully at the portrait photograph of the President of the Republic that hung on the wall by the door.

'You want him to lose the election,' he said. The Brigadier shrugged, poured himself another drink and waved the bottle towards Bruno, who put his hand over his glass.

'I couldn't care less who wins the election, they're all pretty much the same,' the Brigadier replied. 'But there's something rotten in the entrails of the state, some of it in my own Ministry. You know what I'm talking about because I'm told you said much the same thing to Isabelle. Phone-tapping journalists and opposition leaders, burglaries, suitcases full of secret campaign funds, crooked deals, planted evidence, enemies lists and worse. That's what I'm sick of. To save France from that requires a change of government.'

'No, it doesn't. It means we need a free press and a fair election.' Bruno pushed the half-full glass of scotch back across the table, picked up his hat and walked out.

Bruno could see from the gate a spray of droplets raining on the young tomato plants, signalling that the Mayor had returned from hospital and was engaged in that most restful of chores, watering his garden. He turned at the sound of Bruno's footsteps, offered him a friendly nod and then raised his eyebrows.

'You look cross,' he said, over the patter of spray on leaves. 'Jacqueline called to tell me about the burglary. She also told me about dinner with your friends in Sarlat. It will be a pleasant change to go there without going to the hospital. She'll be here shortly. We can have a drink before we head over there.'

Bruno took a deep breath and asked: 'How's Cécile?'

'Asleep in a morphine dream. Her hand twitched when I held it. We grew these plants from seedlings, and now she won't live to eat them. I've accepted that. What's the matter with you?'

Bruno recounted his conversation with the Brigadier.

'I wish I could identify for you one election when nobody in the state apparatus tried to put his thumb on the scales,' the Mayor said. 'It's what they do, part of the price we have to pay for the existence of an intelligence service. We expect them to keep us safe from terrorists, but we've never been very good at defining the lines they should not cross.'

The Mayor walked back to the tap on the side of the house, turned it off and wound the hose into neat loops. 'You know what I mean, Bruno, you cross a few lines yourself from time to time and so do I. It's an imperfect world so it comes down to personal judgement. I let you get away with a few things because on the whole I trust your instincts and your motives. It's for you to decide how far you trust the Brigadier.'

'I'm not sure there's anything I can do,' Bruno said. 'I thought I was doing the right thing in advising Jacqueline to release a summary of her work, so at least she keeps control of it and it doesn't get suppressed. But now it turns out that's what the Brigadier wanted all along.'

'Not quite. The Brigadier wants it released. So do you and so does Jacqueline. But if you're worried that the Brigadier wants a wave of heated headlines to emerge like a bombshell in the final days of the campaign, you don't have to let him get away with that. Ah, there she is now.'

The white BMW pulled into the drive and Jacqueline stepped out. She was wearing high heels again and a silk dress in pale green. She kissed the Mayor on the lips and hugged him briefly before turning to Bruno and offering her cheek.

'I took your advice,' she said to Bruno, and pulled two folded pages of typescript from her bag. 'Here's a first draft of an article I'm thinking of sending to *Le Monde*.'

Bruno read out loud. 'Recently declassified documents from American archives suggest that US–European nuclear cooperation went further than has been hitherto believed and that like Britain, France's development of missiles and nuclear weapons benefited from the discreet sharing of US technology . . .'

'It reads like *Le Monde*,' he said, handing it to the Mayor, who skimmed it quickly.

'Those who know will understand the significance of this, and those who don't will probably not get past the first paragraph,' the Mayor said. 'Perfect; it's all there but not sensationalized.' He gestured to the table on the terrace where a bowl of olives and another of nuts awaited, and invited his guests to sit before he went into the kitchen and returned with a tray bearing three champagne flutes and a half-bottle of champagne.

'Just enough to wet our lips before we head for Sarlat,' he said, and turned to Bruno as he opened the bottle. 'I hope you're not planning to go in uniform.'

'I've got a jacket in the van. I'll look like a boringly dressed civilian.'

'Talking of wetting our lips,' said Jacqueline, 'I was thinking about Bruno's friend at *Paris Match*. It might be a good idea to have him run a small item first, a teaser to whet *Le Monde*'s appetite. In my limited experience of the media, they seem all the more interested when they know a rival publication is sniffing after the same story. Would your friend be amenable to that?'

'He might be, if we pitch it the right way,' Bruno said, raising his glass to her. 'You may have to succumb to the *Paris Match* treatment, a flattering photo and an interview with the glamorous historian who straddles two continents.'

'That doesn't sound too bad.'

'That's not all. You can expect quite a lot about your past, May '68, Vietnam protests, SDS, radical feminist, Greenham Common.'

The Mayor raised his eyebrows and Jacqueline gave him a sharp look. 'You've been doing your homework.'

'Not at all,' Bruno replied. 'It was just read out to me from an Interior Ministry file on you that's currently sitting in the Gendarmerie.'

18

They were climbing into Jacqueline's car for the journey to Sarlat when Bruno's phone rang, and J-J's gruff voice told him that new evidence had emerged. Yves Valentoux would be arrested that evening for questioning.

'It looks bad.' J-J went on. 'Yveline has evidence that he wasn't at home in Paris all evening, like he said. And she went through all his credit-card statements and then through the individual bills. He bought a disposable phone about six weeks ago which we've tracked moving down here from Paris on the day that Fullerton was killed. It's as if the guy was being followed as he drove down here.'

'How do we know it was Valentoux's phone?'

'It's on his credit card. He bought it at a Leclerc when he was doing his groceries. At the same time he put twenty euros onto it prepaid, so we were able to identify the SIM card.'

'What does he say?'

'I haven't spoken to him yet. I'm on my way to Sarlat to arrest him. I cleared it with the magistrate. Ardouin will join me at the police station. I thought you might want to be there.'

Bruno explained to Jacqueline and the Mayor and then rang Annette.

'I know about it,' she said as soon as she answered. 'Ardouin just rang me. So much for our happy dinner party.'

'Does Yves know?'

'Yes. He's sitting beside me, shattered. He's agreed to go to the station and I'll go with him. All we know is there is supposed to be new evidence. Will I see you here?'

'Yes, J-J invited me to the station. They can't keep you on the case, not now you're sharing a house, and obviously I can't talk about the new evidence. But I'm sure you can find him a good lawyer. I'll stay in touch.'

Bruno rang off and called first Pamela and then Gilles to explain, and felt relieved when Gilles offered to take Pamela and Fabiola to dinner instead. Driving to Sarlat, he welcomed the time to himself as he drove, time to consider just how little he really knew of Yves. Bruno knew that he was a skilled actor, able to perform and entertain at a dinner table within a day of finding his lover's body. He had abundant charm, and Bruno and his friends had all warmed to him. Bruno had been touched when Yves showed him the photograph of his daughter, but could that have been a theatrical ploy to secure his sympathy?

He would have to wait until he saw the details of the new evidence. And there would be questions to answer. If Yves had driven down with his disposable phone, it was clear from the distance counter he hadn't used his own car. What transport had he used? Could he have driven down earlier, parked at a station and then used the trains to get back and provide himself with an alibi from the motorway tolls? He tried to remember exactly what Yves had said about the evening he spent at his apartment in Paris. And if he had followed

Fullerton down to the Périgord and killed him then he'd have needed to clean up and change. Where had he done that? The forensics guys were sure nobody had stayed at the *gîte* since Dougal's people had cleaned it.

As he navigated the series of roundabouts that led into Sarlat, Bruno concluded that the crucial point was that if Yves had not been at home in Paris when Fullerton was killed, then he'd been lying. That need not mean he was the killer but it made him into a top suspect along with Paul Murcoing. Could they have somehow been in it together?

Bruno usually enjoyed being in Sarlat, a town where he half-expected to walk into a film crew making yet another version of *The Three Musketeers*. The set designers might need to tidy up a few shop fronts and remove the chairs from a few café terraces, but otherwise they wouldn't have to change a thing. The town had been preserved as if in aspic since the sixteenth century, a glorious jumble of medieval houses and narrow alleyways, dark tunnels and grand Renaissance town houses, all built around a monastery and an abbey that dated back to Charlemagne's time. Now the capital of the Périgord Noir and one of the most visited towns in France, Bruno never tired of wandering its cobbled streets on those evenings when he made the journey to its cinemas with Pamela and Fabiola. Like Annette, they were passionate about film and Annette's decision to settle in the centre of the old town had made their own visits more frequent.

This was a more sombre visit, and when Bruno arrived at the town's *sous-Préfecture*, which housed the Commissariat of Police, Ardouin was already questioning Yves. J-J and Yveline were side by side at the desk normally used by the duty officer and going through the file of her researches.

'Valentoux lied about being in his apartment that evening,' she said, flashing him a triumphant smile. 'I checked his landline records with France Télécom and he got two calls that he didn't answer. I rang the number and it was an actress he knew. She wanted him to engage her for the festival here. And he didn't reply, so it looks as if he wasn't home.'

Bruno nodded. 'Sounds like good work on your part. What does he say about the disposable phone he bought?'

'He hasn't said anything to us. He said he'd wait until he spoke to the magistrate.'

'What was the timing on those two phone calls?'

'The first was seven twenty, the second at seven twenty-four,' she replied.

'So he could have slipped out to buy a paper or some cigarettes, something so routine it could have slipped his mind.'

'It's possible,' J-J said. 'But when he's being questioned for murder, I think he'd have remembered. And then there's the disposable phone. Anyway, it's up to Ardouin now. I've ordered some pizzas, I think it could be a long night.'

J-J pushed the file across to Bruno and he scanned through the coordinates for the cellphone tracking. The scan had started at noon on the day of the murder and the first location was Villejuif, just south of Paris, and then the phone had followed the Aquitaine autoroute through Orléans and Limoges. The tracking had stopped at six in the evening when the location was St Denis.

'Do we have any more data for before noon and after six?' Bruno asked. 'And were any calls made or received on the phone?'

'I just picked those as the relevant times,' Yveline replied.

'There were a couple of calls, one to a St Denis number and the other to a disposable phone somewhere in Bergerac, but we don't know who owns it. I've asked France Télécom to let us have the records of the number, so at least we should learn something, but they can't do that until Monday.'

'Do we know whom he rang in St Denis?'

'Delightful Dordogne, a rental agency. That's all we've got.'

Bruno asked himself why would Yves be calling Dougal's agency when Fullerton had been making the arrangements.

'Can we get some more tracking on the phone, before noon and after six?' he asked.

'What's the point?'

'If Valentoux was the killer, we need to know how he faked his alibi with the autoroute tolls. The phone tracking could tell us that.'

'That makes sense,' said J-J and asked Yveline to see to it. The pizzas arrived as she was on the line to France Télécom and Bruno took some slices in to Ardouin and Yves, who looked relieved to see him.

'Monsieur Valentoux says he bought the disposable phone when shopping for groceries with his friend Fullerton when they were together in Paris,' Ardouin said. 'It seems Fullerton had wanted one because he didn't want to pay the roaming charges on his English one. Did you find any such phone among his possessions or in his van?'

'No, sir. But we didn't know we should be looking for one specially.'

'Monsieur Valentoux also insists he was home on the evening in question but might have gone out briefly to buy cigarettes at a local *tabac* on the Avenue Moreau, where he says they know him,' Ardouin continued. 'They may be able to confirm this. Could you call them, please, and check?'

'It's called the Café Moreau,' Yves added. 'I always buy my cigarettes there.'

Bruno went out and called directory inquiries and then the café. A woman answered and he introduced himself and explained his business.

'I remember Yves bought a lottery ticket early in the week because he said he was leaving Paris the next day. That was why he bought a couple of extra packs for the journey,' the woman said. 'But I can't remember whether it was Monday or Tuesday or Wednesday. If he still has his ticket, it should give the date and time. They'll be drawing in a few minutes, that's why we've got the TV on.'

Bruno thanked her, put the phone down and knocked on the interview room door. Ardouin told him to enter and Bruno asked Yves if he still had his lottery ticket. He opened his wallet and handed Bruno the ticket.

'Purchased at Café Moreau in Paris on the third, that's Tuesday evening, at seven twenty-four,' Bruno read aloud. He scribbled down the number and handed the ticket to Ardouin. 'The woman in the café remembers selling it to him along with some cigarettes. And that would explain why he didn't answer his phone.'

Ardouin nodded and closed the file before him. 'So your story holds up, Monsieur Valentoux. One of those rare occasions when cigarettes may actually have done you some good.'

Bruno excused himself and went to the front desk, where the sergeant on duty had a small TV set and like millions of his compatriots was watching the weekly lottery draw with his ticket in his hand. Bruno watched the little balls bouncing in their swirling currents of air until one popped out and rolled down into the first container. When the final ball had landed, he called the Café Moreau again and told the woman that Yves had three numbers and the joker. What was that worth?

'Too much for me to give him his winnings in cash,' she replied. 'It has to be a banker's draft, at least five hundred. Depends how many other people have the joker.'

Ardouin and Yves were just coming out of the interview room when Yveline put down the phone, ran a hand over her face and said: 'France Télécom can't give us the different times on the phone track until Monday.'

'I'd like to know more about the travels of this mysterious phone, but even so, I don't think we need detain Monsieur Valentoux any longer,' said Ardouin. 'We now have proof that he was in Paris around the time that Fullerton was murdered.'

'It's his lucky day,' said Bruno. 'He's just won five hundred on the lottery.'

Disappointed in their hope of dinner in Sarlat, the whole St Denis contingent had gathered at Pamela's place for an impromptu meal of Fabiola's risotto. The Mayor had brought wine and two tins of his own pâté and Pamela had salad from the garden and cheese. After calling to see where they had all gone Bruno was able to join them in time for coffee and relate the dramas of the evening.

'So you're back looking for Paul Murcoing,' said Pamela, when his tale was complete and a toast drunk to Yves's release.

'Well, I am,' said Bruno. 'He was the last person we can place at the murder scene, so we have to find him so we can talk to him. But the *Proc* says the evidence against Murcoing is only circumstantial and there's no obvious motive. Yveline still has her eye on Valentoux and J-J wants to start looking at other antiques dealers who might have had a motive to kill Fullerton.'

'Maybe there's an English connection, somebody living here who knew him,' Pamela mused.

She was looking well, the pallor of a Scottish winter beginning to give way to the beginnings of a tan, her bronze hair piled loosely atop her head to display her long neck and the emerald earrings that suited her. She was wearing a pale blue blouse of heavy silk over perfectly cut jeans. Bruno smiled, enjoying the look of her, the clear skin and bold eyes, the shape of her neck and the delicate scent of her hair. She returned his gaze, a fondness in her eyes, and placed her hand on his where it rested on the table. That was unusual; Pamela seldom showed her affection in public.

His attention was distracted by sounds of argument from the other side of the table, where Gilles and Jacqueline had been locked in discussion. With the events of the evening, Bruno had forgotten that Jacqueline had wanted him to help promote her story in *Paris Match*.

'Bruno, could you explain to Jacqueline that I'm not a little clockwork toy that can be wound up and sent marching away and then turned off?' Gilles said, filling his glass with the fresh wine. 'There's a big story here, but all I'm getting is hints about nuclear strategy and warnings not to make a big sensation. You know I can't work like that.'

'I'm just saying that I don't want my work to be over-interpreted,' said Jacqueline crisply. 'This is a serious matter.'

'I've known Gilles a long time and I trust him,' Bruno replied. 'Why not show him that draft you showed me earlier and then explain how you would like the story to emerge? He knows more about the way the media works than anybody else here, and I'd like to hear his views.'

Giving Bruno a dubious look, Jacqueline shrugged, took the folded typescript from her bag and passed it to Gilles. He pulled a candelabra closer, put on a pair of reading glasses and began to study it closely.

'Lousy intro,' he muttered, and Jacqueline's lips tightened.

This was not going well. Bruno helped himself to some cheese and bread. Gilles finished reading, took his glasses off and handed back the typescript.

'This is based on your book, which won't be published in the US until the end of this year, early next year. Is that right?' Gilles waited for Jacqueline's nod of agreement. 'But you want to get the facts out now because you're worried that the government wants it suppressed and you think the French people have a right to know how they've been lied to for forty years about our precious *force de frappe*. How that nuclear arsenal isn't really ours, it comes courtesy of the Americans, just like the British. The technology for our missiles, our guidance system, our multi-warheads, our test sites, even the triggers for the bomb itself, all come from the USA, even though we have been proclaiming for decades that we are independent. In return for this, our President agreed to modify French foreign policy. And you want me to run a vague little teaser piece in the *Match* to build up interest before you run this as an op-ed piece in *Le Monde*. Am I right so far?'

'Yes, rather histrionically phrased, but in the essentials you're quite right,' said Jacqueline in a clipped voice.

Gilles put his hands together, looked from Jacqueline to Bruno and back again. 'And in return for running this teaser, rather than getting the credit for breaking what could be one of the stories of the year, all I get is the offer to write a nice soft feature with a full-colour photo all about this intriguing Franco-American historian who's blowing the whistle on one of the biggest strategic secrets of the Fifth Republic. It doesn't sound to me like a good deal.'

'That depends how you write the teaser and what you put in it,' said Bruno.

'I could also let you have some of the documents to publish, but I'd also insist on approving whatever you write in this teaser, as you call it,' Jacqueline said stiffly, sitting back and folding her arms. The body language between her and Gilles was cold, verging on hostile. 'I have transcripts of Kissinger's meetings, the jokes about France having the world's worst nuclear programme, all headed with the words Top Secret.'

'Let me explain my problem,' Gilles said, leaning back and sipping at his drink. 'I go to my editor with the teaser and tell him what comes next week. He looks at me like I'm an idiot and he wants to know why we don't keep the story to ourselves and screw *Le Monde*. That's what I'd be asking, in his shoes.'

'You get the exclusive on the documents,' said Bruno, before Jacqueline could respond. From the way she was bristling, he was sure she was about to make some cutting remark about *Paris Match* not being taken as seriously as *Le Monde*, which would only make matters worse.

'The documents have been declassified,' Gilles replied. 'That means we could get our US correspondent to hire a history graduate student tomorrow and tell him to go to the Nixon Library first thing Monday morning and find them.'

'What might help you persuade your editor to do it our way?' Bruno asked.

'What else have you got?'

'Another story altogether. Have you ever heard of the great train robbery and the mystery of the Resistance billions?'

19

Bruno woke to the smell of coffee, a tongue licking briskly at his ears and the weight of a soft, squirming basset puppy on his chest. He opened his eyes, moved Balzac's rump out of the way and saw Pamela, already dressed in riding clothes, standing by the bed with a tray.

'Breakfast in bed, what a treat,' he said, wriggling his way upright. She put the tray on his lap, plumped up the pillows on her side of the bed to sit beside him and took hold of Balzac before the puppy could attack the croissants. They were still hot from the bakery; she must have slipped out of bed and gone down to town for them. There was also orange juice for him and a bowl of Stéphane's thick yoghurt and a banana for her. Balzac turned to lie on his back, legs pedalling the air. The pads on his paws were already starting to darken from the pink of puppyhood but his tummy was a lovely soft rose colour.

Bruno scratched Balzac's belly and looked out of Pamela's window at the sky, bright with a few high streaks of cirrus; it should be a fine day. He glanced at his watch, almost nine. The others had left around midnight and they had said good-night to Fabiola and taken Balzac into Hector's stall so he could sleep beside his friend the gelding. Then they had stood a while, Pamela leaning her back against him as they looked at the vast reach of the stars against the clear night sky. When he began to kiss her neck she'd unpinned her hair to let it float down around his head, turned to kiss him properly and then taken his hand to lead him to her bed.

'Thank you for this,' he said, gesturing at the tray. 'And thank you for last night. I feel wonderful.'

'You know, there was a moment last night when I thought Gilles might be staying the night with Fabiola,' she said. 'They lingered together over coffee and exchanged what my mother would have called meaningful looks.'

'You mean like the looks I was giving you?' He took her hand and raised it to his lips.

'No, you knew exactly what would be coming next. And so did I. But they didn't. The looks were exploratory, aware of possibilities in one another, looks full of uncertainty about how the evening might end. It was quite romantic, just watching them. Maybe she's finally ready to have an affair, but I don't think she's yet made up her mind about him.'

'Gilles is a good guy, she could do a lot worse.'

'He's a few years older than her, which might not be a bad thing,' Pamela said. 'And he's a bit plump. But she could always take him in hand, get him down here at weekends. I'm sure he lives on pizzas and sandwiches in Paris and he probably drinks too much.'

'You sound like you're planning the wedding and thinking about names for their first child,' he said, surreptitiously giving Balzac the final bite of his croissant as Pamela stared up at the ceiling.

'I saw that, and you'd better be sure he leaves no crumbs in the bed,' she said, turning onto her side to face him and

191

putting a hand on his bare chest. Her face bore a serious look. 'Do you think Fabiola's happy?'

'She seems to be. She's got an interesting job, earns more money than me, has lots of friends, horses to ride and she's passionate about that women's shelter in Bergerac she volunteers at.'

'Does it worry you that she earns more than you do?'

'No, because I don't spend the money I do earn. I get my food for free from the garden or hunting or cheaply from my farming friends. My uniforms are free so I don't spend much on clothes. The *Mairie* pays for my petrol and my phone bills. I don't owe a penny on my house, I have a wonderful horse and good wine in my cellar. Other than raffle tickets at the tennis club I don't gamble and I just spent the night with a beautiful woman who brings me hot croissants in bed, all of which makes me the richest man in St Denis.'

'Do you think Fabiola's attractive? She's so sensitive about that scar.'

'I think she's very attractive with a lovely figure and that scar's not prominent and it's the kind of feature that makes a man look twice, and be curious about how she got it. When she says it was a mountaineering accident, it's like she's handed him a rope. Once he starts talking to her about where she's climbed and why she likes it then he'll realize what an interesting, intelligent woman she is, quite apart from being a doctor. Plus she makes a great risotto and those fondues of hers are irresistible.'

'But that's the thing. Intelligent women make men nervous. Maybe that's why she's started learning to cook.'

'You don't make me nervous.' He kissed her hand again.

She gave him a playful slap and said: 'Time to get up. The horses need riding. I'll go and see if Fabiola's awake while you get dressed. See you in the stables.' She kissed him on the forehead and headed for the stairs. As his eyes followed her appreciatively, he was sure she was putting a deliberate extra wiggle in her hips.

An hour later Bruno arrived at the Gendarmerie. Summoned by a message on his phone from J-J, he was dressed in civilian clothes. It was Sunday, after all.

'We've got a camper van Murcoing's sister rented but we can't find it,' said J-J, averting his eyes from the little red monkey that still sat atop Yveline's computer. 'One of the Bergerac cops was trawling through every ad on the Internet and came up with a guy in Issigeac who rented it to her. We're checking every campsite and layby and the *motards* are checking every camper van on the roads. We've even got checks on the Spanish border. Any ideas?'

'We're still watching his mum's house in Bergerac and checking every day with his aunts,' said Yveline. She looked exhausted, nothing like the fighting-fit athlete in the photos on her wall. 'We'll get him eventually when he runs out of cash. They've got to turn up somewhere.'

'I've had a detective taking Paul's photo around all the gay bars,' said J-J. 'A lot of people know him but he's not popular. We followed a few leads and called on some old boyfriends, but no result.'

'What about the *brocante* route?' Bruno asked. Some of the antiques fairs had already begun, early in the season though it was. Bruno supposed that Murcoing could be raising cash by selling off some of the more portable items from his loot, jewellery and silver, either at the fairs or directly to antiques dealers.

'We've visited the dodgy ones, at least the ones we know about, and we've had a cop looking at every *brocante* that's advertised in the whole of southern France,' J-J said. 'We can't afford to keep up this level of manpower much longer, so we need some new ideas.'

'If he's not on the road with the camper van then either he's found a place to hole up or he's already out of the country,' said Yveline. 'It would have taken him just four hours to get to Spain. I know we've got Interpol on this, but can't we get the Spanish police to make more effort?'

J-J looked at her, glanced at the stuffed toy on her computer and rolled his eyes at Bruno.

'There's no shortage of holiday homes all over southern France, places he could go looking, find one that's empty and hole up there, just as he did at Fullerton's place,' said Bruno.

'That's where the manpower problem comes in. There'd be thousands of such places and we can't just send a solitary cop to check out each one. This guy's armed.'

'Was there nothing on Fullerton's laptop that might give us a lead?' Bruno asked.

J-J looked up sharply. 'Fullerton's laptop, where's that?'

'The Apple laptop that belonged to the murdered man, the one we found in the van in the Corrèze barn.'

'*Putain*, now you tell me. I didn't see any laptop.' He leafed through his file and pulled out some papers stapled together. It looked like a long list and he ran his finger swiftly down each page. 'There's nothing on the inventory about a computer. Where the hell is it?'

Bruno remembered Brian Fullerton's cry of triumph when he found his brother's password for the laptop.

'The brother must still have it' he said.

'Where is he now?'

Bruno was pulling out his phone and looking up the number in the address book even as he answered. 'Hôtel St Denis, I'm calling them now.'

Fullerton was still checked in but had gone to church, he was told by Mauricette on the reception desk.

'It's my fault,' Bruno said. 'I should have made sure you knew about the laptop but I was just so pleased we'd found all the stolen goods. *Merde*, J-J, I'm sorry.'

Yveline made a sound of disgust and shook her head.

'It's our fault as much as yours,' said J-J. 'I remember seeing that power cord on the desk in the study where the guns were. I should have made the connection.'

'I'll go to church and bring Fullerton out, get the computer and bring it back here,' said Bruno, heading for the door.

'These village coppers are all the same,' he heard Yveline say as he left. 'Bloody amateur night, the lot of them. God knows how we'll explain this to the *juge d'instruction*.'

Bruno almost ran down the steps of the Gendarmerie, heading for the Rue de Paris towards the church, when he heard the cheerful toot of a horn and managed to stop just before he had dashed into the path of Dougal's daughter Kirsten on her Mobylette.

'You want to look where you're going, Bruno,' she said. 'You'd have done more damage to my bike than we'd have done to you.'

'Sorry, something's come up,' he said, and suddenly thought: Dougal's list. If Murcoing wanted to be sure of finding an empty holiday home, his sister would have seen the list. He strode after Kirsten, who was already turning into the offices of Delightful Dordogne.

'Could you print me out your work list for this week?' he asked. 'I need to see which houses will be vacant, it's about the burglaries.'

'No problem, just give me a minute to turn on the computer,' she replied, taking off her helmet and shaking out her white-blonde hair.

'I'll be back in five minutes.' This time he looked both ways before he crossed the road and headed for the twelfth-century church of St Louis that dominated this part of the town. Built in an age of faith to hold hundreds, today it could count only a handful of worshippers who seemed to be outnumbered by the choir. Father Sentout's sonorous voice was stressing the importance of these weeks after Easter in the lives of the faithful and rolled on undeterred by Bruno's entry. From habit rather than devotion, Bruno dipped a knee and crossed himself, then moved discreetly to the shadow of a pillar and looked for Fullerton. He spotted him in the centre of an empty row of chairs, kneeling and apparently in prayer, and waited until Fullerton resumed his seat.

'Sorry to disturb you, but the chief of detectives for the region wants to see you and we also need to check your brother's computer,' he whispered.

'Can't it wait?'

'Sorry, no. There's a bit of a fuss about your taking them.'

Fullerton sighed at Bruno's words, but nodded agreement

and the two men crept as quietly as they could along the row and out of the church. Father Sentout ignored their movement and the rest of the congregation seemed too intent on his sermon to notice, or perhaps they were simply asleep.

'Sorry to have caused a problem. Once I had the password and got in I couldn't wait to find out what was on the hard drive,' Fullerton said. 'I didn't think you'd need it right away, you all seemed so caught up in the stolen goods. Anyway, I hope you'll be pleased with my progress.'

He explained that he'd found a long trail of emails between his brother and Paul, some about *brocante* sales, some personal and a lot about their shared interest in the history of the local Resistance and the Neuvic robbery. There were also exchanges of emails with other men, including Yves. Francis Fullerton had kept a separate file for his travel bookings and expenses, and each of his many trips to France had been carefully itemized with dates and hotel costs. It was pretty clear from the exchanges with Paul about which houses would be empty, Fullerton explained, that his brother had been up to his old tricks with stolen goods again. And there were hundreds of photos on the hard drive of furniture, each one labelled with a reference number for the house it came from.

'Will you give me a receipt for it, since I want to be sure to get it back?'

'Yes, of course. I'll wait here and you can bring it down. I presume it's in your hotel room?'

He returned within two minutes and Bruno handed him a receipt torn from his notebook, and checked that Fullerton was planning to stay at least three more days. The magistrates had said they hoped to release the body on Tuesday and he had tentatively booked a cremation for Wednesday. Fullerton ducked back into the church.

Armed with Dougal's list and the laptop, Bruno re-entered the room where J-J and Yveline were comparing photos of items of furniture against the inventory of the barn. He put the laptop on the desk, scribbled down the password and explained how Dougal's list showed the holiday homes that Paul Murcoing and his sister would know to be empty.

'It's a total of twenty-two houses, but I know some of these addresses and they're close to a town or to neighbours who would spot people coming and going. I reckon there are maybe fifteen that are remote enough to give Murcoing the security he'd need. One of them is Crimson's house, so that cuts it down to fourteen.'

J-J looked at Yveline, who pursed her lips and said: 'We can't do fourteen simultaneous raids, not without bringing in *Mobiles* from all over France. They won't do that just for a murder. Three at a time is the best we could do, and that would mean getting onto Bordeaux for an extra squad.'

She picked up the little red monkey from the top of her computer and began to pace the room. As if talking to herself she went on: 'Then we'd have to get approval from the *juge d'instruction* and that would mean full precautions, helicopters, thorough reconnaissance, warnings through a bullhorn. Each squad could do a maximum of two hits a day and you can't keep that kind of activity quiet, so then it would be all over the local radio. And what if they're moving around from place to place?'

Yveline replaced the monkey on top of the computer and glared from one man to the other. 'Well?' she demanded. 'It's not going to work, is it?'

J-J cleared his throat and said: 'She's got a point, Bruno. We'd have to bring in the *juge*.'

'What about sending out singles in plain clothes, dressed like ramblers, with a pair of binoculars to see if they see any movement or spot the camper van?'

'They'd be fools to move round outside,' said J-J. 'I'm not sending anybody poking around in range of the houses because this guy is armed and dangerous. What we need is to set some kind of trap, something that would tempt him out. Still, I like the idea of taking a careful look at these places. You're the local man, Bruno, get me some big maps and mark down each house, see if you can locate a likely place nearby where you could stay in cover and watch. Meanwhile, Yveline and I will have a look at the laptop.'

'Leave it with me,' said Bruno, an idea forming in his head of a way to take a discreet look at each of the houses without needing the elite *Mobiles* squads from the Gendarmes. Armed to the teeth and encased in body armour, they were trained for terrorist and hostage situations; they'd blunder all over an unfamiliar countryside. It was hunting season, when men with guns and a sense of fieldcraft were a common sight around the woods and farms of the region. He began making a mental list of the friends he could trust enough to call out on a job like this.

'I've got to do a report for the *Procureur* on that burglary yesterday, the one with the American coffee pot,' Yveline said, giving Bruno a suspicious look. 'I don't suppose you'd know why his office seems to be taking a special interest in it.'

It was on the tip of his tongue to respond with a sharp comment that it was because whoever broke in used the same method as the Crimson burglary. He restrained himself. She was a young woman, nervous at this first job in command, and she was evidently under strain. Older and wiser people had helped him when he was making the inevitable mistakes that came with lack of experience. He should do the same for her.

'Maybe it's just that they've heard of this famous American, Paul Revere,' he replied from the doorway. 'I'm off to pick up a sheaf of maps from my office. If you want some advice from a village copper, I'd get ready for a few calls from the local papers about the value of this coffee pot.'

20

Hector picked his way down the steep bridle trail through the woods until Bruno reined his horse in at a place where there was a break in the trees and he had a clear view of the isolated house below. For once the binoculars case was being used for its proper purpose rather than as a way to carry Balzac while on horseback. He took out the heavy Second World War binoculars that had belonged to Pamela's father and brought the house into focus. The shutters were all closed, the cover was still on the swimming pool and there was no sign of heat from the chimney. A tarpaulin was snugly tied down on the wood-pile, covered in last autumn's leaves and bird droppings. There was a barn, but its door was too low to take a camper van. He scratched it off his list.

'It's empty,' he said to Pamela, settling his shotgun back more comfortably on its strap around his shoulder. He was dressed as a hunter: camouflage jacket and brown trousers and a brown woollen cap instead of the usual riding helmet. If he had to dismount and search on foot, he had to look the part. 'Give me a moment to check with the others.'

He pulled out his phone to scroll through the text messages. There was one from the Baron to say that the first house he'd been assigned was certainly empty, and similar ones from

Stéphane, Maurice and Raoul. Bruno had been confident that his friends, experienced hunters who had tramped over these valleys for years and knew each fold of ground, would be the most natural and least obtrusive way of checking the rental homes on Dougal's list. He acknowledged each message and sent a query to the other hunters about their progress.

He knew this was a long shot. There were many rentals not on Dougal's list, and Paul Murcoing might be smart enough to have worked out that the police would make the connection between his sister and Dougal's spreadsheet. But at least Bruno felt he was doing something positive in this increasingly frustrating hunt for Fullerton's murderer. He put his phone away, checked that his handgun was still on safety and spoke to Pamela in a low voice.

'If we head across the field below and up the next ridge, we should be able to see the third house. There's just the one gate in our way that I can see.'

'Good, I could do with a canter and so could Bess. These woodland trails can get tiresome.'

Bruno decided not to retort that Pamela had insisted on joining him, asserting that two people out riding would look much less suspicious than one and nobody would ever mistake her for a policewoman. She was probably right, but her presence made him nervous. There was an outside chance that this mission could be dangerous and a small voice in the back of Bruno's head murmured that he was putting her at risk because of his own pride, his desire to show Yveline that with his friends and local knowledge he could achieve results that her Gendarmes would never match.

He flicked at the reins and Hector walked on until the woods gave way to moorland. At the prospect of an open field Bruno's horse tossed his head and moved smoothly into his stride. He seemed to have overcome his initial urge to race ahead of any other horse in sight, now sufficiently at ease with Pamela's mares to accept the way Bess had moved alongside to keep pace.

At the gate, Bruno looked back at the house before he dismounted, but the place remained still, no flicker of sunlight reflecting from some lens in one of the upstairs rooms, no empty bottles or rubbish bags outside the kitchen door. They rode on, making their way up the ridge and then skirting some woods and hedges before getting to the long arm of woodland that slanted down towards the next house on the list, promising good cover. There was no trail and the undergrowth was thick, so he went forward on foot, then pulled himself up on a couple of low-lying branches until he had a clear view of another isolated house. He checked carefully with the glasses but saw no sign of habitation. The barn was big enough to take a camper van but he couldn't see its doors from this side. The dirt lane up to the house was thick with weeds that looked unbroken by any passing wheels. He walked back to Pamela and the horses.

'You go on ahead along this ridge. There's a firebreak through the forest that leads towards that hunters' shack where we had a picnic, remember? I'll meet you there. We can look at one more house and that's it for today.'

'I remember the hunters' shack, but what are you going to do?'

'I need to skirt round and take a look at the barn doors on

the other side, see if they're big enough for the van. Don't worry, I won't get close.'

'If it's safe enough for you, it's safe enough for me. Besides, I'm getting bored. Let's go.'

Pamela put her heels into Bess's side and cantered down the hill, gathering speed as she headed directly for the house. Quickly he mounted and chased after her until he was alongside and she could see him gesture to his left. He merely wanted to stay on the high ground, but she thought he was inviting her to race and bent forward in the saddle to urge Bess to go faster.

'No, no,' he shouted, feeling a sense of alarm as he tried to catch up with her to head her off. 'Go left, up the slope.'

Hector stretched out his neck and stepped up his pace, soon outpacing Pamela's much older mare, but the gelding ignored Bruno's efforts to stay in front so he could start nudging Pamela to the left. Hector raced on ahead and only then would consent to heed the rein, veer to the left and back up the hill. Bruno reined him in and risked a look behind, to see Pamela, whooping with joy at the thrill of her speed, continuing her gallop down the hill on a course that would take her within a hundred metres of the house.

Bruno's heart was in his mouth. If Murcoing was hiding inside, a burst from his Sten gun could be lethal at that range. Cursing, Bruno took Hector on a tight rein down the hill after her, conscious of the gun bouncing on his hip. He hoped it was covered by the hunting windcheater he wore as a riding jacket. Suddenly his horse jinked to one side, surprising him. Bruno looked down and saw Hector had sidestepped to avoid a fold in the ground, the grass scratched away at one side.

Then he saw the holes, and realized they were riding into a rabbit burrow.

Even as he began to shout a warning he heard a scream. He looked up to see Pamela tumbling through the air and her horse sprawling, one foreleg still trapped in one of the dozens of holes that rabbits had made.

Skirting the burrows, he rode as fast as he dared to where Pamela lay, dreading what he might find as he jumped down from the saddle and bent over her still form, willing his ears not to hear the hideous screeching from her stricken mare. He felt the pulse at her neck and it was still beating. He didn't dare to move her, fearing a broken neck. Her limbs were lying straight, and when he pinched the tendon above her knee her lower leg twitched. The spinal column was still functioning.

He fumbled for his phone and rang Fabiola, who was supposed to be waiting for them with the horse van near the next house they were to check. Bruno told her what had happened and where he was.

'I'm in the next valley but I'll get there as soon as I can,' she said. 'Listen, Bruno, calm down. Call an ambulance right away. Above all don't move Pamela.'

Dully, feeling as if his mind was working slowly, he dialled 15, the number for medical emergencies, and found himself connected to Ahmed at the St Denis fire station, and was told they'd be there within fifteen minutes.

'What's that screaming?' Ahmed asked, and when Bruno said it was her horse, he replied: 'Shoot the poor bugger.'

As he trudged back towards Bess, he realized that no sign of life had come from the house. Nobody could have ignored the dreadful noise that Bess was making, and his eyes filled with tears when he saw that Hector was standing over Pamela's mare and tenderly nuzzling her, as if giving what comfort he could. Bess didn't seem to notice. Her foreleg was still trapped inside the hole and the rest of her leg lay at a brutal angle. Her entire weight must have pivoted on the trapped hoof and snapped all the delicate bones. There was no way Bess's leg could be saved, and she was an old horse.

He didn't give a damn if Murcoing and his sister were inside the house and alerted to flee as soon as they heard gunfire. He pulled his automatic from the holster on his belt and flicked off the safety catch. He slapped Hector's rump to push him away, kneeled beside Bess and tried in vain to hold still her tossing head. He could barely think with the noise, but tried to remember the drill as he looked at this faithful horse on whom he had learned to ride. He drew an imaginary X from right ear to left eye, and right eye to left ear.

Bess suddenly seemed to be looking at him and the thrashing of her head stopped for a moment. Aiming for the centre of the X he put the muzzle close to the mare's forehead to avoid any chance of a ricochet and fired twice into the skull. That was the rule; if the first shot failed to penetrate the second one would. Bess's great head jerked and then sank to the ground.

The echo of the shots, so different from the sound of a shotgun, seemed to rock the air around him as he closed the safety catch, reholstered the weapon and went back to Pamela. He slipped the shotgun from his shoulder and took off his jacket to cover her. There was no movement on her face, no flickering of eyelids, but her hands were warm, her pulse still firm.

He tried to remember how she had fallen. She had tumbled over Bess's head, exactly as if turning a somersault. Thanks to the way she'd been galloping, her waist and knees had been bent and her head tucked low. That was the shape he remembered seeing as she turned through the air, rising almost slowly before she came down fast, her body still curved. Had she landed on her head or her back? He tried to remember. She had rolled once and again, then her limbs had gone loose and she'd sprawled. He closed his eyes and squeezed them tight, forcing the visual memory of her landing, but it had been too fast, too shocking to him. The exact way she had hit the ground was not clear in his mind.

A sound came from behind him; Hector, stepping slowly, looking from Bess's body to Bruno. He came another step, lowered his head and moved again, close to Bruno, shaking his head nervously. Bruno remained still until Hector brought his nostrils down to breathe on Bruno's neck. Slowly, his hand stroking Hector's neck, Bruno rose to his feet and mounted his horse.

He turned Hector's head away and trotted around the side of the isolated house to check the far side of the barn. It was open to the elements, no wall and no door. Half a dozen camper vans could have parked inside but there wasn't a single one, just some scattered, ancient hay. As he completed the circuit, he heard the sound of the ambulance siren in the distance and checked his phone. All the hunters had now reported in. Each of the houses on Dougal's list had been checked and pronounced empty. It had all been for nothing. He dismounted and led Hector back to Pamela's still form.

Fabiola arrived first, the horse van that was attached to Bruno's Land Rover bouncing and jolting on the dirt track. She left the engine running, glanced at Bruno without speaking and went to Pamela, the medical bag she always kept close jerking as she ran. Kneeling, she checked for a pulse and then gently pulled back an eyelid. She opened her bag, took out an instrument and used it to peer into Pamela's eyes, into her ears and then up her nose. Finally she ran her hands carefully over Pamela's limbs and then stood as the ambulance came into view.

'She's concussed, unconscious, no sign of bleeding from the ears,' she said. 'How did she land?'

'I'm trying to remember, but all I can be sure of is that she was tucked in like a ball, as if somersaulting. She rolled once when she hit the ground and then again before she sprawled.'

Fabiola glanced at the dead horse. 'You took care of Bess? I thought I heard two shots.'

'That was me.'

Ahmed and Fabrice ran from the ambulance with a stretcher. Doctor Gelletreau heaved his bulk along behind, carrying a neck brace. He slowed to a walk as he recognized Fabiola.

'I was nearby with the horse van,' she explained, and repeated what she had told Bruno. 'We'll need an X-ray and a scan so that means we take her straight to Sarlat. I'll go with her,' she concluded.

'I'll come, too,' said Bruno.

'No, you won't,' she said, in a tone so harsh that Bruno felt she was accusing him of doing more than enough damage already. He felt a savage sense of guilt. He should never have allowed Pamela to come with him. And it had all been point-less, his little glow of pride at thinking of his quarry's access to Dougal's list now destroyed. If he'd been a better rider, perhaps he could have headed Pamela off before she reached the rabbit warren. He should have found the words to dissuade her from joining him on the search. At the least he should have realized that his slow, cautious searching of the deserted houses was leaving her bored and eager for a gallop. He'd been so focused on his task that he'd barely thought of her at all.

And now as he watched Fabiola help Ahmed and Fabrice put the brace on Pamela's back and head before gingerly edging her onto the stretcher, he felt a surge of something much deeper than concern flood through him as he pondered what Pamela meant to him. She had created a private world for herself with her pool and horses and tennis court and her own little community with Fabiola. And she had generously and without any demands shared it with him. There was always good food and a welcome, horses to ride, companionship and easy conversation, and above all that sensuous warmth and pleasure that she offered him in the privacy of her bed. There were many forms of love, Bruno reflected, but he had no doubt that many of the deepest and sweetest kinds were embodied for him in this woman who was now being placed in the back of the ambulance.

Fabiola stared at him impassively from the bench inside until Fabrice closed the rear doors. After it pulled away, Bruno with difficulty took the saddle and bridle from Bess's body and then called the vet to arrange for Bess's removal. He unsaddled Hector, led him into the horse van and drove gingerly down over the rough field and onto the track that led to the road. As he reached it, his phone rang.

'I'm at the hospital,' said the Mayor, his voice hollow. 'Cécile passed away peacefully this afternoon.' He hung up before Bruno could say a word.

21

There was no sign of the Mayor's Peugeot when Bruno pulled into the parking lot of the hospital just east of Sarlat. He asked for Pamela in the emergency wing and was told she'd been taken to the main hospital for X-rays. He found his way to the right department and a tired-looking nurse told him to wait. He showed her his police ID. Again she told him to wait but this time added that she'd fetch a doctor. A young man in a white coat arrived to say she was concussed and the X-rays had shown a broken collarbone. Pamela had now been admitted at least for the night and was scheduled for a scan sometime the next day. If complications developed she might have to be moved to Bordeaux.

'Has she come round?'

The young man told him no, adding that the woman doctor who had brought her in was still with her. He gave Bruno the room number.

Fabiola was sitting beside the bed where Pamela lay. She had an intravenous drip in her arm and a small tube feeding oxygen into her nostrils. Electrodes were attached to her temples and more wires snaked under the hospital nightgown and onto her chest. Displays on the machines behind the bed showed bright lines dancing rhythmically. Her face was white, her lips pale, her neck and throat encased in a foam brace.

'How serious is it?' he asked.

'It's always serious when someone's unconscious, and the longer it lasts the more serious it is. It looks like there's no cervical spine injury, but we're watching for any build-up of intercranial pressure or any lesions. From the marks on the back of her helmet and riding jacket it looks like she landed partly on her head but mainly on her shoulders and back. You said she was rolling when she landed, it may have saved her from a broken neck. Were the two of you racing?'

'No, she was galloping but I wasn't. I was some way behind her, it took twenty or thirty seconds to reach her and she was completely still by the time I did. I'd been trying to get her to turn away from that house. It was Hector who spotted the rabbit warren and I tried to shout a warning, but too late. I should never have allowed her to come with me.'

'Probably not.' Fabiola turned her face away to look at the machines.

He couldn't tell if there was some medical duty she had to perform or if she couldn't bear the sight of him. He knew from the look she had given him as the ambulance doors closed that Fabiola was furious with him and probably blamed him for Pamela's fall. That was fair enough; he blamed himself. Was this the end of his friendship with Fabiola or an anger that would pass as Pamela recovered? He hadn't really considered the prospect that Pamela might not recover fully. He'd assumed that since her neck was not broken and her limbs seemed to work she would wake up and be back to normal in a day or so. But what if it wasn't so simple, or if she had suffered lasting brain damage or would eventually awaken with some change in her personality?

He quelled the thought and looked around. There were three more beds in the room, two of them empty and someone lying still in the third, bandages wrapped so thickly around the head that Bruno could not tell if it was a man or a woman. There were no paintings, no TV set or radio in the room. It was entirely functional.

'Are you planning to stay here?' he asked.

'No, I'll come back with you. I'm just giving the staff a bit of a break by being here, otherwise that nurse would have to be in and out. I'll come back tomorrow to have a look at the scan results. They'll tell us more. If she's not awake by then . . .' She broke off and glanced at her watch.

'Can I touch her?'

Fabiola nodded. 'Could be a good thing.'

Bruno went to the far side of the bed, took Pamela's hand and stroked it, thinking how odd it was to feel no returning pressure. Trying to avoid the wires and tubes, he bent forward to kiss her cheek, smelling the antiseptic wipes they had used on her.

'What worries me is that she told me once that she'd fallen before and had been concussed,' Fabiola said. 'Over dinner one evening she was explaining why she'd given up show-jumping. She came off when her horse shied at a fence and she blacked out then for a few minutes. A second time can make it much more serious.'

'Can I come back with you tomorrow?' Bruno felt that dismaying sense of helplessness that a non-medical person feels in a hospital, dependent on the staff for information, for reason to hope.

'I'll call you after we look at the scan, but I expect she should

213

have surfaced by then, at least I'm hoping for that. We can go when you're ready. I'll tell the nurse and have a word with the doctor. They're pretty good here.' She left the door open when she left the room.

Bruno didn't know if he was imagining things but he thought he felt some movement of Pamela's hand where it lay in his. He looked at her eyelids but there was no sign of any quivering. He told Fabiola when she returned and she checked the screens on the machines.

'Her pulse rate is up a little.' She lifted Pamela's eyelids again, looked for a long moment. 'No change.'

'What are you looking for?'

'If the pupils are of different size, that's a clue to look for brain damage. It doesn't mean there is any, it's just an indicator. And you want to see how the pupils react to light.'

'You think there might be brain damage?' The words were out before Bruno could stop himself.

Fabiola paused before she answered and turned to look him in the eye. 'We're at one of those unpleasant moments when doctors are as much in the dark as you. Until we see the scan, or until she recovers consciousness and we can start to assess her state, we don't know what the outlook is going to be and there's not much point in speculating.

'I know it was an accident and I know how Pamela sometimes rides like a mad thing. But I'm not just a doctor, I'm her friend and I'm human. Right now I'm furious with you and looking for someone to blame. So please just drive me home with the radio on and let's not talk. There's nothing more I can tell you.'

*

214

Back in St Denis after dropping the still silent Fabiola and collecting Balzac from the stables, Bruno called at the Mayor's house only to find it empty and no Peugeot in the garage. He debated whether to drive to Jacqueline's to see if the Mayor was there and decided against it. But he felt the urge to do something, anything, rather than sit and worry about Pamela and feed his sense of guilt. He called J-J and the automated voice told him to leave a message. Then he rang the incident room at the Bergerac station where the hunt for Murcoing was being coordinated and reported the empty houses to Inspector Jofflin. There was no news from the search of the campsites nor from the road patrols.

He remembered he had to call Crimson to tell him of Pamela's fall and to postpone the dinner he'd been planning. When he explained how he and Pamela had been looking for Paul Murcoing, Crimson interrupted: 'Was that the chap who burgled me?'

'Yes, but he's now a murder suspect, either on the run or in hiding somewhere. That's why we were searching the *gîtes* that were listed as empty.'

'Do you have some way to smoke him out?'

'Maybe.' Bruno remembered that J-J had wondered whether Murcoing could be lured out of hiding into some kind of trap. Maybe his obsession with the Neuvic money could be used as bait. It was worth a try. He explained his thinking and then asked: 'What kind of bait would we need?'

'That's simple,' said Crimson. 'You'd need some new documents being released from the archives that cast new light on it all, maybe giving the names of which Resistance leaders were authorized to control the money.'

'You mean like some new documents from the SOE records, not yet declassified?' Bruno asked.

'Exactly,' Crimson replied. 'You wouldn't even need real documents, just forge a couple of file references and a page of contents from an archive catalogue and a sample page, scan it and post it on an email message to Murcoing. I presume he's got Internet access of some kind, if only through a phone.'

'We'd have to send it to Murcoing in a way he'd believe it,' Bruno said. 'I'm not sure how we could do that. We know that Fullerton was equally fascinated by the Neuvic business. Maybe we could concoct a message to Fullerton about new documents with a copy to Murcoing. That might work.'

'Let me think about this,' Crimson replied. 'I have one or two old friends who're familiar with those archives, including the ones still sealed. We have our quarry, we need a trap, and I think I may be able to provide the bait. I'll need someone here who's good with computers. Who's that woman teacher, the one who set up the computer system for the schoolkids?'

Bruno gave him Florence's phone number and then set off in search of the person who had best known the murdered man. He found Brian Fullerton at the Hôtel St Denis, sitting in the courtyard under the plane trees with his pipe and a glass of kir. A bowl of olives and an open laptop lay on the table before him. This was his own computer, he explained, and he was looking forward to replacing it with his brother's once the police had finished with it. He made much of Balzac, who was always delighted to make a new friend, and offered Bruno a drink. Bruno joined him in a kir and when Brian asked how the search for Murcoing was progressing, Bruno simply shrugged.

'I'm getting quite a sense of the guy from the emails,' Brian said, gesturing with his pipe at the laptop.

'But they're on your brother's machine,' Bruno said, and then saw the small thumb drive fixed into a socket on the side of the device. 'Ah, I see, you copied your brother's stuff onto that.'

'Not all of it, but the emails,' Brian replied. 'It's going to be a hell of a job working out which parts of his stock are really his and which were stolen. Sorting out his will and his financial affairs will be difficult enough, so I thought I'd try to do some work on that while waiting for the body to be released. But instead, I've been going through the emails with Murcoing.'

There was material in here for half a dozen police inquiries, he explained, including Murcoing's role in helping buy some of Francis's guns from some shady types running a bar in Toulouse. There were several long emails from Murcoing, recounting all his grandfather's theories and suspicions about who got the money from the Neuvic train. The old man saw suspects everywhere, starting with Malraux and some Russian who was in the Maquis in the Limousin, and going on to claim some big insurance firm had been started with part of the loot. There was a long account of some impoverished mechanic from Cadouin who was suddenly able to buy three trucks as the war ended and set up a successful haulage firm.

'Hard to tell what's true, what contains a grain of truth and how much of it is pure invention,' Brian concluded.

'Did your brother have anything to contribute?'

'Yes, indeed. He took it all very seriously.' Brian lit his pipe and sat back as he began to explain that Francis had made several visits to the Public Records Office in Kew, just outside London, looking up the SOE archives. Many of them had been declassified and Francis had scanned photocopies into the computer and sent them off to Murcoing with a rough translation. There were desperate missives to London from Resistance chiefs about how broke they were and how they needed money to feed their men and help support their families.

'But nothing more about the Neuvic train?'

'Yes, that's what Murcoing was really interested in, but my brother only found snippets in the SOE archives. But he told Murcoing that more files were scheduled to be declassified and he'd hired a researcher to keep an eye out for them. One of the last emails, setting up this last trip he made to France, said he'd gathered lots of new photocopies that he was bringing with him.'

'We didn't find those at your brother's house,' Bruno said, thinking that this could fit with Crimson's idea for new documents to lure Murcoing out of hiding.

'So Murcoing must have taken them,' Brian replied. 'He's obviously obsessed with this Neuvic business. He has a list of names of Maquis types from the Groupe Valmy and other networks, people he claimed were suspects, or ones that he or his grandfather believed had got away with some of the loot. Lord knows there was enough money at stake. He gives their addresses, the names and addresses of their heirs, the family businesses and farms that suddenly had money to expand after the war. Two or three of his emails ended up with the phrase "They will pay for this!" But he doesn't say whether he wants to denounce them or blackmail them or what.'

'Could you collect those names for me and email them to

me at my office?' Bruno asked. 'I'd like to check them against our list of burglaries. What was your brother's reaction to this kind of thing?'

'It didn't seem to surprise him. But that was Francis, he was always an enthusiast. Even as a little boy he'd take up some hobby like stamps or aircraft recognition and hurl himself into it for weeks at a time, just like he did with Grandpa Freddy's wartime career and this venture with Murcoing. We went to see his specialist when he was in one of those expensive treatment centres where they try to wean people off drugs, and he told us that Francis had an addictive personality.'

'What about their personal relationship? Did Murcoing know about Francis's affair with Yves or his liaisons with other men?'

'Francis was emailing all sorts of different men in ways that made the sexual relationship pretty clear, but he was at pains to keep them all separate,' Brian replied. 'With Murcoing, I think there was much more devotion on Murcoing's side. It reminded me a bit of that line from La Rochefoucauld, that in love there is always one who kisses and one who offers the cheek. Murcoing was very much the one doing the kissing.'

'I'm wondering if that could have been a motive for the murder,' Bruno said. 'Murcoing could have felt betrayed if or when he found that Francis was about to have a romantic holiday with another man.'

'I've asked myself the same question. The relationship with Murcoing had lasted for a long time, according to the emails. That was unusual for Francis. I used to wonder if Francis ever really loved anybody, except maybe his nephews and nieces, my children. It's hard to tell, and even harder to match the charming little brother I knew with what he later became. He could be quite a monster when he was on drugs.'

Brian called up the final exchange of emails and turned the laptop so Bruno could read.

The last email from Francis had been sent on Monday and he'd arranged to meet Murcoing at his Corrèze farm 'after the weekend', presumably meaning this weekend. Francis had added that he was bringing a full load of furniture from England to be unloaded and would then return across the Channel with French furniture from the barn. Bruno worked out the timing. Today was Sunday. The email had been sent the previous Monday, and on the Tuesday Francis had taken the Chunnel train and called at Dougal's to pay for the extra days' lease and to pick up the keys.

'So my brother would not have been expecting Murcoing when he suddenly showed up at the gîte. There could have been an angry scene,' Brian said. 'But I don't understand how Murcoing knew that Francis planned to arrive early for a romantic interlude with this other man.'

'His sister works for the rental agency,' Bruno replied 'She knew which gîtes were going to be occupied and when. And the name of the tenant is also listed for the relevant week so the cleaners and gardeners know who'll be there. She'd certainly have recognized his name, since this affair with Murcoing had been going on for over a year, you say.'

'Maybe even longer. Look at this.' He scrolled back to the beginning of the chain of emails between the two men, the first one dated in September, over eighteen months earlier, and sent by Murcoing when Francis had returned to England after their affair had begun, or perhaps resumed. He pointed to a line in the rather rambling and passionate message.

'I have often thought of you even before that magical reunion when I saw you at the fair in Monpazier,' Bruno read, and wondered just how long it had been between the reunion and their previous meeting.

That triggered a memory, something he had noted at the time and planned to follow up, but it had slipped his mind. It was to do with Valentoux and the night he had told Bruno about his daughter. Valentoux had been asking around the gay community for information about Paul Murcoing and had been told he was known as a mercenary youth.

The conversation began to play back in Bruno's head. They had been standing on the steps of his home because Yves had wanted a cigarette. Yves recalled that Francis Fullerton had recounted some story of being in this region and meeting a boy a decade or so ago. And then an image suddenly appeared in Bruno's mind of the studio portrait of a sultry-looking Murcoing that had been on Francis Fullerton's bedside table in Corrèze and of Yves mentioning a poem that Francis had written about a boy named Paul.

Mon Dieu, he thought to himself, it's the missing boy from Bergerac who gave the medical clinic a false name on that case I could never resolve, the one that kept me awake at nights. It will be in one of my first notebooks.

He began to rise clumsily, jolting the table and startling Brian, who reached out to steady his drink. Bruno was thinking of the pile of cardboard boxes in his barn where he stored his old papers.

'Sorry, I just remembered something,' he said.

'Is it to do with the case?'

'Maybe, but it's probably not that important, it's just that there may be a connection with something that happened a long time ago.'

'Can you tell me about it? Does it involve Francis?'

'I think it might, it happened about ten years ago. A group of English gays rented a *gîte* and invited some French boys back to their pool. But the fathers turned up as well and beat the hell out of them. I tried to sort it out but the English guys all left the area. The French boys were sent away on sudden holidays and everybody clammed up. There was one boy I could never track down, who may have been young Murcoing.'

'Ten years ago, that's just before Francis went to prison. And I recall that he did go on holiday not long before he was arrested. I don't remember him being beaten up.'

'Did your brother drive a Range Rover?'

'No,' Brian answered. 'But his partner did, Sam Berenson, the one who died and left him the antiques business.'

The names of the Englishmen had been on the rental agreement and on the car registration forms. Bruno was sure he'd have copied them down in his notebook.

'Do you recall any poems on your brother's laptop?' he asked.

'Yes, he wrote a lot, poems, short stories. He even wrote a few songs when he was in New York, made a couple of CDs which I still have. I don't know if his writings were all in his computer but they probably are. Why?'

'Yves Valentoux told me the other day that he remembered Francis reciting a poem he'd written about a French boy. That may have been where all this started. I'm going to have to look out my old notebooks.'

'That's a shame, because I was just about to invite you to dinner, if you're free, that is,' said Brian. 'I've had enough of going through these emails and the mess of my brother's life.'

'You're very kind, but I have some horses to take care of and a friend who's just gone into hospital. I may have to leave at any moment.'

22

It was Bruno's day off, and after he'd phoned the hospital and Fabiola hoping in vain for some news of Pamela, he decided to plunge into activity rather than sit around worrying. He'd started by hunting through the cardboard boxes containing his old notebooks. Each box was sealed with sticky tape and numbered with years. Inside, wrapped in the plastic bags the dry cleaner used to protect Bruno's uniforms, the notebooks were in rough chronological order. He found the relevant one, resisted the temptation to read it through and relive old events and cases, and checked on the names of the Englishmen he'd written down from their car insurance forms. One of them was Francis Fullerton and another was Samuel Berenson, the name of the older man whose home and business Francis had inherited.

The only French name he found was Edouard Marty, the boy who'd disappeared to England before taking his place at university. While his notebook didn't say so, Bruno was sure he remembered that it had been the university of Bordeaux. And he'd planned to study architecture. His parents had been old when he was born and Bruno knew the father had died and the mother had moved away to be with her sisters. He called the faculty of architecture, asked to speak to the director's office, identified himself and explained that he was trying to trace a former student, Edouard Marty.

'He's still here,' she said. 'What are you after him for, speeding again in that new Jaguar of his?'

Nothing like that, he replied with a laugh, just a routine inquiry about a possible witness. But what did she mean, that Edouard was still at the university?

'He's not teaching today, he's only part-time,' he was told, and then he was given the name and number of a company named Arch-Inter where Edouard Marty could be found, when he was not teaching a course on the history of interior design as an associate professor. Bruno searched for the company on his computer and found an elegant website, with the words Arch-Inter forking out to say *Inter-national* and *Inter-iors*. To his great surprise, it boasted offices in Bordeaux, Cannes, London and Los Angeles.

The company offered services in architecture, interior design and furnishings in different traditions, from English country house and minimalist modern to French *ancien régime* or Empire. There were photographs of very grand-looking rooms furnished in various styles, each of them captioned in Russian and in English. It seemed to be a one-stop service for wealthy Russians, who would buy a house or apartment and have it filled by Arch-Inter in whichever style the client chose. How long, Bruno wondered, before they added Shanghai to their list of offices?

Bruno clicked on the section titled About Us and saw that Francis Fullerton was listed as the London representative. He sat back, reflecting on the chain of circumstance that connected the beating-up of some foreign gays a decade ago with this international company today. And what better outlet could there be for Fullerton's haul of French and English antiques? This was clearly a much bigger and more lucrative operation than Bruno had assumed, and one that could throw up some alternative explanations for Fullerton's murder.

He phoned Bernard Ardouin, the *juge d'instruction*, who called up the website on his own computer as they spoke. Ardouin asked whether Bruno recognized as stolen any of the items in the photographs. No, he replied, but the art squad of the *Police Nationale* might do so, and the place to start would be to compare the website pictures with the photographs on Fullerton's computer. Bruno explained the original connection between Fullerton and Edouard and asked whether Ardouin had any objections to Bruno's driving to Bordeaux to interview the architect.

'I'd rather you didn't do that yet,' said Ardouin. 'We don't want to alert him before we're sure stolen goods are involved. And as you say, this looks like a matter for the art squad rather than you, but all credit to you for opening up this lead. I'd better brief J-J and get him to print out those photographs on Fullerton's laptop.'

'Still no sign of Murcoing?' Bruno asked.

'Nothing from J-J or the Bergerac police and he's not used his bank card. He'll have to show his face at some point, it's just a matter of time. I've asked J-J to have some plain-clothes types mixing discreetly with the crowd at the funeral tomorrow.'

As he rang off, Bruno wasn't so sure that finding Murcoing would be quite that simp.e. He shrugged. It was neither his patch nor his responsibility, and he had chores enough to occupy him. It was high time to resume his training session with Balzac, who was by now so accustomed to being hugged and caressed by every human he met that Bruno had some difficulty in getting him to associate achievement with reward.

His special dog biscuits helped. Each month, Bruno mixed together a litre of milk, a bag of brown flour, an egg and a handful of brown sugar and added some salt. He cut a slice of fat from the ham that hung from the beam in his kitchen, fried it and then poured the fat into the mix along with a shredded clove of garlic. He then cut into tiny slices the crisp remnants of the ham. If he had any gravy left from one of his own meals, or any other useful leftovers, they went into the mix. If it was still too moist, he added breadcrumbs. Baked for thirty minutes in a hot oven, the biscuits had proved irresistible to his previous dog, Gigi, and now to Balzac. Lured by the scent, Balzac would come when called and had learned to approach Bruno from the left with one whistle tone and from the right with another.

It was when he'd ended the training session with a grooming session and was cleaning Balzac's ears that he'd been reminded of one avenue he had not tried. It was the identifying tattoo inside Balzac's ear that did it.

Bruno went into his study and pulled out the phone book, turned to *Tatouages* in the *pages jaunes* and found two tattooing parlours in Bergerac. He checked his watch, donned his uniform and headed into town, where he'd be in time to catch Pascal at the Post Office taking his mid-morning break. He dropped off Balzac in Hector's stable and armed with Paul Murcoing's photograph and the sketch Pascal drew from memory of the tattoo on the arm of the driver of the white van, he drove to Bergerac. Stopping to buy diesel, he made the obligatory courtesy call to Inspector Jofflin to say he'd be coming onto Jofflin's turf and might have a lead on Murcoing. To Bruno's relief, he was passed to voicemail and left a message without having to explain his hunch.

At the first parlour, a place in a run-down part of town that seemed to specialize in gothic images, he drew a blank. The second place was just off the old town, not far from the river, in a street where flower shops alternated with bio food stores, hairdressers and vegetarian restaurants. Ahead of him two women, one with a severe crew cut, were strolling hand in hand. The shop window of the tattoo parlour was dominated by a dramatic collage composed of posters advertising local concerts. Inside, a shaven-headed man in black leather pants and a matching waistcoat, his arms and chest covered in ornate and colourful designs, glanced at Pascal's sketch and said proudly: 'That's my Maori warrior.'

'Your what?' Bruno asked.

'Maori warrior, from New Zealand, I saw it on one of their players in a rugby match on TV. Different designs say different things about how many fights you've been in, how many enemy you killed. I adapted it and made my own design.'

'Did you do one for this guy?' Bruno showed him Paul's photo.

'Paul, yes, I did that one, and another that only his best friends would see. But I haven't seen him for a few days. He's usually in Marcel's of an evening.'

'Is that a bar?'

'Bar, bistro, little theatre in the back, its real name is Proust but we all call it Marcel's. It won't be open now, though. Weekend nights run late so they don't open Mondays until the evening. Is he in trouble again?'

'No, he's a witness in a case, but what was he in trouble for?'

'I don't know, it's just something you say. But I make sure he pays me cash in advance,' the man said. 'You know what I mean?'

'Do you know where he lives?'

'You might find him at Marcel's, he's got one of the rooms upstairs. I don't know if he lives there or just uses it for pickups, but like I said, I haven't seen him for a bit. And if you find him, don't tell him it was me that told you.'

Bruno found the place easily enough, between a dog-grooming parlour and an antiques shop with a single Buddha head in grey stone dominating its window. Proust was painted black, and the windows were filled with movie posters of Jane Russell and Lana Turner, flanking a blown-up photo of a beautiful woman's eyes. Bruno thought they might have belonged to Elizabeth Taylor. Below the eyes was a photo of Marcel Proust in profile. The door to the bar was closed, but it opened when he tried the handle. Inside, chairs were piled atop tables, the floor was wet and a black woman who was mopping it looked up guardedly at his police uniform.

'Looking for Paul Murcoing,' he said, showing the photo.

She shrugged and slopped water on the floor. 'Boss not here,' she said, not looking at him.

He walked across and put the photo in front of her face. 'Do you know this man?'

She closed her eyes. 'You talk to boss.'

Bruno sighed. She was almost certainly an illegal immigrant. He disliked doing this but he did not want to waste time.

'Your papers, please, Madame.'

'Papers at home.' Now she had stopped mopping and was standing still, head down.

'You have a choice, Madame, you either show me his room right now or we go to the police station and check your papers.'

She shrugged again, this time with an air of defeat, pulled a large ring of keys from the pocket of her apron and led the way up two flights of narrow stairs to an unpainted wooden door. She unlocked it and let him step into a room that was clearly unoccupied. There was a plain double bed, with a mattress and a pillow but no bedding, a small table with a water jug and basin, a hard-backed chair and a handsome armoire that had seen better days. It was empty.

'Paul gone,' she said, a phrase she repeated when he asked when he had gone, how long he had been there and who else had stayed.

'His things, his possessions?' he asked. 'Where are they?' He knew the police lore, that when you wanted to intimidate, you took out a notebook. He fished in his jacket pocket for something to write with, remembering with a sinking feeling that he had left his pen in his car when checking the tattoo-parlour addresses on the map. The notebook was sufficient. Sullenly, she led the way downstairs to the cellar and pointed to two cardboard boxes.

'Boss packed these when Paul gone. He leave Tuesday.'

That was the day of Fullerton's murder. He put the notebook away and opened the first box, full of unwashed clothes and a pair of dirty sheets. The second box contained shoes, toiletries, a small TV set, some books and what Bruno assumed were sex toys. They included leather manacles with straps, a battery-driven vibrator and what looked like clothes pegs in brass. He

230

assumed they were nipple clamps. There was a small brown bottle with a label describing it as leather cleaner, which Bruno suspected was amyl nitrate, a drug that was sniffed and supposedly enhanced sexual pleasure. At the bottom was some mail. The biggest envelope had an English stamp and postmark and inside was a printout of two crude photos that appeared to have been taken with a cell phone. One was of Yves Valentoux and Francis Fullerton standing together, eyes only for each other, at a bar. On a counter behind them was the kind of beer glass, a dimpled jug, that you only found in English pubs. The second photo was in the same place and showed the two men kissing. Was this the trigger for Paul's jealous rage? Who might have sent it, and with what motive?

Most of the mail was junk, but he found an insurance form for the white van, a pharmacist's receipt for eighty-three euros that had not yet been claimed back from the *mutuel*, the health insurance fund of the transport employees section of the Force Ouvrière trade union. Finally he found a bank statement that showed Paul with just over two thousand euros in his account. The address for the account was the bar downstairs.

'No more,' said the woman, and made no objection when Bruno took the papers. She followed him upstairs, and by the time he was at the door she was mopping the floor again. He suspected her boss would never learn of his visit. He left messages for both J-J and Jofflin to pass on Murcoing's old address and to suggest that a visit to Marcel's bar might produce some leads. Since he was in Bergerac he looked up the address he had for Joséphine, Murcoing's aunt. She worked with old people, Father Sentout had said. She lived not far from the first tattoo place he had visited, a crumbling neighbourhood where the butchers advertised halal meat and several of the women were veiled.

She answered the door in a housecoat with a towel wrapped turban-style around her head and flapping her hands in a way that suggested she was drying her nail polish.

'I've come to give you fifty euros,' he said, showing the banknote.

'I thought you'd pay me at the funeral tomorrow.'

'I was nearby so I thought I'd deal with it now. You might be busy tomorrow. If you'll just sign this receipt for two of your father's old banknotes, one for the *Mairie* and the other for the Resistance museum, and I'll be on my way.'

She invited him in, offered a cup of coffee, and as her kettle boiled she glanced casually at the receipt he'd brought and pocketed the fifty euros. Bruno had drafted the receipt with care, saying that the sum was received 'in return for two invalid banknotes of a thousand francs, dated 1940, said notes to be used for historical display only'. The space to be signed and dated by Joséphine identified her as representing the lawful heirs of Loïc Murcoing.

She sat at the kitchen table to sign it, and made no objection when he pulled out a chair and joined her, resting his arms on the slightly sticky waxed tablecloth. The kitchen looked as though it hadn't been changed for decades. There were none of the usual fitted cupboards, but racks of shelves for the plates and a small refrigerator that growled and wheezed. Joséphine wrote clumsily, as one not much accustomed to writing, and then turned aside to make the coffee, grinding the beans and then using a cafetière. It was good and he said so.

'I'm never one to scrimp on a good cup of coffee,' she said, adding three lumps of sugar to her cup. 'One of my only treats these days.'

'Everybody in the family coming to the funeral?' he asked.

She eyed him narrowly, her hand sliding down to the pocket of her housecoat as if to make sure the banknote was still there. 'I'll say this for you, you're the first copper who didn't push his way in and start asking where I was hiding Paul. And before you ask, I don't know where he is and nor do my sisters. And nobody will be more surprised than me if he shows his face at the funeral and gets arrested.'

'I heard he was living over a bar near the centre, a place called Proust, known to the customers as Marcel's.'

'You know more than the coppers round here then. He was supposed to have part-ownership of that place, but I don't know what came of it. Probably nothing, like most of Paul's big ideas.' The words were harsh but her tone was fond, Bruno noted.

'He seemed a bright lad from what I hear, someone who should be going places rather than just driving a van.'

'His grandpa was so proud of him, always top of the class,' she said. 'We all were when he passed his *Bac* and went off to the university, first time anyone in our family ever did that. He was always clever, but a sweet kid. Everybody liked him, even animals. He always had one in tow, a dog or a cat. He had a way with them, stray dogs used to follow him home. He always wanted to keep them but his dad had walked out soon after he was born so there was no money.'

'He did well to get to university,' said Bruno.

'That's when it all went wrong. He was easily led astray was Paul, fell in with the wrong sort, and that's why he dropped

233

out. I blame those damn drugs, or he'd really have made something of himself.'

'What did he study?' Bruno was happy to have got her talking. He still didn't feel he knew much about Murcoing.

'He was specializing in architecture. He could always draw beautifully, even as a little boy. Portraits, landscapes, he had a real gift. He drew one of me and I didn't even know he was watching me. It was so good I framed it, look.' She heaved herself to her feet, went into the sitting room and brought back a cheap plastic frame. The pencil sketch it contained was not simply recognizable as her, but it conveyed something of the determination with which she had endured a hard and ill-paid life.

'That's very good.'

'He was only fourteen when he did that. You ought to see his landscapes, ones he did when he was a bit older.' She gestured to the kitchen wall behind Bruno and he turned to look at something that had not registered when he first glanced around the kitchen. Now that he looked more carefully he saw a framed watercolour of a Bergerac street scene in autumn, leaves turning brown and the stone of the buildings merging with the grey sky. It felt sympathetic rather than gloomy, an attempt to find some beauty in a drab scene.

'He could make a living at this.'

'He made a few francs in the summer, doing sketches of tourists down by the statue of Cyrano, but they wanted quick caricatures, not the little portraits he liked to make. Come and look at this.'

She led him back into the sitting room, dominated by an elderly three-piece suite around a TV set, and from the cupboard beneath the TV she drew a thick sheaf of paintings, all sketches in pencil or chalk and some more watercolours. Bruno leafed through, thinking of the waste of talent that Paul's life represented. There were a couple of scenes of Périgord villages and churches that he'd have been proud to own, and some more fine portraits. He stopped at one that looked familiar and he suddenly realized that it was Edouard Marty as a grown man in his late twenties. There were three exquisite portraits of Francis Fullerton, one dozing in a summer hammock, another in a formal pose in a chair, and a third on a beachfront, hair ruffled by the wind. There was an intimacy about them, a depth of affectionate knowledge that suggested love.

'He's really gifted. I wouldn't mind buying some of these from him, or from you maybe.' He pulled out a watercolour of a river scene and another of a Périgord village. 'If I gave you the money, I know you'd see he got it eventually.'

'Give it him in prison, you mean, once you buggers round him up?' The moment of shared appreciation had gone and Joséphine was back in her defensive stance.

'I'd forgotten about that, I just like the paintings,' he said, genuinely. Her glance softened.

'He used to charge twenty, thirty euros down at the statue. Give us fifty and you can have 'em both.'

23

This time his police uniform ensured that Bruno was shown directly to Pamela's room in the hospital. Fabiola's phone call with the good news had reached him as he was leaving Bergerac. Pamela was awake and lucid; the scan had shown no lasting damage beyond a broken collarbone and two cracked ribs. The tubes and wires had all been removed. She was sitting up with one arm in a sling, reading an English newspaper with a pen in her good hand, when he poked his head around the open door. He gave her the overpriced flowers he'd bought at the hospital shop.

'They're lovely, Bruno, thank you,' she said, returning his kiss. She tasted of toothpaste and there was a scent of lavender he'd not known her to wear before. She filled in one of the clues in her *Times* crossword before continuing. 'Fabiola was here earlier and told me about Bess. It's very sad and I'll miss her, but she was an old horse and you obviously had no choice.'

'When will they let you go home?' There was a rather battered metal vase on the cupboard. He filled it with water from the tap.

'Maybe tomorrow, the doctor said, since Fabiola will be there to keep an eye on me. But why the uniform? Isn't today your day off?'

'Something came up on this murder case so I had to go to Bergerac and look official.' He placed the flowers in the vase and turned back to her.

'Bruno, really, you can't just dump them in like that,' she said in mock reproof. 'Bring the vase to me and hold it while I arrange them. Honestly, you men have no idea.' She began with her good hand to arrange the mixed red and white roses, making him strip some leaves and bend some of the stems to change their height. 'At least I can afford to buy a new horse now, thanks to my mother's will. That's something to look forward to.'

'Make sure it has a rabbit-hole detector.' He was pleased to hear her sounding so normal and looking so much better than he'd expected. Fabiola must have brought in some make-up and the pretty white nightgown that he recognized. The newspaper was probably her idea, too.

'I hope these are tough enough for you.' Bruno laid on the bed beside her a booklet of Sudoku puzzles. Normally she raced through them almost as quickly as she could fill in the numbers.

'Lovely, such a treat, but now I want to hear all about the murder case. Have you traced Murcoing yet?'

No, but he now knew a lot more about the young man, and he explained his findings in Bergerac and the Arch-Inter connection.

'So who would have sent the photo to Murcoing of his lover kissing Yves? Who might have had an interest in driving him into a fit of jealous rage? And who would benefit from Fullerton's death? It's obvious, it must be the brother. He stands to inherit, after all.'

Bruno shook his head. 'Brian says his brother's will leaves everything to Brian's kids, to be held in trust. He may be lying but we can check that through the British police. Now they have a death certificate there's no reason for the will to be secret. If Brian is lying about the will, then obviously he becomes the main suspect. But how would Brian or anybody else have known that Paul would be driven to kill just by that photograph? He doesn't strike me as a man so concerned with sexual fidelity that he'd murder a lover who cheated on him. And we might never have known about the Corrèze farm if Brian hadn't told us. It doesn't hang together.'

She nodded. 'How certain are you that Murcoing is the killer?'

He shrugged. 'We can place him at the murder scene at about the relevant time, but mainly it's because he's gone on the run. That always feeds suspicion. He had a romantic motive and maybe also a financial one, if he thought Fullerton was cheating him. Certainly Fullerton had a lot of money and Paul seems to have been getting very little.'

Not wanting interruption, he'd switched both his phones to vibrate that morning before going to see Joséphine. The second, private one vibrated now. He glanced at the screen, recognized the number that was calling and said: 'I have to take this.' He excused himself, heading into the corridor and out of earshot as he answered Isabelle.

'Have you seen the *Paris Match* website?' she began, her voice neutral rather than angry. 'Your friend Gilles is making news again.'

'I haven't seen it but I think I know what it's about.'

'The Brigadier knows you're behind it. And there's a rumour that there's something coming in *Le Monde*.'

'I don't understand why he thinks I'm involved. Gilles talked directly to Jacqueline Morgan. Her book is finished and she's looking for publicity. I know she's written something for *Le Monde* but it's up to them to decide what to do with it.'

'Don't be coy, Bruno, not with me. And I don't care whether her story runs or not, but there are aspects of this that you don't know. Can we meet?'

'Did the Brigadier tell you about the difference of opinion between him and me at our last meeting?'

'Yes, and that's partly what I want to talk about.'

'Where are you?'

'I'm in Périgueux. It needs to be discreet, so can I come to your place?'

Bruno checked his watch. 'Alright, let's say five this afternoon.'

They rang off and he went back to Pamela, who greeted him with a question. 'Are you absolutely certain that your corpse is the man you think it is? The head has been destroyed so how did the brother identify him?'

'They're doing a DNA test and the usual fingerprints. He'd served a prison term, so they're on file. We'd have used dental records but as you said, the head was smashed.'

'But right now you're assuming that your dead man is who you think he is and not the brother. Am I right? What if your corpse is the brother and the man you think is the brother is in fact the crooked antiques dealer and also the murderer?'

Pamela had been doing too many crossword puzzles, he thought. 'If it's the crooked antiques dealer who's alive, why would he have led me to his hoard of stolen goods? And he must assume that we'll check the fingerprints. That's routine.'

'Who was it called you?'

'It was about Gilles. His piece on Jacqueline's nuclear secrets is on the *Paris Match* website.'

'Are you trying to avoid telling me that your caller was the person you refer to as my favourite French policewoman?'

He nodded, feeling guilty and reminding himself that he should never underestimate Pamela's powers of perception.

'Will this *Paris Match* story mean trouble for you?' she asked.

'Maybe, I don't know. As long as the Mayor stays in office, there's not much they can do, beyond taking my special phone away, and I wouldn't mind that at all. Life was a lot simpler before the Brigadier had me on speed dial.'

'Presumably Isabelle wants to see you about it.'

He nodded again and warily scanned her face. She looked neither cross nor suspicious, simply thoughtful.

'Have you looked into this Arch-Inter group you mentioned? If they have offices in California they must be a big operation. Wouldn't they have to fill in some kind of customs form if they ship goods overseas?'

'Not within Europe. Fullerton could bring in and take back vanloads of antiques to Italy or England with no problem. For Russia, he'd need a customs declaration, and for America they'd have to go by container, so there'd be records. The art squad can handle all that, they do it all the time.'

'Pass me my laptop. Fabiola brought it.' She asked him to plug it into the wall socket and inserted the little plug that connected to the Internet through the cellphone system. While she booted up, he took the opportunity to visit the men's room, his uniform provoking the usual range of curious and worried glances.

'This Arch-Inter firm is pretty big in the States,' she said when he returned, gesturing for him to look over her shoulder. 'That's quite a showroom they have in Santa Monica and they're promising regular new deliveries of English and European antiques. Hmm, I wonder . . .'

She typed in a Google search for Companies House, London, accessed the website for the register of British companies and typed in Arch-Inter. Up came the name and a number. She tapped twice on the number and up came a list of documents filed by the company, each of which could be downloaded for one pound.

'We don't even need to pay. Here are the names of new directors added to the board. Surprise, surprise, look who we find.'

Over her shoulder he read the names of the new directors, Paul Murcoing, Brian Fullerton and Edouard Marty, all added on the same date three years earlier. Francis Fullerton had been a director since the company was formed in 1996. There was another English-sounding name, Alan McAllister, which Bruno recognized from the California branch of Arch-Inter.

'The plot thickens,' she said, sitting back and looking extraordinarily pleased with herself.

'You should be doing my job.'

'Too easy,' she replied with a grin. 'And you might want to check whether Murcoing had a company credit card. If it's attached to a British bank he could have access to money that your systems aren't tracking.'

'*Mon Dieu*, we never thought of that . . .' He wondered how Pamela knew about such matters and then remembered her account of spending hours with lawyers and accountants, sorting out her mother's estate.

'Now you need to get your *juge d'instruction* to check the annual reports to see just how much money the company is making,' she went on. 'Above all he needs to check the share register and find out how many shares each director owns. That's how you can tell who's really in charge.'

'With Fullerton dead, the question now is what happens to his shares. Presumably that'll be in his will,' Bruno said, reaching for his hat. 'I have to go and see Ardouin, the *juge*, and then relate all this to J-J.' He bent down and kissed her. 'Did anybody ever tell you that you're as brainy as you're beautiful?'

'Never in quite this context, with me lying in bed and a man who ought to be much more grateful just about to don his hat and leave me to languish.'

He kissed her again. 'Close your eyes and think of justice.'

Delayed by his meeting with the *juge* and the need to brief J-J on the startling news that Paul Murcoing had been a director of Arch-Inter, Bruno collected Balzac and then drove to his home. He saw no sign of Isabelle's rental car when he pulled onto his land. But seeming to know she was there, Balzac scooted from the back of the Land Rover and round the side of the house to the chicken coop where Isabelle was sitting on a tree stump in the late afternoon sun, watching the birds and smoking. She tossed her cigarette aside as Balzac leaped onto her lap and used his back legs to pedal his way up to lick her neck. Holding the puppy in both hands, she rose and offered the cheek Balzac was not monopolizing to be kissed.

'You walked here?' She was dressed like a hiker in walking boots and windcheater and somehow still managed to look chic. A light rucksack was on the ground beside her.

'I parked at the hunter's hide on the far side of the ridge and walked the trail. You should be impressed that I remembered the way.'

'Why the discretion?'

She gave a slow smile. 'I could say I was thinking about your reputation or maybe I just fancied a gentle walk through the woods to see how my leg had recovered.' She took a paper-wrapped bottle from the rucksack and passed it to him. 'But I'm also bringing a message from the Brigadier along with this peace offering. He says you passed the test.'

Did the Brigadier never stop playing games? He opened the tissue paper and found a bottle of Balvenie, the Brigadier's favourite scotch. 'It didn't seem like a test to me.'

'I know, he put me through a similar interview. The mood in Paris is poisonous right now with the election so close, people worried for their jobs, lots of documents being shredded, files being sanitized. It's hard to know who to trust.'

'That's the life you chose, Isabelle.'

She nodded. 'It's what I thought I wanted, what I still want, if only it weren't so damn political all the time. It's like living in Machiavelli's kitchen. Anyway, it looks like I could be getting that European job. I'm on a shortlist of three and I'm the only candidate who speaks English and has experience of international liaison. I go up to The Hague for the formal interview on Friday morning. You ever been to Holland?'

Bruno shook his head. He knew there were discount flights from the airports at Bordeaux and Bergerac.

She gestured to his house. 'I see you finally put the windows in the roof. Will you show me?' She picked up Balzac to carry him with her.

Bruno led the way inside, remembering how he had talked of his plan as they had lain in bed together, sharing that special territory of new lovers as they spoke of plans and dreams and explored possible futures together. Always practical, Isabelle had said he'd have to knock down walls to install stairs. So Bruno was shyly proud of the solution he'd found, to put the staircase into the small room he'd used as a study, fitting his desk and books beneath the stairs and not taking space from his sitting room. He was a little nervous of her reaction. When she climbed the stairs ahead of him, her limp was still noticeable.

'It's great, Bruno,' she said, putting Balzac down to explore as she looked into the smaller room to the left and the much larger room to the right and then poked her head into the small shower room he'd inserted between them. They were still empty of furniture. She looked again into the smaller room.

'The children's room you always planned,' she said. Her voice was flat.

'That depends if there's more than one, then they get the big room, or maybe both of them.'

'Aren't you planning to move up here yourself?'

'Not yet, at least,' he said. 'There's the painting to finish, blinds and curtains to choose. And I like that bedroom downstairs.' He did not have to add that it was the bedroom that they had shared.

'How will you get the beds up that staircase?'

'I just have to get the mattresses up. The beds I can build myself.'

She walked across to the window, opened it and looked out at the view across the steadily rising ridges, fields and woodlands and not another house or road in sight. Then she turned, leaned against the sill and looked carefully around the big room as if furnishing it in her mind. He wondered if she was thinking of what might have been, but she pushed herself off from the windowsill, flashed him a determined smile and headed down the stairs, speaking over her shoulder.

'I've got something for you as well.'

Balzac was too small to get down the stairs without tripping over his ears so Bruno scooped him up and followed her. Outside, she went back to her rucksack and pulled out a stiff cardboard envelope and handed it to him.

'It was her we were interested in, not just Crimson,' she explained as Bruno pulled out a grainy surveillance photo of Jacqueline taken at a hotel entrance. She was with a tall and slender man with a thick head of flowing white hair, a man instantly recognizable to anyone who read French newspapers. The next photo showed the two of them embracing in the shadows of an entrance courtyard to what looked like a very plush apartment building.

'That's your boss,' Bruno said, finally realizing why anything to do with Jacqueline could set off alarm bells in Paris.

'That was before he became a minister, five or six years ago when he was still mayor of Orléans and she was teaching at the Sorbonne. The building is where he kept a discreet *pied-à-terre* on a fancy street behind the Parc Monceau.'

'Did the RG get photos like this of everybody?' he asked. The *Renseignements Généraux* had been famous for their voluminous files on the left-wing parties, but he wasn't so very surprised that they had been keeping an eye on fast-rising politicians of all stripes.

Isabelle shrugged. 'Who knows if they were watching her or him? Does it matter? They both turn out to be people of interest, particularly now.'

Bruno was trying to work out the political implications. 'So now your Minister is worried that Jacqueline's book might rebound on him and he takes the blame if they lose the election?'

'That's why he needs to find someone else to take the rap. That's one of the first laws of politics,' Isabelle replied. 'And if the blame somehow falls onto the Americans or the British and their shadowy secret services trying to manipulate our elections and blacken the names of our patriotic politicians . . . I don't need to spell out the rest, do I?'

She took the cardboard folder and the photos back from Bruno. 'You understand that I can't leave these with you. I'd better go. Will you walk back to the car with me, you and Balzac?'

He printed some names on a page of his notebook and gave it to her, explaining the results of the web search at Companies House. 'We need to see a copy of the will Fullerton made in England. J-J is trying to get them through the usual channels. If you can find out faster through your Scotland Yard connection, it may help. And I'd like to hear if anything is known about these people, directors of this Arch-Inter company.'

'I thought you already had your suspect, this Paul Murcoing who's one of the directors. Or are you following one of your hunches?'

'Never leave potentially useful information unchecked – isn't that what you used to tell me?'

She shouldered her rucksack and began to walk around his

chicken coop to pick up the track into the woods. Bruno saw her grimace and her limp was suddenly more apparent. He caught her up, took her arm and turned her round and steered her towards his Land Rover.

'I'm getting a bit pressed for time,' he lied. 'I'd better drive you back to your car.'

She gave him a sharp look but agreed, saying: 'I've something to tell you, and it might be easier to tell you in the car when I don't have to look you in the eye.'

'If you want to tell me that it's all over between you and me, I've been expecting it,' he said, carefully keeping his voice neutral. 'We've both known long enough that there's no future for us. You're not coming back to Périgord, even if you give up the career in Paris.'

To get to her car by road would mean driving two long sides of a triangle, so he was taking the short cut along the bridle way and the hunters' track. It meant driving slowly but they would still be there in a fraction of the time and this was not a conversation that he wanted to prolong.

'We've lived with that,' she said. 'This is something else.' She paused and they drove on in silence, Balzac resting quietly on her lap, quite content just to lie there and feel her hand stroking his back.

'I don't really know how to begin, because I know that as soon as I say this it really is over between us.' Her voice didn't sound like Isabelle at all, none of that energy and eagerness he knew so well. 'There'll be no more surprise reunions, no more fantasies of having you for a weekend in Paris. It's final. You'll never want to speak to me again.'

He rounded a bend and saw her car parked by the hunters'

shack, perhaps a hundred metres ahead. He had a sudden presentiment of what she might be about to say and felt a great hollowness begin to gather somewhere deep in his gut.

'I have done something unforgivable,' she said as he drew up beside her car. Her head was bowed and she seemed to be speaking to Balzac more than to him, or perhaps making her farewell to the puppy she had always called 'ours'.

'It was that night before the summit, the night before Gigi was shot, when we were together.'

Bruno was sure of it now. Her voice seemed to be coming from a long distance away. He wasn't sure that he could speak.

'I got pregnant and I didn't tell you.' He heard her open the car door and felt her place Balzac gently on his lap but he couldn't turn his head to look at her. 'I had the abortion and never told you. I think I knew that you'd talk me out of it, or you'd try, and that was a conversation I couldn't face.'

Her hand touched his cheek and he felt the vehicle shift as her weight left it. 'I know what this means to you. I'm sorry, Bruno.'

He sat immobile, stunned, barely registering the way she limped to her car without looking back, unlocked it, climbed stiffly in and drove away. It was Balzac who brought him back to reality, clambering up the steering wheel to get close enough to lick Bruno's chin before tumbling back onto his lap.

24

'Why did you race off like that? I said I was sorry, that I knew it wasn't your fault. Pamela told me all about it.' Fabiola was breathing hard as she brought her mare to a halt beside Bruno.

'It's nothing to do with you. It's me,' he replied. 'I had a bit of a shock today so I felt a need to clear my head with a gallop. I'm the one who should apologize.'

'What shock? Pamela's fine, as good as new.'

'It's not that. Forget it.'

Even during the ride, Hector racing beneath him faster than they had ever gone together, the finality of Isabelle's revelation still stunned him. There had been a new life and now there was not. It was not just the wind of his reckless ride that was blurring Bruno's eyes. It would have been kinder of Isabelle never to have told him, but that was not her way.

Fabiola eyed him curiously. 'So if it's not me you're angry with, let's not take it out on the horses. Can we go back more slowly? Victoria's too old for a ride like that and I don't think Balzac enjoyed it.'

Bruno looked down to where the puppy was huddled up as deep inside the binoculars case as he could go, staring up at Bruno with wide eyes. He was being selfish, Bruno chided himself, and foolish to think that he could escape dealing with this by pushing his horse and his own horsemanship to their limit. He turned Hector and began to walk him back along the forest ride, Fabiola falling in alongside but too wise to speak. He knew that some unpleasant nights lay ahead of him, failing to sleep or waking in the small hours and thinking of the way Isabelle had looked at the extra rooms he had built into his house and what the sight and reality of them would have done to her.

But that was for the future. He had a job to do, a murderer to hunt down, a suspicion to pursue and friends like Fabiola to whom he owed more than this surly silence. At that moment, duty itself vibrated for his attention from the phone at his belt. He answered and heard J-J's voice.

'We found the stolen camper van, or at least the plates. Some Dutch tourist realized his own van had suddenly grown French plates, the ones we were looking for. It looks like Paul put the Dutch plates on his own van.'

'Where was this?'

'A campsite just outside Hendaye, down by the border. It looks like he got over into Spain. Or that's what he wants us to think. Still, we've got the Spanish police alerted.'

'Have you got anywhere with those wills yet?'

'We have the one with the *notaire* in Ussel. It's boilerplate. All his French property goes to his nearest family, which means his brother and sister. He cites the Corrèze farm and a bank account. We're still waiting for the British will. And we're having trouble with Fullerton's computer. A lot of stuff had been deleted and the files written over, so it's not so straightforward to dig stuff out from the hard drive. We'll have to send it to the specialists in Paris and that costs a fortune. This job's breaking my budget as it is. And we heard back from the phone trackers. Valentoux's story about that disposable phone he bought holds up. It was switched on in Calais on the morning Fullerton was killed and the cellphone masts tracked it all the way down to St Denis. It looks like it was with him all the time and it hasn't been switched on since.'

'Murcoing could have taken it and used a different SIM card,' said Bruno. 'What about this guy in Bordeaux, Edouard? I asked the *juge* if I could go and interview him but he said he wanted the art squad brought in. Have they been in touch with you?'

'Yes, two of their guys are going through Fullerton's photos and the Arch-Inter customs forms; that also goes on my budget. There won't be anything left for my salary at this rate.'

Bruno rang off and turned to Fabiola. 'Do you have plans for dinner or shall I make us an omelette?'

'I've got plans, I'm afraid, but thanks.' She coloured a little and changed the subject. 'Whatever it is that's on your mind, you know I'll help if I can.'

'I know. Maybe we can talk later. If you're in a rush, I can rub the horses down.' He carefully didn't ask where she was going.

She looked at her watch. 'Thanks, that would help.' As soon as they reached the stables, she darted into Pamela's house, taking off her riding jacket as she ran.

That gave Bruno time to do something that had been on his mind. Once the horses were settled and fed, he climbed into his Land Rover and took the road to the farther end of the commune, to the holiday rental cottage he remembered from his first year as the policeman of St Denis. He knew his district so well by now that he could have found it blindfold, and rather than let his thoughts dwell on Isabelle's decision, he turned on Radio Périgord for the news, none of which concerned him, except for the final item.

'Police are still searching for Paul Murcoing, said to be the chief suspect in the St Denis murder case of Englishman Francis Fullerton. *Juge d'instruction* Bernard Ardouin refused to comment on reports that Murcoing was believed to have fled to Spain. And finally, who was Paul Revere, and why is his coffee pot said to be worth as much as a hundred thousand euros? Coming up next, on Radio . . .'

Bruno switched off as the *gîte* came into view, looking a great deal more battered by time than when he had last seen it. The roof was no longer new but the tiles had weathered to the soft red that typified the region, and the gravel of the drive and forecourt had turned grey. One gable end was now green with ivy and some badly pruned roses straggled around the door. A Volvo with Dutch licence plates was parked at the side of the place and a child's bike lay on its side on the bumpy lawn. Ten years, no eleven, and hundreds of holidaymakers must have lived and eaten and swum and sunbathed here since his last visit, overlaying his own grim memories of the place when he had walked to the rear and seen blood on the tiles and those wisps of blood, hanging like red smoke in the water.

Balzac had clambered forward from the back of the Land Rover and over the handbrake to sit in the passenger footwell. Bruno scooped him up and put him in his lap. Maybe at last he was on the way to finding some resolution of that case that had haunted him and kept him awake in the early hours, thinking how he could have handled it differently.

Ironic, therefore, that his future nights would be troubled

by the far more personal anguish at what Isabelle had done. He would try to understand it from Isabelle's point of view as well as his own. He would argue to himself that it was Isabelle's life, her body, her future, and that she alone was entitled to make the decision. The baby that had been aborted was the promise of new life, but for Isabelle it must have seemed like an almost mortal threat to the life she had planned for herself.

But could she not have had the child and given it to him to raise? He'd have found nurses, babysitters, taken it to the crèche and the infants' school, taught it to fish and to cook, to know the woods and the ways of dogs and horses. Why had she never even given him the chance to make that suggestion? Did not a father have rights over the future, over the life and death of his child? Isabelle understood this; it was why she herself had admitted that what she had done was unforgivable.

No, he understood that Isabelle must have thought this through. She would be aware of the physical changes that would come as the pregnancy progressed. And she would understand the impact on her psyche as the hormonal shifts brought forth the maternal instincts that would wrench at her whole being when it came to part with her child. Even if she gave the child to Bruno and returned to Paris or to Holland to resume her career, there would have been the guilt as her child grew up without her. She must have looked ahead to desperate Christmases and birthdays, brief reunions and heart-rending farewells, and decided against that course. Unlike him, she was trapped by the iron laws of biology.

He was suddenly aware that tears were running down his face and onto Balzac and that a man had come out of the *gîte* ahead and was staring curiously at him. He put on his cap and climbed out of the vehicle so that the tourist could see his uniform, and waved.

'*Tout va bien?*' he called. 'All OK?'

The Dutchman nodded and waved back. Bruno returned to his seat, noticed that the engine was still running, turned his car and drove away, heading automatically to St Denis but not sure if he was in any mood to go home and spend the evening alone.

He was saved by a phone call. He glanced at the screen and saw it was Florence calling, so he pulled in to the side of the road to answer.

'Bruno, I'm with Monsieur Crimson and he wants to invite us both to dinner if you are free. I have a babysitter. Here, he wants to talk to you.'

'Bruno,' came the familiar cheery voice. 'I just got a call from the Vieux Logis, they have a cancellation and can do me a table for three in an hour. Can you join us? I want the three of us to put our heads together over an idea I've had.'

'That's very kind of you and I'll see you there in an hour,' Bruno said. 'I just need to go home and change and look after the dog then I'll head straight for Trémolat.'

'Bring your puppy. The waiters will love spoiling him. See you there.'

They sat in the garden, beneath the plane trees whose leaves seemed almost to be growing as Bruno watched, surging with the energy of a Périgord springtime that was about to burst into summer. Whether indoors in winter or outside as the warmth came, it was the restaurant that Bruno would choose if it were to be the last meal of his life. He could only afford to dine here rarely, but always ordered the same *menu du marché*; whatever the chef had managed to acquire that day and assemble into a wonderfully balanced meal.

There were always little *amuse-bouches* to begin, baby pizzas the size of eggcups or a morsel of *boudin noir* stuffed into a fig or something equally inventive. Then the meal took its usual course, a *crème brûlée* of foie gras or a chilled soup, and then some confection of fish, sometimes a ceviche of raw fish cooked in the acid of some exotic fruit rather than the usual lime juice. The meat could be rabbit or a small noix of lamb, veal or venison, whatever the chef had to hand, but always with perfectly cooked vegetables. That was the difference between his own efforts and the meal of a professional chef, Bruno thought, the blending and balance of dishes and the arrival of each component at just the right moment.

This evening's pleasure was enhanced by the sight of Florence, seated between himself and Crimson, in a simply cut linen dress of pale blue which brought out the colour in her grey eyes. Her hair, which had been lifeless and dry when he had first met her at the truffle market in Ste Alvère, now shone with life and had been shaped to bring out her fine bones and slim neck. She looked around the gardens and eyed the ordered shapes of the topiary, the obelisks and spheres, with cool interest rather than open curiosity, as if she were accustomed to dine at a place such as this.

'This dinner seems small thanks for your efforts in recovering my rugs and paintings, Bruno, and for your remarkable skills with a computer, Florence,' said Crimson. 'I wish you'd been on the team in my old job. Take a look at this document she cooked up, Bruno. That should smoke our quarry out.'

He pushed an iPad across the table, and on its screen was what looked like a photocopy of an aged document from some official archive. It looked genuine down to the ancient typescript, the utilitarian grey of the official paper and the marks of little holes where papers had been pinned together. It looked like the contents page of a file, and Bruno recognized some of the words and acronyms – Neuvic, Valmy, FFI, FTP. Other names were new to him, and some words, DIGGER and ARCHER and WHEELWRIGHT, were in capital letters. He asked Crimson to explain.

'The names are simple enough,' Crimson replied. 'Maurice Buckmaster was the head of SOE's section F, which ran operations in France, and Gubbins was the Major-General in overall charge. The document refers to Buckmaster's report to his boss on the Neuvic train, which makes it look as though London was much more involved in the whole business. The words in capital letters are the names of operational networks. DIGGER was one of the SOE networks active around here in 1944, run by a Frenchman called Jacques Poirier who joined the British army and was known as Captain Jack. He became friendly with Malraux and that document is supposed to be Poirier's account of what happened to the money. You know the other acronyms, *Francs-Tireurs et Partisans* and so on?'

'They look very convincing. Well done, Florence,' Bruno said, nodding that he understood the terms. 'But do these documents exist?'

Crimson pursed his lips. 'Some of them do, like the reports from Buckmaster and Poirier, but they haven't been declassified yet. I know roughly what's in them and there's no smoking gun, as our American friends say. It's fairly routine stuff, reporting rumours about the Neuvic money and saying there's no confirmation. The fact is, we didn't really want to know. What we've concocted here is just the contents page, but that should be enough to smoke Murcoing out. And Florence also cooked up a new email to Fullerton, with a copy to Murcoing, claiming to come from the Public Records Office as a notice that new files which Fullerton had requested have now been declassified. She copied their official format and it all looks very persuasive.'

'So it does, but now that we have the bait how do you propose to draw Murcoing out into the open if he bites?'

Crimson ran his fingers over his iPad and another document appeared that looked like an email. It was in serviceable French, but obviously written by a foreigner.

'I set up a new email account with a fake name, and emailed Murcoing,' Florence said, evidently proud of her work. There was a slight flush to her cheeks as if she were excited by her unexpected role in the venture.

Bruno quickly read the email, which purported to come from a professional researcher in London who claimed to have done regular archive work for Fullerton at the Public Records Office. It said he'd been sorry to see news of Fullerton's death in the British press, but Fullerton had earlier given him Murcoing's address and the researcher wanted to know if Murcoing was still interested in the documents. Murcoing should know that much of the contents of the supposedly declassified files had been blacked out but the researcher had personal contacts who had given him the uncensored version. He was coming to France and would be happy to arrange a meeting, if Murcoing was able to pay the sum agreed with Fullerton.

'We attached the faked contents page to the email,' Crimson explained. 'I'm rather proud of that last document, the one dated 1946 that claims to come from the British Embassy in Paris reporting a meeting with American and French government officials on the Neuvic affair.'

As two black-clad waiters approached the table bearing plates, Crimson ran his fingers over his device and the documents disappeared. He slipped the iPad into a briefcase that rested against his chair. The sommelier arrived and refilled their glasses with the champagne Crimson had ordered, a Celebris from Gosset, one of the oldest of the champagne houses. Bruno had heard of it but never tasted it before. With just a faint hint of sweetness, it went perfectly with the scallops in *beurre blanc*.

'So now we wait for Murcoing to log on to his emails and then to contact you at your fake email address,' Bruno said. 'And then you arrange a meeting. What do you suggest should happen then?'

'I assume we can arrange the meeting at a place where you can organize a police ambush.'

'We know he's armed and dangerous and he's already killed once. I don't think you should be anywhere near the meeting place,' Bruno replied firmly.

'I hope you're not planning to be involved yourself, Bruno,' Florence said. 'This is a job for a specialist police unit.'

'Of course, you're right,' Bruno said. 'What worries me is that we may be underestimating Murcoing. He's no fool, and he must be suspicious of something like this falling so conveniently into his lap. I'm not sure he'll just come waltzing to some prearranged meeting spot. If he takes the bait he'll try to set up a meeting at a place he can control and he'll certainly check it out beforehand for any sign of an ambush. That's what I'd do. Still, we may be lucky. Filial piety may bring him to his grandfather's funeral tomorrow, which would save us all a great deal of trouble.'

The sommelier brought the decanter with the red wine Crimson had ordered, laying the cork beside it so Bruno could make out the stamped capital letters that spelled out Château Haut-Brion.

'*Le quatre-vingts-quatorze, Monsieur,*' murmured the sommelier, a man who had learned his art in the old school. Instead of pouring some wine for the customer to taste, he poured a tiny sip for himself and then sniffed and tasted it to pronounce it good before half-filling the three glasses.

The ninety-four, thought Bruno, a wine made when he'd been dodging mortar bombs in Sarajevo, when Paul Murcoing had been a young teenager and Francis Fullerton had been attending funerals in New York of friends who had died of AIDS. Crimson had been doing whatever the interests of the British crown required and Florence had been at school amid the dying coalfields of northern France.

Bruno's eye was caught by a movement at the far side of the garden, where two diners had been hidden by the trees, and he was only a little surprised to see Gilles offering his arm to help Fabiola rise from her seat. The couple then strolled hand in hand from the garden and out into the night. Well, well, he thought, sniffing again at the wine and thinking that if Fabiola had been at school when it was made, Gilles had been darting across Sniper's Alley in that same wretched Bosnian siege that he had known. Curious, the strength of the bond that such a shared experience could forge, and it left him confident that his dear friend Fabiola was in good hands.

25

Bruno was always proud of his town, but he felt an extra glow as he stood at the big wooden doors of St Denis's church greeting the steady flow of mourners arriving for Murcoing's funeral. Some he had expected, like his friend the Baron wearing his medals from the Algerian war, and Joe, Bruno's predecessor as the town policeman. Joe wore in his lapel the small red rosette of the *Légion d'Honneur*, awarded for his boyhood exploits as a Resistance courier. Then came those inhabitants of the retirement home who could still walk; they always enjoyed a good funeral, if only to remind themselves their turn had not yet come. What Bruno had not expected was the turnout of youngsters. He assumed at first it was because of Florence, their favourite teacher, in the choir. Then he saw Rollo the headmaster bringing up the rear.

'I thought it made a good teaching moment,' Rollo said, shaking hands. He spoke over the slow, sad tolling of the church bell. 'We held a special lesson this morning on the history of the local Resistance for the senior classes and then asked if any of them wanted to join me at the funeral. I'm proud of them, not one stayed behind.'

Crimson murmured: 'No reply from Murcoing yet,' as he arrived with Brian Fullerton, followed by Monsieur Simpson, the retired English schoolteacher who had been called up in the closing weeks of the Second World War and thus counted as comrade-in-arms of the dead man. He was flanked by the only two other citizens of St Denis who could claim the honour, Jean-Pierre and Bachelot, one a veteran of the Gaullist Resistance and the other who had fought for the Communist FTP. After a lifetime of enmity which had made their families the Montagues and Capulets of St Denis, they had finally in old age and retirement become friends.

Jacqueline arrived discreetly alone, rather than coming with the Mayor, who stood beside Bruno at the door to greet the mourners. Since he was to give the eulogy, the Mayor was wearing his sash of office and accepted with quiet dignity the murmured condolences on the death of Cécile. 'Friday,' he kept saying, again and again, as the old folk asked when her funeral would be.

Joséphine and her sisters were already installed in the front row, Gilles sitting behind them, his notebook open to scribble details. Plain-clothes police were scattered throughout the congregation. More police were in the nearby cafés and J-J himself stood just inside the door of the *Maison de la Presse*, pretending to study the magazines. But of Paul and his sister there was no sign.

From respect, Bruno was wearing the medal of the Croix de Guerre he had won in Bosnia, which he normally kept in a drawer at his home. He was in full-dress uniform, freshly pressed, and his boots and leather belt polished that morning. Philippe Delaron was taking photographs of the honour guard; eight soldiers and a junior officer from the garrison at Agen stood at ease in the churchyard. The officer looked at his watch.

The Mayor looked at Bruno, who glanced across to J-J in the shadows of the shop and shrugged. It was time.

'*Escadron, garde à vous*,' the officer called. The troops came to attention and marched in pairs into the church, down the nave and as Bruno and the Mayor followed them, took their places at each side of the coffin. The futuristic shape of their FAMAS rifles looked oddly out of place amid the ancient stones. Murcoing lay in state before the altar, on which stood giant photographs of the young fighter he had been. The coffin was closed and on its lid rested his Resistance medal.

The tolling bell had fallen silent and from his place before the choir, a schoolboy began to beat the slow, steady rhythm of a march on his drum. The choir began quietly and then with slowly increasing force to hum the familiar chords of the Resistance anthem, *le Chant des Partisans*. And then Florence's pure soprano rang out high and clear throughout the church.

'*Ami, entends-tu le vol noir des corbeaux sur nos plaines?*' Friend, do you hear the dark flight of the crows across our land?

Just a handful of words, a tune and some phrases made heavy by the weight of history. Yet as Bruno shifted his eyes from Florence to the coffin and the photographs of the young fighter behind it, he felt the tears begin to gather. He was not alone.

He saw the eyes of the young officer glisten and Father Sentout weeping openly as Florence reached the line: '*Ce soir l'ennemi connaîtra le prix du sang et des larmes.*' Tonight the enemy will learn the price of blood and tears.

'Bring the guns from the haystacks, careful with the dynamite.' Behind him he heard the quavering voices of the old people take up the words and then the full choir joined in with, '*Si tu tombes, un ami sort de l'ombre à ta place.*' If you fall, a friend will come from the shadows to take your place.

It had all happened a lifetime ago, a generation before he had been born, and Bruno wondered why it moved him so. He suspected it was less the words and the music than the images they summoned in his head: jackboots marching through the Arc de Triomphe, De Gaulle speaking from London to pledge that France would fight on, General Leclerc's Free French troops racing into Paris as young men like Loïc Murcoing fought against tanks with a handful of weapons in their own streets and villages. He thought of Joe, recounting how as a boy he'd watched as the collaborators of St Denis had been lined up on the bridge Bruno knew so well and shot so that their bodies crumpled into the timeless flow of the river below.

But as Father Sentout began the Mass there was something else that stirred Bruno deeply, beyond these wartime pictures flickering in his mind. It was the presence around him of the folk of St Denis, young and old, conservatives and communists, men who had worn uniform and women who had kissed them farewell and waited for their return. It was this gathering to commemorate and to remember, to pay tribute to one of the last of the old men who had gone to the hills to take up arms against the invader, knowing that death would be the price of defeat. It was fitting, Bruno believed, that the young people were here, to understand what it had meant to France to be vanquished and occupied by foreign troops who did not bother to hide their contempt for the conquered. And it was right for those youngsters to know that in a nation like France, no defeat was ever final, no fate was ever foreordained, that even amid the ruins and corpses of defeat, rebirth and recovery and renewal could always come.

The Mass ended and the Mayor came forward to stand by the coffin, his head bowed in homage before he turned to address the crowded church.

'*Françaises et français*,' the mayor began. 'Dear friends and citizens of St Denis, we are here to pay honour to a brave son of France and to the cause of freedom for which he fought. Nothing I could say here would match the courage and sacrifice of thousands of our young men and women who stood for France in our bleakest hour, when that dark flight of the crows haunted our sweet land and the panzers rolled through our villages. We thank them for what they have taught us about this France that we love. We stand in awe of their courage and we extend our sympathies to their families for their loss. And we give thanks to the Lord, in this church where our ancestors have prayed for a thousand years, that Loïc Murcoing was able to live the rest of his life in pride and dignity in this valley that he had helped to free. And we pray that our sons and daughters will never again have to bear such burdens. *Vive la France, vive la République*.'

While the soldiers presented arms and the choir burst into the *Marseillaise*, Bruno joined in the words as he reflected that his Mayor had a rare gift among politicians, never to speak too long. Along with the Mayor, Jacquot, Joe, the Baron and Montsouris, Bruno took his place beside the coffin, and as the anthem came to its end he gave a quiet word of command and they lifted it onto their shoulders. The officer ordered his men to port arms, and stooping a little under the burden the coffin-bearers followed Father Sentout and the file of troops down the nave and out through the churchyard to the cemetery.

'Now,' said Bruno and the six men began to pay out the ropes and the coffin sank slowly as the first shots of the salute rang out. As the echo of the third and final volley died away, Loïc Murcoing rested on the soil for which he had fought. One by one, his relatives and neighbours came up to pick more of that soil from the heap by the grave and toss it onto the coffin lid. By the time they had all done, and each of those present had dropped a handful of earth, the coffin was no more to be seen.

Bruno looked up to scan the wooded hill behind the cemetery, and then across beyond the church to the hedges that lined the winding road to the hamlet of St Félix. He felt certain that somewhere in that shadowy terrain Paul Murcoing was watching the interment of his grandfather. A cruel irony, thought Bruno, that Loïc Murcoing was being honoured for taking to the hills to fight the enemy, while his grandson was now hiding in those same hills to evade the justice of France.

In Paris, *Le Monde* was published as an evening newspaper, but it did not reach the provinces until the following morning. The Internet, however, had made it universally available as soon as the print edition was published, and Jacqueline was reading the text of her article on her smartphone, the Mayor peering over her shoulder to make out the words on the tiny screen. Around them in the council chamber of the *Mairie* the crowd lined up for glasses of wine and tiny sandwiches and canapés. The *vin d'honneur* the Mayor had arranged to follow Murcoing's funeral was in full swing.

'It's weird,' said Gilles, squeezing his way through to Bruno with two glasses of red wine and handing one to him. 'My teaser piece on the nuclear stuff ran on the website yesterday and got almost zero reaction. But this morning's article on the great train robbery has really started something. There was so much traffic that it crashed the website and everybody's trying to follow it up. My editor's ecstatic.'

'That's another dinner you owe me,' said Bruno.

'I know, but I've been working non-stop.'

'That's not what I hear. The word is that you were dining with a beautiful brunette at my favourite restaurant last night. Hand in hand, is what I heard.'

Gilles eyed Bruno. 'Do you know everything that goes on round here?'

Bruno grinned at him and clinked their glasses together. 'She's a fine woman and you're a lucky man. But watch yourself; if you trifle with her, you'll have me to deal with and you'll wish you were back in Sarajevo.'

'Trifling is not what I had in mind, Bruno, not with Fabiola. I'm serious about her, in fact I'm smitten.'

'She's a serious woman and she's also the best doctor we've ever had in this town, so don't even think about trying to lure her away. Meanwhile, tell me about the reaction to your Neuvic article.'

'A couple of deputies have called for a parliamentary inquiry, the Banque de France is under pressure to hold a press conference and the Socialists have issued a statement denying that they got any of the money.'

'Never believe anything until it's been officially denied,' Bruno said with a chuckle.

'But something else has come up you ought to know about. I've had an email from Paul Murcoing. It came through on my phone just now as I was coming into the *Mairie*, and there's a big document attached. Can we get out of this crowd and find a quiet place to read it?'

Bruno led the way back to his office, noting with approval that Gilles managed to pick up two full glasses as he ducked and darted through the thickening crowd. He turned on his own computer and gestured for Gilles to take the chair and use the big screen to read whatever Paul had sent.

It began with an email, sent to the electronic address listed for Gilles on the *Paris Match* website, congratulating him for 'bringing this scandal from the shadows of our history into the light of day'. But he'd only scratched the surface of the story, Paul went on, and the real truth had yet to emerge. Gilles clicked on the attachment to open the document.

'*J'accuse*,' read the title page, a cliché in French political journalism since Emile Zola had used it on the front page of *L'Aurore* to condemn the miscarriage of justice in the Dreyfus case.

'I accuse André Malraux of theft from the people of France . . . I accuse the British government of using their influence over the Resistance to manipulate French politics in their own interests . . . I accuse the government of the United States . . . I accuse De Gaulle . . . I accuse François Mitterrand . . .' And on and on it went, some of it taken wholesale from the rants he had posted on the Resistance history websites, some of it about his grandfather. And the attack on British intelligence contained a scan of the concocted document Bruno had seen on Crimson's iPad the previous evening.

'In the old days before the Internet,' said Gilles, 'this sort of stuff used to be written in green ink with lots of underlinings and capital letters and usually finished up claiming they were being bugged through the fillings in their teeth. Except this British document looks new. Is this for real?'

Bruno made a quick decision. You either trusted a man or you didn't. 'No, it's a fake,' he said. 'It was cooked up and sent to him to smoke him out. It looks like Paul's taking the bait.'

'*Putain*, this story gets better and better and *Paris Match* is at the heart of it. Dead Resistance hero, gay grandson on the run for murder, British spymaster faking documents to help French cops capture him, all this and a conspiracy theory around the great train robbery. And he's got his sister with him. You couldn't make it up.'

'Are you planning to use some of this?' Bruno asked, a little nervous at the prospect of a media circus.

'You bet I am. This is a manhunt story made for the Internet age – and I'm in touch with the target. I'll send out a tweet that he's reached me and then do something for the website, but first I have to call Paris and brief them.'

'Just don't say anything about the document being faked. And make me a couple of printouts of that rant of his while you're sitting there. I'd better find Crimson.'

He pulled J-J out of the party and took him onto the balcony outside the Mayor's office to brief him and give him one of the printouts.

'It was all your idea, J-J,' Bruno explained. 'You were the one who asked if we could set a trap for Murcoing. He didn't show for the funeral but he's biting at this. We need to find out where this computer is that he used to email Gilles, but I'm betting he's still in France and that camper van with the Dutch plates was just a ruse.'

'You haven't thought this through,' J-J replied, looking cross. 'So he gets in touch with Crimson. What then?'

'Then I go to whatever rendezvous he nominates and bring him in. I wear a tracker in my shoes so you know where I am. You can have cars and a helicopter on standby somewhere close in case we need reinforcements.'

'This is a job for the *Jaunes*, not for you. They're trained for this.'

'It has to be one man, someone who knows him.'

'You don't know him.'

'I know enough about him and his family to have a chance of talking him into giving himself up. With the *Jaunes* a shoot-out is just about guaranteed. Let's find Crimson and see if he's heard from Murcoing. He should be inside, fighting his way to the bar to get a drink.'

They found the Englishman squeezed into a corner by the window that overlooked the river Vézère, trying to rescue Florence from the admiring attentions of the young officer who had led the guard of honour. J-J used his bulk to clear some space around them, introduced himself to the officer and asked him to give them some privacy. With the sensitive antennae of a lifetime in politics, the Mayor realized that something important was happening and suddenly appeared alongside Bruno just as he was explaining that Murcoing had swallowed the bait.

'We won't know if he's contacted us until we can get to a computer and check that email address I set up,' Florence said. 'I've got my laptop in my bag.'

The Mayor led the way to his own spacious office, which to Bruno's knowledge had never yet been polluted by the presence of a computer. Florence sat down at his desk and fired up her machine.

'Don't you need a plug or something?' the Mayor asked.

Florence gave him a maternal look and shook her head before turning back to open the emails. 'He's sent something. He wants a phone number to reach you,' she told Crimson.

'We'd better buy you a disposable,' Bruno said. 'He's going to be expecting to hear an Englishman and someone who knows what he's talking about.'

'Can you find out where he sent the email from?' J-J asked.

'Not discreetly and we don't want him to know we're looking. But you should have experts with the equipment to track it.'

'The first thing I have to do now is call the *juge d'instruction* and tell him what's happening,' said J-J. 'He's in charge of this inquiry.'

'But it isn't just an inquiry any more. It's a manhunt,' said Bruno. 'And we have some time. When Crimson answers that email and gives Murcoing the phone number, we have to say that he's just arrived in France, let's say in Paris, coming in from London on the Eurostar train. It will take him some time to get down here so there'll be no meeting until tomorrow. And Murcoing will need time to arrange the right place for a rendezvous.'

Crimson let out a short, excited laugh. 'I'm almost beginning to enjoy this.'

26

'The English are mad,' said J-J as his aide Josette powered the big Peugeot up the road to the autoroute that led to Bordeaux. 'Did you hear him? Saying he was enjoying himself. We won't even be there in time for lunch.'

Bruno had persuaded J-J to make a last appeal to the *juge d'instruction* on the need to interview Edouard Marty, even though the art squad had reported they could find nothing questionable in his accounts. Bruno was convinced that Edouard must know something more than the bland statement he'd given to the art squad. Yes, he was a director of the company that Francis Fullerton had founded, he had claimed, but he was a very minor shareholder and he was concerned solely with the interior design side of the company and specialized in modern and minimalist design. He had nothing to do with the antiques. And his work for Arch-Inter was simply a sideline to his own architecture practice and his teaching at the university.

But that left out the connection from a decade ago, when Paul Murcoing and Edouard Marty had been the boys at the swimming pool. The link between Fullerton, Paul and Edouard had to be important. An old friend from his youth, with whom he remained connected in Fullerton's crooked business, was someone to whom a man on the run could turn for help or money or transport.

'How do you want to handle the questioning?' Bruno asked. He knew from experience that J-J was a relentless interrogator, and while his sheer bulk could intimidate most suspects he also had a subtle sense of the psychology and timing of the art of questioning. 'Shall we do it the usual way, you play the tough guy and I'm the understanding one, or what?'

'Probably,' grunted J-J. He was flicking through a file of spreadsheets. 'If this goes on much longer it's going to eat up ten per cent of my investigation budget for the year. And with the new cuts there's no reserve fund. Christ, look at the overtime for the plain-clothes guys at the funeral, a complete waste of money.'

This was no time to say 'I told you so,' thought Bruno. Instead, he reminded J-J how many burglaries had been cleared up from the haul at the Corrèze farm. And he was dubious about Edouard's protestations of innocence over the antiques trade. The website of the showroom in California had shown a lot of antiques and Edouard's office seemed to be the place that organized the shipping. The art squad concentrated on the high-cost items like old master paintings, Impressionists and the treasures that would win them headlines, rather than the bulk trade of moderately priced antiques and lesser paintings that had been Fullerton's speciality.

'How are things between you and Isabelle?' J-J asked, closing his file and thrusting it into the overstuffed briefcase at his feet.

'Over,' said Bruno.

'That's what you always say, but she keeps coming back.'

'Not any more. She's moving to Holland to join Eurojust, has her interview Friday but it sounds like a formality.'

'*Putain*, and I've just about persuaded the Prefect to let her take my job when I retire. I was hoping to get her down here before the election and all the backstabbing starts at her Ministry. You've heard the rumours about that?'

'No, but I know what I've read in the papers. And who knows how the election will turn out? If this lot get re-elected, there'll be no change.'

'That's where you're wrong. Even his own party is just looking for an excuse to get rid of this minister of the interior. He's a liability. And this new super-agency he's set up is a menace. That's why I want Isabelle out of it before the shit hits the fan.'

Bruno seldom talked national politics, partly because his interest was limited and partly because he reckoned there wasn't that much difference between the parties. He remembered some graffiti he'd seen: 'It doesn't matter who you vote for, the government always gets in.' But he'd rather talk politics than talk about Isabelle. The wound was still fresh.

'What worries me is that every time I raise it with her, she says she doesn't want to come back here,' J-J went on.

'I think she means it,' Bruno said, when it was plain that J-J was waiting for him to respond.

'She's under a lot of strain,' said Josette from the driver's seat. It was the first time she had spoken. 'She was crying in the ladies' room the other day. It's not like her at all.'

Bruno felt her cast an accusing glance at him in the rear-view mirror. He turned his eyes away to look at the countryside flashing by the autoroute. Josette had put the magnetized blue light on the roof and they were doing a hundred and eighty. At this speed, they'd be in Bordeaux in less than an hour.

When they reached the Pont d'Aquitaine, the great bridge over the river, J-J made a courtesy call to his *Police Nationale* counterpart in the Gironde *département* to explain his presence in the city. The *juge d'instruction* had already telephoned, J-J was told, and if any assistance was required Bordeaux would be happy to help. Josette's satnav system directed them to the plush suburb of Caudéran, and then to the most exclusive area of all where the gardens backed onto the Parc Bordelais. Bruno and J-J exchanged glances and J-J rubbed a finger and thumb together to signify the price of such a property as the Peugeot pulled up in the driveway of the distinctly grand *maison de maître* where Edouard lived and kept his showroom.

'Very tax-efficient, home and showroom in one,' grumbled J-J. 'I dislike the little *pédé* already.'

'Stop it, J-J,' chided Josette. 'You aren't allowed to say that kind of thing anymore, not even you. You know I'm supposed to report it.'

'See what I have to put up with?' J-J sighed, and hauled himself out of the car and up the wide steps to the double doors. A discreet brass plaque on one of the columns that flanked the doors read Arch-Inter.

'Commissaire Jalipeau and Chief of Police Courrèges to see Monsieur Marty,' he announced, loud enough for the echoes to reverberate throughout the house, to the elegant young woman in black silk who answered the doorbell. Behind her, the hallway was uniformly white, the stairs, the tiles, the walls and woodwork and the single tall-backed wooden chair that was the only furniture.

'Do you have an appointment?' she asked, coldly.

'Do you want an appointment with the inside of a jail cell, Mademoiselle?'

'It's alright, Clarisse,' came a voice from the upper landing, and Edouard appeared. 'May I help you, gentlemen?'

'Where do you want to start being questioned, here or in my police HQ? Since I suspect you'll end up in custody, it might save time if we went straight there.'

'Let me see if I can help you here,' Edouard replied calmly, descending the staircase as if making an entrance. He was wearing a black suit over a T-shirt so white that it gleamed. 'I thought this had all been settled with your colleagues from the art squad.'

'They're not colleagues. They're specialists who sip tea and make polite small-talk about Monet and Manet and money. I deal in murder and violence and that's what I want to question you about.'

Edouard led them into a large room, opposite the one to which Clarisse returned. It was again all in white except for a strikingly red chaise longue with chrome legs at one side of the fireplace and two very modern chrome and black leather chairs facing it. A block of polished steel sat between them to serve as a table and inside the large fireplace stood an African carving of a woman with row upon row of breasts descending the length of her torso. Above it hung a bizarre and multi-coloured modern tapestry of jazzy abstract shapes from which hung festoons of blue and yellow fabric.

'Where is your old boyfriend Paul Murcoing?' J-J began.

'I have no idea. I haven't seen him for several weeks.'

'Where were you last Tuesday afternoon and evening?' J-J was referring to the time of Fullerton's murder.

'I think I was out of town with clients. It will be in my diary.'

'Have you communicated with Paul in the last week in any way?'

Edouard paused and examined his fingernails. 'A couple of phone calls, perhaps, and some emails, all to do with business.'

'You'll have no objection to our going through your phone bills and emails?' J-J's aggressive delivery made it clear this was no question.

'Perhaps I'd better discuss that with my lawyer.'

'Discuss all you want, I've got an order from the *juge*.' J-J waved the document he'd collected from Bernard Ardouin and turned to Bruno. 'Call Josette in and tell her to get that computer from the secretary and have a look around for any more. Also she's to bring down any mobile phones she finds.'

'Don't I know you?' asked Edouard, studying Bruno.

'The last time we met you were naked and your friends' fathers had been beating the hell out of you. That was at the holiday home where you and Paul Murcoing and Francis Fullerton were first together.'

Edouard nodded. 'I remember. You pestered my parents and my school friends until you got bored and gave up.'

'You're wrong,' J-J said. 'He never gives up. That's why he's here. But compared with me, he's a pussy-cat. Now, about your little playmate Paul . . .'

Bruno went outside to call in Josette from the car. She was scanning a list of numbers on the screen of her phone when Bruno passed on J-J's instructions. She handed him the phone.

'I just downloaded his phone records from France Télécom. There's a lot of calls in the last week from a number that looks like a disposable phone and some more from public call boxes, paid for with one of those cards you can buy. J-J will recognize them if you give it to him.'

She slipped on a pair of evidence gloves and went into the house and into Clarisse's room. Bruno heard angry female voices as he handed J-J the phone.

'You get a lot of calls from public phone boxes, do you?' J-J inquired. 'No, only in the last few days. I wonder who that could have been. Wouldn't have been the man we're hunting for murder, would it?'

'I don't know where Paul was calling from, but yes, he has called several times in recent days.'

'What about?'

'Business, the legal position of the company after the death of Monsieur Fullerton, that sort of thing.'

'Did you discuss anything else?'

'No.'

'Did you know that we had put out public statements in the press and on TV saying we wanted urgently to interview him?'

Edouard paused and then nodded his head.

'And you want to tell me that that important little detail never came up in your business chats?'

'I told him that he should go to a police station and offer to help you all he could. I cannot believe he's a murderer, least of all that he killed Francis. They were very close.'

'So you knew how to get in touch with him but decided against doing your duty as a law-abiding citizen and informing the police. You're in big trouble, Edouard.'

'I didn't know where he was. He said he was moving around.'

'I'm getting bored with this,' J-J said, turning to Bruno. 'Let's take him back to the station, charge him with obstruction of justice, conspiracy. We'll get around to the murder later. Get the handcuffs from the car and let the press office know we can offer everybody a nice picture of Edouard here being led out of his fancy house in chains.'

'No need to rush things,' Bruno said, and turned to Edouard, who was now looking alarmed. Bruno let the silence build as J-J thumbed through the phone records.

'What did Paul use for money?' Bruno finally asked. 'Did you give him any?'

'No, I didn't see him so I gave him nothing. I don't know what Paul did for money.' Edouard was sweating and his immaculate T-shirt was starting to look rumpled at the neck.

Bruno knew the signs. Soon there would be a little act of resistance, a token defiance to retain some shred of self-respect. Then Edouard would break and start to treat J-J as some father confessor whose approval he could win by telling everything he knew.

'What company records do you keep here?' Bruno went on.

'Your art squad colleagues went through all the records.' There it was, the moment of defiance. Now J-J would move in for the kill.

'No, they didn't,' said J-J. 'They didn't put a freeze on your bank accounts and company credit cards, which is what I'm about to do. I want all chequebooks, statements and credit cards. Does Paul have a company credit card?'

'Yes,' Edouard said, as if suddenly eager to help. 'I have the number on file, I can get it for you . . .'

Josette came thumping down from the stairs carrying an expensive-looking weekend bag. She put it on the steel cube and began to pull out phones, an iPad and laptop. Edouard put a hand to his mouth and stared in disbelief at this lawful rifling of his life, as if finally understanding the sweeping investigative powers of the police backed with a signed order from a *juge d'instruction*.

'This one's a disposable,' Josette said, holding up a cheap handset. 'It was by the bed. Its memory goes back as far as the day after the murder and all the calls in and out are with the same number, that other disposable on the list. I bet it's Murcoing's.'

'*Putain*, you really are in trouble,' said J-J. He pulled a notepad from his briefcase and began copying down the times and dates of the various phone calls. 'You've been in touch with him never less than twice a day. So where is Murcoing now?'

'I don't know, he never tells me. I really tried to persuade him to give himself up. He gets this way sometimes, single-minded, determined . . .' Edouard's shoulders heaved as if he were about to be sick, but instead he gave a sound that was half-cough and half-sob.

'Has he been here, to this house?'

'Not lately, not since this all this began.' Edouard was wiping a handkerchief at his mouth, his brow, his neck.

'Do you know how much money he's pulled out on the company's English credit card?' Bruno asked. 'We know about that.'

Edouard swallowed and nodded. 'I checked online this morning, it's just over three thousand euros.'

'Maybe we won't freeze it just yet,' said J-J. 'If he tries to get more out and finds it's frozen, he'll suspect we've got Edouard. We'll keep the phone line going as well, so long as Edouard can only answer in our presence and we tell him what to say.'

He told Josette to set up a tracing system on the phone, then asked Edouard for the code required to open his iPad. Edouard shook his head and remained silent.

J-J sighed and pulled out the *attestation* from the *juge d'instruction* and handed it to him. 'See that, where it says electronic records? You've got no choice, Edouard. The law says so.'

When Edouard stayed silent, J-J shrugged and said: 'Give me your ID card.'

Edouard took out his wallet and handed it across. J-J put it beside the iPad and said conversationally: 'Over seventy per cent of people use four-digit codes for their PIN numbers that are taken from their birth date. Let's try that.'

He tapped four numbers but nothing happened. He tried another combination and the screen opened. Edouard stared at him as if witnessing some magical trick and then shook his head. He looked at J-J scrolling through various icons on the screen and seemed to reach a decision. Another little act of defiance, thought Bruno, another confession now due to come.

'He said he keeps his phone turned off except that he calls me every day at eight in the morning and eight in the evening,' Edouard burst out. 'You can see that from the dialling logs.'

'And do you have any little code between friends to say that all is well and the stupid police haven't yet caught on?' J-J asked.

Edouard began to babble, as if he could not wait to tell them everything that he knew or suspected. But Bruno noted that everything he said was about Paul, not a word about himself, about Arch-Inter or even about Francis Fullerton. Maybe Edouard was made of sterner stuff, after all, giving up whatever he thought the police wanted to know. But perhaps there were other secrets still unspoken and still protected behind this flood of confession. Maybe it was time to push Edouard a bit harder.

Bruno waited until Edouard stopped talking and then spoke thoughtfully, as though thinking aloud. 'Why don't we get the art squad back in here to have another crack at him? They'll be really angry that they missed all this so they'll drop the kid gloves this time. We've got enough to hold him so we might as well let them have some credit.'

'I think we can bring in more than just the art squad,' said J-J, swivelling the iPad so Bruno could see the images of naked boys on the screen. 'This looks like a different kind of art to me. I'm disappointed in you, Edouard, I didn't expect this. Tell me, Bruno, how old do you think these kids are? These two are under-age, I'll take my oath. Josette, who runs the paedophile squad in Bordeaux these days? Is it still that old brute Pontin?'

'It's still him, *chef*, the last I heard.' She rose and turned to look at the images. 'Definitely under-age, I'd say.'

'Inspector Pontin's a legend in this business,' J-J said conversationally, scrolling through more photos. 'You're going to have a very interesting time with him, Edouard. Oh dear, this little boy can't be more than thirteen. Old Pontin won't like these pictures at all. And you a professor at the university. Well, I think we can say your teaching career's over. And do you have any idea what happens to paedos in prison?'

Edouard had drawn up his legs and shrunk into a crouch on the chaise longue, his hands over his face.

'Last chance, Edouard,' said Bruno. 'Maybe there's some more help you can give us on finding Paul.'

27

Bruno had the Mayor's formal permission to be late for work so that he could collect Pamela from hospital. Even so, he was outside the Moulin bakery when it opened at seven. In his Land Rover was a thermos flask with fresh coffee, in the cooler a half-bottle of champagne and some fresh-squeezed orange juice, butter and his own home-made blackcurrant jam. He bought three croissants, three *pains au chocolat* and a baguette, all still hot from the oven, handed them to Fabiola in the passenger seat and drove to the Sarlat hospital to give Pamela a special breakfast before taking her home.

It had been the Mayor's idea. When Bruno had called him late the previous afternoon from Bordeaux to say he was driving back to Périgueux with J-J and Edouard, their prisoner, the Mayor insisted on driving to Périgueux to collect him. When Fabiola had called Bruno's mobile to say they could bring Pamela home the next day, the Mayor suggested Bruno should leave the town to police itself until Pamela was safely installed back in St Denis.

The Mayor had taken him to Jacqueline's for supper and found her on the phone, doing an interview with *France-Inter* on her article in *Le Monde*.

'Just before the two of you returned, I had a rather more

difficult call from Paris,' Jacqueline said when she put down the phone. 'It came from the minister of the interior, a deeply unpleasant man with whom I was foolish enough to have a fling some years ago. He asked if I was seeking to destroy his career.'

'I don't see the connection,' the Mayor said, looking startled and confused.

'Our affair was not exactly secret, although he was married at the time. I'd met some of his political colleagues at dinner parties and receptions, you know how it is in Paris. And of course when they saw my name on the piece in *Le Monde* they assumed that he was somehow behind it and began wondering at his motives. He must have had some rather angry phone calls as a result, and hence his call to me.'

'You must have seen that coming,' said the Mayor.

'Of course I did, which was an excellent reason for publishing the article. He was a charmer, of course, and very good-looking, but I found that I couldn't stand his utter pomposity, which is why I ended the liaison. His subsequent political career has plunged him even further down in my estimation. He was a bully in private and he's been a bully as minister. The man's a disgrace. I won't be at all embarrassed if this becomes public so long as it ends his political career.'

Bruno exchanged looks with his Mayor and felt himself grinning. 'You have been warned,' he said.

The Mayor looked fondly at Jacqueline and said: 'I'll take my chances.'

After the meal, the Mayor had driven Bruno back to St Denis, saying he had something to discuss.

'I don't sleep there, you know,' the Mayor said as they set

out. 'It wouldn't feel right, certainly until Cécile's funeral is over.'

'And perhaps the election,' Bruno replied, thinking of the impact on the voters of the Mayor embarking on an affair when his wife had just died.

'Perhaps. But when you get to my age, Bruno, and you find yourself fascinated by a woman and feeling like a youngster again, that's not something you can afford to ignore. I'd rather be with Jacqueline than get re-elected. To be in love again is like a gift.'

'It always is, at any age.' Bruno felt the Mayor take his eyes briefly from the road to glance at him as if about to speak, and was relieved when he didn't. He didn't want any conversation about Isabelle.

'I spoke to Monsieur Crimson today about this trap you are setting for young Murcoing,' the Mayor said after a silence. 'Are you planning on going yourself?'

'Yes, to try and talk him into giving himself up.'

'But you'll be armed?'

'No, I don't think so.'

'Are you mad? He's killed already and now he has these guns.'

'If he sees I'm armed, he'll be tempted to shoot. If he knows I'm unarmed, we have a chance to settle this peacefully. We are all assuming that Paul killed Fullerton in a *crime passionnel*, but from what I've learned about him, I'm not sure it's as simple as that.'

'But it's an insane risk to take, Bruno. I can't allow it.'

'You'd rather Crimson went instead?'

'No, of course not. Some hostage expert from the special Gendarme unit, that's who we need to send.'

'Yes, but to send him where? And with what instructions? To shoot him like a dog? That would be illegal. Paul's in charge of arranging a meeting place. He'll set this up carefully, probably insist that the documents he's been promised are placed in such a way that he can inspect them before he shows himself. I've thought this through and it's the only way.'

'What does J-J say?'

'He began by objecting, but he came to see that it makes sense to do it this way. I'm not convinced that Paul did it, or that he acted alone, or that he's so crazy that he's staying on the run with no plan to get out of France and make a new life somewhere.'

'You sound as though you know him.'

'I don't, but I know about his grandfather and his obsession with Neuvic. I've met his aunt, Joséphine, and I was the one who organized the funeral for the old man. He was close to his grandfather and he'll have heard about that. I wouldn't be at all surprised if he has given his aunt or his mum a disposable phone so they can stay in touch. A lot of planning has gone into this, which is why I think he must have an escape route planned. And then there's his painting.'

'What do you mean?' the Mayor asked, as he pulled into the parking lot behind the St Denis *Mairie* alongside Bruno's police van.

'I bought a couple of his paintings from his aunt. They're very good, landscapes. His portraits may be even better. There's a sensibility . . . I don't know how to put it but I find it hard to equate Paul the artist with the brutal way Fullerton was killed.'

'So how do you explain it?'

'I don't, I can't.'

The two men sat together in companionable silence, the engine still running. Finally the Mayor spoke.

'Give my regards to Pamela when you collect her from hospital. And take my tip, make an occasion of it. Take her some flowers. Maybe you should take her some croissants. The food at that hospital leaves a lot to be desired.'

'Thanks for the tip, and for the dinner and the ride,' said Bruno, climbing out of the car. 'I'll let you know how things develop. Sleep well.'

'What a wonderful breakfast,' Pamela exclaimed as Bruno placed the tray on her lap, poured her a glass of champagne mixed with orange juice and kissed her on the forehead. Somehow she'd managed to fix her hair and face and look fetching for their arrival. Fabiola held Balzac back from leaping onto the bed and allowed him to give Pamela a single token lick on the neck before putting him on the floor with his own chunk of baguette.

'It's a special occasion,' said Pamela. 'I think he deserves a corner of my croissant.'

'I'll fit you with a bandage we call a figure eight. It will keep your collarbone in place,' Fabiola said, passing the treat down to Balzac. 'You should still wear the sling most of the time because otherwise you'll try to do too much with that arm. I'll be there to help you dress until you get used to it.'

'Presumably that means I can help you undress,' said Bruno, pouring the coffee. He pondered making some light remark about Gilles, but thought better of it. He had no idea if or how their relationship had developed, and no doubt Fabiola would prefer to impart any news to Pamela herself.

'You'd better learn to restrain yourself,' Fabiola chided him. 'We want this collarbone to heal quickly.'

'The doctor here said it would be at least six weeks,' Pamela said. 'And longer before I can ride again.'

'He's right,' said Fabiola. 'I'd like you to wait three months.'

'But that's my peak season. If I can't look after the guests I'll lose my regular visitors.'

'We've taken care of that,' said Bruno. 'Florence has recruited two girls from her oldest class who'll come and clean the *gîtes* and your house and change the bedding. They'll also take care of the washing and ironing every Saturday morning for twenty euros a week each. And Yannick who lives at the bottom of your lane will look after the garden for ten euros an hour . . .'

'Thank you both, you've been marvellous. But what about Bess?'

'All taken care of,' said Bruno. 'No charge. Since I reported that the accident took place while you were helping the town police, the council paid the fifty euros for the disposal.'

'I've been looking on the Internet and there's a *jument* for sale up near Limoges,' Pamela said, her eyes bright. 'She's a Selle Français, Bruno, like your Hector, and I'm thinking about breeding her. It would be lovely to have some foals around the place.'

'You can't buy a horse till you've ridden it and that's a good three months away,' said Fabiola. 'Now let's get you packed up and dressed and we'll take you home. Bruno, you take the food and the suitcase and the dog down to the car and I'll help Pamela dress. I want to fit this new figure-eight strap. Then come back and get us, but knock first.'

He was delayed at the Land Rover by a phone call from Yves, who apologized for calling so early but he'd been having breakfast with Annette. He'd mentioned something about Paul Murcoing and she had insisted he call Bruno at once. Bruno told him to go ahead.

'When I last spoke to you about him, I'd talked to someone who evidently disliked him. Last night at one of the rehearsal dinners I spoke to somebody who liked him, or at least thought well of him. Apparently he'd met Paul when they were both volunteering at a hospice in Bergerac. He said he thought Paul was a kindly boy and found it hard to believe he'd killed anybody. That's it, Bruno. If I hear any more, good or bad, I'll let you know.'

The Land Rover had just passed through Meyrals on the way back when Bruno's phone rang again. Fabiola, who had dealt with too many car-crash victims to let a driver use a cellphone, took it from the pouch at his waist, accepted the call and held it to his ear.

'It's Crimson, and it's all gone wrong. I've just heard from Murcoing. He doesn't want to meet me and says that instead I should get in touch with Gilles from *Paris Match* and let him have the new documents. He's even sent Gilles's email address. What do we do now?'

'*Putain*, let me think. I'll call you back as soon as I can.'

Fabiola put the phone away. 'Bad news?'

'Our clever little plan to smoke out Paul Murcoing just collapsed and I don't have another.'

289

He explained the ploy that he, Crimson and Florence had developed, and his scheme to go to the rendezvous instead of Crimson to talk him into giving himself up.

'Thank heavens that's not going to happen,' said Pamela from the rear seat. 'It's a ridiculous risk for you to take. Why not just leave it to J-J and the rest of the police? They're bound to pick him up eventually.'

'I don't think it's that simple,' said Bruno.

'Didn't I hear Gilles's name being mentioned on the phone?' asked Fabiola, a note of concern in her voice. 'How does he come into this?'

'Gilles has been in touch with him, or rather Paul emailed Gilles after his piece appeared on the *Paris Match* website. Now Paul wants Crimson to give the documents to Gilles.'

'These are the documents you faked?'

'No, we only faked the title page of a file. The documents don't actually exist but Paul doesn't know that.'

'Why should Crimson do what Paul wants and hand the documents over to the press?' Pamela asked. 'I thought you said this researcher you invented wanted money for them.'

'You're right,' Bruno replied. 'And he was expecting them to go to a private person, not to the press.'

Might the plan be saved, Bruno asked himself, if Crimson just said no and insisted on the original arrangement? He'd have to think this through and keep his thoughts to himself. He didn't need the distraction of Pamela trying to talk him out of it.

'How much money did this researcher want?'

'I'm not sure any deal was reached. The story is that this was a professional researcher who used to do occasional work in the archives for Fullerton, paid by the day. Crimson thought that would be at least two hundred euros a day, but these documents are supposed to be special, classified papers that have not been publicly released. I imagine the price would be two or three thousand, maybe more.'

'Where would Paul get that sort of money?'

'He got three thousand on the company credit card.' Bruno turned on to the long lane that led to Pamela's house. 'Maybe that was why he wanted the cash. Look, we're almost home.'

He always enjoyed this approach, the long ridge climbing to the left and then the fringe of poplars that shielded the house and grounds from the north and east, the ivy-covered pigeon tower and the welcoming sight of the house itself, the courtyard formed by the flanking barns that Pamela rented as *gîtes*.

'The sooner that gardener gets here the better,' said Pamela. 'I've got three families arriving Saturday.'

'And I have to get to work,' said Bruno, helping her from the car.

'Dinner tonight after you ride Hector?'

'Let me call you.' He kissed them both and headed back towards town, punching Crimson's number into the phone as he drove.

28

Crimson's house was not quite in order. The rugs had been laid, the pictures hung, and most of the furniture was back in place. But the dining-room table was still to be reassembled and cases of wine were stacked beside it. Crimson took Bruno to his study, where a desk phone, an iPhone and a cheap disposable were lined up on the desk. It was covered with a large-scale map of the area and a laptop stood open on a small table beside the desk.

'You dyed your hair,' said Bruno. As arranged, both men were wearing khaki slacks and blue shirts.

'It was the nearest I could get to looking like you. Even with binoculars, if we have the same clothes and hair colour he won't be able to tell us apart. We'd better synchronize watches and be sure we have each other's phones on speed dial.'

'Quite a little operations room,' said Bruno.

'I've got other maps as well, notepads and tape recorders, and there's coffee in the thermos. Why did you bring the dog? I mean I'm delighted to see the little fellow, but you can't intend to take him along.'

'He's my secret weapon. Murcoing likes dogs.' Bruno looked around the study. 'It looks like you've done this sort of thing before.'

As soon as he was out of sight of Pamela's house, Bruno had called Crimson and suggested that he reply to Paul by saying he had no intention of giving the documents to the press. He wanted to deal only with someone who was personally known to and trusted by Fullerton. Otherwise he'd return to England and forget the whole thing. Crimson had agreed and sent the email.

'Florence is teaching but she wants to drop by after school. She's arranged babysitters,' Crimson said. 'Now we just wait.'

'Not quite,' said Bruno. 'If you can find a screwdriver we could put that dining table of yours back together.'

It took them twenty minutes and would have taken longer but for J-J's arrival with Josette, who explained that she and her husband had just furnished their new house from IKEA and so she knew about putting furniture together. She added that she loved dogs and Balzac was the friendliest little charmer she'd seen in years, which sent her soaring in Bruno's estimation. She took off her jacket, rolled up her sleeves and took charge. Crimson excused himself to make more coffee. When he returned with a tray, the table was assembled.

'Well done, we can spread out the other maps now,' he said, gingerly resting the tray on it as if unsure of Josette's skills.

'Don't worry, Monsieur. I sat on it to be sure I'd done it right.'

'Before we start on today's operation, I have some interesting news,' said J-J. 'When Josette looked at Edouard's mail, she found a letter from the traffic police. His Jaguar was caught by a speed camera on the autoroute from Périgueux to Bordeaux just after eight on the evening of Fullerton's murder.'

'That means he was there,' said Bruno.

'He was certainly in the general vicinity. And the *juge d'instruction* shares your suspicions, but Edouard now has a lawyer and he's not saying a word.'

'*Putain*, I was sure you'd broken him yesterday.'

'Me too, but it seems we were wrong. I'll get back to him when this is over. Now listen carefully because I have something I'm required to say,' said J-J. 'This is not an officially sanctioned operation. You are doing this at your own risk and I know nothing about it, understood?'

'Yes, I understand.'

'Here's a slim-line flak vest, not the latest model but it will stop a handgun. We've changed the number plates on your car so it looks like it was hired in Paris,' J-J went on. 'And here are the shoes.' He handed over a pair of black hiking boots. 'The tracker's in the heel and Josette has the monitor. We'll need to be no more than two or three kilometres away for it to work, so keep me informed by phone of where you are. Inspector Jofflin has a second car waiting outside Bergerac with another monitor.'

'Any support?' Crimson asked.

'Somebody owes me a favour, so a team of *Gendarmes Mobiles* will be doing an anti-terrorist training exercise with live weapons and a helicopter at the Golfech nuclear power plant near Agen. They're about eighty kilometres away, say thirty minutes, but give me some notice and I'll have them moved closer. They've been informally briefed and we're on the same communications net.'

Bruno nodded, and inquired innocently: 'The favour would be the Brigadier?'

'Don't ask. And here's a wire for each of you so we know

294

what you're saying if you can't use the phones. It goes under your clothes and we have to attach the transmitter to your backs with tape, so get your shirts off. It's very short-distance, maybe three hundred metres if we're lucky.'

Bruno and Crimson began to strip. J-J waited until they were taped, the system tested and Bruno had the flak vest under his shirt.

'And here's the gun I want you to use.' He put his foot up on a chair and drew up his trouser leg to reveal an ankle holster in black webbing and Velcro and drew out the gun.

'It's a Smith & Wesson Centennial Airweight, designed for this holster. It's an American thirty-eight, which is pretty much the same as our nine-millimetre. It's a revolver because it's less likely to get jammed by sock lint or any kind of debris you pick up walking through rough ground. And I want it back.'

'I don't want to carry a gun.'

'Take it, and don't be a fool.'

'At least this way you have the option,' said Crimson. 'And it really is concealed.'

Reluctantly Bruno strapped it on, privately suspecting with a soldier's superstition that this would probably ensure that Paul never made contact again. Crimson's disposable phone rang.

'Hello,' he said, his English accent more evident than usual. A pause, but Bruno saw the little cogs on the cassette recorder moving. Josette turned away to make a call, presumably to start the trace.

'Yes, I have a car, a rental, a white Peugeot, a two-o-seven.' Crimson was speaking in English.

Another pause. 'I'm at a hotel on the autoroute outside Périgueux, Francis told me he had a place nearby.

'Yes, I have a map. Yes, I've found Les Eyzies. The public telephone outside the Post Office on the main street. How long will it take me to get there?'

Bruno felt frustrated hearing only one side of this conversation. Couldn't they have rigged up some extra earphones?

'You'll call me there at one precisely. I understand.'

Another pause. 'Francis promised me two thousand pounds. Let's say twenty-five hundred euros.'

'Very well, at one.' He closed the phone.

'Fifty seconds,' said J-J looking at his watch. 'That should be long enough to trace it. Josette?'

She held up a hand to silence him as she listened and scribbled on a notepad.

'It came from a public phone booth outside the *Mairie* in Coux,' she said, and turned back to speak into her phone. 'We expect the next call at eleven to the public box outside La Poste in Les Eyzies. Can you set the trace up now? Thanks.'

'Call Jofflin, tell him to get to Coux and then call in,' said J-J. 'Murcoing won't still be there but this looks like the area.'

'He might be watching the phone box, or Yvonne might be watching,' said Bruno. 'He's not alone.'

'We'll be careful.' J-J turned to Crimson. 'We'll follow you to Les Eyzies and we'll park down the road but in line of sight. There's a filling station on the corner we should be able to use. I want Bruno hiding on the floor of your car at the rear. I suspect Murcoing will have a second phone box arranged after Les Eyzies, one he can watch for any funny business. When you have the final rendezvous, or one that is not a phone box, you hand the car over to Bruno. You'll have to find a spot which is under cover. When Bruno drives off, stay under cover until you see my car and we'll collect you. Make sure you can recognize it and keep talking so we can pick you up on the mike.'

'You've done this before,' Crimson said to J-J.

'Kidnapping case a few years ago, we set up a similar tracking system for the plain-clothes guy who carried the ransom.'

'And how did that turn out?'

'The plain-clothes guy lived, took one bullet but got their pickup team. One of them led us to their safe house and the hostage team did the rest. We saved the kidnap victim.'

'Don't be so modest, *chef*,' said Josette. 'You were the one that took the bullet.'

'And if I hadn't been given the ankle holster, I'd be dead. Remember that.' J-J looked at his watch. 'Right, let's run through the check-list. Radios, phones, tracker shoes, ankle gun, pen and notepad. Anything else?'

Josette checked her list. 'A file for the documents he's supposed to be carrying. Phone cards in case they need to use a call box.' She looked at Bruno. 'Don't you need a leash for the dog?'

'You're not taking the dog along?' J-J said.

'I've got the leash in my back pocket. Paul Murcoing loves animals but was never allowed to have one as a kid. His aunt told me. This gives me an edge.'

J-J shook his head and rolled his eyes at Josette. 'Let's go.'

Bruno lay hunched and sweating under a blanket in the rear footwell of the Peugeot. Even with the passenger seat as far forward as it would go it was a squeeze, particularly with Balzac squirming on his chest. He had an open phone line with J-J as Crimson came back from the phone booth.

'The next phone booth is at Campagne in fifteen minutes,' he said, and drove back to the small roundabout by the Centenaire hotel and turned off on the Campagne road.

'OK, we heard that,' said J-J over the phone that Bruno held to his ear. 'We'll take the lower road past St Cirq so he won't see you're being followed. We can park at the place where they sell foie gras, we should still be in range.'

Another uncomfortable ride and then a further hot and stuffy wait until Crimson returned from the Campagne phone booth and reported: 'He says I have to drive on to the next phone box, in Audrix, by the *Mairie*. I take a left on the road to Coux and then a right at the top of the hill. He must have scouted this all out carefully.'

'*Putain*, he'll see us coming up that long hill if we follow,' said J-J. 'Josette, get Jofflin to drive up from Coux, go past Audrix and then he can wait at that cheese shop just below the village. We'll go the long way round through St Denis and use the parking lot at the big cave. And see if they can get a trace on the Audrix phone booth.'

Another drive up a long hill with endless bends until Bruno felt his right leg start to cramp. He braced it against the door and tried to bend himself double at the waist so he could straighten the leg. Realizing something was wrong, Balzac wriggled up Bruno's trunk to lick his face and then found his way out from under the blanket. Audrix was one of the highest villages in the region, a good place for a watcher with binoculars to follow the progress of approaching cars.

'Are you alright?' Crimson asked.

'Just a cramp, I'll be fine.'

'Sorry, we're almost there. If I'd thought, I'd have rented a bigger car. By the way, I told Paul I have my dog with me. He asked what it was and I said a basset hound puppy. He laughed.'

At Audrix, the wait for Crimson to return was considerably longer and J-J told Bruno over the phone that he could not hear the mike. His voice was nervous and J-J kept asking what was the delay and why was Crimson not returning. Bruno replied that he had no answer. He could see nothing and it would be too risky for a head to suddenly appear from the rear seat of the Peugeot.

'It's probably taking time for Crimson to write down the directions,' Bruno said into his phone. 'It means we're on the last lap. Wait, I hear footsteps. That's probably Crimson coming back to the car.'

The driver's door opened and Crimson spoke as he settled himself and attached the safety belt.

'I'm to drive on down the hill, cross the railway line and then take the first road on the left, at a sign marked Tennis,' he reported. 'Are you hearing this alright, J-J?'

'Yes, it's faint but we can hear you. Speak the directions slowly and Bruno, could you hold the phone out from under the rug? We should be able to hear it better.'

Crimson repeated the directions. The terrain was all familiar and Bruno followed the route in his head. He'd visited the tennis club, had even played on its courts in tournaments, and he'd warmed up on that rugby field before playing against the local team. He knew the track to the motocross circuit, as part of a route he'd occasionally taken on horseback.

'We'll do the switch immediately you turn left at the sign for the tennis club,' Bruno said. 'There's good cover there from hedges. Leave the engine running and wait for J-J.'

'I heard all that,' said J-J. 'But be sure Crimson stays in hiding when he's out of the car. I'm coming but I don't want to be there immediately, it would look too suspicious. And the chopper's on its way. I'll hold it at Le Buisson until I hear from you.'

'Turning now to the tennis club and stopping,' said Crimson, and Bruno felt the weight shift as he left the car. 'Good luck.'

29

Bruno clambered over the seats and behind the wheel, closed the door and drove on into the parking area. He turned off the engine, left the key in the ignition, picked up the file on the passenger seat and caught sight of himself in the mirror. His hair was a mess from being beneath the blanket so he ran his fingers through to straighten it. He climbed out of the Peugeot and freed Balzac to scurry around the car. The dog lifted his leg against a wheel, darted to the tennis-club building and sniffed around the door. When Bruno began to walk, certain that binoculars would be watching, Balzac followed.

The shoes he'd been given felt odd, as if one heel was higher than the other, presumably for the tracker. It was a warm day and the flak vest was already damp against his singlet from being beneath that damn blanket. Bruno checked his watch when he passed the small vineyard. He'd been walking five minutes. Another eight minutes took him to the railway crossing, where a pair of Alsatians barked at Balzac when he went up to their fence to make friends.

Bruno smiled wryly to himself as Balzac, looking puzzled at his harsh welcome, scuttled back to his master's side. They continued to follow the route he'd been given. As he turned up the gravel path that led to the woods where the rendezvous would take place, Bruno wondered whether that might be an omen for his own reception. What might he expect from this encounter? He went through the traditional soldier's catechism; he either secured his objective of persuading Paul to give himself up, in which case there were no worries, or he didn't. If he failed, either he'd walk away free, in which case there were no worries, or he wouldn't. If he did not walk away free, either he would not take a bullet, in which case, no worries. If he was shot, he'd either recover which meant no worries, or he wouldn't, in which latter case he wouldn't be able to worry.

The crude fatalism cheered him a little, but that was not the calculus that had sent him trudging up this winding slope in the hot sun. Bruno's knowledge of Paul Murcoing had gone beyond the crude caricature of a violent gay psychopath who had butchered his lover. Bruno saw him as a human being, close to his sister and his grandfather, and as an accomplished artist who refused to do cheap sketches for cash and preferred more serious works. Paul possessed an easy charm that worked on women as well as men, and on dogs too, Bruno recalled. He had volunteered at a hospice for the dying. And just like his grandfather, he was obsessed with discovering the truth about the Neuvic train. Bruno could not make all this fit with the simplistic category of killer. Paul must know the game could not go on much longer and he had his sister to think of.

Up to Bruno's left was a hill topped by a water tower and a mast for cellphones. Was that the flash of sunlight on binoculars he saw? It would be a perfect location to track Bruno as he walked to the rendezvous and keep watch for any suspicious cars. Ten more minutes took him along the dirt track and

Bruno started the climb through the woods to the enormous clearing which had been turned into a motocross circuit.

As he looked at the plunges and humps and muddied curves of the circuit, he felt certain that Paul would be using one of the motorbikes designed for such tracks. It would take him cross-country and through woods in a way that would laugh off any pursuit. Why hadn't he thought of that and advised J-J to have some *motards* on standby? He checked his watch; it had taken him twenty-five minutes and he'd gone at least two kilometres, probably maximum range for the tracker. The trees would cut that even further.

Jofflin's car would be the closer of the two. There was no other discreet place nearby for J-J to park and no proper roads, only dirt tracks that would challenge even his own Land Rover. This was an area Bruno knew. He'd hunted here, ridden over the land on horseback with Fabiola and Pamela and even come looking for mushrooms with the Baron. The nearest road in the other direction was three or four kilometres away and J-J's car could not handle the rough forest tracks. Bruno would have to assume he was on his own.

He got to the concrete stand and waited, Crimson's disposable phone in his hand. This would be the difficult moment, when Paul would be expecting the English accent that he already recognized and which Bruno could not possibly hope to impersonate.

The phone rang and he put it to his ear and began working his mouth as though saying 'Hello' again and again but keeping silent. He heard a male voice speaking English and carried on miming his response. He took the phone from his ear, looked at it, shook it, returned it to his ear and began once more miming his 'Hello.' Faking a bad connection was his only chance.

Across the clearing perhaps two hundred metres away he saw a flash of movement through the woods. Then he saw it again, further along through the trees, and realized it was someone on a mountain bike, wearing a cycling helmet and shorts. Very clever, he thought. Nobody could catch a mountain bike in these woods and they could avoid all the roads. And cyclists were so common that they could probably risk the Gendarme patrols, and go cross-country again if they had to.

There was a sound behind him and he turned to see another mountain bike, the rider in helmet, shorts and a long-sleeved cycling vest in green, coming slowly down the slope from the woods towards him. The cyclist stopped, perhaps thirty metres away, feet on the ground but poised to pedal swiftly away. From a waist pouch, the cyclist took an automatic pistol and pointed it at Bruno. It was big and flat, an automatic, probably the Browning.

No matter how good his training or how thoroughly he had tried to think through this moment, Bruno learned anew that there was nothing quite like the adrenalin shock of a gun being aimed at him. He told himself that the vest was designed to stop a nine-millimetre round and tried to repress the thought that an untrained shooter usually fired high and there was no vest to protect his head.

The file in one hand, the phone in the other, Bruno ignored the tremor in his legs and raised his hands above his head as Balzac wagged his tail and trotted up to the bike to sniff at the cyclist's feet.

The second cyclist came out of the woods to Bruno's right

and paused, perhaps twenty metres away. He took off a small backpack and removed a slim black weapon, its magazine sticking out sideways from the barrel. Bruno recognized the Sten gun. After he'd learned that it was missing from Fullerton's collection, Bruno had looked it up. Thirty-two rounds, nine-millimetre bullets, a tendency to rise when fired and very prone to jam. The cyclist held the butt in his right hand, finger on the trigger, and his left hand on the magazine. That meant he didn't know the gun well. Holding it there meant pressure on the magazine which could alter the angle at which the bullets were fed into the chamber and cause a jam.

'It's not him,' shouted the first cyclist, the one holding the automatic. It was a female voice. 'I know this guy, he's a cop from St Denis. It's a trap.'

'*Bonjour Yvonne, bonjour Paul*,' Bruno said, his arms still high and his eyes fixed on the gun that threatened him. He was conscious that his voice was a notch or two higher than usual and there was a chill lump of fear in his belly. 'I've come to ask you to give yourselves up before anybody gets hurt.'

'Did you see any cars, anybody else following him?' Paul asked his sister. His face was covered in a fashionable stubble. The sleeve of his cycling vest had ridden up enough for Bruno to see the beginning of the Maori warrior tattoo.

'No, but it's got to be a trap.'

'The bikes are a good idea,' said Bruno, straining to keep his voice calm even though his throat was dry. He settled back on his heels to stop the quivering in his legs. 'Even if there were any cars, you can get away again. I'm hoping you won't do that. There are no charges against Yvonne. Think of her future.'

'Go back up the hill and keep watch,' Paul told his sister.

He pulled back the bolt to cock the Sten, holding it steady and aiming low. Bruno's heart thumped as he realized that he was now one pull of the trigger away from all thirty-two rounds of the magazine hitting him in less than three seconds. 'You expect me to believe that you came just to tell me to give up? Have you got the documents?'

As Yvonne stood on her pedals to cycle back up the hill, Balzac trotted across to Paul and made a friendly bark of greeting. Paul ignored him, not taking his eyes away from Bruno for a moment.

'There are no documents, Paul. We cooked up that page as bait to get a chance to talk to you. I knew about your grandfather's war record, about the Neuvic train, about his suspicions.' The words came out in a rush and he knew that he was not sounding persuasive, even to himself.

'They aren't suspicions. He spent half his life trying to find out what happened to that money. What about the contents page you sent me from the archive? Was that faked too?'

'Not entirely,' he said, straining his ears for the sound of a helicopter or even a car engine for some indication that he was not alone facing a submachine gun. He had seen the way the bullets could stitch their way up a human body. 'Most of the documents exist, they're just not declassified yet. But I'm told they don't provide much evidence for your theories. The British really didn't know what happened to the Neuvic money.'

'You'll have heard that from Crimson, the guy the papers call the spymaster. So he's in on this as well.'

Paul's voice was even, not carrying any tone of anger or frustration. Bruno hoped he would stay this calm.

'Crimson got involved when you burgled his house. But we got all the stuff back from Fullerton's place in the Corrèze. We very nearly caught up with you both there.'

Paul nodded. 'So what brings the St Denis policeman into this?'

'Apart from the burglaries being on my turf, I was at your grandfather's deathbed. He had one of the Neuvic banknotes in his hands as he died. I'm keeping his Resistance medal for you and the photos he had of himself in the Groupe Valmy.'

Bruno's legs had stopped trembling and he felt the first glimmer of relief that this encounter was turning into a dialogue, just as the book on hostage negotiations said it should.

'One of the photos was of the Neuvic operation. And after he died I found some photos of you and him together. I've got one in my shirt pocket. I thought you'd like to have it. Can I get it out and show you?'

'Just keep your hands in the air. Does that mean you were the one who organized the funeral?'

Bruno nodded. 'Your grandfather got a good send-off. Half the town was there with a military honour guard and we sang the *Chant des Partisans*. Did you get close enough to see anything of it?'

'Not as close as I'd have liked. But I heard the music.'

'I went to see your aunt, Joséphine.'

'So I heard. You bought a couple of my pictures, got them cheap, just as you did with the Neuvic banknotes.'

'I paid what I was asked.'

Paul considered that and nodded. He glanced down at Balzac, who was sniffing around his ankles. 'That's a nice basset, what's his name?'

'Balzac.'

Paul smiled, that same smile Bruno had seen in the surveillance photo at the printing shop. Bruno understood why the shop girl had been charmed.

'Tell me, why did you bring Balzac?'

'Because I know you like animals.'

Paul laughed. He looked calm and self-possessed, with none of the nervous stress Bruno had expected. Bruno found that at last he was able to swallow as his own tension began to ease.

'You're a strange kind of cop. What's your name?'

'Bruno, Bruno Courrèges. I'm the town policeman at St Denis, as your sister said.'

'Bruno, I've heard that name before. I seem to remember seeing something in the papers about pulling a Chinese kid out of a fire, and that thing in the big cave, was that you?'

Bruno nodded. Paul eyed him curiously.

'How did you get on to me?'

'A postman remembered the van and the France-Chauffage sign you faked, so I went to the sign shop, where they had a security camera. Then I took your picture to the *Zone Industriel* in Belvès and met one of your admirers, a woman called Nicolle. She recognized you from the photo. So then I had a name and we began to check known addresses and went to see your aunt and began looking for Yvonne.'

Paul laughed. 'I haven't thought of Nicolle in a while. So it was all because a postman saw the van. Would that have been somewhere near the place where Francis was killed?'

'On the track to the house. He was leaving after delivering some post, you were heading towards it. I presume Francis was still alive then.'

'Assume all you like.' He paused and then cocked his head as if remembering something. 'How long have you had this job?'

'Ten years, and yes, I was the cop who came to investigate the attack on that holiday place ten years ago when you and Edouard Marty were beaten up with the older English guys. You were the one taken to the clinic with the broken nose where you gave a false name and address, and either Francis Fullerton drove or he was the one with the broken arm.'

Paul nodded slowly and studied Bruno without speaking. The Sten did not waver. 'Are you armed?' he asked.

'I have a small gun in an ankle holster. A snub-nose revolver. It couldn't reach you at this range. I wouldn't have worn it but senior colleagues insisted. They think you're a murderer. I'm not so sure.'

'Why do you say that?' Paul sounded genuinely curious. 'The papers and the radio are all saying I'm guilty.'

'Partly it's the hospice where you volunteered, partly it's your paintings, but it's mainly because I can't bring myself to believe you killed Francis in a *crime passionnel*. I think you loved him but I can't see you being jealous in that way. And I can't see you beating him to death like that, so brutally.'

'Well, you're right about that.' He gave a short laugh. 'All of it.'

'Tell me what happened, Paul. If you didn't do it, who did? Give yourself up and come along with me and we can find out what really happened. You haven't got much time. We know about the British credit card and we're blocking it. You'll have no more money. There's a helicopter nearby with a team of *Gendarmes Mobiles* aboard. You know how they're trained.

They'll take one look at that Sten and they'll shoot first and ask questions later. Think about Yvonne, do you want them gunning her down alongside you?'

'It needn't be like that,' Paul replied. 'Thanks for the warning but this isn't over.'

'So what now?'

Paul looked at Bruno thoughtfully. 'It's a pity there are no documents. That story needs to come out.'

'Gilles from *Paris Match* is a good reporter. Once he gets his teeth into something, he keeps on chewing.'

'You know him?'

'We've been friends for a long time. We met in Sarajevo during the siege. He was a reporter. I was in the army.'

'Interesting, Grandpa would have approved. Now since I don't want to make more trouble by shooting you, I'd like you to put that phone down and take your shirt off. Leave the photo in the pocket.'

'I'm wearing a flak vest and a wire.'

'That's what I expected, so take them off. I imagine you've got a cordon forming around this area while you engage me in friendly chit-chat.'

Bruno complied, wincing as he ripped off the tape that held the transmitter to his back, and laid them on the ground in front of him. He opened the button on the shirt pocket and slightly withdrew the photo so Paul could see it.

'Now, sit down on the ground. Keeping your hands well away from that ankle holster, take your shoes off. Use your feet to prise them off, that's right. Now take off that ankle holster. If you try to open it I'll shoot you. Don't get up. Just raise your arms and put your hands on your head and keep them there.

Now start shuffling back on your bum and call your dog to join you. Keep on backing away.'

Bruno called Balzac from sniffing at his abandoned shoes and wriggled back down the slope. Paul kept the Sten gun aimed at him as he stepped off the bike and put Bruno's shoes, phone and the transmitter into his rucksack. He left the gun in its holster. Finally he took the photo from Bruno's shirt pocket and then remounted his bike.

'Good luck, Bruno. Sorry your feet are going to get a bit torn up, but stay in touch with Gilles. I may have something to communicate and I'll do it through him.'

'Can you at least tell me who killed Francis?' From far in the distance, Bruno could hear the first, faint chattering of a helicopter.

'It wasn't me. I was there, but I didn't kill him. I couldn't have, despite what he was doing to us.' Paul cocked his head, hearing the rotor blades.

'That's the *Gendarmes Mobiles*,' Bruno said. 'For God's sake, think of your sister. This doesn't have to end with you both dead.'

Paul shook his head, looked up the hill and whistled and after a moment his sister appeared. He stuffed his gun into his rucksack, shouldered it and rode off along the side of the hill, disappearing into the woods, his sister following close behind.

Bruno lowered his arms at last, and they felt so light they seemed to want to rise again of their own accord. His body was sending waves of relief through his frame that the danger was over while his mind felt disappointment that he had failed to bring Paul in. He took a deep breath and stretched. The Gendarme chopper was still too far away to be seen.

He went back for his shirt, flak vest and the ankle holster, wincing as the sharp pebbles bit into his stockinged feet. Feeling a curious mixture of elation and humiliation, he hobbled very carefully down the motocross circuit to the track that led back to where Jofflin's car was waiting. When he saw it he waved and then heard the engine start up. He'd met Paul, given him the photograph with his grandfather, tried his best to persuade him to surrender and heard him say he didn't kill Fullerton. He might not have brought him in, but he'd held the suspect in place for over twenty minutes, which should have been long enough for whatever plans J-J had prepared for an ambush. That wasn't a bad afternoon's work.

30

J-J had not been happy. His car had got stuck on a trail in the woods far behind the motocross circuit and required a breakdown truck to come and tow it out. His phone couldn't get a signal and the helicopter with the *Gendarmes Mobiles* had beaten its way back and forth along the ragged edges of the woods and never seen a soul, let alone two cyclists. He grudgingly accepted the return of his revolver and flak jacket, listened to Bruno's account of the conversation with Paul and only smiled when he saw Bruno's bare feet. The ruined socks had been thrown away, but Balzac had gleefully rescued one and carried it dangling from his mouth.

Jofflin drove Bruno and Crimson back to Crimson's house, where Bruno borrowed a pair of socks and put his old shoes back on. Thanking Crimson for his trouble he drove back to his office to report to the Mayor, who warned him that Delaron was asking questions about unusual police activity.

'You met this young man, Paul?' the Mayor asked.

'Yes, and we had an interesting conversation given that he was holding me at gunpoint. He wouldn't explain what had really happened, just that he was at the scene but hadn't killed Fullerton, despite "what he was doing to us". That's the bit I don't understand. I've no idea what Fullerton was doing, nor who Murcoing meant when he talked of "us". But he was very self-confident, as though he knew something that would ensure it all worked out for him. I never saw anyone who looked less like a hunted man on the run.'

'What happens now?'

'I tried to tempt him out of hiding and bring him in and it didn't work. I suppose now it's up to J-J and the *Mobiles*, which means there's a strong chance that he gets killed and we never learn the truth.'

'It's out of your hands now. And I imagine you haven't heard the news. The minister of the interior has resigned, pleading reasons of health, which is a most unusual development this close to the elections. Jacqueline is delighted and rang to say she's putting some champagne on ice to celebrate. Gilles will be joining us, since she now sees him as a worthy fellow conspirator. She made a point of saying that you were also invited along with Balzac and what she called your various womenfolk. I think that was meant to be a joke.'

'I suppose you can never be sure with a woman like Jacqueline.'

'*Bien entendu*, it makes life much more interesting.'

Back in his office, where a full in-tray and a pile of unopened mail awaited him, Bruno opened his computer and groaned as he saw screen after screen of emails. It would take him days to clear the backlog. He looked out of his window. The cars at the roundabout had stopped for a line of cyclists to pedal through. They were all on racing bikes with dropped handlebars rather than mountain bikes and none of them was wearing a green vest, but he studied them anyway, wondering how far away Paul and Yvonne could have gone by now.

His desk phone rang, and he looked at it glumly. What would it be this time? A lost cat, a denunciation of some poor unemployed guy working for cash, perhaps a complaint about the new parking restrictions.

'Bruno, it's Jack Crimson. I'm at home and Florence is here along with Brian Fullerton. But so are Paul Murcoing and his sister and they're pointing guns at us.' He was trying to make his voice sound calm, but Bruno could almost feel his tension through the phone line. 'They're holding us all hostage . . .' Crimson's voice cracked but he went on: 'And he wants to speak to you.'

'Bruno, I told you this wasn't over,' came the now familiar voice. 'This is why.'

'*Putain*, I didn't think you could possibly get into worse trouble but now you have.' Bruno's mind was racing as he tried to recall the check-list of procedures for a hostage situation. 'What do you want, Paul?'

'A presidential pardon, a safe passage out of the country for Yvonne and me and the promise of a public inquiry into the Neuvic money. I'll release Crimson when those conditions are met.'

'What about the others, Fullerton and Florence? You don't need them; you could let them go.'

'After what you told me about the *Mobiles*? I don't think so. Call me back on Crimson's landline in one hour from now or things start to get unpleasant. I have three hostages, don't forget, and I only need the one.'

He rang off. Bruno immediately dialled J-J, walking briskly back to the Mayor's office as the call connected. He saw the Mayor's startled face as for the first time in his career Bruno entered without knocking. His eyes on his Mayor, Bruno said into the phone: 'J-J, I've just had a call from Paul Murcoing at Crimson's house. He's taken Crimson hostage at gunpoint along with two other guests.'

The Mayor rose, looking stunned, and then sank back into his chair as Bruno recounted Paul's conditions.

'J-J, I'll meet you there at Crimson's house and I'll arrange for a doctor and an ambulance to be on standby. I have my mobile phone and for anything else the Mayor will be here at the *Mairie*. I'll patch my phone through to his office and rig up a tape recorder.'

'Mother of God,' said the Mayor as Bruno rang off and called Fabiola's cell phone.

'I'll be right back with the recorder,' said Bruno and left for his office. When Fabiola answered, he briefed her and asked her to arrange an ambulance, and for someone to check on Florence's children. One of her pupils was probably babysitting but could not be expected to stay all night. He opened his safe and took out his gun and a spare magazine and put on his holster and uniform jacket. He forwarded all his calls to the Mayor's extension and took the recorder back with him along with two spare cassettes and rigged it to the Mayor's phone.

'I'm going to Crimson's house where I'll meet J-J,' he said. 'You're the communications backstop. Get Roberte in to answer your phone rather than Claire, she's more level-headed. Fend off all calls that aren't related to this hostage situation and make sure you keep your mobile charged and ready, since I'll use that to stay in touch with you. Is that clear, sir?'

'Yes, Bruno.'

'Please make a note to call me in exactly fifty minutes to remind me that's when Paul is expecting me to call him again.'

The Mayor looked at his watch, took the top from his fountain pen and scribbled a note to himself on a clean pad.

'And nobody, nobody is to talk to the press. If Delaron gets hold of this we'll have a circus.'

Bruno was already dialling again, the special number that he was only to use in emergencies.

The phone was answered but there was no reply, just a silence. 'This is Bruno Courrèges in St Denis and I need to speak to the Brigadier urgently.'

'Bruno?'

Oh God, it was Isabelle's voice. Of all the people in the Ministry she had to be the duty officer of the day. Firmly squashing all the emotions and recriminations that flooded through him, he kept his voice crisp and neutral.

'Crimson has just been taken hostage at his home,' he began, and explained the details.

'*Putain*, the Brigadier's not here. He's gone to the Elysée and there's complete chaos here. You heard our minister just resigned? I'll try to patch you through but if he's with the President he can't take the call.'

'Stay on the line to see if he answers and if not, keep calling him until you can brief him. I'm on my way to Crimson's house where J-J will join me. We have some *Jaunes* in the vicinity with a chopper but they're trained in anti-terrorist response, not hostage rescue. So do your best to keep them out of the way.'

'You got it. If the Brigadier doesn't answer in ten seconds leave it to me. And Bruno, please take care.'

He waited the ten seconds but the Brigadier did not pick up. He rang off and then began to dial the Gendarmerie when the Mayor coughed and said: 'Er, Bruno?'

He stopped at the door, about to trot down the *Mairie* stairs, phone to his ear.

'I'll look after Balzac, don't worry.'

The pup was sitting on the rug beside the Mayor, looking up at Bruno in perplexity. Was his master going for a walk without him?

'Thank you, sir, I know he's in good hands.'

He ran down the stairs as the call went through, hoping that Sergeant Jules would answer rather than Yveline.

'Gendarmerie, St Denis,' came a female voice, but it was Françoise.

'It's Bruno. Is Jules there? It's an emergency.'

'He's right here. I'll put him on.'

As he got to his Land Rover Bruno explained to the unflappable Sergeant Jules that he wanted all available Gendarmes deployed to form a distant cordon around Crimson's house. They were to stay out of sight and keep all traffic away unless it was official.

'It's a hostage situation, so you know the procedure. I've informed J-J. Perhaps you could inform the Prefect's office and the *Proc*. We'll probably need more Gendarmes from St Cyprien on standby if this goes through the night. Tell Ivan to start making sandwiches and pots of coffee. If you call the Mayor he'll arrange for someone to bring them out. Where's Yveline?'

'It's her day off. She said she was going shopping in Périgueux.'

'Call her and brief her and suggest that when she gets back she holds the fort at the Gendarmerie but I need you and the rest of the squadron out there as soon as you can.'

'Understood. I'll see you there. I'll get Ivan to make ham and cheese, they're always the most popular.'

Bruno grinned. He could always count on Sergeant Jules for the essentials. He put his phone in his breast pocket and tried to concentrate on his driving while despite himself his brain kept building mental maps of Crimson's house and grounds, access points and vulnerabilities. He told himself it was for the eventual arrival of the hostage rescue squad. He knew the rough technique: plastic explosives on front and rear doors simultaneously, as flash-bang grenades went through each of the windows and a ladder team broke into the upper floor.

But he remembered wooden shutters on Crimson's ground-floor windows, which made the flash-bangs more of a problem. Drenching the place in tear gas and smoke was the usual alternative but it was risky. The other options were even worse: snipers, starvation and stealthy entry.

When he arrived at the entrance to Crimson's drive, Bruno was alone. He parked out of sight, leaving the sidelights on. Avoiding the drive he slipped through the woods at the side of Crimson's property to scout the sides and rear of the house. The shutters had all been closed and he could see no open windows on the upper floors. Inside the garage was Crimson's rented car and Brian's car was parked in front of the doors. Florence's bicycle leaned against the side wall. There was good cover by the garage for an assault team to form up, and only a single window, probably for a staircase landing, on the nearest wall. The *Mobiles* could cover that window with a silenced gun, put up two ladders and break in that way. That's how he would do it.

Bruno crept close to the shuttered windows, each of which showed chinks of light from inside, but there was no sound from the rooms at the rear. One of the mountain bikes was leaning against the kitchen door, something that might give them a warning if it was moved. Gently he felt along the frame and his fingers touched a taut piece of string that led through the keyhole into the house. There would probably be a bell or something on the other end that would make a noise if the bike was moved.

At the front of the house, in the room he recalled as Crimson's study and which had earlier that day been his makeshift operations room, he heard the murmur of voices. The sound was not clear enough for him to tell who was talking but he was sure he heard a woman's tones and it sounded like Florence. At least he knew where some of them were. The other bike lay against the front door. Paul had probably rigged a warning system on that one, too.

As he withdrew to the fringe of trees and back to his Land Rover he was sure he was forgetting something. Had there been another door into the house? Perhaps he could find a way to break silently through the French windows. He cast his mind back to his previous visits and remembered the descent to the wine cellar and the hatch for the fuel-oil delivery. He crept back to the rear of the house and felt for the metal plates and the padlock that sealed them. Bolt-cutters could take care of it. Damn, he should have made a sketch of what he could recall of the interior for J-J. There would be five in the house, Paul and Yvonne, Crimson, Florence and Brian.

Crimson had explained that Florence would be coming to his house after school to hear what had happened with the trap they had set. But why was Brian Fullerton inside? Had he not been supposed to be flying back to England today with his brother's ashes? Bruno had heard nothing about any delay in the release of the body, but that must be the explanation, and Brian had become friendly with Crimson. Maybe he'd simply dropped by to say goodbye and walked into the kidnapping. Bruno knew from Pamela's trips that the Ryanair flight left at around five, so Brian would have missed his flight back from Bergerac by now.

Bruno stopped, struck by something he had not considered before. That flight usually landed around four, so how had Brian arrived in Bruno's office on Friday morning? Brian said he had changed the flight to Bordeaux the consulate had booked for him and flown into Bergerac instead. And he added that he'd come straight to Bruno's office from the airport and had not even checked in to his hotel.

The thought nagged at him, so he called the security office at the airport where Marco, one of the shift chiefs, had been in his class at the Police Academy. Bruno asked about the inbound flights from Britain on Friday morning. There had been none. He asked Marco to check if there were any records last week of a Brian Fullerton arriving. He heard the sound of a keyboard being tapped.

'Nothing on the computer,' said Marco. 'Want me to check other airports? It's all on the same database now. Here he is, flew into Bordeaux Monday last week on British Airways from London Gatwick. Open return.'

'Thanks, Marco. You're sure it was Monday? Could there be any mistake?'

'No, this comes from the airline boarding lists. If they're not on the flight they're not listed.'

Monday last week was the day before his brother was murdered. Why was Brian flying in then? And why had he misled him? Brian had flown into Bordeaux. Edouard was in Bordeaux and his Jaguar had been caught by a speed camera returning from Périgueux to Bordeaux on the evening Brian's brother was killed. And one thing that Brian, Edouard and Paul had in common was that they were all directors of Francis's company. But this couldn't be about inheritance; Francis's will put everything in trust for Brian's children.

Was he sure about that? Hadn't he asked Isabelle and J-J and even Crimson if there was some way to check Francis's will? Suddenly he remembered Pamela telling him that unlike France, under English law you could leave your property to anyone you chose. If Francis was planning to leave his property elsewhere that could be a motive for murder.

As he reached for the phone at his belt, he felt it vibrate.

'Bruno, it's J-J. On my way, I'll be with you in ten minutes or so. The Brigadier just rang me. They can't get a hostage rescue team here before tomorrow morning and he suggests we use the *Mobiles*. He's not too bothered about taking Murcoing alive and we can have them here in ninety minutes. What do you say?'

'If they go in guns blazing, there's always a risk to the hostages. Is the Brigadier ready for that?'

'He says he is. But that kind of operation has to be authorized by a minister and we don't have one. That's the problem.'

'We'll talk it through when you get here.'

He saw headlights coming around the bend from St Denis and stepped into the middle of the road to flag down the vehicle. It was the Gendarmerie van, Françoise at the wheel and Sergeant Jules beside her, with the ambulance following close behind. He was just advising Jules where to post his men when his phone vibrated yet again. It was the Mayor.

'Bruno, it's time to call Paul Murcoing again.'

'Thanks, sir. Any developments?'

'Everything's fine. Roberte is handling the phones and Jacqueline is looking after Florence's children. I'll call if anything happens. Isabelle rang, asking for news.'

'Could you call her back and ask if she had any reply from England about Francis Fullerton's will?'

'Very well, but you'd better phone Paul.'

From his address book Bruno tapped Crimson's home number. It was picked up at once, as though Paul had been standing by the phone.

'It's Bruno. Your conditions have been relayed to the proper authorities but there's a problem. If you turn on the TV or radio you'll realize this is no trick. The interior minister has just resigned for personal reasons. Normally that's the man who would have to make a decision about your conditions but right now the post is vacant.'

There was a silence as if a hand had been placed over the mouthpiece at the other end. Bruno could hear faintly the sound of a female voice, high and angry, Paul's sister. Then Paul spoke, trying to sound calm but not succeeding. 'There must be a deputy or an acting minister.'

'Yes, but without lawful authority. We're trying to get this clarified and I've asked my Mayor whether this can go to the Elysée and the President can make a decision. Can I ring you back as soon as I hear anything?'

'Where are you now?'

'Near the house and there's just me, so far. A couple of Gendarmes are setting up a roadblock to keep other traffic away. We're waiting for the *Police Nationale* from Périgueux.'

'Call me back in an hour, and tell those people in Paris that if they don't have a decision by then, I start putting bullets into hostages. I'll start with feet and knees, unless I think you're dicking me around and then I'll get serious. One hour, Bruno.'

'Don't make this worse . . .' Paul had hung up. Bruno rang the Mayor to pass on the message.

'I spoke to Isabelle,' the Mayor said when Bruno had finished. 'She had a copy of the will in her emails and she said to tell you she's sorry she'd forgotten to pass it on. Apparently the will was changed very recently. Fullerton's estate goes to any natural child of his own, and failing that to Yves Valentoux to be held in trust for a girl called Odile. Who on earth is she?'

'I think she might be the key to all this, and that's exactly what I needed to know. Thank you and thank Isabelle for me when you speak again. What do you think the chances are of the Elysée intervening?'

'Very slim. It would mean taking responsibility for the death of Crimson and the others. The fact that there's a vacuum at the top of the Interior Ministry is just the kind of escape clause politicians like.'

Bruno rang off and instantly called Yves Valentoux. From the background sound, he was in a bar or restaurant.

'Yves, this is really important. Lives may hang on it. How serious was Francis about asking you to marry him?'

'He was planning a trip to the States for both of us to do it there, where it's legal. I hadn't agreed but he was always so confident about everything . . .'

'Would it be legal for a non-American?'

'He was American, or at least he'd taken out US citizenship

when he lived there in the Nineties. Apparently it was quite easy before nine-eleven. He always said the Queen wouldn't mind and he also kept his British passport.'

'And you told me he wanted to give Odile a little brother or sister. What about his HIV?'

'He said he'd researched it and there were ways to sanitize his sperm. I never took it that seriously but he certainly did.'

'I think this plan to marry you and have a child was what got Francis killed. It would have changed the inheritance.'

31

J-J closed his phone with a snap. 'They won't make any decision in Paris and they won't authorize using the *Jaunes*. I guess it's down to you now.' He looked with sympathy at Bernard Ardouin, the *Procureur*, who had joined them at Sergeant Jules's Gendarmerie van. It was the nearest they had to a mobile operations room until the real one arrived from Périgueux with reinforcements.

'You could order the Gendarme general for the *Département* to send in the *Jaunes*,' J-J went on. 'But he'd probably refer back to the defence ministry and we'd be back where we started. The only people you can be sure will carry out your orders are my team and Bruno here.'

Ardouin's own boss, the chief *Procureur* for the *Département*, was at a gala dinner and opera in Bordeaux along with the Prefect. Their phones were turned off.

'I have to call Paul again in ten minutes,' said Bruno. 'Dammit, does nobody have the balls to make a decision?'

'I'm sure they'll find him soon,' Ardouin said, trying to sound decisive. 'There must be an intermission coming up.'

Bruno had expected better from Ardouin. He turned away to hide the disgust on his face and called the Mayor.

'Nobody wants to take a decision. Will you authorize me to go in? I think Paul will be prepared to speak to me.'

'Bruno, whatever you decide to do will have my full support and Roberte who's sitting here heard me say that. Just remember the oath you swore when you took office, "to defend the constitution and the laws of *la République* and the citizens of St Denis". I don't have to remind you that Florence is indeed a citizen and her children need her back.'

Bruno was dialling Crimson's number when a shot came from inside the house followed by the piercing note of a woman shrieking, once, twice, and then the sound bubbled away into silence.

'I'm sorry I had to do that,' Paul said as he answered Crimson's phone. 'I warned you this would happen.'

'I have no news and no official response from Paris on your conditions but a superior officer is now here, Commissaire Jalipeau, head of detectives for the *Département*. The *Procureur* is with him and he wants to talk to you.'

Bruno handed the phone to J-J and went back to Sergeant Jules, who was chewing on a sandwich. He offered another to Bruno, who shook his head.

'Since nobody else will do anything, I'm going to try,' he said. 'I'll need you to break a window on the upper floor and pull down the bike that's leaning against the front door, both at the same time. Ten seconds after that, I want the bike leaning against the back door to be pulled away. There's an alarm rigged to each one and it will distract them. And I'll need those bolt-cutters you have for traffic accidents.'

'Alright, do you want me to come with you?'

'I'm not sure you'd squeeze through the gap I'm planning to use, old friend, but thanks for offering. Who's the best of your team?'

'Françoise, no question. She's also the best shot. By the way, Yveline's back, holding the fort like you asked, and calling every few minutes to ask if anything's happened. She had one bit of news. Somebody left a cardboard box on the steps of the Gendarmerie with an old silver coffee pot inside. It must have happened just after I left. She says it looks like the American one that was stolen and what do you want her to do?'

'Tell her to call the owner and see if she can identify it,' Bruno replied. 'But first, let's talk to Françoise.'

Jules beckoned Françoise to join them and asked if she was ready to volunteer to go in with Bruno.

'About time somebody did something,' she said. 'If he's shot Florence . . .'

Bruno explained his plan. He went to the back of his Land Rover, pulled out his spare roll of fishing line and measured out two lengths of twenty metres each. He gave one to Françoise and sent her to creep to the front door and tie the line to the bike while he did the same at the rear.

They rejoined Sergeant Jules, who had collected a handful of fist-sized stones and positioned himself by the landing window that looked onto the garage. Each of them gave the sergeant an end of fishing line.

'Pull on that and the bike topples and the alarm goes off,' said Bruno. 'When you hear the click of the bolt-cutters, count to twenty and then pull the back-door bike.'

Jules repeated the instructions.

'Then count to ten and break that bloody window and start shouting. Stay tucked up against the wall so they can't see you or shoot you but keep on throwing stones until that glass breaks.'

'Count to ten, window.'

'Then count to ten again and pull the front-door bike. I'll go first and try to get up the stairs to the landing to get the high ground and Françoise stays at the top of the cellar stairs.'

'What's this?' J-J demanded, joining them. 'What are you up to, Bruno?'

'Since you lot won't do anything, the Mayor has told me to do something.'

'You're not doing anything.'

'You're not my boss.'

'No, you damn fool, I'm your friend. What have you got in mind?'

Bruno explained his plan. J-J nodded. 'I suppose it might help if I were to call him and say we'd just heard from Paris when I hear your bolt-cutters.'

'It would help a lot. If I can open the front door on the way up, I'll try it.'

Bolt-cutters in hand, with Françoise carrying an aerosol can of lubricant, they crept around the rear of the house to the edge of the terrace and the access for the fuel oil. Françoise sprayed the lubricant onto the hinges and then held the padlock so Bruno could get a purchase. With a powerful heave of his shoulders he closed the long handles of the cutters and heard a loud snap. Françoise pulled out the broken padlock and then Bruno took a deep breath, seized the edges of the two metal plates and in a swift move pulled them up and open. Better a short, sharp sound than a long-drawn-out squeak of protesting rust.

He let himself into the hole, counting under his breath, lowered himself on his arms until his feet touched the floor and the count was ten. He whispered to Françoise to follow, helped her down and then took out his gun. He released the safety catch. Fifteen.

He opened the door to find the cellar in darkness. He groped his way to the stairs and began climbing at the count of eighteen. He had just reached the top of the stairs when he heard glass break and then a noisy clatter. He opened the door, the light suddenly very bright, and heard a woman's voice shout 'Back door.' Footsteps ran down the stairs from the upper floor. This was a count of ten and he had reached three, now four.

To get to the back door she'd have to come past him, and he used a technique that somebody had once used on him in a rugby game and it had put him out of action and left him unable to speak. He'd never hit a woman but this would be better than shooting her. As Yvonne jumped down the last stairs and turned to face the back door Bruno put his entire weight into a punch that started at his knees and ended in the centre of her stomach, just below the rib cage. There was a great whoosh of air being expelled from her lungs and she bent over double and then fell as if she'd been poleaxed. The automatic pistol fell from her hand.

The count was seven as he collected her gun and tucked it into the back of his waistband so there was no time to open the front door. The count was ten as he began leaping up the stairs as the first rock came in through the landing window.

Bruno lay flat on the landing, pointing his gun down the stairs and planning to shoot Paul somewhere around his waist, to stop him but perhaps not kill him. He would have one clean shot at a moving target before Paul's Sten began hosing the stairs with bullets.

Then he heard the sound of a blow, a grunt and something clattering as it fell. Confused voices, shouting, protesting. Then came a burst of automatic fire from inside the study, shockingly loud.

Then silence.

'*C'est fini, c'est fini*,' came a shout. 'It's over. I got him. Here's the gun.'

The study door was opened and the Sten gun, minus its magazine, was pushed out into the hall.

'Can we come out now? This is Brian Fullerton. Murcoing is dead and we are all safe.'

At that point Sergeant Jules pulled the second length of fishing line and a new clattering came as the bike toppled and the glass jug filled with teaspoons that had been resting on a chair was pulled down by the falling bike to tinkle against the door.

'Françoise, secure the prisoner on the floor,' Bruno called. 'Then go out and get J-J and the sergeant, the doctor and a stretcher.'

'She's choking, it sounds very bad,' Françoise said. 'I've cuffed her.' Her gun poised, she went to the front door, clambered over the bike and shouted for the others to come.

'Come out one at a time with your hands up,' Bruno called.

Brian came first, looking defiantly around him, then Florence, her face drained and her hands and lips trembling, but she looked unhurt. There were no bullet wounds in her hands or feet. Paul had been bluffing with that shot. Finally came Crimson, looking back into the study, from which drifted whiffs of cordite.

'It's clear,' said Crimson.

'What happened in there?' Bruno asked. 'Keep your hands up.'

'I tripped him, grabbed the Sten and shot him,' said Brian. 'It was him or us.'

'There was a shot earlier and a woman's scream,' said Bruno. 'We thought he might have shot Florence.'

'He fired into the ceiling and his sister did the screams,' said Crimson. 'It was a bit of theatre.'

J-J was the first in the door, Fabiola on his heels, and then Sergeant Jules and the *Procureur*. Bruno pointed Fabiola to Yvonne, still straining for breath, rocking back and forward from her waist, her eyes wide with terror. The three hostages dropped their hands and Florence turned accusingly to Brian Fullerton.

'You didn't have to shoot him,' she said. 'He was helpless, spreadeagled on the floor. He'd dropped the gun.'

'We'll sort this out later,' Bruno said, and told them all to get back as he looked into the study.

Paul Murcoing lay in a spreading lake of blood. His handsome face was unmarked but a trail of bullet holes rose from his left hip, across his stomach and up his right chest. His eyes and mouth were open, with a look that might have been surprise.

'Good result,' said J-J, coming into the room, the others following. 'Hostages all saved, the bad guy dead, the girl lives to go on trial. We charge her with kidnapping, resisting arrest.'

'I think there might be another trial,' said Bruno. He turned to Crimson. 'Tell us what happened in there.'

'They panicked when the first bike fell. Paul had sent his sister upstairs, he was worried about the landing window being vulnerable. Then he took a phone call and as he was speaking we heard her shouting and running downstairs and then nothing until the windows started breaking. That's when Paul dropped the phone and ran out.'

'I tripped him,' Brian interrupted. 'That's when I grabbed the Sten and shot him. I thought he might have another gun.'

'How convenient for you that he's dead,' Bruno said. 'Paul can take the blame for all of it, the thefts and the murder of your brother.'

'You didn't have to kill him,' Florence repeated. 'He'd fallen, lost the gun and you had him covered. I couldn't believe it when you opened fire.'

'He killed my brother and he would have killed us, too,' Brian retorted angrily. 'I was saving our lives.'

'It didn't look like that to me,' said Crimson. 'Florence is right. I won't mourn for him but there was no need to shoot the man.'

Brian ignored him and lifted his head defiantly. Bruno stared at him a moment, remembering what he'd learned about Brian's flight times, and then addressed him.

'When we met last Friday you told me you had just flown into Bergerac, hired a car and come straight to St Denis. Is that right?'

'That's right. I changed the flight the consulate had booked.'

Now Bruno knew he was lying and everything fell into place, Brian's attempt to sanitize his brother's laptop, his false arrival date, his shooting of Paul even when he was helpless and unarmed. He felt he even understood Paul Murcoing's phrase, 'what he was doing to us'.

'When did your brother tell you he was intending to marry Yves Valentoux?' Bruno asked.

'What, my brother marry?' Brian scoffed. 'He was gay.'

'But he wanted a family. He wanted a child, he wanted a spouse and he had found a partner he loved and wanted to live with. He told you that, didn't he?'

'My brother had all sorts of wild ideas, adoption, fatherhood. His enthusiasms never lasted more than a week or two.'

'This one did. Francis told you he was going to father a child and have it brought up by two friends of Yves who were already raising Yves's daughter. And you realized that he would thus disinherit you and your children and leave the control of his company to strangers.'

Brian glared at him, his fingers curling into fists, but Bruno carried on.

'So with Paul and Edouard Marty, your fellow directors in Arch-Inter, you decided to take steps to ensure the company, not to mention the house in Chelsea and the Porsche, stayed in your hands.'

'This is all bullshit, Bruno . . .'

'Did you not know Edouard Marty was arrested yesterday and is telling us everything? How he picked you up at Bordeaux airport last Monday, drove you out to confront your brother . . .'

Bruno was making it up as he went along but had never been more certain of anything.

'You hated him, hated him because he was your mother's favourite, because of all the money they spent on his debts and his rehabilitation, while you were the dutiful son, the hard worker. He was gay and you were straight. You gave them the grandchildren but he had all the love. He goes to prison but his old sugar-daddy dies and leaves him the house and the business. As your wife said, not bad for two years inside. Then his business took off and he had all the money. And all you had was a token shareholding and the hope that your children might inherit something, and then you learned that even that was going to be taken away from you.'

Brian stared coldly at Bruno and said nothing.

'We have Edouard's testimony, we have your flight details, we have a speed camera that took your photo as you drove back in Edouard's Jaguar and we'll have your clothes, where I think we will find microscopic specks of your brother's blood from when you beat him to death. And now you killed Paul so that he conveniently takes the blame for it all.'

'Brian Fullerton,' said J-J, and Bruno turned to listen. 'You are under arrest for the murder of your brother, Francis . . .'

Bruno felt a punch on his back, stumbled forward and the pistol that Yvonne had dropped and that he had stuffed into his waistband was wrenched from its place. For the second time that day the adrenalin flooded his body. Brian was pointing the weapon at him.

'You think you're so bloody clever but you've no idea what it was like. He was a monster. My parents had to sell their house to pay for the little queer's treatment and what do you think there was left for me? I'm glad I did it . . .'

There was a great clunk and Brian's eyes went glassy, his knees buckled and he fell as Florence completed her follow-through after the forehand drive had slammed her precious laptop into his temple. The sheer metallic case cracked open and components and letters from the keyboard tinkled to the floor.

'Thank you,' Bruno said, his legs still trembling and his mouth dry. Painfully, he swallowed and bent to collect the pistol that had fallen from Brian's hand. 'We'll get you a new computer.'

Florence let out a great sob, threw down the wrecked computer, put her hands to her face and crumpled into Bruno's arms.

'Can you please take me home to my children?' she asked him as J-J handcuffed the unconscious man.

Bruno led her out, leaving J-J and the rest of them to clear up, complete the paperwork and file the charges. He settled her in the passenger seat of his Land Rover and called the Mayor.

'It's over. Paul is dead, shot by Brian Fullerton, who has now been charged with the murder of his brother. No hostages hurt. I'm taking Florence home to her children. If Paris calls, tell them it's all ended well. If Pamela calls, tell her I'm on my way. I'll see you tomorrow.'

Bruno rang off, feeling a great wave of tiredness that slowed him as he climbed behind the wheel and set off back to St Denis. He thought of Yves and the way he'd spoken of his daughter, Odile. He thought of the murdered Francis Fullerton and his yearning to be a father. He felt himself groping to understand these deep and potent tides of parenthood and family, the waves of ancestry and succession that tied past and present together.

He looked at Florence, aching to be back with her children, and he thought of the risks he had taken that evening. And he wondered if he'd ever have stepped into such danger if Isabelle had still been carrying his child.

Acknowledgements

This is a work of fiction and all characters, places and institutions are inventions, except for the historical facts cited below.

The Resistance train robbery at Neuvic in July 1944 took place exactly as described here, and the haul was 2,280 million francs. The final months of the war were a period of sharp inflation, so comparative values are difficult to establish, but the exchange rate calculated for the US Federal Reserve by the US Embassy in Paris in 1945 suggests that the sum taken was around 300 million euros in today's money, or $400 million. See:

http://www.federalreserve.gov/pubs/rfd/1946/47/rfd47.pdf

In financial terms, it was by far the greatest train robbery of all time. In suggesting that this was five times the national budget for education, I used the best detailed analysis of the French state budget for 1946, which can be found online at:

http://www.persee.fr/web/revues/home/prescript/article/pop_0032-4663_1947_num_2_4_1873

I am grateful to my friend Jean-Jacques Gillot, an eminent local historian and co-author of *Résistants du Périgord*, an authoritative encyclopaedia of the Resistance in Périgord, for his invaluable researches into the Neuvic affair. He generously shared his archives with me, including those of the *Paix et Liberté* movement, a shadowy anti-Communist group with access to police archives which was set up after the war to monitor the French left, apparently with clandestine US support. M. Gillot is also the author of the best account of the fate of the Neuvic money, *Le partage des milliards de la Résistance*, and of *Doublemètre*, an enthralling account of the Resistance leader Orlov, almost certainly a Soviet spy, who suddenly became exceedingly wealthy after the war. So did many others, including André Malraux, and despite repeated official inquiries, the fate of much of the Neuvic money remains unknown.

The use of the Marshall Plan slush-funds to finance US intelligence operations in Europe after the war is a matter of historical record. My own book, *The Cold War: A History* (London and New York, 1993), covers much of the ground. Preventing a Communist takeover in France and Italy after 1945, when the Communists were the largest and best-organized of all political parties, was a top priority for the US and Britain. George F. Kennan, the career US diplomat whose famous Long Telegram from Moscow in 1946 sketched out the grand strategy of containment that was to guide US policy throughout the Cold War, argued for US military intervention if the Communists looked like winning power through elections.

My account of Jacqueline's researches into secret US assistance to the French nuclear programme after 1970 is historically accurate, thanks to the work of my colleagues at the Woodrow Wilson International Center for Scholars in Washington DC. Their Cold War research centre has assembled an extraordinary archive of documents and astute analysis which illuminates much of the secret history of modern times. Some of the documents I cite on French dependence on US nuclear technology may be consulted at:

http://digitalarchive.wilsoncenter.org/document/113232
http://digitalarchive.wilsoncenter.org/document/112388
http://digitalarchive.wilsoncenter.org/document/113238f

In the last of these selected documents, the transcript at a Pentagon meeting on 5 September 1973, with Defense Secretary James Schlesinger and future national security advisor Brent Scowcroft, Dr Kissinger notes that 'the real quid pro quo is the basic orientation of French policy'.

The interpretation of the likely impact of such revelations on French politics is my own invention for fictional purposes.

The brunochiefofpolice.com website has had several queries about some of the foods mentioned in the Bruno novels. The splendid *Tomme d'Audrix* cheese and the *aillou* are indeed made by my friend Stéphane Bounichou, who can be found in the markets of Le Bugue on Tuesday and Saturday mornings, Le Buisson on Fridays and St Cyprien on Sundays. Mail order is possible in some European countries. He can be reached via:

http://www.facebook.com/pages/Fromagerie-Le-Ptit-Jean-De-Mai/171737676196647?sk=info

Like Bruno, I am torn between trumpeting the excellence of the wines of Bergerac and particularly of the Pécharmants, and worrying that greater renown might make them too expensive to afford. For the moment, they remain very reasonably priced and details of some of my favourites may be found on Bruno's website. The magnificent wines of Château de Tiregand, particularly the *grands millésimes* of 2005 and 2009, can be found at:

www.chateau-de-tiregand.com/index1.html

I am grateful to the Dordogne tourist board for their enthusiastic support for Bruno's adventures. They are offering to provide by post a book of vouchers for reduced admission to the Lascaux cave and many other caves, castles, gardens and tourist attractions in the region to any reader who sends their name and address to:

bruno.perigord.tourisme@orange.fr

As always, the real heroes of the Bruno books are the astute and kindly people of the Périgord and the wonderful *paysage* and way of life they have crafted over the centuries. It is a privilege to live among them and to share it. Once again I must ask forgiveness from my friend and tennis partner Pierrot, our local policeman whose genial personality and wisdom first inspired the Bruno stories, for covering his placid and law-abiding countryside with fictional corpses.

Bruno would not be Bruno without Jane and Caroline Wood in Britain and Jonathan Segal in New York, and without Anna von Planta and Ruth Geiger in Zurich. My wife Julia and our daughters Kate and Fanny have always been the first to read each new Bruno and have been as perceptive as they are supportive. The food in the Bruno novels owes just about everything to Julia, Pierrot, Raymond the retired gendarme and my other friends and neighbours. Much of this book has been written with Benson, our basset hound, sitting or more often sleeping at my feet until I take him out for a walk and a *p'tit apéro* with Raymond or the Baron or Joe my neighbour, and often with all three.